W9-BOR-022

☙ PRAISE FOR ❧

TRICIA LEVENSELLER

"One of my favorite YA books ever. The action!
The world-building! The voice! This book kicks so much ass."

—CALE DIETRICH, author of *The Love Interest*, on *Warrior of the Wild*

"Levenseller presents a fully rounded portrait of a girl whose strength
in battle is tempered by her very human anxieties. Rasmira's quest is
thrilling, her emotional journey compelling; this adventure sings."

—*BOOKLIST* on *Warrior of the Wild*

"This high-octane novel is filled with mythical creatures and showcases a
heroine who wants to be a warrior, a woman, and a leader."

—*SCHOOL LIBRARY JOURNAL* on *Warrior of the Wild*

"The real gratification lies in Rasmira's transformation
from broken, betrayed girl to resourceful, confident victor.
Her final clash with the god is heart pounding, and her
triumph in front of her village and father is satisfyingly righteous."

—*THE BULLETIN OF THE CENTER FOR CHILDREN'S BOOKS* on *Warrior of the Wild*

>—○—<

"Levenseller has created a formidable female character who can
take care of herself as she makes some hard decisions."

—*SCHOOL LIBRARY JOURNAL* on *Daughter of the Pirate King*

"With a cunning plot, robust writing, and complicated characters, any
reader will enjoy being manipulated in Levenseller's capable hands."

—ANNA BANKS, author of the *New York Times* bestseller *Of Triton*,
on *Daughter of the Pirate King*

★ "Levenseller makes an impressive debut with this funny, fast-paced, and romance-dashed nautical fantasy, set in an alternate world of pirates, sirens, and myriad islands . . . This one's not to be missed."

—PUBLISHERS WEEKLY on *Daughter of the Pirate King*, starred review

"Tricia Levenseller's vivacious debut novel, the first in a duology, boasts stormy seas, sexy pirates, swordplay and a heroine who conquers all three with aplomb . . . A rip-roaring high seas escapade with a tinge of fantasy, *Daughter of the Pirate King* will engage and enthrall its teen audience."

—SHELF AWARENESS on *Daughter of the Pirate King*

>‑◉‑◄

"[Levenseller's] words will pull you in, and there's no escaping them."

—CHARLIE N. HOLMBERG, author of the Paper Magician Series, on *Daughter of the Siren Queen*

"Fiercer and wittier than ever!"

—ELLY BLAKE, *New York Times*–bestselling author of *Frostblood*, on *Daughter of the Siren Queen*

"Levenseller comes into her own . . . penning an argh-worthy blend of pirate derring-do and lively romance."

—BOOKLIST on *Daughter of the Siren Queen*

"The author has yet again captured the adventure, romance, and ruthless ways of the high seas . . . This fast-moving adventure with strong female characters would be great for those who love a good pirate story, a touch of romance, and action-packed sword fighting."

—SCHOOL LIBRARY JOURNAL on *Daughter of the Siren Queen*

THE SHADOWS BETWEEN US

ALSO BY TRICIA LEVENSELLER

Daughter of the Pirate King
Daughter of the Siren Queen

Warrior of the Wild

THE SHADOWS BETWEEN US

TRICIA LEVENSELLER

FEIWEL AND FRIENDS

NEW YORK

A FEIWEL AND FRIENDS BOOK
An imprint of Macmillan Publishing Group, LLC
120 Broadway, New York, NY 10271

THE SHADOWS BETWEEN US. Copyright © 2020 by Tricia Levenseller. All rights reserved.
Printed in the United States of America.

Our books may be purchased in bulk for promotional, educational, or business use. Please
contact your local bookseller or the Macmillan Corporate and Premium Sales Department
at (800) 221-7945 ext. 5442 or by email at MacmillanSpecialMarkets@macmillan.com.

Library of Congress Cataloging-in-Publication Data
Names: Levenseller, Tricia, author.
Title: The shadows between us / Tricia Levenseller.
Description: First edition. | New York : Feiwel and Friends, 2020. | Summary: Eighteen-
year-old Alessandra Stathos, the second daughter of a minor nobleman, makes a plan to
seduce, marry, and kill the king, then rule the world, and only love can stop her.
Identifiers: LCCN 2019018601 | ISBN 9781250189967 (hardcover)
Subjects: | CYAC: Fantasy. | Ambition—Fiction. | Kings, queens, rulers, etc.—Fiction. |
Love—Fiction.
Classification: LCC PZ7.1.L4858 Sh 2020 | DDC [Fic]—dc23
LC record available at https://lccn.loc.gov/2019018601

Book design by Liz Dresner
Feiwel and Friends logo designed by Filomena Tuosto
First edition, 2020
20 19 18 17 16 15
fiercereads.com

For Becki

I can't think of anyone more deserving of this Slytherin romance.

Thanks for reading it first!

>—○—<

It's cool not growing old. I like being the eternal stud.

—Damon Salvatore, *The Vampire Diaries,*

Season 1, Episode 4

CHAPTER

1

They've never found the body of the first and only boy who broke my heart.

And they never will.

I buried Hektor Galanis in a hole so deep, even the devils of the earth couldn't reach him.

My dream was of him, of the day he told me it had been fun but he was done. Some other girl had caught his fancy. I don't even remember her name. At the time, all I could think of was the fact that I'd given everything to Hektor: my first kiss, my love, my body.

And when I told him I loved him, all he had to say was "Thanks, but I think it's time we moved on."

He had other things to say, too. When I sank my knife into his chest, words came spilling out of him almost as fast as the blood.

He couldn't make sense of it. I couldn't, either. I barely remembered grabbing the knife Father had given to me for my fifteenth birthday, three months previous, with its jeweled handle and silver sheen, but I do remember that Hektor's blood matched the inlaid rubies.

I also remember what finally helped my head catch up with my pounding heart: the last word out of Hektor's lips.

Alessandra.

His last word was my name. His last thought was of me.

I won.

That knowledge settles within me now just as it did three years ago. That sense of rightness, of peace.

I lift my arms into the air, stretching like a cat, before rolling over in bed.

A pair of brown eyes is only inches from my own.

"Devils, Myron, why are you staring at me?" I ask.

He presses a kiss to my bare shoulder. "Because you're beautiful." Myron lies on his side, his head propped up on a closed fist. My bedsheets cover him from the waist down. It's a wonder he fits in my bed, he's so tall. Floppy curls sprawl across his forehead, and he flicks back his head to clear his vision. The scent of sandalwood and sweat wafts over me.

With a hand, I keep the sheets held up over my chest as I rise to a sitting position. "Last night was fun, but you should go. I have much to do today."

Myron stares at my chest, and I roll my eyes.

"Perhaps again later?" I ask.

He looks up at me, before his eyes flit meaningfully to my chest once more.

No, wait. Not my chest. To the hand holding the sheets in place and the extra weight I now feel there.

There's a diamond on my finger. It's beautiful, cut in an egg shape and buried in gold. It winks in the morning light as I tilt my hand from side to side. The ring is by far the most expensive trinket he's ever given me.

"Alessandra Stathos, I love you. Will you marry me?"

Laughter fills the room, and Myron flinches at it. I quickly place my free hand over my lips.

"What are you thinking?" I say a moment later. "Of course not." I stare down at the gorgeous ring once more. With this gift, Myron has outlived his usefulness. For some reason, my lovers cease to give me expensive presents once I turn down their proposals.

Alas.

"But we're so happy together," he says. "I will cherish you every day. Give you everything you deserve. I will treat you like a princess."

If only he knew I have my sights set a bit higher than that. "It's a very kind offer, but I'm not ready to settle down just yet."

"But—I've shared your bed," he splutters.

Yes, he and three other boys this month.

"And now it's time for you to leave it." I move to rise from the bed when the door to my chambers bursts open.

Myron freezes with his hand outstretched toward me, and my father, Sergios Stathos, Lord Masis, looks down at what he can see of our naked bodies.

"Leave," he bites out in a deathly quiet voice. My father is shorter than my five and a half feet, but he's built like a bull with a thick neck, wide shoulders, and keen eyes that pierce to the soul.

Myron tries to take the sheets with him, but I've got them firmly clamped around myself. When he fails to wrest them from me, he reaches down to grab his pants.

"Leave now," Father specifies.

"But—"

"Listen or I will have you whipped!"

Myron stands. Barely. He hunches as though he can hide his tall frame. He makes it halfway to the door before turning. "My ring?"

"Surely you want me to keep it? So I can remember our time together?"

Myron's face twists. He has one foot pointed toward the door and the other toward me.

Father growls.

Myron takes off at a run, nearly tripping over my father's boots as he bolts over the threshold. Once he's gone, Father turns to me.

"You make it difficult for me to find you a suitable match when you're caught with a new bedfellow every night."

"Don't be ridiculous, Father. That was Myron's fifth stay."

"Alessandra! You must stop this. It is time for you to grow up. To settle down."

"Has Chrysantha found a husband, then?" Father knows very well the law forbids me to marry until my older sister does. There is an order to things.

Father treads over to the bed. "The Shadow King has dismissed a number of single women from the palace, Chrysantha among them. I'd hoped your sister would catch his eye, rare beauty that she is."

Oh, yes. Chrysantha is a rare beauty. And she's as dumb as a rock.

"But it was not to be," Father concludes.

"Myron's free," I offer.

Father levels a glare at me. "She will not wed Myron. Chrysantha will be a duchess. I've already made arrangements with the Duke of Pholios. He's an aging man who wants a pretty girl on his arm. It's done. That means it's your turn."

Finally.

"You've suddenly taken an interest in my future, have you?" I ask, just to be difficult.

"I've always had your best interests in mind."

A complete untruth. The only time Father bothers to think of me is when he catches me doing something he thinks I shouldn't. Chrysantha has been his focus my entire life.

Father continues, "I'm going to approach the Earl of Oricos to discuss the match of you and his son, who will inherit one day. Soon, I should think, given Aterxes's ailing health. That should make you happy."

"It doesn't."

"You're certainly not going to remain my problem forever."

"So touching, Father, but I've got my sights set on another man."

"And just whom would that be?"

I stand, pulling the sheet up with me, before tucking it under my arms. "The Shadow King, of course."

Father guffaws. "I think not. With your reputation, it'll be a miracle if I can get any nobleman's son to have you."

"My reputation is known by none, save those whom it directly concerns."

"Men do not keep the exploits of the bedroom to themselves."

I smile. "They do when it's me."

"What is that supposed to mean?"

"I'm not stupid, Father. I have something on every man who has seen the inside of this room. Myron has an unfortunate gambling problem. He lost a family heirloom in a game of cards. Blamed the missing pendant on a servant and got him whipped and fired. His father wouldn't be happy to hear of it. And Damon? I happen to know he's part of a group of smugglers importing illegal weapons into the city. He'd be sent to prison if anyone knew the truth. And let's not forget Nestor, who's quite fond of the opium dens. I could go on naming all my lovers, but I think you get the idea."

Though his face doesn't change, Father's shoulders lose some of their tension. "Such winning gentlemen you keep around, darling."

"The point is, Father, I know what I'm doing. And I'm going to keep doing whatever I wish, because I am the master of myself. And you? You're going to send me to the palace with the next wave of women to see the king, because if there's anything I'm good at, it's getting men to propose to me." I flash the diamond on my finger in his direction.

Father's eyes narrow. "How long have you been planning this?"

"Years."

"You said nothing when I sent Chrysantha to the palace."

"Father, Chrysantha couldn't catch the attention of a rabid dog. Besides, beauty isn't enough to catch the eye of the Shadow King. He has beauties paraded in front of him all year long.

"Send me. I will get us all a palace," I finish.

The room is quiet for a full minute.

"You'll need new dresses," Father says at last, "and I won't get your sister's bride-price for weeks yet. That won't be enough time."

I pull the ring from my finger and stare down at it lovingly. Why does he think I've taken so many lovers? They're fun, to be sure, but most important, they're going to finance my stay at the palace.

I hold up the ring where my father can see it. "There's plenty more where this came from."

>—I—◆>—○—◇<—I—<

SEWING HAS ALWAYS BEEN a hobby of mine, but it is impossible for me to make all the new clothing required for my upcoming plans in such a short amount of time. Working with my favorite seamstress, I design and commission ten new day outfits, five evening gowns, and three appropriately indecent nightgowns (although those I make myself—Eudora doesn't need to know how I intend to spend my nights).

Father takes no part in the planning, as he is much too busy with his accountant, worrying over the estate. He's bankrupt and desperately trying to hide it. It's not his fault. Father's quite competent, but the land just isn't producing as it once was. Disease swept through a few years ago and killed most of the livestock. Every year, the crops grow thinner. A well has already gone dry, and more and more tenants are leaving.

The Masis estate is dying, and Father needs to acquire decent bride-prices for my sister and me in order to keep his lands running.

Though I'm aware of the situation, I haven't bothered to worry about it. My lovers all feel the need to give me nice things. Very expensive things. It's been a fun game. Learning their secrets. Seducing them. Getting them to shower me with gifts.

But to be honest?

I'm bored with it.

I have a new game in mind.

I'm going to woo the king.

I suspect it won't be longer than a month before he's helplessly in love with me. And when he proposes, I will say yes for the first time.

For once the marriage is official and consummated?

I will kill the Shadow King and take his kingdom for myself.

Only this time, I won't have to bury the body. I'll find a convenient scapegoat and leave the Shadow King for someone to discover. The world will need to know that I'm the last royal left.

Their queen.

CHAPTER

2

Father exits the carriage first and holds out his arm to me. I grasp it with one gloved hand, hold up my heavy overskirt in the other, and descend the steps.

The palace is a grand structure painted entirely in black. It's positively gothic in appearance, with winged creatures resting atop the columns. Round towers sweep up the sides, roofed with shingles, a recent architectural style.

The entire length of the palace is built near the top of a mountain, with most of the city winding its way downward. The Shadow King is a grand conqueror, spreading his influence slowly across all the world, just like his father before him. Since the surrounding kingdoms try to retaliate from time to time, a well-protected city is vital, and the grand palace is said to be impregnable. Guards patrol the grounds with rifles slung over their shoulders, a further deterrent to our enemies.

"I'm not sure black was the best color choice for your attire," Father says as he leads me up the steps to the main entrance. "Everyone knows the king's favorite color is green."

"Every single girl in attendance will be wearing green. The point is to stand out, Father. Not blend in."

"I think you might have erred in excess."

I think not. With the king's conquering of Pegai, some of the ladies at court tried the Pegain style of loose pants with jeweled hems below a fitted top. After a while, the style faded away. It was too different for most ladies to adapt to.

I've designed a combination of the Pegain style and our heavy-skirted Naxosian style. I wear close-fitted pants beneath a floor-length overskirt, which parts in the middle to show off the pants. Heeled boots raise me an extra inch off the floor. The overskirt is short-sleeved, but I wear gloves so long they overlap the sleeves. My top is tied in the back beneath the overskirt, the neckline just short of my collarbone. Modest and yet not matronly.

A black rose pendant rests on a choker around my neck. Matching earrings dangle from my lobes, and my hair is half up in a loose twist.

"I assume you have a plan for once you're introduced to the king?" Father asks. "He will receive each lady one by one up to the dais. He barely even looked at Chrysantha when it was her turn. The Shadow King never descends the steps to interact with the partygoers. He doesn't even ask anyone to dance."

"Of course I have a plan," I respond. One doesn't go into battle unprepared.

"Are you going to tell me this plan?"

"It doesn't involve you. You don't need to know."

The muscles in his arm bunch slightly. "But I could weigh in. Help you. You're not the only one who wants you to succeed."

I pause at the top of the steps. "Have you ever seduced a man before?"

Father's cheeks redden. "Of course not!"

"Then I don't see why I should need you to weigh in on anything. Rest assured, Father, if there's any way in which you could prove useful, I will tell you. For now, I can handle things."

We continue on at a leisurely pace. The doorman nods a greeting at us as we pass him by, and Father leads me toward the ballroom.

But we can't come within a hundred feet of it, because a line of green extends nearly all the way back to the far wall. Nigh a hundred girls chitter with their families and one another, all waiting for an introduction with the king. I'm certain they can't all be eligible for marriage. Many look like younger sisters of the older ladies in line. Still, should the king show any interest in the younger ladies, I'm certain their fathers will *make* them available.

Father tries to take me to the end of that line, and though it appears to be moving at a somewhat quick pace, that simply won't do.

"No, we're not waiting in line," I say.

"That's the only way to get an introduction with the king."

"Let's go into the ballroom first."

"You'll be lost in a sea of people in there. That's not going to catch his attention."

I blow out a breath through my nose before turning to face Father. "If you cannot do as you're told, then you can leave. Remember, Father, all your tutelage with Chrysantha did nothing. Your way doesn't work. I am in charge of this plan, and I will execute it as I see fit. It simply won't do to have us quarreling once we enter the party, so make a decision now."

Father's lips press into a thin line. He doesn't like being told what to do, least of all by me, his youngest child. Perhaps if Mother were still alive, he'd be more gentle and kind, but illness took her when I was eleven.

Finally, Father nods and holds out his free hand in front of us, inviting me to lead the way.

I do.

The upbeat music of an orchestra wafts out a set of open doors farther down the way. They appear to be used primarily for exiting the party, however. I watch girls with handkerchiefs pressed to their noses to muffle their sniveling and angry mothers chastising them for it scamper into the hallway, making hasty retreats.

Has the king been openly rejecting the women who come to get an introduction? I smile at the thought of his forwardness. That's exactly the sort of thing I would do in his position.

Father and I push past a few more nobles leaving before we're finally caught in the thick of the party.

Couples glide together on the dance floor. Gentlemen drink wine from goblets, and mothers gossip to one another from the sidelines. Groups of girls giggle behind fans or shawls as they stare up at the dais.

At the Shadow King.

I've never laid eyes on the man before, and now I'm free to observe him as long as I like while momentarily hidden among the other guests.

His name, it would seem, is well deserved and in line with the rumors I've heard. Tendrils of shadow halo his entire outline. They swirl as though alive, caressing his skin and dissolving into nothing before reappearing again.

It's fascinating to watch.

They say the Shadow King has some sort of power, but no one knows what it is. Some say he can command the shadows to do his bidding, that he can use them to kill—choke the life out of his enemies. Others say they're a shield. That no blade can pierce his skin. And even others say that the shadows speak to him, whispering the thoughts of those all around.

I certainly hope that last one isn't true.

Knowing what I have in store for him after our wedding night simply won't do.

Once I adjust to the outline of shadow, I'm able to take in other features. His hair is as black as the shadows around him. The sides are cropped short, but the hair up top has some volume to it, parted to the side. A strong brow shades his eyes. The lines of his jaw are so sharp they could cut glass, and a healthy dose of stubble covers them. With a straight nose and full lips—

He's the most beautiful thing I've ever seen, even when his features are set somewhere between boredom and irritation.

Seducing the king will prove to be a most enjoyable task, indeed.

We match, I note, as I take in his clothing. While all the dresses around us vary from mint to teal to olive, we are both decked in head-to-toe black. The king wears sleek dress pants. A black undershirt, tie, waistcoat, and overcoat. Brilliant silver buttons don his jacket. A chain dangles from the shoulder to a pocket above his left breast, holding a watch, no doubt. Black leather gloves cover his hands, which rest on the arms of his chair. A sheathed rapier leans against his throne, one for style, not use, I'm sure.

Though he doesn't bother with a crown, there is no doubt as to the man's status.

"He's so striking," I say at last. And young. I know he was only crowned about a year ago, but he can't be much older than I am.

"Remember, if you approach him, you're not permitted within five feet of him."

Yes, I know the law. No one is allowed to touch the king. To do so is punishable by death.

Oh, he is a delightful mystery that I can't wait to solve.

"Dance with me, Father."

Having learned his lesson, Father places a hand at my waist and leads me into a slow-moving Naxosian dance without question. We turn along the outskirts of the dance floor, but I order Father to lead us closer to the center.

To our left, two gentlemen dance together. The taller one twirls the shorter one in perfect form. To our right, a man and woman scoot indecently close to each other, and I silently cheer them on. The rebel in me loves to throw dirt in the face of decorum.

After a minute passes, I spot a few men looking over the heads of their dance partners to catch a glimpse of me. My black attire is doing its job splendidly.

But mostly, I think it's the fact that my pant-clad legs are a rarity in the room. Most men aren't used to the style. And I've opted for tight-fitted ones that show my curves to their best effect.

"People are staring," Father says.

"That's the point, isn't it?"

I imagine what the scene must look like from up on the dais—the black center of a daisy amid sage petals.

More and more girls exit the ballroom after obtaining their introductions. I hope the line ends soon. There can't be *that* many girls of noble blood.

A sudden spark of heat lands on my neck and spreads down to my toes. I'm being watched. "Tell me, Father, have we attracted the notice of the king yet?"

Father glimpses the throne out of the corner of his eye. They widen. "I believe we have."

"Excellent. Keep dancing."

"But—"

"Father," I warn.

I let myself get lost in the steps. I do so love dancing. I love the way my body becomes light and fluid when I go through the motions, the way the spins send my hair over my shoulders, the way my skirt twirls around my legs.

When the song is nearly over, I ask, "How many women are left in line?"

"Ten."

The song ends, and the orchestra strikes up another.

"Should we—?" Father starts.

"I'm parched. Let's go to the tables for some refreshment."

"But—"

At my glare, he takes my arm once more and leads me up to a table laden with red-filled glasses and tiny samples of food on trays.

I select a glass, holding it in my fingers by the long stem, and bring it to my lips.

"Lord Masis," a bright voice says from the other side of the thin table.

I look up. Before us is a golden-haired noble older than I. Perhaps thirty. He still appears young in the face, but he's much broader in the shoulders than the men I'm used to entertaining.

"Lord Eliades!" Father greets, forgetting me for a moment. "Where have you been? We haven't seen you in weeks at the club."

I haven't the faintest idea what club he's referencing, but I suppose I should have known Father wasn't spending his evenings at a mistress's. He never has gotten over Mother.

Father stretches out a hand to shake Eliades's, and I note that the younger gentleman has quite the calluses on his right hand. How unusual for a lord. But as I take note of the distinct muscles visible through his dress pants, I'd deem him an accomplished horseman.

"Alas, my estates have needed my full attention this long while. I've needed to . . ."

Already bored with the conversation, I don't bother listening in. Instead, I turn around to survey those dancing. One gentleman steps on his partner's foot during a turn because he has his eyes on my legs.

"Ow," she protests.

I smile down into my glass, taking another sip, careful not to look anywhere near the throne. I swear I can still feel a ray of heat bearing down on me from that direction.

"Forgive my rudeness!" Father suddenly exclaims more loudly.

"Orrin, this is my daughter Alessandra. Now that Chrysantha is betrothed, I'm permitting her an outing at the palace."

I stifle a groan before turning. I suppose it only helps my cause to be seen interacting with other guests and not showing any interest in the king. But I'm also certain I will find any friend of my father's to be intolerable.

I grasp my overskirt in my free hand and curtsy. "A pleasure."

Eliades's eyes sparkle before he dips into a bow. "She's as beautiful as the elder. Is her temperament just as sweet?"

Before Father has to scramble for an answer to that question, Eliades adds, "I'm still put out that you did not give Chrysantha to me. My money is just as good as a duke's!"

"As an earl, I'm sure you understand that I had to give her the best title offered. As much as I appreciate our friendship, my dearest Chrysantha . . ."

I close my eyes tightly. Chrysantha is the last thing I want everyone to be discussing. This night is about *me*.

"Father, another dance is starting." I set my empty glass on the table and tug at his arm.

Remembering the purpose for this excursion, Father excuses us and pulls me in line with the other dancers. I try to hide my ire. Even at a party where Chrysantha is absent and Father is bent on helping me catch the eye of the king, he can't help but speak of his favorite. The daughter who looks like Mother and shares her gentle demeanor.

"The line is gone," Father says as we perform the first steps, his focus now returning to the king.

"Just keep dancing. Do not look at the king any longer."

"But he's watching us."

"Ignore him."

In my periphery, I see the king shift in his seat, as though he caught himself in one position for too long because he was occupied.

Occupied with me.

My anger drifts away at the thought. This song is faster, requiring more dexterity and concentration. As Father's face blurs in front of me, I'm able to forget all about the king. There is nothing but the tempo pounding in time to my heartbeat and the feel of my feet sweeping across the floor.

Before the song can come to a close, the music cuts off abruptly. The couples around us scatter, and Father brings our dance to a halt.

The king is approaching, his shadows sweeping behind him as he moves. I try to quiet my breathing from the exerting dance as Father takes my arm in his and turns to greet our sovereign.

"Your Majesty," Father says, bowing.

I curtsy along with him.

"Lord Masis," the king says with a nod. "I don't believe I'm acquainted with your dance partner."

I keep my eyes just to the right of the king. Though I don't see it, I can feel the king's eyes taking me in from head to toe. He's been watching me for the last fifteen minutes at least, but now he takes his time with his close-up view.

"Forgive me, sire," Father says. "May I introduce my second-born, Lady Alessandra Stathos."

The king tilts his head at an angle. "You did not get in line with the other ladies, Lady Stathos. Is the dance floor more interesting than I am?" His voice is a deep baritone; not quite soothing, but powerful.

I fight a smile as I allow our eyes to meet for the first time. A delicious jolt shoots through my entire body at the connection.

His eyes are the green of the sea, of crashing waves and violent winds. There's something dangerous in the depths of them, something exciting, and I realize right then that feigning disinterest will be difficult.

When I finally manage to pull my gaze away, I let it travel downward, taking in the king slowly while he watches. Assessing him properly from the tips of his black hair to the base of his shined boots.

"Yes," I conclude.

The air leaves my father in a painful-sounding squeak.

But the Shadow King lets out one low laugh.

"I saw ladies leaving the ball in tears," I continue. "It seemed speaking with Your Majesty was a sure way to get kicked out. I wasn't about to let that happen before I joined in the dancing."

"Is it the dancing you like? Or are you merely looking to show off your"—he darts a quick look down to my legs—"dress?"

"Are you mocking my outfit? I designed it myself."

"Quite the opposite. I rather like it." A pinch of humor lurks at the edges of his lips. I think it might be at my expense, and I don't like that one bit.

I say, "Give me your measurements, and I can have one made for you."

Another grin stretches across the king's lips, and I can't help but admire how much more handsome he becomes with the movement.

"Dance with me," he says.

Father goes so still, one would think he'd been turned to stone.

"Is that an order or a request? I'm told you hang girls who get too close to you."

"Not hang. Those girls are asked to leave the party. So long as you mind your distance, I will not have you dismissed as well."

Still, I'm not ready to concede just yet. "Is there any fun in a dance when you can't touch your partner?"

"Accept my invitation and you will find out."

CHAPTER

3

The dance floor clears until it is only the king and me. The orchestra strikes up a new song, one that only we can share.

Keeping his eyes on mine, the king advances a step, and I move backward with the motion, following his lead. This style of dance is more improvised, rather than having a set choreography to adhere to, and I can't help but wonder if the king is somehow testing me with it, seeing if I can keep up. When he steps to the side, I mirror him. He keeps his arms crossed behind his back, but dancing is not meant to be so stiff, so I let mine move with me.

At first, it's difficult not to become distracted by the tendrils of black dancing around him. The shadows are so unusual, so fascinating. I wonder what would happen if I reached out to one. Would it curl around my finger? Dissipate at the touch of my skin? Feel as though I'd plunged into a fog?

I remember myself when the Shadow King holds an arm out to me. I know I'm not meant to take it, so instead I twirl for him, letting my overskirt lift off the floor to show more of the tight-fitted pants beneath. I close my eyes and feel the motion more deeply.

The tempo picks up and so do the king's movements. I seem to sense his actions rather than watch for them. The dance turns exhilarating and frantic, almost as if there's something desperate in the music itself. As the song grows faster and faster and the king's eyes burrow into mine, I can't help but feel as though he's trying to communicate something to me through dancing alone.

I see nothing but those green eyes, feel nothing but the floor against my feet. I lose all sense of time and purpose.

When the music comes to a crushing halt, I dip my head backward as the Shadow King lets one gloved hand tilt toward me in the imitation of a caress.

I'm breathing heavily while staring up into two swirls of emerald green. We right ourselves seconds later.

When the king finally looks away from me, he raises his voice for all to hear. "That's enough revelry for one night."

And without another word, the king turns on one heel and stalks from the room, grabbing his sword on the way out.

I'm staring at the spot where he disappeared in stunned silence.

In the next instant, servants dressed in silly wigs usher everyone from the room. Father takes my arm, and I silently follow his lead.

What just happened?

I thought the dance was perfect. I didn't touch him. I didn't get too close.

The king, who has never publicly danced with anyone since his coronation, asked *me* to dance.

And then he left without another word.

Men do not dismiss me. No one has since Hektor. I feel my nostrils flare and my face heat up.

"It was a valiant attempt," Father says as he hands me up into the carriage. "Devils know you achieved more than any other woman has. Not only did His Majesty bother to look at you, he asked for a dance. He will remember you. This isn't necessarily over."

The carriage moves slowly, halting and rolling in small increments as the traffic backs up from all the other people leaving the palace.

"Just a moment!" a voice calls out. The carriage comes to another jerking stop.

The head of a man appears in the open window of the carriage. A palace servant, by the way he's dressed.

"Lady Stathos?" he asks.

"I am she."

He sticks an arm into the carriage and presents me with a black envelope. When I take it, he doesn't leave. He waits patiently for me to open it.

Forgive me, Lady Stathos, but I've changed my mind. I do not wish for you to leave just yet. You're far too interesting for that. Will you come join my court? Consider this an invitation, not a demand. My man will await your reading of this note in the event of your acquiescence.

—RM

I wonder at the signature. Could those be the king's real initials? I suppose I shouldn't have expected him to sign *SK*. *Shadow King* isn't his name, after all.

Elation rushes through me as I realize what this means.

"What is it?" Father asks.

"The king asks for me to stay at court."

"Then why are we still sitting in this carriage?"

I turn toward the servant. "I will accept His Majesty's invitation."

"Very good, my lady." He opens the carriage door for me but shuts it before Father can descend the steps. "I'm afraid the invitation extends only to the lady, my lord. You're free to return home."

And before my father can utter a word of protest, the servant leads me back toward the palace.

WE DON'T GO THROUGH the main doors. Instead, I'm taken through a side entrance, something that appears to be used only by the servants.

Indeed, curious laundresses and kitchen workers stare at me as I'm taken down long corridors with black carpeting. Past sconces in the shape of thorny vines. Through doorways lined with vases painted with stallions and eagles.

Is the king trying to hide me? Or perhaps simply not make a spectacle of my more permanent arrival?

Eventually, the servant deposits me in front of a door. He reaches for a key within his coat and lets us in.

The room is grander than anything I've ever stayed in, with thick light-blocking drapes, wooden furniture detailed with exquisite roses, and cushions of the softest down, but it is nothing compared to what a queen's rooms would look like, I'm sure.

A maid is waiting in the room, likely having just finished turning down the bed.

"The king has already sent for your things, my lady. They should be here first thing tomorrow," the man who led me here says.

"But I've only just agreed, and you haven't yet told him I accepted."

The servant holds himself a little higher. "The king was hopeful you would accept."

Hopeful? More like presumptuous. Arrogant.

"I see."

I have a lot of work ahead of me.

CHAPTER

4

The next morning, breakfast is delivered to my room, along with my possessions. I spend the morning ordering servants about. The wardrobes are filled with all the dresses I've designed. A vanity has my powders, perfumes, and jewelry placed upon it.

I'm not especially fond of reading, but I did bring several books with me to the palace. Most are works on philosophy, mathematics, agriculture, and other topics of importance. They exist to hide the only three books of interest. To the outward eye, they appear harmless: three tomes full of plants and herbs used for medicinal purposes. But in each one, there are several chapters on poisons and antidotes, highly useful for me because I will have to kill the Shadow King once I've secured his hand in marriage.

Hektor's death was messy, disgusting, so very difficult to hide and clean up. I'm reluctant to stab anyone ever again. Poison is a much cleaner way to kill, and it will prove much easier. Not to mention, it's nigh impossible to root out the poisoner.

I order the maids to place the books on an empty shelf in the room. Then I step back to admire the entire ensemble.

Yes, it'll do.

A maid helps me to dress. I select a deep blue overskirt to wear over matching pants. The fabric is a simple cotton, unlike the taffeta of last night's outfit. Lace hems my ankles, the pattern that of a trail of roses. Instead of boots, I opt for day slippers. My blouse laces up the front in a fashion similar to a corset. It will be highly scandalous, and I suspect none of the men at court will be able to keep their eyes off me.

That's the point. When a man sees something that several other men want, he can't help but want it, too.

The maid pulls all my hair up onto the top of my head, heating tendrils into curls spilling down my neck and over my ears.

Just when I'm starting to feel ready for the day, another servant is admitted into my rooms.

He bows low. "My lady, the king hopes you will join him and the rest of the courtiers in the orchards for tea."

"Have I missed lunch?"

"I'm afraid so, but the king expected you would. He assumed settling into your new room would take most of the day."

I'm glad to know the king is thinking of me even when I am not around.

"If I may also add, my lady, the king doesn't usually make an event of afternoon tea. I expect he's arranged it all for you."

"For me?"

He crosses his white-gloved hands behind his back. "It is my understanding that this is your first time at court. There are many new people with whom to become acquainted."

That brings a small smile to my lips. "Then I suppose I shouldn't disappoint His Majesty by not showing up."

>—+—+>—O—<+—+—<

BRICK-LINED TRAILS WEND UNDER trees filled with cherry blossoms. A thin creek trickles by to one side, and the birds fill the air with their music.

Plenty of cushioned seating has been added outdoors, and a long table filled with thin sandwiches, sliced fruit, biscuits, cakes, and other sweets is constantly replenished by servants.

Excitement sparks through me at the thought of all the opportunities ahead. My father isn't here to ruin things this time, and I'm surrounded by the most influential people in the world.

A group of ladies sits by the creek, sharing the newest gossip. Three gentlemen stand huddled together under one of the cherry trees, teacups in hand, laughing over something one of them said. A few couples have branched off from other groups. I watch a pair of courting ladies walk with hands clasped together, the hoops of their skirts touching. Really, the ladies at court could do with some fashion advice from me. I hope I will start some new trends.

With all the courtiers distracted by their current companions, no one takes notice of my arrival yet.

I make a show of walking toward the refreshment table, letting my eyes wander in search of the king, when something barrels into me from behind.

I nearly lose my footing, but I catch myself, though a huge pressure impedes my overskirt.

A reprimand is already on my lips as I turn, but I'm brought up short.

There's a dog panting before me.

At least I think it's a dog. It also has a startling likeness to a bear. In both size and color.

"Hello," I say, bending over and holding out my hand.

The dog takes a few sniffs before nudging my fingers with its nose. An invitation to pet it if I've ever seen one.

I've always wanted a dog, but my father forbade it because he has such a terrible reaction to them.

I stroke it—*him*, I correct after a quick look down to confirm the sex—behind the ears.

"Good boy," I say, "though I'd appreciate it if you got off my skirt."

He lies down, covering even *more* of my skirt, his wet nose digging into the fabric.

"What are you doing, silly creature?" I adjust myself to avoid losing my balance and end up bumping into something with my foot.

A ball the size of an apple. Hidden beneath my skirts. I reach down for it.

"Oh, is this what you're looking for?" I ask.

The dog jumps to a standing position, tail wagging, finally freeing my skirt. I cock back my arm, throw the ball as far as I can, and watch the giant mongrel race after it.

And then, out of the corner of my eye, a wisp of shadow.

The king is watching me. His shadows darken once our eyes meet, swirling more thickly about his form. I wonder if they change with his thoughts. If I could learn to read them if I studied them long enough.

He stands in the shade cast by one of the trees, leaning his frame against the trunk. Today he has his hair brushed back from his forehead, and I can't begin to guess what sorcery manages to hold the strands in place with such volume. He wears a long-sleeved black dress shirt, matching gloves, a waistcoat of deep blue brocade, and a black cravat.

I hadn't realized I'd been smiling at the dog until I feel my features shift into surprise.

And then I watch the dog trot over to the king and drop the ball at his feet.

With a quick adjustment, I right my overskirt and sweep toward the king, stopping when I'm five feet away. I cross my arms over my chest.

"Is that your dog?" I accuse, even though I already know the answer.

"Good boy, Demodocus," the Shadow King says, picking up the ball and tossing it away again. Demodocus races after it once more. To me, he says, "You have a good arm."

"And you have impressive aim."

He lifts a brow. "Surely you're not accusing me of intentionally throwing the ball at you."

"That's exactly what you did." But why? "If you wanted my attention, all you had to do was ask for it. Though I'm disinclined to give it now that I know you practically ordered your dog to tackle me."

The corners of his mouth turn up. "It wasn't your attention I wanted. I was curious to see how you would react to Demodocus."

"Why?" I ask, baffled.

Demodocus gallops toward us before dropping the ball at the king's perfectly polished shoes. He raises it in a black-gloved hand before hurling it toward a group of ladies sitting in chairs along the creek. Demodocus streaks in front of them, racing to catch his prize, and a volley of shrieks rises into the air.

The king arches his neck slightly, as though this proves his point. Whatever that may be.

"You react well to the unexpected," he says at last. "And you like animals. That's two things I didn't know about you before."

"And you are devious." Siccing his dog on unsuspecting ladies.

"Now surely you'd already guessed that about me," he says, pushing off from the tree. He steps into the light, and I step backward with the movement, keeping the appropriate distance. His grin grows as he looks me up and down.

"Something funny?" I ask.

"I'm merely admiring your attire once again. Tell me, is the corset not meant to go underneath the blouse?"

"It's not a corset. It's merely styled after one. I like the way the laces look. Why hide them?"

The king takes a moment to digest that. "You are going to cause all kinds of trouble in my court."

I can't tell if he's worried or amused by that.

"Just look at how you've already changed things. If you will excuse me." He turns to the side. "Demodocus! Come, boy!"

Demodocus reaches the king, and the two take off at a brisk jog through the trees, shadows streaking after the king like a comet.

Already changed things? But whatever could he mean?

I put my back to where the king disappeared and instead focus on the other forms in the garden.

Oh.

The ladies at court—they're dressed in head-to-toe black. Not a speck of green in sight.

They're imitating me from last night. How did I not notice this immediately?

I caught the eye of the king. He asked me to dance, and now he was seen talking with me in the orchards. People are staring openly at me now. And—

And a group of older lords and ladies is walking toward me. There are five of them, each somewhere in their forties or fifties, I expect. They look important. I can tell by the way they don't spare glances at anyone else around them, the way individuals move for them to pass.

And in the way other people who were about to approach me halt to let these five reach me first.

"Lady Alessandra Stathos, isn't it?" the man at the front of the group asks, holding out a hand. "My name is Ikaros Vasco. I am the head of the king's council."

I offer my hand, and he bows over it with a head of hair more white than brown. Lord Vasco has aged well, save for wrinkles about his eyes.

"Yes. It's a pleasure to meet you, Lord Vasco."

He doesn't bother to introduce the rest of his companions, who must be the other advisers to the king.

"I'm afraid I don't know much about you," he says when he rights himself. "Second daughter to an earl. Never seen in society until last night. Although there are a few gentlemen at court who claim to know you, having done business with your father."

He's looked into me. Gone digging into my background. Of course he did. It's his job to know everything he can about those whom the king spends his time with. The real question is, was the king the one who ordered my past looked into? Or is the council acting on its own?

"I'm afraid you have the law to blame for that," I answer honestly. "My sister just became engaged. I wasn't permitted to attend events until recently. The only people I've had a chance to meet are those whom my father does business with."

"And their sons, it would seem."

I blink. "Excuse me?"

"I found it rather curious that none of the ladies at court have ever heard of you. I mean, your sister was here at the last ball. She stayed at court. Made friends. And yet she never once mentioned you. It's like you didn't exist then."

I smile politely as a lead weight rests at the bottom of my stomach. Trust Chrysantha to cause problems without even being here. Once again.

"And yet," Vasco continues, "Myron Calligaris and Orrin, Lord Eliades, say they know you. They had a lot to say about you, in fact. Eliades couldn't speak enough on your charms." Vasco makes a face. "Calligaris had . . . other things to say about your character."

I'll bet he did. Myron is still bitter over my rejection.

My sister and my gentlemen friends are painting a horrible picture of me without even saying anything damning against me. But I can fix this.

"I'm afraid Lord Calligaris had asked my father for permission to court me *before* my sister was engaged. As a law-abiding gentleman, my father was obliged to refuse his request." I let my face fall into a look of sadness. "I'm afraid Lord Calligaris blames me for it. Can you believe it? It's as though he has no respect for those who set and carry out our kingdom's laws."

Which, of course, would be the five men and women before me.

Lord Vasco nods with new understanding. "Indeed. I shall have to revisit my earlier conversation with him."

And before then, I shall have to remind Myron about what will happen should he divulge the nature of our previous acquaintance. Ladies aren't permitted lovers before marriage. Just one of the many laws I will change once I'm sitting on the throne.

Just a hint of a rumor like that would ruin me and all my plans.

"Do enjoy your time at court, Lady Stathos," Vasco says. "I'm sure you will be happy to see many old faces, but might I suggest—if you're hoping to spend more time with the king, that is—that you make some *female* friends. Hmm? And perhaps try for some more traditional attire?" He looks down at my clothes with some distaste.

"I already have female friends, Lord Vasco. Perhaps you didn't question as many ladies as you ought to have at court."

"Is that so?" he asks.

"Yes, if you will excuse me."

I have three seconds to survey the orchards. First my eyes land on the group of ladies who screamed when Demodocus bounded in front of them. I mentally shake my head. *Not them.* Then my eyes light on a gathering of lords and ladies in a huddle. They look far too friendly for me to be seen there.

And then I spot two ladies apart from the rest. They sit on a bench before the creek a ways down, enjoying some quiet away from everyone else.

Yes, they'll do.

I stride with purpose toward them. I feel the council's heated gaze on my back. They watch me the entire distance, which thankfully is much too far to be overheard.

"Hello," I say when I reach the pair. "My name is Alessandra Stathos. Might I join you?"

The first girl brightens instantly, and I let my shoulders slump with relief. This is exactly the kind of response I needed the council to see.

"Of course, please sit! I'm Hestia Lazos. Please, call me Hestia."

I like her instantly, for that alone. Only friends exchange first names.

Then I take in her attire. She's wearing pants underneath her over-skirt. I doubt she had the outfit on hand. I wonder how many seam-stresses had to stay up all night in order for her to wear it the next day.

Hestia's coloring is a rich umber with yellow undertones. She wears her hair short, only about an inch from her scalp, the strands wrapping in tight coils. The lack of length shows off her gorgeous earrings, a pair of garnets encased in complicated brasswork.

"And this is my good friend Rhoda Nikolaides."

"It's a pleasure to meet you, Lady Stathos," Rhoda says. She wears a black gown with terribly heavy-looking petticoats. She barely man-ages to fit on the bench with the thickness of her skirts. Though all the nobles are dressed in fine clothing, I can tell that this lady is fabulously wealthy. Her skirts shine so brightly, I can practically see my reflection in them. Her hair is done up in a coiffure so intricate, it would take no fewer than three ladies to manage it. The strands are the same color as my black hair, but her skin is a bit darker, more amber than my dark beige.

"Please call me Alessandra," I say, following Hestia's lead. Besides, I need to make friends quickly, don't I? I haven't had many opportunities to make friends, and it has been my experience that most ladies do not like me. Not when I'm their competition for the attentions of men.

But these two are all sincere smiles.

"At last we meet!" Hestia says. "I was going to approach you, but then I thought perhaps I shouldn't, since I didn't want to overwhelm you. What with everyone wanting to know who you are! And then I saw the council, which made the decision for me. I'm so relieved you've asked to join us. I've been dying to ask you who made the gown you wore last night. It was simply darling!"

"And deliciously scandalous," Rhoda adds. "I adore how adventurous you are with your wardrobe. It certainly caught the king's attention quickly." She smiles as though we've just shared some wicked secret.

They both look at me expectantly.

I say, "I actually design the outfits myself. I love to sew, and I hire a seamstress to help when I run short on time to make everything."

"You're joking!" Hestia says, her long earrings swaying with the turning of her head. "No wonder you wore it so well. You designed it with your own figure in mind. I wrote to my seamstress as soon as the ball was over and offered her triple her usual rate if she could finish this outfit for me. She did her best to heed my written instructions, but I still don't quite like the fit of the pants. It's simply brilliant to wear an overskirt over the top of them. Did you know? The reason the Pegain style faded away so quickly was that"—she lowers her voice to a whisper—"most girls couldn't handle having their bottoms so exposed. But you solved that problem, didn't you?"

I don't quite know what to make of the conversation, but a voice suddenly sounds from behind us, making me jump.

"Forgive me for interrupting talk of bottoms. I would gladly continue the conversation, but I simply must secure an introduction."

The newcomer strides around the bench to stand before us. "Leandros Vasco. At your service, my lady."

"Vasco?" I ask as he takes my hand and kisses it. "You're related to Ikaros Vasco, the head of the king's council?"

Leandros sighs. "I'm afraid he's my uncle."

I don't see the resemblance. Leandros looks a couple of years older than me. He's long and lean—like the king, but his hair is a light brown, which he wears down to his shoulders. His short beard is neatly trimmed. He wears a red silk waistcoat atop a black shirt, his cuff links in the shape of roses. His nose was broken once, but it was set well. Only a small notch near the bridge gives anything of it away. It manages to make him look dangerous and dashing all at once. Were it not for the fact that I have to give the king my full attention, Leandros is exactly the sort of man I would find myself dallying with.

Rhoda presses her lips to my ear. "Leandros wasn't able to take his eyes off you at the ball last night. I think he's already taken with you. But, then again, who isn't?"

"I certainly can't fault you for your relatives. It is a pleasure to meet you, Leandros," I say, daring to use his first name. Just because I can't bed him, it doesn't mean I can't flirt. Our eyes meet, and he suddenly sizes me up in a new light. As a possibility. It's terribly mean to give him hope, but I just can't help myself.

"And where are your companions?" I ask. I'd seen Leandros earlier in the orchards. Before Demodocus plowed into me. He was talking with two other men his age.

"Distracting the masses, of course." He nods over my shoulder.

I turn to see his friends intercepting other gentlemen coming my way.

"Wanted me to yourself, did you?" I ask.

"Can you blame me?" he asks.

I grin. "How long have the three of you been at the palace?" I ask, including the girls in the conversation.

"About six months," Rhoda says, "but Leandros has been here far longer, haven't you?"

"Yes," he says. "I've lived at the palace for years. Being on the king's council necessitates my uncle's living here. I asked to join him. I'm not really fond of living out in the country."

"Did you grow up with the king, then?" I ask.

Something on Leandros's face looks saddened by the question. "During our adolescence, yes. We were quite close actually. Along with my friends."

"Were?" I catch on to his use of the past tense.

"He pushed everyone away once he became king. He doesn't trust a soul. I suspect that's why no one is allowed near him."

"I suppose," Rhoda says after a pause in the conversation, "that I would be distrustful, too, if I were a king, knowing that the last one had been murdered."

I don't know much about the late king and queen or their murders, but I do know that the culprit was never caught. Some, of course, speculate that the new king is responsible. But that hardly matters to me.

It has no bearing on my plans.

CHAPTER 5

As we rise from our bench, Hestia and Rhoda invite me to join them and the rest of the ladies in the sitting room for some embroidery before suppertime.

"And that's my cue," Leandros says. "Farewell, ladies. Alessandra, I do hope to see more of you in the future."

I nod, shading my eyes slightly with my lashes, before turning to Rhoda and Hestia. "I'm not much for embroidery, but I could bring one of the new outfits I'm working on."

"Yes!" Hestia exclaims. "Then you can teach me some stitches. Oh, won't you, Alessandra?"

There's something so genuine behind the question. I can't help but answer with "Of course."

"Wonderful," she answers. "I can already tell we'll be fast friends."

We start for the palace together, and a servant standing farther down the creek joins us. I don't usually take note of servants, but this one is quite handsome.

"Oh, this is Galen, my manservant," Rhoda explains. "He accompanies me most places and will be carrying the embroidery supplies to the sitting room for us."

"My lady." He bows, a head of chocolate-colored curls dipping toward the ground.

Unaccustomed to being introduced to servants, I merely incline my head, but neither Rhoda nor Galen seems offended. In fact, as soon as we reach the castle, they both start off in what must be the direction of Rhoda's embroidery supplies, the two already deep in conversation.

After I gather my own things, I have a servant escort me to the sitting room. I'm told the room belonged to the late queen, which she used for social activities with the ladies at court. Apparently, the Shadow King has permitted the female nobility to continue their needlework there, since there isn't a current queen to make use of it.

The doors are opened for me, and I enter into a circular room with marbled floors and a beautifully painted ceiling made to look like the night sky, stars and all. Tall windows let in plenty of natural light, and a chandelier dangles down, lit with a hundred candles. Though the palace has already been fitted with wires for electricity, I love that the queen kept such a beautiful light fixture.

Plush cushions and chairs spiral around the room, most of them already occupied. The few empty ones I spot are embroidered with black roses on the seats and backs. I've noticed the design throughout the entire castle, and I wonder the reason for it. The royal family's coat of arms is a black stallion kicking its front legs into the air. So this must symbolize something else.

"Alessandra!"

I startle at the voice.

"Over here. I've saved you a seat!"

Right in the center of everything, Hestia stands and waves me over. She's somehow managed to change her entire outfit, grab her embroidery, and beat me down here. Now she wears a blue overskirt over the top of her black pants. Little bluebirds are sewn over the fabric.

I'm not sure whether to be flattered or annoyed by the blatant imitation of my blue attire.

I tread over to her, clutching a swath of fabric in my arms.

Ladies have their skirts settled around them so they can sit more comfortably on the settees and chairs. Since I'm wearing pants, I opt for a large pillow on the floor, crossing my legs at the ankles as I sit.

Whatever conversation had been ongoing when I entered continues. Hestia babbles on about the lord she spent the most time dancing with at the ball last night.

Rhoda joins me on the ground, uncaring that her ankles are exposed when she sits.

"If it's not too rude to ask, may I inquire as to your age, Alessandra?" she asks.

"I'm eighteen," I say. "And you?"

She huffs out a breath. "Twenty-four. I'm fairly certain I'm the oldest unmarried lady at court."

"Surely not," I say, spreading out the fabric along my lap so I can find where I left off.

Rhoda nods. "I must admit, however, that I've already been married once. So perhaps it doesn't matter that I'm currently single?"

"What happened to your first husband?" I ask.

"Oh, nothing so dreadful as leaving me. He only died. Not even the richest man can escape old age."

I raise a gloved hand to hide a smile. "Not a love match, then?"

"No, but he left me quite a lot of money, so I suppose I shouldn't complain too much. And he gave me Galen! Galen was his valet, you see. And after my husband died, I just sort of kept him. He was such a huge help in making all the funeral arrangements and helping me adjust."

"Yet you're in a hurry to be wed again?" I ask.

She straightens her skirts. "Oh, I don't have to marry again. Not with my fortune, but I would very much like to have something heated and passionate. I was wed at far too young an age to a shriveled old man. I'm ready to be with someone young and healthy. Someone I can love. Don't you want that?"

I've done passion before. That's what it was with Hektor. It didn't go over well. Passion doesn't lead anywhere good. It turned me into a murderess.

However, I'm beyond flattered that she would confide in me about her desire for passion without marriage. She's trusting me with this information. It prompts me to answer her honestly.

"I've already had my love match."

She quirks a brow. "But you are unwed. How did it end?"

"He decided he didn't want me anymore. Passion leads to fierce heartbreak, Rhoda. You might think twice about how badly you wish for it."

"I hadn't thought of that." She looks off into the distance at nothing, lost in thought for a moment. "Either way, I'm getting ahead of myself. I still have four months of mourning left."

"Mourning," I repeat.

"Yes, I'm not wearing black because I wish to. A wife is required to be in mourning for a year after her husband's death. I'm to only wear black, and if I attend social functions, I'm not allowed to fully participate; I must watch from the sidelines."

My mouth drops open. "You can't be serious!"

"Very serious, I'm afraid."

"No, no, no. This won't do at all, Rhoda! I take back what I said. You *do* need a passionate tryst. There's no sense in mourning after a man you never loved. We must find you someone immediately. Is there anyone at court who brings out a passion in you?"

It turns out there are several men Rhoda is interested in. I promptly forget all the names she tells me, but she titters on about their looks and titles.

At first, I'd chosen my two new friends as a way to appease the council, but I'm realizing now just how useful the two will prove to be. Rhoda is knowledgeable about all the men at court. She's been observing them carefully (from afar, of course) since her husband died. She might be my opportunity to better fit in with those at court. And Hestia is almost obsessed with how I dress. I suspect she'll be the primary source on all gossip about me, since she's making such an effort to be like me. Knowing how those at court view me at all times is invaluable. It was only luck that the council revealed what little they knew of me already. I need to be on top of how I'm perceived constantly if I'm to know what the king and his court think of me.

At a break in Rhoda's discourse, I ask her, "Is this why you came to court? For the men?"

"Oh, no. I came to court because the king requested it."

"He requested it?"

"Yes, many of us were invited to stay. Well, to be honest, it's almost a bit of a command. I don't think I could leave if I wanted to, but I'm having such a fun time sizing up all the men at court, I don't mind one bit."

A command.

A thought strikes me. "Rhoda, were you in the palace on the night the king's parents were murdered?"

Sadness shadows her features. "Yes, oh, it was a horrible night."

"And Hestia was here, too? And Leandros?"

She thinks. "I believe so."

"And he's commanded you all to stay at court? He's commanded everyone here to stay at court?"

She looks up at me suddenly. "Oh, you think—"

"Yes."

The Shadow King is trying to root out his parents' murderer. He's invited everyone who was there the night they died to stay at the palace. He's *ordered* their indefinite stay so he can keep an eye on them and find the culprit.

But that can't be why I'm here. I wasn't here when his parents died. And according to Leandros, the king doesn't let anyone get close to him. All his social interactions are elusive at best.

So why has he invited me to stay at the palace? Can it truly be simply because my plan is working?

I ponder this as I finish the hem on the skirt I'm working on. I'm fashioning something new, a skirt that hangs down to the floor in the back but rises to above midthigh in the front. I will, of course, be wearing tight pants underneath the outfit. I don't think even the king could avoid kicking me out of court if I showed off my legs outright.

The finished product is even better than I imagined, but I need to fashion a top to match, and I haven't thought of the design for that yet. I'd hoped the skirt would inspire me. I hang the garment in my wardrobe for now.

The note arrives just as my stomach grumbles for supper.

My dear Lady Stathos,
I'd be honored to have you join me for dinner tonight.

—JM

❦

ANOTHER SERVANT LEADS ME through the palace. I take careful note of all the turns and staircases, trying to acquire a mental map of the place in which I'm now living. Eventually I'm taken through a doorway and led into a large room. I was expecting a parlor, but this is a library. Books span shelves that reach clear up to the twenty-foot ceiling. As far as I can tell, not a speck of dust coats a single tome, despite how old some of them look.

A fire has already been built into the hearth on one wall, and two rather large armchairs stretch out before it, one on either side of a short table. Tea has already been laid out.

The servant holds out one of the chairs for me, and I sit.

"His Majesty will be just a moment." And with a bow, he leaves me alone in the room.

At a hint of movement on the floor, I snap my neck in that direction. What I'd written off as a fur rug placed between the table and the fireplace, I now realize is Demodocus.

"Hello again," I say.

Demodocus cracks open one eye for a brief second before resuming his nap in front of the fire.

"Had a busy day, did you? All that fetching got the better of you, I suppose."

Demodocus rolls over, putting his back to me.

"Message received. I'll let you get back to it. But where is your master?"

I glance around the room, taking in the colors on the spines, when the king arrives.

Only he doesn't use the door.

He walks right through a wall of books.

My back snaps straight in my chair as I watch the Shadow King take shape through the books, the shadows around him growing lighter when he's all the way through the wall.

He's already watching me when his eyes take shape beyond the tomes, and I wonder if he was observing me, waiting for my eyes to land on that exact spot on the wall before stepping through solid shelves.

My eyes harden of their own accord. "Is that supposed to impress me?" Belatedly, I tack on, "Your Majesty."

His knee-high boots tread softly on the carpet as he crosses the room. "I have already guessed it takes quite a lot to impress you." He pulls the opposite chair out for himself and sits.

We watch each other for a moment in silence, but finally, curiosity gets the best of me. "How long have you been able to do that?"

"Walk through walls? The ability runs in the royal family, though it doesn't develop until a child starts to grow into adulthood."

"A side effect of the shadows, no doubt."

The Shadow King grins as he brings his teacup to his lips. "No doubt," he says after a swallow.

I can tell he's greatly amused by my questions, and that realization has me shutting up. I put my full focus on my teacup instead, drinking while looking around at the great expanse of a room. I can neither give him exactly what he wants nor be too predictable. I have to walk a very fine line. It is the same with every man.

"I see Demodocus is performing his duties excellently as watchdog," the king says to the dog's back.

I stifle a smile. "Is that really what he's for?"

"When he's around, I've noticed those at court are less likely to approach me. When I bought him, he was meant to be a source of protection."

"And instead you were stuck with a teddy bear," I say with a fond look at the dog.

After a knock and the king's call of "Enter," servants bring in our supper. It would appear they've brought all four courses at once. A bowl of soup is set before me, and the smell of squash and cream wafts upward, making my mouth water. Next to it is placed a tray of fruits, neatly sliced, with a serving bowl of sweet yogurt for dipping. The main course is cured elk, cut in spiced strips and placed on a bed of greens.

And finally, a slice of chocolate cake for each of us is positioned in the center of the table, chocolate drizzle steaming along the sides.

The men in tights and wigs halt along the edges of the room.

"Leave us," the king says. "We won't need anything else."

There's something about watching him give orders that has my blood flowing faster in my veins. He has such power. Men are forced to obey him without a word of protest. They would do anything he commanded.

I want that power.

Seeing it up close has my resolve hardening.

When the door closes, I shift the plates and bowls in front of me, moving everything to the sides of the table until my path is clear to the chocolate cake. That, I bring forward, until it's directly in front of me.

I don't look at the king, but I get the sense that he's watching me closely. As I take a bite, the soft cake practically melts in my mouth, and I know I made the right choice to start with it while it's still warm.

When I can't take the awkwardness any longer, I deign to look up. The king has his own slice of cake in front of him.

"How alike we are," he says after licking a drop of drizzle from his lips.

"Because we both enjoy chocolate? You can't get out much if you think that an uncommon trait."

He takes a drink from one of the goblets that was brought in with the food. "I didn't mean the chocolate. When I see something I want, I reach for it without hesitation."

Perhaps if he were looking at me another way, I would think he also meant to convey that he wanted me. But his gaze isn't heated. It is relaxed, and I am getting the distinct impression that he doesn't get to do that often.

"What are you reaching for now?" I ask.

He takes only a moment to think. "The world," he says simply. "I want to own all of it. For every city to bear my coat of arms and for every person throughout the continent to know my name and recognize my reign."

I let myself imagine it for a moment. For the whole world to know my name and live under my rule. What better way to feel complete and whole and accomplished?

"And you?" he asks, cutting into thoughts of me standing on a tower, overlooking all that is mine. "What do you reach for?"

Perhaps I should think longer about my answer. I should be careful and calculated, but I say truthfully, "Acknowledgment."

He tilts his head to the side.

"I am a second daughter. Practically ignored. Never invited to parties or balls. Never thought of or really seen. I long to truly live. To be a part of everything." No longer kept hidden away while Chrysantha experiences it all. I never wanted to wait my turn.

"I see you," the king says, and the shadows around him heighten ever so slightly, as if they, too, are acknowledging me. "Tell me, Lady Stathos, what would you do with the acknowledgment you so desire if it was suddenly given to you?"

"How do you mean?"

"It can't be just the attention you're after, can it? That would be very petty, and you do not strike me as the petty type. So tell me—this acknowledgment. Why do you want it?"

I take a slow sip of wine while I think through my answer, wondering what he expects me to say. In the end, I opt for the truth again.

"I want friends. I want to be a bigger part of the world around me. If I'm seen and respected, others will value my opinion. I want the power to change things."

"Change? Such as changing a law that prevents younger daughters from entering society until the eldest is engaged?"

"Exactly," I answer.

"I think we might have some common goals, Lady Stathos."

I remember my earlier conversation with Rhoda and the realization that the king is looking for a murderer among those at court. That, coupled with all the questions he's presented me with tonight, prompts my outburst.

"Why am I here?" I ask.

The king interlaces his fingers in front of him and leans his chin over the top. "I have a council breathing down my neck. I am nineteen. A young king, they say, and until I am twenty-one, I have to go to them for permission for everything I do and heed their counsel in all things. What they want most is for me to find a wife and ensure that, should anything happen to me, an heir is already taken care of."

I don't breathe as he says the next bit.

"I have no intention of taking a wife or making heirs. I have an empire to build and traitors to root out of my very court. What I need is for the council to stop hounding me, and if I were to have the appearance of courting someone, they would do just that.

"You are here, Lady Stathos, because I'm looking for a friend. Someone who isn't seeking to be a queen, as you are not. Someone who isn't afraid to tell me what they are thinking, no matter if they think I will dislike it. And our friendship will also have the benefit of appeasing the council.

"You are beautiful," he continues. "But not so beautiful as to tempt me. You are everything I am looking for. You are perfect."

I don't have words. So as not to have my jaw hanging down to the table, I put another bite of cake on my tongue.

You are perfect, he'd said. Right after *not so beautiful as to tempt me*.

I want to slap him. I want to kiss him. I want to throw the rest of my cake in his face as much as I want to finish off the delicious dessert.

I take another bite. I have too many thoughts swarming my mind, but I can grasp one thing.

"You would use me," I say. Flat. Deadpan.

He sets his fork back onto the plate beside his cake. "I'm not looking to use you. I'm offering you a trade. Remain here at court. Allow everyone to draw their own conclusions about the two of us. And in return, everyone in this castle will know your name. You won't miss another party or ball ever again. Every invitation will be given to you, so many that you couldn't possibly accept them all."

"What makes you think I don't want to be queen?" I ask.

"If you had, you would have gotten in line with the rest of the girls. You wouldn't try to insult me every chance you get."

Good. He doesn't see through my charade.

I stare at the goblet on the table. After leaving him to squirm in his chair for a while longer, I say, "You will have to make up for the incredibly rude comment you just made if you expect us to become friends."

"Rude?"

"You said I wasn't beautiful enough."

His mouth drops open. "No, I said you were the right amount of beautiful. I said you're perfect."

Now I am just being petty.

Tamp it down for now. Put on a smile and accept his offer.

"Forgive me," he says a second later, surprising me. "It has been a long time since I've had a friend who didn't walk around on all fours. My words didn't come out the way I'd meant them."

But they did. And that's what's so infuriating.

But I say, "I accept your offer and all that comes with it."

"Excellent." The Shadow King switches out his cake for the still-steaming soup. "If we are to be friends, then surely I should call you Alessandra when we are alone?"

"We are not friends just yet, Your Majesty, but once we are, what shall I call you?"

A faint smile still lingers on his lips. "My name is Kallias. Kallias Maheras."

"Kallias," I say, letting the syllables drift off my tongue: *kuh-LIE-us.*

I have been entrusted with the name of a king.

Now I need him to give me his heart.

CHAPTER 6

fume as I walk back to my rooms.

Not beautiful enough to tempt him, am I? We'll see about that. I'm going to make him fall so in love with me, he'll forget he ever saw another woman. He will be *begging* for me by the time I'm done with him.

And then he'll beg for his life right before I end him.

That sweet thought sustains me as I reach my rooms and tread toward my bed.

The king was not wrong. A large pile of letters rests on the table in my room, but I don't get to open them right away.

There's a man next to my bed. I half hoped it would be handsome Leandros, just so I could have a story to tell the king about chasing men away from my room. But alas.

It's Myron.

"What do you think you're doing?" I demand. "How did you even get in here?"

He's so tall his head is only a foot away from the ceiling. Impeccably dressed in black pants and a plum-colored coat, he turns at the sound of my voice.

"Alessandra, fancy seeing you here."

"It's my room!"

"Yes, and your maid was all too happy to let me in. All I had to do was smile and make up some story about leaving a trinket for you to find on your vanity. Apparently, she's a romantic."

I grimace. "For your sake, you'd better hope she doesn't talk."

"Why? Would it be so terrible for people to know I'd left you something?"

I stare at him, trying to make sense of why he could possibly be here, when he kicks off his shoes and reclines on my bed.

"Come here," he purrs.

"Get out," I say, my voice turning abrupt and sharp.

"Just because you didn't want my ring, it doesn't mean you don't want this. I know you."

"Since you've failed to notice, allow me to spell things out for you. *I don't want you.* The king is courting me now. The king, Myron. Why would I want the second son of a viscount, when I can have the Shadow King?"

Myron rises so quickly, the bed creaks. "He won't have you. You're not a virgin. Not after I was done with you."

I sigh. "Myron, just because you were a virgin when we met, it doesn't mean I was."

His mouth drops open.

"What did you say to Lord Vasco and the council?" I demand. "They said they spoke with you."

"I wasn't your first?"

I tug off my gloves and toss them aside, then do the same with my slippers. "Here's how this works. You don't say *anything* about knowing me ever again. You came to my father's estate a couple of times with your father on business. Nothing more. You saw me in passing. That is all."

"I didn't see you in passing. I saw you naked. More than once," he says threateningly. "I bet the council and your beloved Shadow King would love to hear that."

I toss my eyes heavenward. "That's not how this game is played. Have you forgotten, Myron? I know what you did. Your father gave you one of his most prized possessions. To *you*, his stupid second-born son. And you gambled it away. And if he found out? I'm betting a disinheritance is in your future."

Myron's jaw clenches.

"Why do you think I don't have a reputation, Myron? It's because I know how to play this game. Now leave, and don't ever speak to me again."

He grabs his shoes on the way out, slamming the door loudly enough for my neighbors to hear. As long as no one is out in the corridor, hopefully no one can guess which room he came from.

⇒·◆⟩·○·⟨◆·⟨

WITH MORNING COMES A fresh set of ideas for scheming. I'm getting my king, and I'm ridding the palace of anyone who gets in my way.

After breakfast, I tend to the pile of letters, rating them by importance. Invitations from duchesses and marchionesses go in one pile. Countesses and viscountesses in another pile. And those from baronesses I don't bother to open. I use my morning to make replies, accepting invitations and declining others. I write up a schedule for myself, so I can keep track of all my appointments, and then I send a letter to Eudora. I will need more evening attire. It won't do to be seen in the same dress twice.

Two hours later, and I call a maid to help me get ready. Naturally I had to fire my first maid, but the new one knows all kinds of fun coiffures. She piles my hair onto my head, placing every strand with an individual amethyst-studded pin. A gift from a previous lover, of course. My face is painted to perfection. I pull on lavender pants with a complicated bead design running down the front of each leg. The violet brocade overskirt is simply divine, with long sleeves and a floor-length hemline. I slip into black boots with a small heel, pull on black wrist-length gloves, and then head down for lunch.

Not so beautiful as to tempt me.

I huff as I remember those hateful words.

I appear to be one of the first to arrive in the great hall. Small groups of courtiers chat animatedly with one another. When I step into the room, a few heads turn, voices quiet to gossiping tones, and ladies pull out their fans.

And then a man approaches me.

"Lady Stathos! I'd hoped I'd get a chance to speak with you again."

Blond. Handsome. Perhaps a decade older than I. Where have I seen him before?

"Orrin, Lord Eliades," he says.

I still must give him a peculiar look because he adds, "Your father introduced us at the ball!"

Ah, that does the trick. He was the only person I met aside from the king. He kept bringing up Chrysantha and trying to compare me to her.

I do not like this man.

"I simply adored your sister while she stayed at the palace," he says before I've even offered a reply, "and I know you are just as wonderful! Since we had such a connection at the king's ball the other night, I hoped you might like to attend the countess's upcoming charity ball with me. I'm sure you've received the invitation. Alekto is a friend, and I adore functions that raise money for the less fortunate. I simply have so much money to spend!" He laughs as though he's told some joke before continuing. "I once bought a blanket for every child in the Naxosian Orphanage. Do you know how many blankets that is? Two hundred and thirty-seven. Can you believe so many poor souls are—"

"Excuse me," I say. Leandros has entered the room, and since he doesn't consider me a consolation prize after failing to wed my sister, I turn my back on Orrin without the slightest bit of guilt.

In fact, I have to physically shake off that last conversation. Charity. Orphans. The devils wasted good looks on such a man.

I put on a smile for Leandros and his companions.

"Lady Stathos!"

"Leandros."

He's quite dashing today, dressed in a teal waistcoat and brown boots. The color really makes his hair shine. He's flanked by two other men. His friends who fended off the courtiers while we were out in the orchards, I believe.

"Alessandra," he amends, since I used his given name. "Lovely to see you."

A not-so-subtle elbow jabs into Leandros's side, and he remembers that we are not alone. "Right. These are my friends, and they are desperate to make your acquaintance. Meet Petros." He points to a tall fellow with a generous helping of freckles across his nose and cheeks. Somehow, the imperfections only make him more handsome. "And Rhouben." Rhouben wears the boldest and most vibrant clothing I've ever seen. He mixes bright blues and greens together in such a daring way, looking as fine as any peacock. I think he might do it to make up for the plainness of his features.

"Gentlemen," I say.

Each takes my hand in turn and offers a kiss atop my glove.

"At last," Rhouben says, when he drops my hand. "I've been dying to meet the only person at court who dresses better than I do."

"I would argue," I say, "but I would only do it to be polite."

He laughs. "And honest on top of it all. You are a rare treasure."

"Careful now," Petros says. "You're an engaged man, Rhouben. Hands off."

"Congratulations," I offer to the first man. "Who is the lucky lady?"

Rhouben grimaces. "Melita Xenakis."

"I haven't met her yet. Is she here?"

Petros looks over his shoulder. "Yes, she's the one looking distastefully at Rhouben's coat."

I find Melita immediately. Perfect blond ringlets rest over her shoulders, covering a blue brocade. In fact, I now note, all the ladies are wearing blue. Which I wore yesterday. I smile in satisfaction. As if sensing my stare, Melita's gaze catches mine. Her features change into a hideous scowl, as though I committed some crime by looking at her. Or by speaking with her betrothed.

"In that case, you have my condolences," I say. "She's awfully protective of you, isn't she?"

Petros slaps his friend on the back and laughs. "You don't know the half of it. She's like a leech, sticking to Rhouben's arm everywhere he goes. And, oh, you'll love this! His father didn't even tell him about the betrothal until it was already done."

Rhouben groans at the memory.

I struggle not to laugh. "And what of you, Petros? Are you courting anyone?"

"Not anymore," he says sadly. "I'd had my eye on Estevan Banis, but at the king's ball, he danced three times in a row with Lord Osias."

"Men can be so fickle," I offer.

"Indeed."

"And you, Leandros?" I ask, including him in the conversation.

"I am completely unattached, so you needn't worry." He gives me a devilish grin.

"Alas, I am now spoken for," I say. "The king requested permission to court me just last night!"

Rhouben and Petros offer their congratulations, but Leandros looks appropriately put out. As the conversation continues, I let my eyes catch on the new noblemen entering the great hall. I offer them bright smiles, which is all it takes to get them to come join in on the conversation. Our group of four quickly grows to ten. All the young men are eager to ask me questions: Which functions will I be attending? Is my dance card all full for the next ball? Why haven't I graced the court with my presence before now?

I haven't mentioned that the king is courting me since I told Leandros and his friends. The new men don't need to know, especially since I need them for this little show I'm putting on for the king.

A herald calls something, but it can't be heard over our chatter in the corner. But out of the corner of my eye, I watch as the Shadow King enters the great hall. In fact, I've been waiting for it. Those seated at the table who spot him rise to show respect.

Kallias doesn't sit right away. He makes those at the table remain standing as his eyes do a sweep around the room. Though I'm not watching him outright, I can feel the moment they land on me. It's as if a current of heat zaps through the air.

At the next thing Petros says, I laugh a little louder than needed.

See? I want to shout. *Most men find me beautiful. Most men find me* irresistible.

"Lady Stathos." The words aren't shouted, but they resonate through the room as much as if they had been. The men around me quiet instantly and turn to bow to their sovereign.

"Yes, my king?" I ask.

"Have you already told everyone our news?"

"No, sire."

He holds out an arm in my direction while addressing the room. "I'm courting Lady Stathos." His gaze flits meaningfully to the next table over, where his councilors are seated.

The men around me suddenly step backward as though caught

doing something naughty. All save Leandros, Petros, and Rhouben, who don't seem to care at all that the king has just publicly claimed me as his.

They were his friends. He cast them aside. Why should they care if they irritate him?

Lord Ikaros Vasco, the head of the council, rises and holds up his glass of wine. "To a happy courtship!"

Those around the room raise their glasses in turn and repeat the words. Vasco keeps his eyes on mine while he sips from his cup.

I'm watching you, that look says.

I offer a sincere smile in response before inclining my head to the room of congratulators.

Then I let my eyes rest back on the king. I cannot tell by his features if he's reacting at all to seeing me surrounded by men, but perhaps his declaration is reaction enough. He *verbally* claimed me. Or was that for the benefit of the council alone? It is them, after all, whom he needs to convince of our betrothal.

The king is wearing a violet waistcoat, I realize then. Somehow, we've managed to match our clothing yet again. It's as if we are trying to look like a united front.

As if I were always meant to be his queen.

Kallias lifts a finger and gestures to the seat at his right. A servant leaps from his place at the wall and rushes to pull out the chair. Carefully. Oh so carefully with his proximity to the king.

That's when I notice that two empty chairs rest to the left and right of the king. No one is permitted to sit within two seats of him.

Except me.

The spot to his immediate right is presented to me, and the hall goes quiet as one after the other, the nobles notice that chair—the one right next to the king—being held open.

I tug at my gloves, making sure they're secure, before I excuse myself from my circle of admirers and cross the distance to Kallias.

Once I'm seated, I keep my hands in my lap, careful not to bump anything or touch a certain someone. We're much closer than the law's five feet, but if Kallias is permitting it, I'm not about to complain. Besides, the most delicious scent of lavender and mint and musk fills my senses at the close proximity. The Shadow King smells delicious.

Kallias brings a mouthful of what looks like some sort of vegetable soup to his lips. "I see you're making friends. Is acknowledgment everything you hoped it would be?"

"Too soon to tell."

A servant places a napkin in my lap before resuming his position along the exterior of the room.

"You look exquisite today," the king says, pitching his voice low. We're separated enough that I don't think anyone else at the table can hear.

"You're trying to make up for what you said yesterday," I say in an equally reserved tone.

"I'm merely speaking the truth."

Well, it's a start.

Down the table, I watch pair after pair of eyes pretending not to be watching me. The men wonder what I've done to have the king claim me. The women watch my every move, wondering how they could get the king to claim *them*.

My eyes land on Myron, briefly, who looks away as soon as he realizes he's been caught staring.

Good boy.

I can't believe how well the king has already delivered on his promise. Those letters in my room are a result of dancing with me, of speaking to me where we could be seen in the orchards. And after his announcement today? I can't even imagine what doors he's opened for me now.

"Do you suppose all the women will be wearing purple tomorrow?" I ask, before turning my attention to my food.

"I suspect they'll try to pay off your maids to tell them what color you put on in the mornings."

At that, my eyes narrow. "Is that what you did?" I look meaningfully at his attire that matches my own. "Or did you simply peer through the wall into my bedroom to take a look for yourself?"

Those teeth flash in the widest grin yet. "I promise it's been years since I peeked in on ladies dressing. I'm not twelve anymore."

I sample my own dish. It's just as delicious as last night's supper. "Were you caught?"

"Oh, yes. When Lady Kalfas spotted me, she ratted me out to my mother, who gave me such a scolding that I was never even tempted to try again."

"What words could have possibly persuaded you not to try again?"

"She told me that if I persisted in looking, it was as far as I would ever get with the ladies. And she said no one would ever respect me if I didn't respect them."

I smile into my bowl. "And was it the idea of never getting respect or never getting to do more than look that did it for you?"

"Both," he admits. "As well as the idea of ever having to discuss such things with my mother again."

I laugh gently at that. Though part of me can't help but wonder if he ever did get to do more than look. Intimate relations would be impossible when the law forbids anyone from touching him, wouldn't they?

After a break in the conversation, I say, "Your council is watching us closely."

It's true, though they're being more subtle about it than those seated at our own table.

"They're put out because I forbade them from sitting with me during mealtimes. I have to talk politics all day, but I refuse to have it grace the luncheon table."

"There are ladies on your council?" I say it like a question. I'd assumed they were part of the council, but I realize now that they could simply be the wives of the men. These are modern times, and ladies have more rights and liberties than ever before. Still, the monarchy tends to be slower to adapt than everyone else.

"Yes, Lady Desma Terzi is the royal treasurer. I've never met anyone better with numbers. And then Lady Tasoula Mangas is my liaison with the common folk here in the city. She keeps tabs on the merchants and the economy, apprising me of anything noteworthy."

"And the other two gentlemen? I've already had the pleasure of meeting Vasco." If I'm to run the kingdom one day, I will need to know the names of all those on the council.

"Lord Vasco can be protective. He was an old friend of my father's. He's the most well-connected man in the kingdom. If there's a problem I need solving, he's the first to have a solution. Then there's Kaiser, the general over the men stationed here in the city. And lastly, Ampelios. He . . . gets things done."

"Assassin?" I guess immediately.

Kallias takes a sip of his drink. "Among other things."

We both watch as Ampelios takes a sharp knife to the meat in front of him, slicing the steak into even pieces and stabbing them with the point to place a morsel on his tongue.

"Those are the five individuals you are putting on a show for," Kallias adds.

"I've been told I would have made an excellent actress were it not for my noble birth."

"I don't doubt it." Kallias sweeps his eyes over the guests seated at our table. "I've placed at my own table those closer to my age. Not that it matters much with the distance I must maintain from them."

I want to ask him *why* he must maintain such a distance. Why does the law prevent people from touching him? Does it have something to do with his shadows? But I do not know the king well enough to ask such questions yet.

CHAPTER 7

After lunch, I take a look at the schedule I've made myself to locate the soonest event. A troupe of performers is attending the Viscount of Christakos's estate this Friday, and a party of guests has been invited to come watch a performance of *The Lovers*, a play in which two people find love despite all the obstacles keeping them apart.

Though Kallias will undoubtedly have received an invitation as well, it would be best to let him know I'm attending, so he may accompany me.

I pull a piece of parchment from a stack on the desk and select a pen. Knowing the letter will only be for his eyes, I begin.

Dear Kallias,

I have received an invitation to attend a play held at the home of the Viscount and Viscountess of Christakos. The performance is supposed to be the story of two lovers coming together despite outstanding odds. Wouldn't it add credence to our ruse to be seen together at such a performance? I do hope you will accompany me.

Your friend,
Alessandra

It is not even an hour later when a servant finds me with a reply.

Dearest Alessandra,

Thank you for your invitation, but I'm afraid I must decline. A new problem has arisen, one that requires me to be in constant meetings all week long. I'll barely have the time to break for meals over this one.

But do enjoy the play without me. I'm sure it will be splendid. At least I can work knowing you won't be bored.

Your friend,
Kallias

I retrieve a fresh piece of paper.

Kallias,

What problem? Is there anything I can do?

Your friend,
Alessandra

Alessandra,

News will spread sooner or later, but it would seem the kingdom has a dangerous bandit on the loose. He's attacking nobles on the road and stealing their money. Lady Mangas of the council informs me that there's a sudden surplus in money flow among the peasants, so we can only conclude the bandit is stealing from the titled and giving it to the common folk. Naturally, I can't have my own people fear traveling. I must put a stop to this at once.

Thank you for your offer of help, but I'm certain we'll put this to rest quickly, so long as we can give it our full attention.

Your friend,
Kallias

Who in the world would steal and then not keep the riches for themselves? That's just bad business. Someone that stupid must surely be caught soon.

Nevertheless, I should be involved in this. The nobles who were robbed will be paying taxes to *me* in the future. If Kallias doesn't solve this problem, it will become mine.

But how does one catch a thief who doesn't retain his finds? That makes it far more difficult to track them down. I will have to think on this. It is a situation that must be handled carefully.

>─┼─◆>─○─<◆─┼─<

ANOTHER LETTER ARRIVES SHORTLY THEREAFTER, again from Kallias. He invites me to join him for dinner. Naturally, I accept.

However, I decide to keep him waiting. I don't want him to think me too eager.

After fifteen minutes pass by, I join the servant waiting outside my rooms. He escorts me to the library once more.

When I enter, a large furry mass darts for me. Demodocus comes to a halt mere inches away. When he sees that he has my full attention, he flops onto the floor, belly up.

"I'm so glad you're happy to see me," I say as I lift one foot to rub his belly.

Kallias, who stood at my entrance, says, "You kept him waiting. Belly rubs are the price you must pay."

"Forgive me, Demodocus," I say, as I rub my foot into longer strokes. The dog's eyes lull back into his skull. "I was working on something and didn't want to leave it unfinished. Are we even now?"

I dare to raise my leg, and the dog rolls over and runs for Kallias's feet before plopping down in front of him, panting.

Kallias waits for me to sit before picking up his silverware and digging in.

Our supper has already been served. Tonight it's chicken legs dripping in a brown gravy, peeled vegetables sprinkled with salt, bread sticks dribbled with butter and honey, and chocolate éclairs for dessert, if I'm not mistaken.

"I took the liberty of arranging the first course for you," he says, indicating the éclair before me. "I suggest you hurry, however, so the rest of the food doesn't grow cold."

If he's irritated by my lateness, he doesn't show any sign of it. Perhaps it's only my imagination that the shadows are moving about him more swiftly.

I dip my finger into the whipped cream atop the éclair and bring it to my lips. Forgoing a fork, I grab the delicate pastry in one hand and bite into it. Chocolate fills my mouth. I think to compliment Kallias on his chef, but I'm brought short by the look on his face.

"Something wrong?" I ask, knowing full well he was distracted by the sensual way in which I sampled my food.

He clears his throat and ignores the question. "What were you working on?"

"The first piece of a new outfit," I say, thinking back to yesterday's sewing project. "I'm trying out a new style of my own design."

"Another scandalous piece, I hope?"

I grin. "I hardly see how my pieces are considered scandalous. All my skin is covered up." More or less. "Not an ankle or wrist to be seen."

He chews slowly on a bite of chicken as his eyes land on my wrist. "I noticed. Is that for my sake? Or do you prefer to keep your hands covered?"

I look at his own gloved hands. "I certainly don't mind gloves. They are a fun accessory to any outfit. But since the law forbids us to touch, it seemed wise for me to keep wearing them when we will be spending quite a lot of time together."

"How very self-preserving of you."

His expression is unreadable. I can't tell if he's toying with me or something else.

Out of curiosity, I ask, "Would you kill me? If I were to touch you?"

He keeps his eyes on me as he takes a swallow from his glass. "Why should you ever need to touch me?"

"It's not uncommon for friends to touch. Handshakes. Hugs. Playful shoves when one says something irritable. Surely you've had friends before? Leandros said you two used to be close."

He doesn't answer, turning his gaze to his food. But I am not to be dismissed so easily.

"Surely you didn't need to push your friends away after you became king? You can't suspect them of killing your parents, can you?"

"Until my parents' murderer is rooted out, I trust no one."

"But what could they possibly gain from such a horrible scheme?" I ask.

He shrugs. "Perhaps they thought they were helping by making me king."

"If they were truly your friends, they would know you had no desire to see your parents hurt."

Kallias swallows the food in his mouth and pauses, as if wondering whether to tell me something.

"It's not the only reason I've kept them at bay."

"What do you mean?"

His eyes meet mine. "It's one thing to be tracking down the late king and queen's murderer. It's another thing entirely to have an assassin after me while trying to root out my parents' murderer."

"Someone is trying to kill you?" I ask, surprised. "How do you know?"

He finishes his chicken and starts on a salted cucumber. "They've failed once already. Last month, my gloves were laced with a topical poison. When I put them on, my hands felt as though they were on fire. The toxin would have spread to my heart in under a minute, I'm told."

I eye the hands hidden behind gloves now. "Are you all right? How did you survive?"

"I am not so easy to kill. My shadows saved me."

I wonder if he also wears his gloves to cover burn marks. Whatever the poison was, it sounds terribly nasty.

"And you think your friends could have had something to do with it?" I ask.

"My friends. The council. Anyone of the nobility. A servant in the palace. It could be anyone. I can't take any chances."

I think of Leandros, Petros, and Rhouben. I honestly doubt any of them are capable of murder, especially with the way they look at their once-friend every time Kallias enters a room. They miss him. And what would they have to gain anyway? I suppose Leandros's uncle is on the council. If there's no king, Ikaros Vasco will remain in power for far longer. But that doesn't gain Leandros anything. He can't obtain the crown. A distant relative of the king would get it first.

And Petros doesn't strike me as the power-hungry type. I know little of his family, but he can't have any claim to the throne. Rhouben wants nothing more than to be free of his betrothed, as far as I can tell.

But I say none of this. If the king has already decided not to trust anyone, there's little I can do to convince him otherwise. And doing so would only put *me* under suspicion.

"Do you have any ideas as to who's responsible? Anything more specific than someone currently in the palace?"

Kallias eyes me suspiciously over the rim of his goblet.

"You are my ticket to acknowledgment. Remember? Without you I have nothing. No parties or respect." Until I can gain the latter on my own, of course. "No one is allowed to kill you on my watch. I want to help."

He nods, as though satisfied with my answer.

"I think someone on the council was involved. Simply because if I'm gone, there's no one in my direct line to pass the crown to. The council would rule my empire indefinitely. Until a new sovereign could be determined. I have many third cousins. They would have to battle for it. And it had to have been a noble or a member of the guard."

"How do you know that?"

"Because the palace was in a lockdown the night of the late king and queen's deaths. There was an insurgent group of peasants who were let into the palace, causing havoc. And no one save nobility would have been allowed into the safe room with my parents. When the room was opened, their bodies were found."

"Where were you?" I ask.

"On the other side of the palace. I'd been engaged in a game of sport with other noblemen's sons. We were taken to another safe room when the shooters were discovered to be within the palace."

"But it wasn't the shooters who got to the king and queen?"

"No. The intruders were all caught before they made it to the royal suites. It was a distraction. Someone let them in so they could have the opportunity to murder my father and mother."

The room goes quiet. Neither Kallias nor I are touching our food any longer.

"Such a dreary topic," Kallias says at last. "I don't wish to burden you with my troubles. I appreciate you wanting to help. But this is not for you to worry about."

"If I am to be your friend, surely you'll wish to share your troubles?"

He doesn't answer, as though just the mention of his troubles has his mind thinking of them.

I've lost him, so I say in a bright tone, "The council seems convinced of our ruse."

In the time it takes me to blink, the shadows lighten, turning to a mere haze, slowing in their movements. "Yes. They couldn't stop con-gratulating me during our meetings today."

"Then they approve of me?" Has Lord Ikaros dropped his suspicions of me?

"At this point, I'm certain they would approve of anything with a womb. They didn't say a word about your eccentricities."

"What eccentricities?"

"Your clothing," he says with a smile.

"That's hardly fair coming from a man clothed in shadows."

"Under my shadows is perfectly normal attire."

"Not that anyone would notice. You stand out like a spark in a dark room all on your own. For someone like me? I have to try to stand out."

"Not anymore," he says. "You are being courted by the king. That fact alone makes you the most popular girl in the world."

CHAPTER

8

A new slew of letters is delivered to me the next morning. For the most part, they're additional invitations to luncheons and balls and banquets. But one letter stands out. It's from Father.

Dear Alessandra,

Word has just reached me that the king has publicly announced your courtship. You have my congratulations. I'm proud of you. Though, I admit I'm disappointed that I had to hear the details from Lord Eliades instead of you. (The poor man appears smitten with you. He was quite upset over the news. It would seem we already have an excellent backup plan in place should you fail with the king. Orrin is very rich, after all.)

I pause in reading to shake off the thought of having to marry Eliades. He's quite handsome, but I wouldn't last two minutes alone with the man. Not if he thinks charity and saving kittens are the most interesting topics of conversation. I continue reading.

Your sister was most glad to hear of your courtship as well. She—

I skip that paragraph.

Finally, I should tell you a constable came by the house, accompanied by Faustus Galanis, Baron of Drivas. You remember Lord Drivas, don't you? I believe you befriended his son, Hektor. Surely you remember the poor lad went missing some three years ago? Lord Drivas is now convinced his son is dead, and he and a Constable Hallas are conducting an investigation. They asked me quite a lot of questions about your relationship with Hektor. I think they're hoping you might have an idea of where he could have gone after he ran away.

I've told them you saw Hektor only a handful of times when he came by the estate with his father, but I wouldn't be surprised if they should wish to question you personally. Anything you can tell them about the last time you saw Hektor would probably prove most useful.

And by the devils, please tell me he was not one of your bedmates. It wouldn't do at all if that came out during their investigation. Not when you're making such headway with the king!

Do be careful, darling, and perhaps do what you can to speed up that courtship. Hmm?

Sincerely,
Your Loving Father

My hand has the letter in a death grip by the time I read the signature. Why the devils would an investigation suddenly be brought up? They couldn't have found Hektor's body, could they?

No, I assure myself. No, they couldn't possibly . . .

IT WAS DIFFICULT GETTING Hektor's body out of my room after I killed him. The only stroke of luck was that he insulted me in my bed, and that's where he drew his last breath. That made it possible to roll him into an empty trunk. I latched the biggest lock I could find onto it and shut the key inside with Hektor's body before closing it.

No one was getting inside that trunk without a hatchet.

But that still left a mess in the room.

I burned my bedsheets in the hearth and told my lady's maid that my monthly bleeding soiled my mattress. I was surprised she believed the lie. I hadn't bled in months due to my tincture that prevents pregnancy.

I knew it wouldn't be long before Hektor started to stink, so the very next day, I rang for a couple of servants to carry my trunk into the carriage. I told them I was off to meet several friends for a picnic, and I drove the team of horses myself.

Once I found the perfect spot, deep into the Undatia Forest, I waited for the cover of darkness. Ever since meeting Hektor, it wasn't unusual for me to be gone overnight, and neither the staff nor my father would think twice about it, though I knew I would get an earful from Father later.

Digging the hole was the most undignified thing I've ever done. It took nearly all night, with many breaks to rest my aching muscles. By the time I deemed the hole deep enough, I realized my mistake.

It was too deep, and I could not get out.

I screamed in my panic, stuck in that hole with nothing but a shovel. I thought to perhaps dig myself stairs, but I wondered if my strength would leave me entirely before I managed it.

It started to rain.

Finally, I thought clearly enough to remove my boots from my feet. I jabbed the heels into the earth and used them to crawl my way out. My muscles spasmed within my body, and my dress was damp with mud, my nostrils full of dirt.

But I would not allow myself to die in the grave I'd dug.

When I finally shoved the trunk over the lip of the cart, the lid cracked open, and Hektor stared up at me as I started to cover his face with dirt.

I was careful. The rain washed away the horses' tracks. And when I returned early the next morning, all that was left was to destroy my dress and make it to my room without being seen.

I handled Hektor as I have handled everything else in my life: alone and with the utmost thoroughness.

They could not have found him. Even if someone went traveling into the Undatia Forest, there's no way they could know they were standing on a grave.

In which case, Lord Drivas must think that Hektor has simply been gone too long to be away on holiday, and he's somehow found it within himself the desire to find his son. Not that he should care that much—what with Hektor being the fourth spare to his heir.

Something's changed, but I shan't let it bother me. To do any searching would only attract more attention to me. I will prepare my answers carefully for when Lord Drivas and his constable come knocking. Otherwise, I shall carry on as before.

>—!—◆>—O—<◆—!—<

SOME DAYS LATER, I stare up at the night-painted ceiling in the queen's sitting room. Once I am queen, I think I will have it redone. I can see the stars outside any night I wish. What I'd like to have painted are things I can't readily see. Perhaps a landscape from each of the five kingdoms Naxos has conquered. Soon to be my kingdoms.

"There," Hestia proclaims. "Did I do it right?"

I look down at her handiwork. "No. The stitches should be even, and you'll want to pull them tighter. This will fall apart as soon as you try to put it on."

She sighs. "All right. Tighter and more even. I can do that. But how do I fix what I've already done?"

I grab the needle from her and pull until the thread slips from the eye. I place the point under the last stitch and use it to pull the thread free.

"Repeat," I say, handing the needle back to her.

Hestia settles back into her seat and concentrates. She's wearing a gown in a lovely shade of turquoise, which I wore yesterday. I wonder if imitating me in all regards is getting her anywhere at court.

Rhoda, however, is dressed in a bright yellow gown that shows off all her curves to their best effect. She is taking my advice to disregard her mourning period quite well.

Rhoda sits on the other side of Hestia, asking Galen for his opinion on which thread she should use for the flower she's stitching. He holds several colors out for her to examine, and they discuss the merits of each. I'm still baffled by how much she interacts with her manservant, but I like her enough not to say anything of it. I can be nice to Galen if it's what Rhoda would want.

But I have to wonder if Rhoda notices the way Galen looks at her. He seems far too distracted by her sudden change in clothing. Or maybe it's just her.

The door to the sitting room opens suddenly, and a stocking- and wig-clad servant enters, holding a box in his hands.

"What are you doing?" Rhoda demands, standing from her chair. "No men are permitted within this room." Apparently Galen doesn't count.

"Forgive me, ladies, but the king sent me. I have something for Lady Stathos."

"Over here," I say, my countenance brightening.

"My lady," the servant says, dipping into a bow before me and holding out the black box.

I take it, the wrapping paper crinkling under my fingers. A bloodred ribbon wraps around the box before ending in a bow on top. The package is fairly light, and the gentlest scent of lavender-mint wafts up from it.

Kallias wrapped it himself.

"Oh, go on, Alessandra," Hestia says, her voice growing higher. "Open the king's present!"

I tug at the bow, and it falls away. Carefully, I unfold the paper. Somehow, it seems indelicate to tear it. Once done, I find the front and pull up on the lid, the hinges snapping upward without a sound.

My breath catches.

I have received countless jewels and precious stones from my lovers, but this—

Nestled in black velvet is a necklace unlike anything I've ever seen. The rubies have been cut into the shapes of petals, spreading outward into a blooming rose the size of a tightly closed fist. Black steel frames each gem, giving a beautiful border to the petals, allowing each jewel to stand out.

The ladies in the room gasp appropriately.

Rhoda bends over my shoulder to give the trinket a proper look.

"My, my," she says. "The king must be head over heels for you." Quieter, she adds, "Well done, Alessandra."

Hestia is so close, her breath is fogging up the gems. I promptly close the lid and hand the box back to the servant.

"See to it that this is placed within my quarters," I say.

"Of course." He goes back out the way he came in.

"What's he like?" Rhoda wants to know. "The king?"

All the needlework is forgotten as the ladies lean forward in their seats.

"He's very smart and capable," I say, thinking of all the meetings and problems he juggles. "And thoughtful."

"Oh, do give us details!" Hestia says.

Drunk on the attention, I can't help but give them some details. I tell them of how we eat our desserts first when we dine together. How he compliments me on my new attire. How he smells of lavender and mint. How fond he is of his giant dog. I also tell them falsehoods. I talk of how Kallias kisses my gloved hands in private. How he whispers into my ear of our future. Of a romantic outing under the stars when everyone else is asleep.

I have to really sell the idea of our courtship, after all.

"He's a romantic," I finish, loving the way the whole room tries to grasp my every word.

>—+—<>—○—<>—+—<

I RECEIVE A NOTE stating Kallias is unavailable for dinner together due to a late-running meeting. I suspect he is still hard at work attempting to put a stop to the bandit. Rumors are everywhere in the palace. Apparently there was another attack. The nobles are putting pressure on their king.

I sup alone in my rooms, arranging the necklace on the table next to me so I can admire it.

Afterward, a maid helps me out of my dress and into a nightgown. If she thinks anything about the nightgowns I've made myself, she says nothing of them.

Tonight I wear a creamy yellow number of silk. The sleeves—or straps, really—dangle off my shoulders, and the gown dips in the front to reveal just a hint of my breasts. Less than a hint, really. A mere line meant not to give too much away, but enough to drive a man mad with wanting to see more.

If only I had someone to show it off to.

I sit on the edge of my bed, my hands behind me, supporting my weight, when he appears.

I jump to my feet before I can stop myself, my heart racing.

Even though I've seen him walk through walls before, it doesn't exactly prepare me. I have a feeling it's not something I could ever get used to.

I'm proud of myself for not shrieking at least.

I catch sight of the king's face once he steps farther into the room and realize he's glaring at me. His fists are clenched tightly at his sides. Despite the late hour, he's clothed from neck to toe in his day attire.

"I thought you were done peering in on ladies while they were dressing," I say.

His jaw shakes slightly as he says, "You're clothed."

"But I might not have been. If you had knocked first—"

"What the hell have you done?"

I cross my arms. I refuse to cower, king or no. "What's the matter with you? I've done nothing."

Unable to bear shouting at me from so far away, he comes forward until we're mere feet apart. "The whole castle is buzzing with it! Did you or did you not tell the ladies in my mother's sitting room that we've touched?"

Cold fingers walk down my spine. I'm unsure whether it's better to lie or not. "Servants gossip. They exaggerate."

"What. Did. You. Say?"

I step away from the bed. "I'm trying to sell our courtship. I embellished our interactions. I said we take midnight strolls together and that you're more intimate when we're alone."

Why is he so worried? It's not as if he has a reputation to protect. He's the king. Royalty may do as they please.

"Did you say that we've touched? What were your exact words?" he demands.

I rack my brain, trying to find the wording. "I said you kissed my gloved hands in private."

"Gloved? You're sure you said gloved?"

"I'm certain. Why?"

He runs a hand through his hair, and the immaculate style falls away, the strands drooping to his ears.

"You cannot tell people that you've broken the law. You cannot—"

"You have no right to be angry with me!" I snap, quite finished with being reprimanded. "You tasked me with selling our courtship. That was the deal. If there were things I wasn't allowed to do, you should have said so. Now tell me why people cannot think that we've touched. And don't you dare try to tell me it's for my safety. You could pardon anyone for anything. You're king. So what do such rumors mean for you?"

The anger falls from his face, and I think he realizes for the first time that I'm in a nightgown. His eyes trail down the length of me. Slowly, just as he did when we were first introduced at the ball.

"They make me weak."

He turns on his heel and disappears through the solid wall of my room.

CHAPTER

9

I demand my maid look for something red in my wardrobe the next morning. I know exactly the garment she will find. A floor-length dress that requires a petticoat to give it some volume. From my waist to the floor, the silk is gathered in bunches, giving it a tastefully wrinkled look. The bodice turns black at the torso and hugs my waist, coming to a little point over each breast, giving me full coverage. The dress is sleeveless, but I wear gloves that climb nearly to my shoulders.

I didn't want to detract from my new necklace by wearing a dress with sleeves.

My maid does the clasp at the back, and the red rose pendant falls over my collarbone, matching everything beautifully.

I am not wearing the dress for the king. Not after last night. No, I'm forced to wear his trinket because all the ladies in the sitting room saw me receive it. How would it look if I were not to wear it?

As soon as I'm done, a tray is brought in and placed on the table, a breakfast of fresh fruits, porridge with sugar, and freshly squeezed juice.

Next to the first tray, a servant brings in a second, setting it on the other side of my little table.

"What is this?" I ask.

Then Kallias walks in, and the servants leave us alone in the parlor.

"I should have known," I grumble as I take my seat, wondering if I should be prepared for more chastising from him.

"I thought I would join you today," he says, holding out my chair for me. "I should visit your chambers to sell our act. We will, of course, avoid the bedchamber, so as not to ruin your reputation."

I take a sip of my juice before saying, "You were in my bedchamber last night. Is that room only to be reserved for when you feel like yelling?"

He looks down, ashamed. "I was hasty to make assumptions. I should have known the ladies would exaggerate their gossip." He looks up from his food, taking a proper look at me. At my neck. "Do you like my present?"

"I liked it better before you yelled at me."

His eyes darken, and he stops the hand that was on its way to run through his hair. He holds absolutely still for a moment, as though thinking through something carefully.

"Ah," he says at last. "I have not yet apologized."

"No, you haven't."

"I'm sorry for behaving like an ass last night. Could you ever forgive me, Alessandra, my friend, if I promise never to do it again?"

"Do what, precisely?" I ask.

"Jump to conclusions without coming to you first, in earnest. Not in anger."

I take my time, making a good show of thinking it over. But of course I forgive him. He has by far given me the sincerest apology I've ever received.

"You could yell at me in turn, if it would make you feel better," he offers.

"I'm not in a mood for yelling."

"Then save it for when you are in the right mood. It's only fair."

I crack a smile. "I forgive you."

The tension in his shoulders relaxes, and he focuses on the meal before him. Without looking up, he says, "The necklace is lovely on you."

He's really fishing for my gratitude. Is he worried I do not like it?

"It's the most exquisite gift I've ever received," I say truthfully.

A small smile reaches the corners of his lips. "No doubt you've received many gifts from men."

"No doubt," I answer playfully.

"Has Lord Eliades tried to woo you with gifts?"

"So you've noticed his attentions toward me?"

"I think everyone in the castle can tell he's smitten with you."

I smile. "Not yet, he hasn't."

"Good." As an afterthought, he adds, "Because it wouldn't do for people to think you're being courted by someone other than me. It would ruin our plans."

"Of course." But could that have been just a smidgeon of jealousy in his tone?

I ENTER MY ROOMS for the evening, having spent a lovely afternoon with the ladies in the sitting room. I didn't see Kallias, save for breakfast. More and more it's becoming important for me to find a way into the meeting rooms. Not only do I wish to get a head start on running the kingdom, but if those rooms are where Kallias spends the majority of his time, then I need to be there.

How else am I to get him to fall in love with me if we're not spending more time together?

I send my maid away as soon as I'm dressed in a simple nightgown and approach the bed.

"Alessandra."

I gasp so loudly, I nearly choke on the air. My hand goes flying to my heart.

"What the *devils*, Myron?"

He emerges from my wardrobe of all places, dressed in pristine brocade, not a wrinkle in sight despite the cramped quarters he was in.

"Why the hell are you coming out of my wardrobe?" I demand.

"The only way I could sneak in here was to wait until a servant was distracted in cleaning. Then I waited for you."

"I thought I made it perfectly clear that we would not be speaking anymore. How *dare* you ignore my wishes? That won't go without consequences."

Myron grins like he's just won his father's inheritance before folding himself into a cushioned chair near my bed. "That's the problem, Alessandra. You no longer have anything to hold over me."

My face remains a mask of indifference, but my skin prickles with fear. "What are you talking about?"

"Haven't you heard the news yet? My father expired this morning. My brother has inherited the viscounty. We're quite close, Proteus and I. I assure you he won't care one whit that I lost that thrice-damned pendant in a game of cards. Proteus also has a love of gaming."

My blood turns cold in my veins. My leverage is gone. "Proteus must be much better at gaming than you, considering he hasn't gambled away every penny he owns."

Myron's jaw clenches, and he stands abruptly. "No, see, you don't get to talk to me like that anymore, Alessandra. Not unless you want the whole palace to know just how much of a strumpet you really are."

My vision goes blurry, and sheer anger buzzes through me. My dagger is in my boot. I contemplate using it for all of a second.

But Hektor's death is being looked into. I can't have another death on my hands. And I'd never get the body out of the palace unseen. No, this situation has to be dealt with very carefully.

Perhaps I could lure Myron away from the palace before killing him?

"Nothing to say?" Myron asks. "Or does your mind need more time to process this? Perhaps I can assist by making your situation perfectly clear." He leans forward. "I own you. You will do whatever I say, whenever I say it. And you're going to start by getting me into that play at the viscount's estate tomorrow night."

"The play?" I ask. "Why should you wish to go?"

"Because it's time I made some more powerful friends. I owe a lot of money to a lot of people. My brother can do only so much for me. But you? The woman courting the king? You're going to get me into the most prestigious estates in the kingdom. And when the world sees you—the king's *chosen*—hanging off my arm, they'll know I'm someone to pay attention to."

No no no no no no no no.

I let out a breath of air as calmly as I can manage before sitting on the edge of my bed, placing a defeated look upon my face.

"I was wrong to treat you as I did, Myron. I'm so sorry. But we don't need to be enemies. We can help each other. I'm happy to get you into the play."

"Save the act," Myron says, unmoved. "I've known you too long to know when you're faking."

"I guarantee you never could tell when I was faking."

Myron's cheeks go red, and his neck looks like it might pop a vein. He strides over to me and raises a hand as though he might hit me. He pauses, then drops it. "I'm not one for violence. I don't need to strike you. Like I said, I own you. Now get me into that play, or I'll tell the king all about how you like to spend your nights."

⊱─┼─◈─○─◈─┼─⊰

THIS COULD NOT BE HAPPENING.

I've always sat at the king's side, all the nobility watching my every move, as though they could learn the secrets to life's greatest mysteries if they only stared at me long enough.

And today?

Today, Myron sits on my left, not the king. Orrin, Lord Eliades, having seen an opportunity, quickly took the seat to my right. Rhoda and Hestia shoot me questioning gazes from across the table. But I can't manage to do much more than glare at my soup.

"We missed you dearly at the charity ball," Orrin says. "I donated two thousand necos to the homeless shelter in Naxos. Such a small amount compared to the vastness of my yearly income, but I intend to give much more throughout the year."

Myron leans over. "Smile, darling; everyone is watching. Come now, or I shall have to strike up a conversation that isn't appropriate for the luncheon table at all."

My lips turn up, but it's more of a grimace than anything else.

I honestly can't say which devil is worse, the one on my right or the one on my left.

I didn't sleep a wink last night. Instead, I've been plotting how to get out of my situation with Myron. So far, I don't have any ideas, save outright murder, but I need to be patient. And somehow make sure Myron doesn't jeopardize my standing with the king.

Leandros, Petros, and Rhouben sit together on the other side of Rhoda, chatting among themselves. Oh, I would give anything to be on that side of the table.

Melita Xenakis, Rhouben's betrothed, keeps a firm grasp on his arm, as though if she doesn't, he'll escape from her. Rhouben attempts to eat his food with his other hand while blatantly ignoring her.

Melita, however, keeps looking over at this side of the table in between each bite of food.

At Orrin, I realize.

Is that admiration in her eyes?

How interesting.

"What do you think of Lord Eliades's charitable acts, Lady Xenakis?" I ask, speaking over the top of Orrin's next dull remark.

Melita jolts as though coming out of a trance. "I beg your pardon?"

"Were you not admiring the earl's generosity? Or was it something else?"

Red flames her cheeks. She turns away from me and leans into Rhouben. I glance back and forth between Rhouben and Orrin. Orrin is certainly more handsome, which would probably entice a vain woman such as Melita. I've had several more conversations with Leandros and his friends since that first lunch meeting. I know Rhouben is the first-born of a viscount. A very rich viscount. He will inherit one day. But Orrin is an earl. Already in possession of his land and title.

An idea begins to form. One that just might rid me of both Orrin and Myron.

"His Majesty, the King!" a herald booms, and everyone is suddenly on their feet. Hestia stands so quickly that her spoon flicks droplets of stew onto Orrin's tunic. My mood improves ever so slightly.

Kallias strides into the room, takes one look at the empty seats at the head of the table, and says, "Lady Stathos?"

"Yes?" I ask, ever relieved that he's here.

"Come join me, won't you?"

I don't wait for a servant to help me out of my chair. I fairly leap from it. Kallias watches me as I sweep past Myron, a look of sheer gratitude upon my face.

"Who is that man? I don't know him," Kallias says as I sit.

"He's nobody," I say in all honesty.

"Now I'm more curious."

The great hall is back to chattering in full force, so I dare to raise my voice a little. "His name is Myron Calligaris. He's the son of a viscount."

"And how are you two acquainted?"

"His father had business with my father. We met on a few occasions when he would come over to the Masis estate."

Kallias has his attention on his food, but I can't help but feel as though the indifference is forced. "You're friends, then?"

"Not anymore." I make the mistake of looking down the table at Myron, who winks at me.

"He seems awfully friendly."

That tone. Oh, how I wish I could read it. "You could group him with Eliades."

"Ah. An admirer who is hesitant to give up. I can hardly fault them for that."

I place my hands on my lap as a servant retrieves my plate from my previous seat and lays it before me.

"Did another meeting keep you?" I ask carefully. "Has the bandit struck again?"

Kallias's shadows darken. "Not since the last time, no. But we've had word of another problem."

I nod, focusing my attention on my food. I don't want to ask. I want him to tell me on his own. I want him to confide in me. To trust me.

My patience is rewarded.

"We've had delegates arrive from Pegai." The most recent kingdom Kallias has conquered. "The news they bring isn't good. There are open acts of rebellion happening right and left. The people kill my soldiers.

Start fires in the barracks. Throw rotten food upon my regent when she travels the streets."

"They oppose your rule?"

A muscle ticks in his jaw. "They were beaten. I conquered them fair and square. Their taxes are hardly more than what they were before, and my soldiers provide protection for the whole city. The only lawlessness to be found is within the insurgent peasants."

"So what's to be done? Public hangings?"

"So far, it's only been public floggings. The smaller the population, the fewer taxes I receive. I plan to move on to conquering Estetia by next year. The army needs the money." He looks up from his food suddenly. "This cannot be interesting to you. We don't need to discuss it."

"I find it fascinating," I answer. "But if I may ask, doesn't flogging a man make it difficult for him to work? How will you obtain your taxes then?"

"Do you have a better idea?"

"Oftentimes, it is not fear of punishment that prevents wrongdoing." As I know too well from my history of disobeying my father. "Sometimes working to gain something is better. What do the Pegains want aside from their independence?"

He turns to me. "I don't know."

"Perhaps a good place to start would be to give them a voice. Allow them to select someone of their own choosing to be on the regent's council—if the attacks cease."

"You would give them more power?" he asks incredulously.

"Of course not. I would give them the illusion of power. Once you know who they've chosen and who that person interacts with the most, you'll have found the ringleaders. And you can put an end to all of them. Crush the entire rebellion underfoot."

He swallows the bite in his mouth. "Alessandra Stathos, that's positively despicable." He says the words like they're the highest compliment he can give me. "You are an absolute gem, do you know that?"

My whole body warms at the praise.

>─┤◆≻─O─≺◆├─<

THAT EVENING, I make inquiries. First to the viscount, Myron's brother, Proteus. Then to the owner of the popular gaming hall I know Myron frequents.

These are the first steps to putting my plan into action.

This is not over. Not by a long shot.

CHAPTER 10

The dress I've selected for tonight is perhaps my most exquisite. For my first outing away from the palace, I want to draw attention. I want everyone to know I'm the one courting the king over six kingdoms.

Even if he's not in attendance with me.

The gown is silver, the skirt showcasing loose ribbons made to look like waterfalls spilling down the sides. Tiny gems, sapphires and emeralds, are shaped to look like fish jumping from the bundled fabric all along the hemline.

My only accessory is a gray fan, perfect for hiding my features should the play turn out to be dull.

And of course to hide my distaste over Myron.

He has his curls pulled back out of his eyes and secured at the back of his head with a band. His jacket is ebony-colored with gold stitching along the hems, across his shoulders, and down the front. Tight-fitted black dress pants with gold buttons adorn his long legs.

"Your arm, Alessandra," Myron says as we exit the carriage.

I refrain from clenching my teeth as I place my arm in his.

Rhoda and Hestia accompany us. And though I've introduced

Myron to both of them as a childhood friend, they keep shooting questioning looks over at him.

"I can't believe you wouldn't tell me what color you were wearing tonight," Hestia moans from beside me. "I should have guessed silver!"

"Your pink gown is lovely," I tell her. "You look like a spring fairy."

"I need to be wearing what the future queen is wearing."

I'm too flattered by the assumption to say anything right away.

"At some point," Rhoda offers, "you really must become your own woman, Hestia. Find your own style. And own it."

Hestia ignores her.

"I believe that's enough chatter, ladies," Myron says. "Come along."

"We can talk as we walk," I bite out. He is not allowed to treat my friends this way. Still, Hestia and Rhoda say nothing as we climb up the drive.

The Viscount and Viscountess of Christakos have a lovely estate. Neatly trimmed hedges line the drive. Steps made of marble lead to the front door, and the viscount and his wife are dressed in only the finest silks and satins.

The lady of the estate takes my hand in hers when it is our turn to be greeted. "Lady Stathos! What an honor it is to greet you in my home, but where is His Majesty?" She stares at Myron, as though by squinting she might be able to transform him into Kallias.

"Detained by work, I'm afraid."

"A pity. Do make yourself comfortable, and I hope you will tell him how you enjoyed our hospitality."

Myron tightens his grip on my arm.

"Instead, I'm accompanied by my friend Myron Calligaris," I say awkwardly, "second son of the late viscount."

"Oh. How do you do?" the viscountess asks politely.

"Quite well considering, my lady. I hope you won't be too wroth with Alessandra for allowing me to escort her in the king's absence. She thought the distraction might do me some good."

The viscountess smiles, but she looks pointedly at the guests behind us, very clearly suggesting that we've taken too much of her time.

"Lady Christakos has many more guests to greet. We should be on our way to enjoy the festivities," I say. Then I start walking, pulling Myron along with me before he can say anything else stupid.

The ballroom has been cleared of everything save cushioned chairs, which are fashioned in a circle around the middle of the floor, which I assume is reserved for the stage.

Our seats are in the front row, because they were selected for royalty.

"Oh, look! It's the Duke of Demetrio. His daughter is coming out into society early next week. Alessandra, you must introduce me."

I know about the ball held in the duke's daughter's honor. I've already accepted an invitation to the event, but I can hardly go over there right now and let Myron make a fool of me yet again.

"The play will start soon," I argue. "There's no time."

Myron answers me with a look. A look that very clearly states what will happen if I don't do as he bids.

But I try again. "There's one seat open beside him. You could snag it before anyone else does. Then you'd have the whole play to talk with him."

Myron thinks it over for only a second before leaving us.

Thank the devils. And I really hope he doesn't do too much damage on his own.

We finally take our seats. Rhoda sits in the middle between me and Hestia, the chair to my left unoccupied.

"Remind me why we brought him with us?" Rhoda asks.

"I had no choice. My father demanded I introduce him to some new people," I lie.

"Quick thinking on getting rid of him, though," Hestia says.

"Thank you. I wish I'd never been—friends—with him." I hurriedly interject the word I'd almost left out. "He's only using me due to my favor with the king." I glance to the girls to my right. "Is that the only reason we're friends?"

Hestia looks affronted. "Of course not! It was your dress that made me want to be your friend! And now that I know you, I couldn't care less about what you wear! Well, for the most part," she amends.

"I admired your ability to snag a man so quickly," Rhoda adds. "It had nothing to do with the king specifically. Aren't we all drawn to our friends in the beginning by trifling things? True bonds develop afterward, when character is revealed."

Satisfied with their answers, I look out toward the empty stage.

A gentleman with tan locks eyes the empty spot beside me and gives me a grin.

Leandros.

"Alessandra," he says after walking over. "I'm so delighted to see you've joined us outside the stuffy palace for a night. However did you manage to separate yourself from the king long enough? You wouldn't be giving me false hopes, now, would you?"

Oh, he's such a flirt. I love it.

"It's all in your head, I'm afraid, Lord Vasco," I say.

He throws his hands over his heart dramatically. "You wound me with your formal address."

"Where are your cohorts this evening?" I ask, looking behind him for signs of Rhouben and Petros.

"I'm surprised you can't sense Rhouben's distaste from here. You'll find him to the right. Third row from the front."

The brightness of his attire stands out like a beacon. I would have seen him if I had but looked. His clothing shimmers with golds and reds. On any other man, it would look ridiculous, but he pulls it off with confidence. To his right, I can see the very reason for his distaste.

Melita Xenakis. She has his arm in a death grip, looking quite pleased with herself. As though Rhouben were a fish she'd just caught. As if sensing my stare, she looks in my direction. Once she sees the empty seat beside me, where the king should be sitting (or perhaps she's thinking of Orrin?), she grins to herself and looks away.

What a little bi—

"And Petros is off giggling in the corner with Lord Osias."

"Isn't that the man who was flirting with his beau at the ball?"

"Yes, well, Petros has decided that two can play at that game."

"How very conniving of him," I say with a smile.

"Oh no!" Hestia suddenly says. "A footman is bringing Lady Zervas this way. Leandros, sit down!"

Leandros attempts to eye me for permission, but Hestia rises and shoves him into the empty seat beside me before regaining her own. The footman doesn't miss a beat, slightly altering his course to deliver Lady Zervas to a new location.

"Why don't we want her sitting with us?" I ask, leaning into Rhoda.

Hestia does the same, bending over Rhoda's lap so I can hear her whisper. "She's a terrible bore. So melancholy all the time. We wouldn't have any fun with her around."

"I don't recognize her from the queen's sitting room," I say.

"That's because she doesn't join the other ladies," Rhoda says. "She keeps to herself most of the time."

"I wonder why she sticks around the palace at all if she doesn't enjoy the company."

"She has to!" Rhoda explains. "Her presence was ordered at the palace just like the rest of us."

Ah, she was there the night the king died. Now the palace is her prison until the culprit is found.

I watch Lady Zervas take her seat. As soon as she does, she looks right at me, her expression practically lethal.

Leandros chuckles from next to me.

"Why is she looking at me like that?" I ask.

"All ladies will look at you like that when you're sitting next to me. It's the jealousy."

I give him a doubtful look.

He grins. "All right, it might not be because of me. But it is the jealousy."

"Because I'm courting the king? He's less than half her age!"

"No, not Kallias. It was the late king whom Lady Zervas fancied. They had a brief courtship before the king's heart was stolen by the late queen. Zervas never got over him. She sees you in a position where she once was, and she envies you for that, I imagine."

Now I look at the lady in a new light. Her voluminous hair is streaked with gray, but it doesn't make her look old so much as dignified. She carries herself with an air of importance but doesn't deign to look at anyone around her now that she's done with me. Yes, she carries herself as if she fancies herself a queen.

"Tonight, she's my favorite person," Leandros continues. "I don't know how else I could have persuaded you to let me sit beside you."

I roll my eyes at him, just as some of the lights in the room turn off, dimming the makeshift stage.

The actors take their places, racing up the gaps between the rows of chairs to reach the center. And the performance begins.

><<>+<>++O++<>++<><

THE PLAY IS SO dreadfully dull. By the end, the two lovers still weren't able to reconcile their differences in order to be together. The entire performance was one long argument, really. There was no swordplay, no fisticuffs, nothing exciting at all.

The next outing I've agreed to attend is the debutante ball for the sixteen-year-old daughter of the Duke and Duchess of Demetrio, far-removed cousins to the king, but relations, nonetheless.

I send another note to Kallias, inviting him to join me, hoping this time it might be different considering he has a connection to the family, but his response is the same.

My dear friend Alessandra,

I do wish I could accompany you. I rather enjoyed the last time we danced. Alas, I am hard at work putting your plan for Pegai into action. With any luck, we'll have the rebels put down before the month is out.

The council and I are also dealing with the latest attack by the masked bandit, this time far too close to the palace for my liking. We at least have a more accurate description of the man. Brown hood. Brown mask over his eyes.

That was, of course, sarcasm.

I'm afraid I will also have to skip dinner this evening. The council will be taking it in the meeting room tonight.

I sincerely hope you are enjoying your time among the nobility. I hear your friend Calligaris accompanied you to the play at the viscount's. I'm glad to see you were able to find a replacement for me.

Yours,
Kallias

A replacement? Is that bitterness I detect in the strokes of his hand? Or perhaps a subtle warning?

I need to get rid of Myron and fast. In order to do that, I need to talk to Rhouben. Yet I also need to speak to Kallias in an attempt to strengthen our courtship. I weigh the two options, trying to decide which to do first. It's been far too long since I've seen the king. I must locate him.

I grow no closer to achieving my goals when days go by without the two of us seeing each other. How is the king supposed to fall in love with me then?

No servant is above bribery, and I use any I can find throughout the palace to direct me to the meeting rooms used by the king and council.

My ultimate task is difficult. I have to have the appearance of courting the king, but I also have to appear to Kallias as though I only want to be friends. All while actually trying to get him to fall in love with me.

It's such a fine line to walk.

I make it as far as a deserted hallway, unsure of where to go next, when a figure rounds a corner.

"Leandros!"

"Alessandra! Are you seeking me out, now? Was it our time together at the play? Have you finally seen reason and broken things off with Kallias?"

I mask the grin that wants to surface. "I'm actually looking for Kallias."

Leandros looks around himself questioningly. "Around my quarters?"

I groan. "Is that where I am? I'm looking for the meeting rooms. A servant directed me this way."

"These are the guest quarters. I assure you the king isn't anywhere on this floor."

"And I paid that last man a necos for directions. Clearly I've been led astray."

"Or you took a wrong turn."

"You dare suggest the blame lies with me?"

A twinkle appears in his eye. "You're being courted by a king. I wouldn't be surprised if your mind was elsewhere while you traveled the castle."

I narrow my eyes. "I'm not the sort of lady to swoon at a title."

"What sort of lady are you?" he asks, his voice taking on a playful tone.

"The kind who likes attention from her would-be intended." I hadn't meant to say it aloud, but the bitter thought surfaced, nonetheless.

Leandros nods, as though that makes perfect sense to him. "May I escort you to the meeting rooms? I have nothing better to do than spend time with a beautiful woman."

I nod gratefully. "Please do. At this rate, the king will have already left by the time a competent servant directs me the right way."

"We're still blaming the servants, are we?"

I'm of half a mind to smack him.

Leandros laughs at the look on my face. "Forgive me. This way." He offers me his arm, and I take it.

After a few moments, I say, "I can't believe I'm reduced to this. Looking for him during his meetings." Leandros will only think I'm put out that the man who is courting me doesn't have time for me.

"A king is very busy," he says. "I'm sure if he could spend more time with you, he would."

"Is that what you told yourself when he pushed you away?" I ask.

The muscles in the arm I'm clinging to tighten. Perhaps that was too harsh.

"No," he says at last. "I knew Kallias needed to heal after the death of his parents. He'd just finished grieving over his brother, only to have his parents taken from him. I gave him time, because I thought, eventually, he would lean on me and his other friends for support. But he hasn't recovered."

"Kallias had a brother?" I ask.

"You don't remember the death of the crown prince?"

I shake my head.

"You would have been young when it happened. Xanthos Maheras was Kallias's older brother of two years. I'm told the king looked up to his brother, but I didn't know him then."

"What happened to Xanthos?"

"A carriage accident, they say."

"How terrible."

Leandros nods. "My uncle brought me to the palace a few years later, thinking the companionship of boys his age might help. I wasn't prepared to actually like him—it being a planned friendship, you see."

I know the sentiment precisely.

"And now with his parents gone," Leandros continues, "Kallias trusts no one. Save you, it would seem." A pause. "How is he?"

I pat Leandros's arm. "He seems well enough. He's so dreadfully busy taking everything on his shoulders. But we have good conversations."

"I just worry he's forgotten entirely how to have fun."

Fun.

Yes, that's exactly what Kallias needs. Someone to remind him what fun is.

"Here we are," Leandros says when we turn onto a new corridor. "Straight ahead. You can't miss it."

"Thank you for your help. I never would have found it on my own."

"You're most welcome." Leandros takes back his arm, and his eyes rest on the necklace at my throat—the ruby-studded rose. "Beautiful."

"It was a gift from Kallias."

"The poets say a virtuous woman's worth is above rubies. I should think the king values you more than all the precious gems in the world combined. I know I would if you were mine."

And he takes his leave, disappearing out of sight.

I'm left staring after him, a peculiar mix of emotions swirling within me.

The poets can say whatever they damned like. A woman's worth is not decided by what's between her legs but by what is in her mind.

But Leandros's flirtations are beyond flattering. Perhaps he might be someone to use in the future should I need to make Kallias jealous. Or, if the two used to be best friends, Leandros would know more than I do about Kallias's interests and hobbies. He could prove to be a valuable source of information, if I could broach the topic naturally.

When I reach the end of the corridor, I'm stopped by a man with overly large spectacles, heeled shoes, tights, and a black tunic. He holds a pen and parchment in his hands.

"My lady, can I help you?" he asks. He tries to be subtle about the look-over he gives me, but I see it clearly.

"My name is Lady Alessandra Stathos. I was hoping to catch His Majesty in between meetings."

The man drops into a bow. "I have heard of your arrival at court, Lady Stathos. I'm sure the king would love to know you stopped by, but I'm afraid he's in back-to-back meetings for the rest of the day."

"Do they switch rooms? Perhaps I could catch him in pass—"

The doors open, and a group of men and women step through. The appointment keeper grabs my arm to pull me out of the way so as not to be run over.

"Forgive me, my lady," he says once the angry horde has passed. He disappears into the room, and I promptly follow him before the door can close.

The room is less a meeting room than an assembly hall. Benches span over half of the space. Against the opposite wall rests a throne and a scattering of smaller chairs. While Kallias occupies the throne, the council members take up the surrounding seats.

This is a room where decisions are made, where power is wielded. Once Kallias is dead, I will be at the head of this room, deciding the fates of others.

Kallias spots me almost at once. He rises and brushes past the appointment keeper to reach me.

"What are you doing here?" he asks quietly.

"Putting on a show," I answer. "I miss my intended. I thought to steal you away. We could go for a horse ride up the mountainside."

"That sounds lovely, but we have more appointments scheduled, I'm afraid. I can't even take a stroll about the room with you."

"Oh," I say, put out. "Well, what was that all about?" I gesture toward the angry nobles who left in a huff.

Kallias rubs at his temple. "Even more of the nobility who have been relieved of their valuables by our masked bandit."

"Have you put a heavier patrol on the roads?"

"That and more. We've done everything we can think of. Lady Tasoula has personally questioned the merchants living in the areas where these thefts have taken place. None of the people will speak against the bandit. He's their hero. They won't turn on him. I suspect, however, that none of them knows his real identity anyway.

"Ampelios has . . . questioned many of the peasants. But we haven't caught any who have accepted the bandit's charity. Without the merchants cooperating by telling us which peasants suddenly have more coin to spare, we have no way of knowing who is receiving the stolen coins.

"We've tried staging attacks to catch him, to no avail. We've issued a reward for his capture, but not a soul is tempted by it. This man is making me look a fool. When I get my hands on him—" Kallias cuts off suddenly, remembering who he's talking to. "I'm sorry. I'm letting my temper get the best of me. You shouldn't be here to deal with this."

The council members are silent, eavesdropping on our conversation without bothering to pretend otherwise. Lord Vasco looks between Kallias and me, waiting to see how I'll respond.

"Your Majesty, I have an idea for dealing with the bandit, if you'd care to hear it. Since you were so appreciative of my advice in dealing with the rebels in Pegai, I hope you will trust me enough to let me speak on this matter as well." The flowery words are for the council's benefit, of course.

Kallias blinks slowly. "Please continue."

"If attempts to trap the bandit have proved unsuccessful, then perhaps a trap for those whom he's giving his stolen goods to would help? Then you could find the right individuals to question as to the thief's identity."

"What would you propose?" Kallias asks.

"Melt down some coins. Create a new seal to stamp them with, something that varies only slightly from the current seal. When the money is stolen and used to purchase things in the market, you can arrest whoever is found carrying them."

The room goes silent.

"That's . . . a lot of work to put into a simple plan," Lady Terzi, the kingdom's treasurer, says. She has a large ledger held out in front of her. "If something should go wrong and we were to lose that money—"

Kallias turns to stare the woman down. "We should put this plan into action. Immediately. It's the best idea to ever come out of this room. Unless anyone else has any other objections?" His teeth clench as he tacks on the question. Until he's twenty-one, he doesn't get the final say, I remember. He has to rely on the council's vote.

When no one speaks, Kallias repeats the order, before returning back to me. He rubs the back of his neck, turning it until a faint *crack* sounds.

"Now that that's underway, will you be free to join me at the Demetrio ball?" I ask hopefully.

"I'm sorry, dearest. I rule six different kingdoms. There's always more to be discussed. I haven't the time for parties or balls or plays. I barely have time to eat and sleep."

I dare to take a step closer, and lavender and mint washes over me. "Just remember, Kallias. If we're to be convincing, we need to have the appearance of a *courting* couple. Courting couples *do* things. They attend festivities together."

He looks at me a moment longer. "I will send you more gifts."

What? Is that supposed to appease me? Or make the facade more convincing?

"Epaphras!" Kallias yells.

I jump as the appointment keeper scurries over.

"Kindly see Lady Stathos out of the meeting room."

I'm escorted away without another word.

CHAPTER

11

can't decide if that went well or not.

On the one hand, I think I just impressed the council. On the other, I'm no closer to getting Kallias to spend more time with me. Perhaps at least my little bit of wisdom will get me invited to future meetings?

That's probably far too much to hope for.

Still, I'll need to wait and see how it plays out, and I have other problems to deal with.

After searching everywhere for Rhouben, a servant finally directs me to one of the billiards rooms in the palace. Ladies don't usually enter gaming rooms, but I'm not about to let that stop me.

He's of course accompanied by Leandros and Petros.

"Alessandra!" Leandros exclaims. "You've sought me out twice in one day. You really are a terrible tease."

"I haven't sought you out at all. I'll remind you I was looking for the king earlier. And now, I'm actually here to see Rhouben."

"He's taken, my lady. You really do like to set your sights on the unattainable, don't you?"

"Not at all, though that does seem to be your strategy."

Petros laughs as he applies chalk to his billiards stick. "She's got you there."

"Why do you need to see me?" Rhouben asks as he leans over the table, sizing up the cue ball and its intended trajectory.

"I have an unwanted suitor I want to get rid of."

"Ouch," Petros says on Leandros's behalf.

I roll my eyes. "I'm of course speaking of Myron Calligaris."

"I thought it was Eliades who was giving you trouble," Leandros states.

"Him too. Actually, my plan should rid me of both of them."

Rhouben hits the cue ball, and a series of clacks results as other colored balls bounce off one another.

"I'm the wrong person to come to," he says as he stands. "If I knew how to get rid of unwanted attention, I wouldn't be engaged to Melita. But my father has threatened me with disinheritance if I don't comply with his wishes."

"Just tell the king about these fops," Petros says to me. "A threat from the most powerful man in the world is sure to get them to back off."

I absolutely cannot do that. If Kallias confronts Myron, then Myron will run his mouth.

"I hope to do this without involving Kallias," I say. "I don't need him fighting my battles for me."

"Want me to challenge him to a duel?" Leandros asks, as he bends over the billiards table for his turn. "This Myron fellow can't seek your favor if he has a sword stuck in his gut."

"I don't need you fighting my battles, either," I say.

"Then *you* challenge him to a duel," Leandros says, a smile in his eyes. He rises from his move, and the play goes to Petros.

"I battle with my mind. Not weapons. Which is why I'm here. I need Rhouben to help me put a plan into action."

"I think we just discussed how abysmal I am at getting rid of unwanted attention," Rhouben says. "The only thing that works with Melita is hiding, like I'm doing now."

"What if I told you I have a plan to free you from Melita?"

Rhouben straightens so quickly I hear his back crack. "Are you serious?"

"Very."

"What do you need? Name it and it's yours." He can barely get the words out fast enough.

Leandros and Petros pause the game to listen.

"First, I need you to answer a few questions, if you would?"

"Of course!"

"What does Melita want more than anything else?"

"To marry a rich and handsome man with a higher title than her father, a baron."

"That's why she snagged you at the first opportunity," I realize. "And why she bats her eyelashes at Orrin. He has a better title than you."

"And he's far more handsome," Petros puts in unhelpfully.

Rhouben reaches over and smacks him.

"Why would your father allow you to marry beneath you?" I ask, curious.

"He's friends with the baron. They've talked of uniting their families since before I was born." The words come out as a grumble.

"Well, we're prepared to stop that. All we need is to arrange for Orrin and Melita to get together," I say.

"How are you going to manage that?" Leandros asks. "Eliades is smitten with you, and I hardly see how that is going to rid you of— Myron, was it?"

"Yes, for that bit, I'm going to need some money."

Rhouben leans his billiards stick against the nearest wall. "You can really get rid of Melita without getting me disinherited?"

I nod.

"How much money do you need?"

Without blinking, I say, "Five thousand necos."

Petros whistles. "That's more than my father makes in a year."

"But not Rhouben's father?" I ask.

Rhouben doesn't need to think twice about it. "I'll get you the money. Just tell me what else you'll need."

"Invite your father to the palace. I don't care how, just get him here. And in the meantime, you need to play the perfect fiancé, so no one will suspect anything."

Petros turns to his friend. "In that case, he's doomed."

>───◆>──O──<◆───<

THE NEXT AFTERNOON, Kallias sends me a bracelet strung with black pearls and black diamonds, a truly impressive design considering Naxos is nowhere near the sea. On Wednesday, I receive an ivory comb studded with blue diamonds, meant to be worn in an elaborate updo. Friday, I'm brought emeralds cut into the shapes of leaves, strung around a necklace band that ends in a large topaz.

Each gift is presented to me when I'm surrounded by people. Knowing that these presents are for their benefit, not mine, has a sharp bitterness taking root in me every time another one is delivered in a gloved servant's hand.

The king is supposed to be in love with me. He's supposed to give me gifts because he's smitten with me.

Not because he's making poor attempts to convince others of our ruse.

He's making this impossible.

>───◆>──O──<◆───<

A SERVANT FINDS ME the day of the Demetrio ball, a letter in hand. I break the bright red wax seal and read:

My dearest Alessandra,

I hope you will forgive my boldness, but word has reached me that the king did not accompany you to your latest outing at the estate of the Christakoses. In fact, it's rumored you spent the evening with a childhood friend. This has dared me to hope that perhaps you've ended things with His Majesty.

You, of course, know of my business travels—

I skip to the bottom to find the signature. It's from Orrin. I didn't even notice he was gone from the palace—

They've kept me from your side for far too long, but I think of you daily. I miss your conversation, your smile, the way you look away from me when you're overcome by my generosity.

When I look at the night sky, I cease to see its beauty. All I can think of is you. Your sable hair and how I long to run my fingers through its lengths. Your lips, ripe as cherries—

The descriptions of my distinct body parts go on for five more paragraphs. I skip to the bottom.

Please write me and tell me you have missed me as much as I have missed you.

Your humble servant,
Orrin Galopas, Earl of Eliades

Dear gods. The man is completely delusional. I look up from the letter and startle to find the servant who delivered it still waiting just outside the doorway to my rooms.

"Begging your pardon, my lady, but my lord hoped you might send a reply back with me."

I want to unleash my fury on Orrin's servant. Instead, I clear my head enough to think reasonably. "How long will Lord Eliades be away from the palace?"

"I should expect another week at least, my lady."

"Good." I start to shut the door, and the servant coughs.

"Oh, there will be no reply for the earl." And I slam the door the rest of the way.

This letter is an opportunity. A way to complete the rest of our plans.

>+‹›+○+‹›+‹

A SHORT LINE EXTENDS down the driveway, but Myron, Hestia, Rhoda, and I don't wait long before we're greeted by the duke and duchess.

After introductions are made, the duke lifts his eyes over my shoulder. "The king is not with you?"

"Kallias so wished to come," I say, daring to use the king's first name in front of the duke. I need to show intimacy between us since Kallias isn't actually here. "Alas, he's hard at work protecting our kingdom."

"I'm here to escort Lady Stathos," Myron says, stepping somewhat in front of me.

The duke's eyes widen as he recognizes Myron from the play. Demetrio glances back at me. "You know this gentleman?"

I can tell from the tone of his voice what he means. *You willingly associate with this man?*

Myron is ruining me. One outing at a time. He elbows me in the ribs.

"Myron is a childhood friend." The words physically pain me to say them. "He's . . . quite charming."

"Oh," the duke says. "Well, do enjoy the ball."

I can tell Myron wishes to stay and talk with the duke longer, but this time it is Rhoda who ushers us along inside.

I momentarily lose my ire once I catch sight of the ballroom. The duke and duchess refer to their young daughter as their shooting star, a reference, I'm told, to her prodigious talent at playing the pianoforte. The decorations have been done to match the endearment. Candles are placed within holders with holes cut in the shape of stars, the designs magnifying and showing on the ceiling and walls. Bundles of flowers in yellows and blues cover every surface in the grand estate, the flowers trailing in the shape of the fading light that appears behind a shooting star. And the young lady's gown rivals my own with diamonds sewn into it every few inches. A long train follows her for ten feet everywhere she goes, making it hard to miss her in the crowd since the partygoers have to mind the chiffon sweeping the floor.

As soon as Hestia, Rhoda, and I take in the sights, my two friends are quickly whisked away by men to the dance floor.

"*He's quite charming?*" Myron repeats when we are alone. "You were supposed to extol my virtues to the duke."

"Showing up with *me* to the ball is telling enough, Myron. You don't want to overdo it. You're going to ruin yourself by overselling yourself. True men of character don't have to try this hard."

"Careful, Alessandra. If you don't sell me enough, I might just have to start extolling your virtues to the court. Or rather, your lack of them." He laughs at his own joke.

Once he composes himself, he pulls me into the dance number among other couples on the floor. "Think what you will of me and my methods," he says after one turn around the ballroom, "but my plan is working splendidly. I've already secured some invitations of my own. I shouldn't need you to get me into any other events."

"In that case, you don't need me anymore."

"Don't be ridiculous. My connection to you is what is giving me the needed credibility. We will continue to associate regularly."

"Credibility?"

"Yes, I'm looking for men to invest in my new business venture—Ow!"

I accidentally step on Myron's foot, so caught off guard by the words. "You're using me to get nobles to *invest in a business venture?*"

Myron takes me through the next set of turns in the dance, acting as though we're not having any sort of argument. "Of course. If you will recall, I'm in quite a lot of debt. I need to get out of it. I'm looking to buy some sailing vessels to open up a trading line with the Kingdom of Estetia."

I'm speechless for a moment. "You. *You*—the man who spends all his money on cards and dice—are convincing courtiers to give you their money so you can open up trade with a kingdom our Shadow King is planning to *invade.*"

Myron glares down at me. "I'm good at getting others to give me money. I've raised quite a lot already. Besides, it's not like Estetia knows the king is planning to conquer them."

My hair should catch fire, such heat emanates from my body. "You are going to sully my good name when you steal all this money to pay off your debts."

"No. I'm not using it to pay off my debts. I'm going to buy trading ships. With the profits of my new business, I will then begin to pay off my debts."

Our second dance together ends, and the orchestra strikes up a third song, but I walk away from Myron.

"Alessandra, I didn't say you could cease dancing with me."

"No, we can't be seen dancing three songs in a row."

He grins. "I own you. You will do whatever I say."

"If we dance another dance, then you might as well tell the whole world my secret, because rumors about me will abound and the king will end our courtship. Three dances in a row is all but an announcement of an engagement. Then you will have nothing to gain from me." The words are desperate, but Myron must see reason.

He sighs. "Oh, very well. I shall go find another partner, but don't you dare go disappear from the party." And blessedly, he leaves me.

I take the rest of the song to compose myself. I am courting the king. I will be rid of Myron very soon. Everything will go according to plan. No one makes a fool of me.

After a few more steadying breaths, I determine to salvage what I can of the evening and enjoy the party.

I stand by the wall, thinking to catch the eye of some man to encourage him to ask me to dance. I find one, a tall stranger with hair a deep red shade, his complexion sun-kissed, and his muscled body practically straining through the well-fitted formal attire. He gives me a polite nod and walks on.

Though somewhat irritated by the rejection, I remain undaunted and try to catch another's gaze. I find a broad-shouldered blond with a handsome mustache and give him a coy smile. He returns the greeting enthusiastically and turns away from me.

What the hell?

"No man here will ask you to dance," a feminine voice says from behind me.

I turn and find the owner, Lady Zervas, her gray-streaked hair falling over her shoulders in perfect ringlets. She hides her mouth behind a cream-colored fan, and her eyes reveal nothing of her expression.

"You are being courted by the king," she says by way of explanation. "No one else would dare to approach you, save your . . . friend."

Orrin also dared, but I suppose he doesn't have a sense of self-preservation. He's too busy saving kittens from drowning.

"If you will permit me to give you some advice," Lady Zervas says, but she doesn't ask it like a question. She plows straight ahead. "Deny the king your favors. You will only be unhappy if you resume this courtship. At best, he will hold you at arm's length always, afraid to touch you."

"And at worst?" I ask.

"That depends on what you fear more. Either he will die and leave you behind in this world, or he will wed another, and you'll be forced to watch him happy with someone else."

"Such bleak options."

"I experienced all three for a time."

"And which was worse? Watching him with another woman or knowing he was dead?"

She snaps her fan closed, a hard line set to her mouth. "The former, dear. Definitely the former."

She turns from me, picking up her skirts in one hand and stalking away.

What a horrible woman.

My eyes catch on a spot of color in the room. Rhouben is dancing with his fiancée, his lips barely concealing a grimace as she prattles on about something. When they turn, she sees me and pulls Rhouben closer, tossing her hair over her shoulder.

I need to speak with Rhouben anyway, and insulting Melita is just a happy bonus. She's been allowed to go far too long unchecked.

I approach the couple, waiting until they reach the outskirts of the dance floor before tapping on Rhouben's shoulder. He stops, and his eyes light up with relief when he sees me.

"May I cut in?" I ask. "You'll be married to the man soon, Lady Xenakis. It's not sporting of you to keep him to yourself before then. And surely you would not deny the future queen?"

Before she can utter a word, Rhouben extricates himself from Melita's clutches and twirls me into the dance.

"You're a goddess," he says into my ear. "You saved me."

"Consider it a mutual saving. No one will dance with me. They all fear the king's ire."

"I don't. And right now, I'm too bored to care about Melita's ire. Or my father's. We should sneak away."

I give him a mischievous grin. "And do what exactly?"

"I should say something naughty, but I honestly don't care as long as it gets me away from that woman. By the way, I have the money you requested in my rooms at the palace. I can get it to you as soon as we return."

"That's wonderful! And I have something that should help us. Eliades sent me a love letter. We can now imitate his handwriting. All I need is to get my hands on his seal to authenticate the letter we send Melita. I'm told Orrin will be back in the palace in just over a week. He no doubt has his seal with him, so we will have to wait until his return to steal it. Have you heard from your father?"

"Not yet. He has a habit of putting off reading my letters, but he'll come once he reads it. I told him I withdrew five thousand necos from my account. That will have him here in no time."

"And what do you intend to tell him when he arrives in a fury?" I rest my head on Rhouben's shoulder as soon as I spot Melita glaring at the two of us.

"That I'm purchasing something spectacular for Melita, of course. But I needed something jarring to prompt his journey to the palace. Once he arrives, I think I can keep him here until Orrin is back from business."

"Good. We need to be careful. Timing is everything."

Another couple sidles up next to us. It's Petros, dancing with a new man I don't recognize. "Are you hogging the king's beau?"

"I'm merely trying to escape mine," Rhouben says.

"You've had Alessandra for two dances already. If it's a third, people will talk. Here, let's switch."

Suddenly I'm pulled into Petros's arms, and Rhouben finds himself holding Petros's partner.

"Hi," Rhouben says awkwardly.

"Would you rather dance with a man or dance with Melita?" Petros asks, as he sweeps me away.

The last thing I see is Rhouben enthusiastically engaging in the dance with Petros's old partner.

Then my eyes are on Petros. I'm laughing at the whole exchange, heady with taking Melita's dance partner, giddy with the relief that there are men still willing to dance with me. Drunk on the thought that Myron will be out of the picture soon enough.

Petros regales me with stories of his recent escapades. Lord Osias and Lord Banis apparently got into a fight over him. They're both nursing mild wounds this evening, so he has had to find other partners to entertain himself with.

After a total of two dances, Petros twirls me outward, sending me into another man's arms.

"Leandros," I say. "Where have you been?"

"Important people never arrive on time to events, but it seems I've missed much of the fun."

"No," I say. "You're just in time for it."

Over his shoulder, I see Petros finding a lady to dance with. Meanwhile, Rhouben is literally walking away from Melita, trying to outdistance her. I suppose my advice to play the perfect fiancé was too much to ask of him.

Leandros is more than an accomplished dancer with the skill in which he lifts me off the floor and spins me in the air. As I feel his hands in mine, feel his arms come around me as we go through the steps of the dance, I can't help but wonder if I will ever feel Kallias in this way.

CHAPTER

12

I t is the dead of night when we return from the ball and Rhouben and I swap money for letter in my rooms. Petros is with us, insisting he wouldn't miss out on the fun. And he also proclaims to be an excellent forger.

Rhouben and I look over his shoulder as he finishes the letter.

Dearest Melita,

I have watched you from afar for too long. I can no longer keep my feelings to myself. Your beauty is like the light of the sun. It almost hurts to look at you, and you make it impossible for me to look at anyone else.

Please, I must speak with you alone. Will you meet me in your rooms at nine o'clock on the evening of the ___? Will you greet me with a kiss, so I may know if your feelings for me burn as brightly as mine do for you?

Your humble servant,
Orrin Galopas, Earl of Eliades

We compare his writing to the note Orrin sent me. Petros has managed the shape of Orrin's letters perfectly. No one would know the difference. It's unlikely that the note will fall into anyone's hands but Melita's, but better safe than sorry. If our plan to save Rhouben from this marriage is to work, it needs to be flawless.

"What now?" Rhouben asks.

"Now all that's left," I say, "is to wait for Orrin to arrive back at the palace. When he does, we add the date to the letter, and then I will seal it with Orrin's crest. Then you must get this letter to Melita without her spotting you delivering it."

"But how will you get his crest?"

Petros stands from his chair and cracks his back. "He's in love with her, you dolt. How do you think she'll gain access to his rooms and get his crest? She'll play him."

Rhouben grips me in a hug, smashing me against his bright red-and-yellow-brocade vest. "You really are the best, Alessandra. If this works, I owe you my life."

"Don't be so dramatic," Petros says.

"Would you want a life with Melita?" Rhouben challenges.

"Fair point. Yes, you owe her your life. And I'll take the fifty necos you promised for the use of my penmanship."

"When did I promise you that?"

I leave the two of them to playfully bicker, my skirts heavily ladened with an envelope full of money.

I SPEND MY MORNING away from the palace, running a few necessary errands. I distribute Rhouben's money carefully, wisely, and when I return to the palace, my smile is full and earnest.

Until I run into Lord Ikaros Vasco on the way back to my rooms.

"Ah, Lady Stathos, just who I was looking for."

"Is everything all right?" I ask.

"Of course. Why shouldn't everything be all right?"

"Because the head of the king's council has sought me out. You practically threatened me during our last conversation."

Vasco tilts his head to the side. "You and I remember that conversation very differently."

I smile politely, but my teeth grind together behind my lips.

"No, I merely wanted to ask how your courtship with the king is coming along. Kallias is so private. The young king won't say a word about it."

"And neither will I."

Vasco nods to himself, as though expecting this answer. "I wonder if that is perhaps because the courtship isn't happening at all?"

I blink. "I beg your pardon?"

"He sends you gifts, and you enjoy each other's company during mealtimes, but what else? To my knowledge, you spend no other time with each other. He does not accompany you to any events. Has he even kissed you yet?"

I round on the man. "That is none of your business. And you know perfectly well just how busy the king is. He doesn't attend events with me because he's in meetings with you and the council."

"To be sure, I know exactly what Kallias spends his time doing. But he has a council to take care of things until he is of age. Now is the perfect opportunity to rely on us to run the kingdom for him while he spends his time with a beautiful young lady such as yourself."

I can't think of a single thing to say to the man in return.

"Unless of course the courtship isn't real. In which case, the council will start arranging for more ladies to meet with the king, and we will have no use for you."

And with that, Vasco leaves.

⊱┈┈◦◯◦┈┈⊰

I HATE NOT HAVING the last word in a conversation. Absolutely loathe it. What's worse, the council isn't falling for our ruse. And if there's no ruse, then Kallias has no need to keep me around. How am I to win him for real, then?

I let myself into my rooms, Vasco's threats ripe within my mind.

"Alessandra."

I jump a foot into the air. How the blazes do people keep getting into my rooms?

"Father."

He crosses his arms over his chest. "I thought perhaps my letters to you were going astray, but it would appear you are receiving your mail just fine." His eyes point toward the mountain of invitations I've already opened and read. Among them is Orrin's love letter. Rhouben returned it to me, having no use for it after Petros made his forgery. I frown at it distastefully.

"I was getting around to writing you."

"Undoubtedly," he says with sarcasm. "You've gotten caught up in the palace. In the finery. In the attention. You've forgotten your entire purpose for being here."

A headache pounds at my temples, and red tinges the corners of my vision. "I've been focusing on winning the king's favor, which is why I haven't had time to write you. Things are progressing perfectly. If there were something to tell you, I'd tell you."

He paces back and forth in front of my wardrobe. "Perfectly, is it? Then perhaps you can tell me why word has reached me that the king never accompanies you to events outside the palace? In fact, I hear you're in the company of that Calligaris boy constantly."

I can't focus on Father as my eye begins to twitch. "I assure you I have everything under control. There's no need to fret. I have the king right where I want him. And Myron will no longer be an issue. In fact, once I have a chat with him, he'll be leaving the palace. Permanently."

Father's face changes. At first, I cannot read it. Then it dawns on me with horror. *Pity.*

"Alessandra, darling, you tried your best. There comes a time when we must admit we've been defeated. You had a good run at the palace, but the king clearly doesn't want you. But don't you worry. We are not ruined. I've made plans."

My fingers slowly curl into fists at my sides. "What did you *do?*"

"I reached out to Lord Eliades. No, don't give me that look. He's rich, and he will give me a nice bride-price for your hand."

"He's an earl!"

"I'm an earl."

"You deemed him unacceptable for Chrysantha but acceptable for me?"

He pauses only a beat before saying, "Your circumstances are different."

Because she is his favorite, and I am not. "The point is to elevate my station! Why would you try to make me a countess when I'm trying to become a queen?"

Father shakes his head sadly. "I'm proud of you for trying, but it's an important lesson to learn to recognize when you've been beaten."

I know when I've been beaten, and I have barely even started.

"You will see reason," he adds. "Once you've had time to come to terms with everything. Now why don't you let me escort you home?"

I look up to the ceiling, gathering my thoughts and calming my tone. "Let me make things perfectly clear, Father. I am not cattle you can sell off, and you can't force me into a marriage I don't want. Not when the king himself is providing for my every comfort."

Father purses his lips. "You will wed Eliades or be disinherited."

"Then disinherit me! The king sends me expensive gifts. I have plenty of money, and I live in the palace. There is nothing you can do to threaten me. You've outlived your usefulness, Father. You got me into the palace, and now I can take it from here. In fact, once I win the king's favor, I'll make sure you don't see *one penny* out of *my* treasury."

The room goes quiet, and Father looks at me in alarm for all of a second. "Take some time before you resort to dramatics, Alessandra. I will check in with you later."

He strides from the room, but his steps are unsure.

⊱･⊰･⊙･⊱･⊰

BEFORE THE SUN IS quite up the next morning—long before the servants should arrive—I let myself into Myron's rooms. He hasn't bothered to lock his doors, so I open one door after the next, until I find the bedroom. The setup is completely identical to my room; however, Myron hasn't gone through any trouble to decorate to his own tastes.

I slide over to the bed on slippered feet and let my gaze take in Myron's sleeping form. So vulnerable. If I wanted to kill him, I could do it now.

But what I've done to Myron is so much sweeter than letting him get off easy with death.

I reach down one gloved hand and flick the end of his nose as hard as I can.

Myron inhales deeply and sits up in one movement, his eyes widening until he realizes it's me in the room. He rubs the sleep from his eyes.

"If you're here because you've changed your mind about the nature of our relationship, I'm afraid I don't want you anymore," Myron says after a long yawn. "Now kindly leave so I can go back to sleep."

He makes to settle back into his blankets.

This time I slap him.

That gets his attention.

"What the hell?" he demands. "Need I remind you—"

I hold a paper before his nose. "You're going to leave the palace immediately. As soon as I walk out that door, you will pack up your things and be gone, never to return. I never want to see your face or hear your name again."

"What is this?" He reaches for the note, but I yank it back lest he get any ideas of destroying it.

"This is a debtor contract."

Myron scrunches his nose in confusion.

"I have purchased all of your debts," I say simply. "From the club. From the men you owe money to. All of it. You now owe me five thousand necos."

His whole body goes perfectly still.

"Nothing to say?" I ask. "Let me make this perfectly clear in case you don't understand. *I own you.* One misstep from you, and I send you to debtors' prison for inability to pay on your substantial debts. How long do you think it would take your brother to get you out of there? Or—do you think he'd even bother?"

I watch every move of Myron's throat as he swallows, relishing every second of his new misery.

"You will give back any money you've accepted from the nobility, and you will cease to claim any connection to me. If you so much as breathe in a direction I don't like, I'll make sure you never see the outside of a jail cell."

I reach forward and pat his cheek mockingly. "There's a good lad. Now off with you."

"You're lying," he says as I reach for the door to leave.

"Am I? Shouldn't take too long for you to verify for yourself. But don't dally. You have until lunch to be gone."

My smile is radiant as I leave his rooms. I only have control over one man, and yet, the power of it washes over me in intoxicating waves of heat. When I am queen, will I experience it a thousandfold, knowing I will command tens of thousands?

⊱⋅ ⟡ ⋅⊰

WITH THE THRILL OF victory still upon me, I go in search of Kallias. It's early in the day still. Surely too early for meetings? After hailing down several servants, I'm finally told the king is breakfasting in the library.

Why didn't he extend me an invitation?

I learn why as soon as a servant admits me into the room. Kallias is surrounded by correspondences. Amid countless papers and writing utensils, I think I see a bowl with hardboiled eggs, and half a piece of toast lies facedown on a book nearby. A book I suspect he is using as a paperweight.

"Now don't you make being king look grand," I say.

The Shadow King looks up from the letter he is composing. "It is good to see you, Alessandra. I feel like it's been ages."

"That's because it has."

He winces slightly. "I hope you can see for yourself that I've had good reasons for my absence." He gestures wildly at the parchment he's drowning in. At the movement, a whirl of shadow follows his arms.

"We have a problem," I say without any more preamble.

"Are you all right?" he asks, looking up and giving me a quick once-over.

"Ikaros Vasco came to see me. He questioned whether our courtship is real. He suspects us. My father even showed up at the palace to take me home, because he was so convinced I'd *failed to win you.*"

Kallias finally sets down his pen. "How is that possible?" Then a look of annoyance crosses his face. "Is this because of the time you've been spending with that Calligaris boy? Dammit, Alessandra, you shouldn't have—"

"It is because of *you,*" I say, daring to cut him off.

He stands and clasps his hands together in front of him, his shadows darkening to midnight tendrils. "I have done nothing but show my interest in you. You sit at my immediate right during meals. I send you gifts."

I wait for him to go on, but I realize he doesn't have anything else to sell his point. "You hardly ever join us for meals anymore. True, you send me gifts, but you never accompany me to events away from the palace. Your neglect of me is showing. Myron started to take advantage of that, but I have done away with him. You need to do more, especially since we cannot behave as a normal courting couple."

"Whatever do you mean by that?"

"Normal courting couples whisper sweet nothings into the other's ear. They laugh when they are close together, sharing breath. Normal couples can't keep their hands off each other."

"We can't do those things," he says, his words clipped.

"We don't have to do those things. That's not what I'm saying. Devils! Do you want to sell our act of courtship? Then *court* me, Kallias. Take me on outings away from the palace. Spend time with me outside of mealtimes. Deliver your gifts to me in person. Act like a man who is infatuated."

He watches me a long moment, considering my words carefully, I hope.

"No," he says slowly. "No." More firmly this time, as though convincing himself. He looks around at the mountain of papers. "I haven't the time for that."

A convenient excuse. What is holding him back?

"I would ask you to join me," he says, "but as you can see, there isn't room at the table. I will see you—when I see you."

He flicks his fingers toward the door, a silent dismissal.

I'm FULLY AWARE THAT I look like a child as I stomp back toward my rooms. But no one is around to see, so I indulge myself.

When I hear someone rounding the corner up ahead, I straighten and allow my slippers to tread normally. I do my best to keep my irritation at the intruder at bay. Yes, this is *my corridor.*

"Two letters for you, my lady," a servant says with a bow, extending a silver platter in my direction. I retrieve the envelopes before disappearing into my room.

The first is from my sister. I stare at her perfect handwriting for a full minute before deciding I should probably read the letter before throwing it into my lit hearth.

> *Dear Sister,*
>
> *I hope this letter finds you in good health. Court life holds many temptations, but I trust you are remaining penitent and chaste.*
>
> *The duke and I are having a marvelous time together. His health is declining, sadly, so our days mostly consist of me reading aloud the greatest works of poetry.*

I skim over more paragraphs of the terribly dull activities she does with the duke and the various gifts he presents her ("Ten carriages! Whatever will I do with so many?").

And then, in true Chrysantha fashion, a few lines of importance buried at the end of her letter:

> *A constable came by the estate today asking what I know about your relationship three years ago with*

Hektor Galanis. I thought all the questions odd, of course, but at the very end, the Baron of Drivas demanded to know if I thought you could have had anything to do with his disappearance.

Fear not. While I told them you were a trollop and undoubtedly slept with the man, you would never do something so terrible as help estrange a noble from his family.

Such an odd exchange, don't you think?

I do hope you will enjoy the rest of your stay at the palace, and I hope you've made some friends who will influence you for good.

Your loving sister,
Chrysantha

I stare at my hands for far too long before I realize I've dropped the letter. I don't even know where to begin processing the various levels of my sister's ineptitude and carelessness.

I hadn't known she was aware of my nighttime relationships, and now the baron knows I slept with his son. As well as a constable, who clearly has his backing. How many more interviews do they plan to conduct before coming to question me personally?

And how long will it take before word of my nighttime activities reaches the palace and destroys my relationship with the king for good?

I snatch the letter and tear it into unreadable pieces before thrusting it amid the flames.

I want to yank handfuls of Chrysantha's hair from her scalp. She's always taken everything from me. But how did she possibly manage to take this, too?

It is only after several minutes of pacing my room that I remember a second letter arrived. Could it possibly be even more bad news? With dread, I break the seal and unfold the parchment.

Dearest Alessandra,

Forgive the impertinence, but I can't help but notice how miserable you seem at the events of late. I thought I might do something to cheer you up. I wonder if you might be up for a different kind of entertainment? Would you permit me to take you out for an evening? Shall we say tomorrow night at eight o'clock? I promise you will not regret it.

Your servant,
Leandros Vasco

Perhaps this is just the opportunity I need. I've been meaning to ask Leandros questions about the king. I need more information to make Kallias mine, and what better way to get it than to ask a man who used to be Kallias's best friend?

Not to mention the fact that Leandros adores me. I deserve to be adored for an evening, don't I? Especially when Kallias won't deign to take the time to see me.

After only a little further deliberation, I write back.

Dear Leandros,
I would be delighted to join you.

Sincerely,
Alessandra Stathos

CHAPTER

13

I look distastefully at the swaths of dark cotton in Leandros's outstretched hands.

"You expect me to *wear* that?" I ask.

Leandros grins from where he stands inside the receiving area of my rooms. "I have an evening planned for us, but you can't go dressed like that."

"What's wrong with how I look?"

I took great care dressing today. My gown is a light purple that clings tightly to my legs. No bustle or petticoats in sight. I've never felt more comfortable. The outfit was, of course, chosen because it matches the new shawl Kallias gifted me. Made from lavender satin, the shawl has woven tassels hanging from the ends, dripping with amethysts. I thought perhaps it might irritate him if he ever learned I wore it while entertaining another man.

Although, that other man is currently dressed like a servant. With cotton trousers, scuffed boots, and a threadbare white shirt, he looks ready to crawl under a bridge to sleep for the night.

"You look rich and irresistible," Leandros says. "That won't do for where we're headed today."

I feel my face scrunch up into an uncomfortable frown, but I can't seem to care. "Where are you taking me?"

"It's a surprise."

I still don't reach for the clothes.

"Look, you can either go to bed early tonight, or you can do something a little dangerous and a lot of fun."

He thrusts the clothes into my arms and shoves me toward my bedchamber.

When I emerge, I look down at myself.

I wear a white blouse with loose sleeves gathered at the wrists. The overskirt is a plain black, wrapping tightly about my breasts and midriff before falling loosely about my legs. It's plain, boring, peasantlike.

Leandros stands behind me and lets down my immaculate hair.

"Stop!"

Too late. The strands fall about my face in loose waves.

"It took my maid an hour to do that."

"And it was lovely," Leandros says. Something about the wicked gleam in his eyes stops me from protesting too much.

This will be an adventure, even if I'm clothed poorly. And Leandros will pay me attention the entire night. It's what I'd told him I wanted from Kallias. And having another man vie for my attention—one who isn't blackmailing me to do so—is too good an opportunity to pass up.

It's petty, I know. But I want to punish Kallias. And I need a distraction—just for a night—from the baron and constable who are set on ruining me.

"Let's get out of here before anyone sees me," I huff.

Grinning, Leandros shuffles me down the hallway before we turn into a servants' stairway and make our way down.

Behind the palace, two horses are saddled and ready for us, a stable boy holding them by the reins. Leandros flicks the boy a coin before bending down next to me and cupping his hands together.

"What are you doing?"

"Helping you onto your horse." Realizing my confusion, he adds, "You can't ride sidesaddle. Peasant girls don't do that sort of thing."

"I am no peasant!"

"Tonight you are; now step up."

I realize right then that I have a choice to make. Either I do this, or I don't. But no more shrieking because I'm a lady. I didn't opt to go off with Leandros because I wanted to be treated like a lady. Ladies don't spend time alone with men who aren't their relations. They don't cavort with the former best friend of the king to get more information about how to seduce said king.

I step onto his cupped hands and swing one leg over the horse. The fabric of my skirt rises up my legs, and Leandros helps to right it, positioning the material so I'm covered.

But as he does so, a finger brushes my bare calf.

I draw in a breath. It's been weeks since I've been touched. Longer than I've gone in years.

"Forgive me," he says. "I didn't mean—"

"No need," I say. "Lead on. I'm ready for this promised entertainment."

Leandros leaps onto his own horse. "Then let's be off."

Down stone-paved lanes and past candlelit lanterns we travel, Leandros's horse ahead of mine. We curve down the streets of the mountain, layer after layer of quiet neighborhoods, run-down inns, and even a bawdy house.

There aren't many out on the streets, not this late at night when it's far too dark for the merchants to sell their wares. Part of me feels guiltier and guiltier the farther we travel from the palace, as though I'm abandoning my entire purpose. But that's not so. I need a night out. An escape. And tonight is not without its purpose.

"Tell me," I say as the horses turn onto another road. "What were you like as a younger man?"

"Ignorant. Hopeful. Carefree."

"More carefree than you are now?"

He grins, his teeth shining in the moonlight. "A great deal more."

"You were friends with the future king. What sort of mischief did the two of you get up to?" I hope the question is a good transition, hiding the fact that I'm hungry for information about Kallias.

He thinks a moment. "We once caught frogs from the lake and put them in his tutor's bed."

"I'm sure she deserved it."

"She had a dreadfully stoic voice, and Kallias wondered if he could do anything to prompt a change in the tone."

I laugh. "And you were all too eager to help him."

"He was my only friend for a while. We did so much together. Fencing. Riding. Gaming. Kallias loves competition. He loves winning. But then, what man doesn't?"

"What *person* doesn't?" I amend for him.

"Do you love competition, Alessandra?"

"Of course."

"Good. Now I'm even more convinced you will enjoy tonight's entertainment."

We come to a stop at an unassuming building, all straight walls and quiet darkness. Leandros ties the horses to a nearby post. I fear they might not still be there when we return, but I'm not about to let that ruin the evening.

Somehow, Leandros finds a staircase. I suppose one must know to look for it in order to find it. He takes my arm and leads me downward, until we're encased in blackness, unable to see a thing.

"I should tell you, I told my maids who I went out with tonight. If I don't return, they'll know you murdered me."

I can hear his smile in the dark. "You won't be dying at my hands. It's only a little farther."

A creak of hinges and rush of air later, we enter through a basement door. A lonely torch sends a flicker of light about the corridor. Distantly, I hear the low rumble of what might be shouting.

As we traverse the new corridor, Leandros says, "Whatever you do, stay close to me the entire time."

We round a corner, travel down a smaller set of stairs, and then finally—finally—we plunge into a doorway spilling out light and noise and the stench of ale.

"Boxing?" I say when I take in the scene before me.

Up ahead, the room slopes gently downward, allowing us a view of the scene in the middle: Two men face each other, bouncing on the toes of their bare feet, their sleeves rolled up to their elbows, sweat dripping down their faces.

Coins exchange hands, girls walk about with cups atop trays, men and women shout to the challengers, booing and cheering.

"Let's get closer," Leandros says, ushering me toward an empty table. We sit, and a girl dressed similarly to me comes forward, asking if we'd like anything to eat or drink.

"An ale for me," Leandros says, before looking at me.

"I'll have the same." Why not? Just because I have a taste for fine wines doesn't mean I can't sample something simpler now and then.

We turn our heads to the scene below, just in time to see the bigger contender catch the smaller one in the chin with a vicious uppercut. The one who was hit flies backward, crashing to the wood floor with an audible *thump*. The crowd explodes with a mixture of cheers and groans.

The barmaid returns with our drinks, plopping one down before each of us. Leandros brings the mug to his lips, downing half the contents in one go.

Not to be outdone, I raise my own cup to my lips, trying not to taste the vulgar liquid as it streams down my throat. Bitter and watered down, it's positively disgusting, but it leaves a warmth in my belly. I drain the whole cup before tossing it back on the table.

"I knew you would appreciate this place," Leandros says. "You play the dignified daughter of the nobility well, but just under the skin there's a girl waiting to have some fun."

My grin isn't forced. "How often do you come here?"

"Not nearly often enough. My uncle expects a lot of me. If he ever knew I were here—" He cuts off with a shudder.

I let out an unladylike grunt. "No talk of responsibilities tonight. Responsibility is why Kallias claims he can't spend any time with me. Utter nonsense. If anyone can make anything happen, it's the king. If he wants a less busy schedule, he should command it."

"If anyone can bring him out of his shell, it's you. Give it time. And if he doesn't ever come around, well, there's always me."

Leandros's cup is now empty as well, and he raises two fingers to the barmaid. Another especially loud exclamation sounds from the crowd as the brutish contender fouls another foe.

"I have to marry a wealthy man," I say. "My father is greedy, and he won't let me have anything less." Oh, wait. No, I suppose that's not true anymore, is it? In the midst of all the things that aren't going my way right now, I forgot my father and his situation are no longer a problem.

"Lucky for you, I'm disgustingly rich," Leandros says.

"And you're content with being a consolation prize?"

"You get used to it when living in the palace with the king."

I fold my arms. "I was under the impression that the king didn't show an interest in any ladies before I came to court."

"He doesn't have to. They still want him and have to settle for me. But I'm sure you won't have that problem."

The second glass of ale is placed before me. This one manages to taste better than the first.

"He won't break his rules," I say. "Not even for me." The ale must be freeing my tongue a bit, but I can't seem to care too much.

"The no-touching is a problem?"

I hide my face behind my glass. "Women have needs just as much as men do."

Leandros's teeth show as he raises his cup. "Perhaps he only needs you to make the first move."

"And end up at the gallows? I think not."

"Then you will have to find someone else to satisfy those needs. At least in the meantime."

"You'd like that, wouldn't you?"

"I am a man of base interests. Ale. Sport. Sex. I have want of nothing else."

"I can't imagine why you don't already have a lady of your own."

"All evidence to the contrary," he says, swaying his mug toward me.

A delicious cloudiness fills my mind, and I find myself offering more smiles to Leandros than I normally would.

"Are you trying to get me drunk?" I ask.

"Even if I were, it wouldn't be to take advantage. Only to help you have a better time. Now come!"

He rises from his seat and grabs one of my hands. I raise my cup to down the rest of its contents, only to find it already empty. How did that happen?

My feet are only slightly unsteady when Leandros and I push into the crowd circling the newest contenders. We manage to squeeze our way to the front. The big brute still remains undefeated.

"Watching is only half the fun!" Leandros shouts to be heard over the shrieks within the room. "Winning is the true sport."

A young boy no older than twelve runs around the outer circle, carrying a large goblet in front of him. "Place your bets here! Ten to one odds for our newest contender!"

A smaller man with a crooked nose has entered the circle of onlookers. After stripping off his shirt, he windmills his arms and bounces from foot to foot.

Leandros holds out a note. "Ten necos says the brute wins."

"Not very sporting of you, sir," the boy says in return, accepting the money and stuffing it into the cup.

"I bet to win."

"And how about the missus? Will you be placing a bet? Do be sporting and root for the smaller man! He may surprise us yet!"

I survey both contenders carefully, watching their movements. The one with the crooked nose is so much smaller, but he is fresh, where the brute has expended much energy already. Still, the larger man looks as though he could pick up Crooked Nose and bend him in half with little effort.

I'm about to decline the bet, when I notice something.

The brute stretches his arms out in front of him, but as he does so, he winces ever so slightly, before rubbing a hand over his right side.

Bruised ribs, likely. Though he's winning the matches, he's taken a few hits. They're wearing on him.

"Why not?" I say finally. "Shall we say . . ." I make a show of rummaging through my pockets. "Twenty-five necos on the little man?"

"A fine bet, miss!" the lad says, ripping the money greedily from my fingers and then scampering off quickly, as though afraid I'll change my mind.

"That was foolish," Leandros says. "You know the boy is only given scraps of what the owner wins off the bets."

"I didn't do it out of charity for the boy. I intend to win."

His scoff turns into a laugh. "I don't want you sour for the rest of the night. You'll blame me for the loss of all your money."

I roll my eyes, and we turn to watch the match. The contestants stand up to a line drawn on the floor and wait for a mediator to slap his hand on the ground before the two tear into each other.

Crooked Nose is quick on his feet, sending jabs at the brute before scampering out of reach. The brute watches him carefully, keeping his eyes on his outstretched fists. After a duck, he brings forward a left fist and connects squarely with the smaller man's chest. He flies back several feet but doesn't lose his footing.

Crooked Nose cracks his neck to the side before plunging forward, throwing a fist toward the brute's face. The larger man shifts out of the way and throws a punch to Crooked Nose's stomach.

He goes down right in front of me.

The floor goes wild. Shouts of "Pontin, Pontin, Pontin" resound, and I assume that must be the brute.

"Get up!" a few voices beg, trying to encourage the young man struggling for breath on the ground.

"Better luck next time," Leandros says to me with a shrug.

But this isn't over yet. I step forward, grab Crooked Nose by his sweaty arm, and yank him to his feet. He leans against me as a huge gulp of air finally whistles through his lungs.

"Now listen," I say in a low growl. "I have a lot of money placed on you, and you're not going to let me lose it, are you?"

"He's too strong, miss," the man says with unsteady breaths.

"He's got at least one bruised rib on the right side. Quit aiming for his face and take a swing lower. Break. His. Bones." Without another word, I get behind him and toss him into the fray.

Leandros wrinkles his nose. "You smell of sweaty male."

"As if you could smell anything over the stench of ale on my breath."

"Would that I were close enough to smell your breath, but—"

The fight continues, and Leandros doesn't finish his sentence. Not as the small contender feints toward Pontin with a left fist toward the head before immediately following with a powerful jab to the ribs.

Spittle goes flying out of Pontin's mouth, but Crooked Nose doesn't stop there. With a flurry of quick punches, he pummels Pontin as ruthlessly as a baker would knead dough.

In only seconds, the bigger man falls.

He doesn't rise.

The crowd silences.

I lift my skirts as I step over the brute and raise my little contender's fist into the air. Then the noise is explosive, my ears fit to bursting from the force of it.

Notes and coins trade hands in a flurry, and the winner leans over to plant a bloody kiss on my cheek.

I'm too high off the victory to care.

Satisfied, I return to my spot, and the boy with the cup is back, brandishing an enormous wad of notes at me.

"Two hundred and fifty necos, miss. An excellent wager. But wouldn't you like to place it on the next match? No one is that lucky only once in the games. You've a natural eye for talent! What say I keep this for you and place it on your victor once again?"

"Maybe next time," I say, taking my money and tucking it away.

I can't keep the smug smile from my lips as I turn to Leandros.

"What did you say to him?" he asks, looking dumbfounded at his champion lying still on the floor.

"He only needed a lady's favor to find the courage to win the fight."

The mediator quiets the room with a whistle. "Who will fight our new champion? Who's ready to earn some money in the ring?"

I reach for Leandros's arm to hoist it into the air for him, but he snatches it back. "I am quite content with watching."

I let out a giggle, the ale still doing wonderful things for my head, as we watch a new contestant enter the circle.

Though I don't place any more money, Leandros and I make our own private bets on who will win.

After three more matches, Leandros has completely lost his pride. "No one guesses right so many times in a row!"

"It's not luck," I say. "It's careful observation."

Despite my having won every private bet between the two of us, Leandros looks doubtful. I suppose I will have to continue proving it to him.

But the floor begins to clear, the men in the circle leaving, soaking people who don't get out of the way quick enough in sweat.

"The night is still young. The matches are done already?" I ask.

Leandros shakes his head, a new grin surfacing. "Only the matches between the men."

"Between the *men*?" I repeat.

A mop swipes over the floor, then some sort of powder is sprinkled in the area meant for the contenders. Chalk, I would guess.

Then a lady walks into the ring. She's dressed plainly, but scandalously, with her skirts hiked up to midthigh, held in place by strings.

So she can fight, I realize.

She's very impressive, all lithe muscle and feminine grace. With round cheeks, small eyes, and a dainty nose, no one would ever guess how she spent her nights. She wears her hair pulled out of her face, pinned tight to her scalp.

Her face is all business, not a smile to be found.

"Who will compete against last night's champion, the Viper!" the mediator asks, walking in a circle to survey the crowd, which has somehow doubled. A body from behind me pushes, and I shove my hips right back at it.

"Why do they have the ladies go last?" I ask.

"Because they're far more entertaining to watch," Leandros answers.

"No doubt it has something to do with the fact that the crowd gets an excellent view of their legs?"

Leandros says nothing, confirming my suspicions.

Finally, a woman steps into the chalked-off circle. She's bigger-boned than the Viper, with more curves on her, but by the slower way she moves, I know she won't win.

"The Viper will beat her," I say to Leandros.

"I'll take that bet."

He loses.

In seconds.

The Viper has well earned her name. Her strikes come rapidly, one after the next, and the bigger woman has no chance of fending them off. She shouldn't have let her opponent strike first.

The Viper faces off against a second opponent.

A third.

The barmaid comes by with more ale, and I lose track of how many more drinks I take from her.

There are things I'm supposed to be asking Leandros. Questions about Kallias and if he's had past lovers. I'm supposed to learn . . . something. Something that will help with my reputation, I think?

But I can't quite remember, and right now, I don't care one bit about any of it. I'm having far too much fun watching the Viper.

And I notice that every time she's about to go in for a jab, she clenches her jaw ever so slightly. Her movements are fairly predictable. She likes to start high, striking the face to disorient her opponents before moving down lower to the stomach and knocking the wind out of them.

"Who's next!" the mediator asks. "Who will face our champion and win a cut of the house's earnings if you're victorious? How about you?"

He singles out a young petite girl at the front of the circle. She shakes her head vehemently.

"You?" He approaches another girl, this one sturdier, better built for fighting, but she, too, declines.

Maybe it's the ale. Or the high from all of my previous victories. Perhaps it's my deep-down desire to be acknowledged by the world.

"I will compete!" I say.

Leandros snaps his neck around, a look of confusion crossing his features, as though someone perhaps threw their voice in my direction.

"Excellent! We have a contender! Step forward, young miss!"

I move my legs, but Leandros grips my arm in a vice. "What are you doing?"

"Competing."

"You can't do that. The king will have my head."

I lean forward. "Good thing we need never tell him of this."

"Alessandra! You're a lady!"

"Not tonight," I remind him, and yank back my arm before stepping into the circle.

I look down at my heavy skirts, but I lose my balance as I do so. Luckily I catch myself before toppling over. "Does anyone have a tie they could lend me?"

No fewer than five men rip hairbands, cravats, belts, or other items from their person to hand over.

I accept a belt and use it to heft my skirts up and away from my legs, before cinching it all in the back.

Several whistles sound appreciatively.

I'm glad Leandros gave me scraps to wear tonight. I'd hate to ruin one of my own dresses.

"What do you call yourself, miss?" the mediator asks me.

I think to give my real first name, but I rather like the idea of something more fun, such as the Viper.

An image of Kallias comes to mind, of the role I desire so fiercely. "Call me the Shadow Queen."

The mediator shouts the title for the crowd to hear. The boy with the cup runs around the outside, and the gentlemen and ladies place their bets.

"Step up to the center, ladies."

I keep my eyes on her chins.

Yes, there are two of them. Didn't she have one when she first started fighting?

"Fight," the mediator says as he slaps his hand on the ground.

The Viper strikes high toward my face immediately, as I knew she would. I drop down in a crouch and shove my fist as hard as it will go into the middle of her stomach.

She careens backward, her arms going to where I struck her. The crowd goes wild, and my hand throbs. I know enough to keep my thumb outside my fist, but my skin and knuckles are unused to such contact.

The Viper recovers an instant later, shaking out her hands as if she can will the pain away. She bounces toward me, and I keep my eyes on her face.

Her jaw clenches, her left fist coming forward. I sidestep, trying to get in a jab toward her face, but she blocks with an arm like steel, the movement sending a jolt up my arm.

She follows with a punch to my face.

I don't dodge in time.

Her fist connects just below my eye, and my neck cracks backward from the force of it.

Gravity claims me, pulling me toward the ground. I can see rows and rows of pant-clad legs from where I land. They're spinning. No, the whole room is. I feel liquid running down my face. Blood? Tears? Spit? Somewhere distantly I think I hear Leandros's voice.

Then everything goes dark.

CHAPTER 14

"You foolish, foolish girl," Leandros says yet again when we reach the castle in the early hours of the morning. Since I regained consciousness, he's done nothing but shove bread and water down my throat. I've sort of sobered up, but the left side of my face feels like someone threw a brick at it. Compliments of the Viper.

We walk up a dead hallway, the servants and staff having long since retired to their beds.

"It seemed like a good idea at the time," I say.

"Next time don't drink so much."

"That peasant ale is deceptively potent."

"All ale is potent when you have six glasses."

I wince as I tentatively touch the area around my eye. "I can't believe I bruised my best feature." I don't know what I'll do about the black eye. I'll need to work a miracle with my face powders to cover it up.

We reach my door, and Leandros drops his voice as he faces me. "All your features are the best. No other woman holds a candle to you."

He leans forward, kissing the black spot around my eye. When he pulls back, he looks down at my lips.

It was an incredible night. One I won't forget anytime soon. And Leandros is handsome. Far too handsome for his own good.

I raise a hand into his golden-brown hair, slide my fingers to the back of his head, about to draw him near.

But then I stop.

I'm here to woo the king. Not his childhood friend.

But would he really find out about one kiss?

It wouldn't be one kiss. I've no doubt Leandros is a fantastic kisser, and I'd be dragging him backward and into my room before long.

Do I want a kingdom or a tumble in the sheets? It shouldn't be so hard to make this decision. But it's been weeks since my last dalliance.

With a sigh, I let my hand drop. "Good night, Leandros. Thank you for tonight. I won't forget it."

A sad grin hits his lips, but ever the gentleman, he nods and strides down the hallway and away from me.

I already regret the decision as I'm left alone and cold in the empty corridor, but it is far too late to change my mind.

I dig out my key from the wads of notes in my pocket and let myself into the room.

I kick off my shoes first, empty my pockets out onto a table.

Then I look up.

Kallias is in the room.

>—·—‹›·—O—·‹›·—·—‹

He sits on my bed, his legs crossed in front of him. His shirtsleeves are unbuttoned, but he still wears his gloves. No vest or jacket, but a small expanse of his upper chest shows without a cravat or top button done up.

Though he looks relaxed, he's perfectly alert.

"Did you have a pleasant evening?" he asks without looking at me, no hint of his mood to be found in his voice.

"I did."

"It would appear Leandros did as well. Why didn't you kiss him good night?"

He was listening. He had to be. Oh, I've never been more grateful for my courage in turning Leandros away.

"A lady never kisses after the first outing."

"So you wanted to?" Now his eyes snap upward. They narrow in on my black eye like an arrow honing for a target. He rises and strides up to me. "What happened? Did Leandros—?"

"Of course not."

He raises a hand up to my face, and I hold perfectly still. A single gloved finger reaches forward and briefly brushes the skin beneath my eye. The leather is smooth and cold.

Kallias's hand tightens into a fist and drops to his side.

"He took me boxing."

"Boxing?"

"He took me to watch the matches. After I won several bets in a row on which player would beat the other, I decided to try my own hand at it."

Kallias looks as though someone has just presented him a question with an impossible answer. "*Why?* Why the devils would you do that? You were beaten!"

I raise myself up tall. "Well, yes. But I had a marvelous time until then."

A breathy laugh escapes the king's lips, and I can tell the humor isn't kind.

"Why are you here?" I snap.

"I canceled my evening of meetings," he says. "I thought to surprise you by taking you out tonight. But you weren't anywhere to be found. I thought to wait for you."

"How many hours have you spent sitting on my bed?"

He runs his fingers through his hair in an angry swipe. "Why would you spend the evening with Leandros?"

"Does it matter who I spent the evening with? He's kind and fun and *actually has time for me.*"

Kallias is quiet for a moment, likely trying to come up with his next argument. I don't give him the chance.

"I agreed to your scheme," I say. "I'm playing the part of your beau. But you know what else came with the deal, Kallias? Friendship. You promised me a friend in you. You weren't delivering. I had to seek friendship elsewhere."

"You have Rhoda and Hestia," he says.

"Rhoda and Hestia aren't going to ask me to dance at parties. Do you know that no men will approach me? I'm off-limits. It's as if I have contracted the plague."

He's silent.

"Leandros and his friends are the only ones who treat me like a person rather than the future queen. Do you know why they empathize with me? Why they befriended me? Because they, too, know what it's like for you to call them friends and then cast them aside.

"Maybe I *was* tempted to kiss Leandros. Maybe I'm lonely. Surely you know what that's like!"

Kallias recoils, as though I slapped him.

I don't feel sorry. Not one bit.

"I'm not a doll that you can dress up and leave alone until you're ready to play with me, Kallias. I'm a person. And if you can't respect that, I'll pack my things and leave tomorrow."

Oh, I really hope it's not the last of the ale talking. Surely it's my sensible mind, knowing that Kallias won't call my bluff. That he'll apologize and beg me to stay. That he'll change his ways and start paying me attention.

Or perhaps I couldn't control the threat, drunk or not. Kallias angers me in a way no person ever has. Not even my father.

I hold my breath, waiting for him to say something.

The king's shadows flare, like flames engulfing his whole body. He turns without looking back and leaves, melting through the wall of solid stone.

Oh dear.

What have I done?

I fall into bed. Despite how terribly wrong everything is going, I can't help but lose myself to exhaustion. Boxing, combined with the late hour, practically drags my mind away into oblivion.

But just before I go, the skin about my blackened eye warms. Not with pain. Not from the memory of the kiss pressed there.

But at the ghost of a gloved hand.

>—+—•◦•—•—◦—•◦•—+—◦

My head throbs as soon as I'm awake. It's a wonderful combination of too much ale and a poor night's sleep.

And on top of that, everything has unraveled.

What choice do I have but to follow up on my threat and order the servants to begin packing my things? The words burn through my throat as I give the orders, and I snap at two different footmen who move too slowly for my liking.

After a moment, I realize this is a job that will take hours. There's no point in my waiting around to watch them finish.

I should try to go about my day as normal.

Rhoda and Hestia hold a conversation while I stare at the empty seat at the head of the long table in the great hall. Kallias isn't there.

Will I see him again before I leave?

And why the devils am I waiting for my things to be packed before leaving? They will arrive at my father's estate whether I accompany them or not.

Actually, I suppose I'm not going back to the Masis estate. How can I after insisting I didn't need Father?

And honestly, I'd rather not see his face too soon. No, I'll go to an inn. Stay on my own for a while until I can rethink everything.

That chair remains empty during the entire luncheon. Of course he doesn't want to see me.

I've lost him. I've lost a throne, a crown, the admiration of a kingdom, the power of being a queen.

I take my time returning to my rooms after spending the afternoon in the sitting room sewing. As though some brilliant plan to salvage everything will come to me if I just have enough time.

What am I going to do? Am I really letting myself lose everything?

First, I should probably take a look at my eye to see if the face powder is still doing its job to cover my bruise. Then—I don't know what will come next.

If my room is all packed, I'll leave. If not, I'll dally a little longer.

I let myself in, dreading the fact that I don't hear the flurry of feet. They must be done! But as I walk through my rooms, I find the unexpected.

It's as if I'd never ordered anything's removal. The room has been cleaned. The bed made. The furniture dusted. But the wardrobe is still full of my clothes. The vanity holds all my cosmetics.

Nothing is packed.

Those lazy, horrible servants. I stomp back out into the hallway, eager to find someone to yell at, and am instantly hailed down by a servant.

"My lady," he says before I can utter a word. "The king requests your presence. Would you care to follow me?"

Yes, I do care very much. Has Kallias more to say about last night's jaunt? Does he want to publicly banish me from the palace? Cast me out for attending an outing with his once friend?

But if there's even a chance that he wishes to forget the argument and have things go back to the way they were, I must take it. I can seduce a king even if I only see him for a half hour two or three times a day, surely? I can get over attending parties where no men will talk to me. It's only for a short time. Until I can secure the king in marriage and then kill him. Then I can have all the male companionship I want.

But blast, why does Kallias have to make everything so damned difficult?

The servant leads me to the first floor, taking me out a back exit of the palace. He stops before a simple carriage and holds open the door for me.

Inside, I see an outline of black pants and fine shoes.

Kallias?

Is he going to personally escort me from the palace? Why?

Grasping my best attempt at maintaining my dignity, I step into the carriage and sit opposite the king.

The door shuts behind me, and Kallias uses the rapier lying on the seat next to him to tap the roof of the carriage twice.

After a slap of reins and the jolting movement of the horses, we're off.

The shadows dance along the cushions about his legs and shoulders. He wears a cotton-white shirt. No jacket or vest. Though he wears his gloves. His pants are very simple today. His shoes are fine, but I suspect it's because he doesn't own anything else.

By his face, I can tell he's waiting for me to ask him a question. *Why are we here? Where are you taking me? Are you still angry?*

But I don't give him the satisfaction.

I turn up my nose and look out the window, watching the passing scenery. It's not much to look at. Homes and stone streets and common folk going about their daily business.

But then the carriage turns, and I'm pitched right out of my seat and toward Kallias's lap.

There's a sensation like smoke from a fire passing over my limbs, and my nose inhales the lavender-mint musky smell of him. But I don't feel the outline of Kallias against my body.

When I open my eyes, I realize I haven't landed on him.

I've gone through him.

I'm inside him.

I'm on my knees on the seat he occupies, him and his shadows engulfing me.

"Ahh!"

I thrust myself backward, worried that he'll somehow stick to me. That I'll have captured the shadows, that I'll be forever encased in darkness.

The smoky sensation abates at the same time the carriage comes to an abrupt halt. I have to plant my feet more firmly not to topple forward into the king once again.

But then I realize—

I touched him.

I broke the law.

He's already cross with me.

Now what will he do?

I look up, see that Kallias is still all in one piece. I haven't somehow scattered him by toppling forward into the swirling, incorporeal mass of him.

His face is still as stone, despite it not being as solid as such.

"Everything all right, sire?" the driver calls down.

Kallias's eyes never leave mine. "We're fine. Continue on."

"Yes, Your Majesty."

We're traversing up the mountain, I realize. Not down. That's why I fell out of my seat, why I feel as though I'm constantly about to lose it once more.

And now I fear the king is taking me somewhere to kill me.

Could I run away? Leap from the carriage and disappear before he can follow? Then what will become of me?

I should try. I should think of something.

"Are you real?" I ask, the words jumping from my lips before I can hold them back.

"Quite real," he says in response.

"But you're not solid. You're . . . all shadows. Did I hurt you? Is that why you don't wish to be touched? Are you going to kill me?" The questions all topple out, each one starting before the last one has quite finished.

He fingers the handle of his rapier. Hopefully for something to do and not because he's contemplating using it.

"No," he says at last. "To all questions."

My heart calms somewhat. He really has no reason to lie to me. If he were going to kill me, I suppose he would just be done with it.

"How is it that you're able to touch that sword but not me?"

Can he not be touched by living things? That would make consummating a marriage very difficult, indeed. But then, I felt the pressure of his glove against my cheek . . .

In the span of a blink, the shadows disappear. All that is left is Kallias. Real, human. Corporeal. Touchable.

Beautiful.

In another blink, he's back to being surrounded by shadow.

"I can turn the ability on and off," he says. "I can force my fingers to solidify in order to pick something up, while the rest of me remains intangible."

"But why the law?" I ask. "If no one can hurt you, why forbid people from touching you? Why bother with gloves? Does *that* pain you? To touch someone skin to skin?"

"It does not pain me to touch anyone. Unless they're maiming me in some way."

Then why? I want to scream. Why push everyone away? Why isolate himself from everyone? Why live alone and untouched?

"If I were to touch someone skin to skin when I'm not in my shadow form, my ability would go away whenever I'm in their presence. I would be corporeal anytime they were around. I would be susceptible to death and pain and all else. My father lived to be over three hundred years old. A long and lonely life until he decided to marry my mother. Then he was mortal. She was the anchor keeping him grounded. And anyone could assassinate him while my mother was near.

"And they did," he finishes. "Falling in love is what got him killed. Now you see why I wish to appease the council without actually fulfilling their wishes. Someone killed my parents, and they will do the same to me if I let myself get close to anyone. Sometimes I even wonder if my brother's death wasn't an accident."

I dare not say anything, for fear he'll stop confiding in me.

"He wasn't like me, you see," Kallias says. "The ability passes from parent to child. But my brother, Xanthos? He didn't get the ability. I believe that's why he died so young. Someone wanted to take him out of the line of succession. My father was much more protected. It took longer to find a way to end him."

I can hardly believe he's trusting me with so much. But I also can't help but wonder if this is some sort of test.

I say, "When you barged into my room that night, you wanted to know exactly what I'd said. Because if people thought we were touching—"

"They'd come after me," he finishes. "And I'd have to be ever on alert."

"Why are you telling me all this?" I ask. "Are you sure you're not going to kill me?"

"You were right, Alessandra. Last night. All of those things you said. I've been afraid to truly live. Being with you outside of closely observed mealtimes makes me vulnerable. If someone learns my secret, if we were to accidentally touch—I could be killed.

"But that's no way to live. I may not be allowed to ever have someone physically close to me. But that doesn't mean I can't let you in. I . . . like you, and I hope that you could like me, too."

Something in me . . . softens. There's something about looking on this dark, powerful man and hearing his hopes for us. It makes me want to make those hopes become real.

Right before I end his life, of course.

"So you're taking me . . . ?" I ask.

"To one of my favorite spots. We're spending time together. Outside the palace. And not because it will further convince the council of our courtship, although that is a benefit. We're doing it because we're friends, and you deserve some real fun."

"Last night was fun."

"Some fun with me," he clarifies, his jaw setting. "No more nights with Leandros."

I raise a brow.

"I'm trying to compromise. I'm spending time with you, and we can't have the council finding out you're sharing your favor with more than one man."

"Fine," I say. "But I reserve the right to see whomever I wish if you start behaving like an ass again."

Sometimes I wonder if it's just a matter of time before I go too far. Before I say something to finally push him over the edge and get rid of me for good.

But I've found that during all our conversations, I haven't had to pretend. When I say things, it's because I truly feel and think that way. I may be trying to win the heart of a king, but . . .

I'm still being myself.

That's never happened before with a mark.

"That's fair," he says.

I reward him with the most charming smile I can find, and it isn't faked in the least.

"Do you think I could sit next to you?" I ask. "So I don't fall out of my seat again? The incline is steep."

He scoots to one side of the plush cushion in answer. I settle next to him, only my skirts brushing his shadows.

"Much better. Thank you."

CHAPTER 15

When the carriage rolls to a stop, the driver climbs down from his perch and opens the door for me, holding out an arm to help me down the single step. Today's overskirt is thin, a green assortment with fabric that glitters in the sun. The pants beneath are fitted and dotted with gathered black fabric in the imitation of flower petals.

"I never got a chance to compliment you on your attire."

"This is one of the few outfits I haven't worn yet. I was angry at you and didn't want to wear your favorite color."

"But then you wore it anyway?"

"I thought it might make you angrier when you were forced to watch me leave with all my things."

He smiles. "It would have." He turns to the driver. "Go for a walk. We won't need your assistance for some time. We'll return when we're ready."

The driver nods before heading for a trail to the left of the carriage. It disappears into a cover of trees. Kallias retrieves his rapier from the carriage and ties it to his belt. Then he grabs a large woven basket from atop the carriage.

"This way," he says.

As he grasps the basket in one hand, the reeds suddenly fade, the shadows eating them up, until the whole thing is just as encased in them as the king is.

"When you touch something, it becomes intangible with you?" I ask.

"I have to grasp it with a corporeal hand. Then when I turn to shadow, the object will turn with me. A blessing," he adds. "Else the court would have quite a stirring when my clothes fell right through me."

I can't help but laugh lightly at that.

The grass is soft and silent beneath my feet as Kallias leads me in the opposite direction of the driver. The ground rolls up and down with the hills. I'm grateful for my pant-clad legs and the sturdier boots I happened to don today.

"Aren't you worried about being alone up here?" I ask.

"Why would I be? I can't be hurt."

"But I can."

"Don't worry. Several riders followed us at a discreet distance. We took a plain carriage instead of the royal carriage. My men are roaming the edges of this spot. Out of sight. Besides, no one travels this way unless they're trying to cross the pass into another kingdom, and why would they do that? Invaders can't make it through to our end because there are men stationed on the other side of the mountain.

"I don't wear this sword just for looks," he adds. "I do know how to use it. Rest assured, the only dangerous thing out here is me."

"And should I fear you?" I ask.

"Never."

Over the next rise, I spot a large oak tree, the branches providing a lovely shade from the warm air. A few dozen feet away, a lake rests, ripples forming from bugs dancing on the water's surface or a fish making a brief appearance.

A field of daffodils surrounds us, the golden petals swaying in the breeze, coloring the whole place in what would make a perfect painting.

It's giving me ideas for dress designs. Next time we come here, I'll have to bring a sketchbook.

From the basket, Kallias removes a red-and-white-checkered blanket, spreading it beneath the shade of the tree. He settles his lean body atop it, crossing his legs beneath him before rummaging through the other contents.

I settle down next to him. Close, but not close enough to touch.

"It's beautiful here," I say.

"My mother used to sneak Xanthos and me out here as boys. We'd play in the mud, catch frogs, pick the flowers. She was never too busy for us, despite being a queen."

"She sounds like fun."

"She was. I . . . miss her." He sweeps his eyes over the daffodils. "She loved flowers. To this day, the groundskeepers take extra measures to maintain her flower gardens outside the palace."

He's finally opening up. This is exactly what I need to draw us closer.

"I'm sorry," I say. "I lost my mother, too. I was eleven when illness took her. For some reason, I barely remember her. Mostly I remember my governess. I didn't see my mother often. Father loved her deeply, and I can't stand my father. So I wonder if maybe I wouldn't have liked her if I had known her well . . . I'm so sorry you lost yours."

"Thank you." He lets out a breath. "But I didn't bring you here to talk about such dreary things. We're here to eat." He waves a hand over all the food he has laid out before us.

There's enough to feed twenty people. I spot at least five different kinds of sandwiches, from cucumber to shredded pork. Strawberries with the stems cut off and some sort of chocolate sauce for dipping. Chicken legs spiced with rosemary. Leafy greens shredded with tomatoes and carrots. Clusters of grapes.

My mouth waters at the sight of it all.

Kallias and I enjoy our food, and this time he listens carefully as I give him blow-by-blow details of last night. I'm proud of the bets I won. I find myself wanting to tell him how I learned the tics of those around me and used it to my advantage.

"You sound like you'd be an excellent general. Perhaps I should fire Kaiser and hire you instead."

I lick chocolate sauce from my fingers. "I'm afraid I have no knowledge of weaponry. Though I do always carry a dagger on me."

The one I used to kill Hektor.

"That's good. One must always be prepared for the unforeseeable." He leans back, enjoying a full stomach, and the two of us just relish in being alone. Being free of the palace. Free of responsibility in this beautiful place.

"I wish I would have thought to pack us swimwear. The water is so refreshing this time of year," he says.

"Who says we need suits?" I ask.

"Your outfit is constricting, and the overskirt would consume water like a sponge to drown you."

"I hadn't meant for us to keep our clothes on." The words are out before I realize they might be too forward.

Kallias turns to me, a wicked grin on his face. "Why, Lady Alessandra, the more I learn about you, the more I like you."

He stands, grabs the neckline at the back of his cotton shirt, and pulls it off in one movement. He looks down at me, calling my bluff, daring me to undress.

I'm only distracted for a moment by the expanse of muscles visible on his chest. They were hidden so well under that loose shirt. Under the layers of vests and waistcoats he's usually to be found in.

But now he's on display, and I decide it's his best look.

I keep my eyes on his as I undo the buttons on my overskirt. Once undone, I shrug off the garment, so I'm clad only in those pants and a tight, sleeveless blouse.

"Your guards?" I ask.

"They're out of sight," he says, his voice growing deeper with each word. Then, as though it takes him great effort, he turns around.

Turns around.

What the devils?

"What are you doing?" I ask.

"I'm waiting for my friend to undress and get in the water."

Oh, is that how it's going to be?

Is that the truth of things between us, or is Kallias trying to force that distinction on our relationship?

Making as much noise as I possibly can, I shrug out of my boots and pants, slip off my blouse and underthings, and then I approach the water, wondering if His Majesty will peek. If it's just an act or if he thinks to catch me unawares.

He doesn't even fidget.

The Shadow King is such a spoilsport.

The water is cold at first, but after a few seconds, I grow used to it, daring to go deeper and deeper, until all the important parts are covered.

"I'm in," I tell him.

He turns around and makes a twirling motion with his finger. My turn to look away while he removes the rest of his clothing.

My toes dig into the smooth mud as I face the other direction. I keep my thoughts away from all the critters living in the lake and instead try to imagine what Kallias looks like naked. All that bronze skin and lean muscle.

I'm so lost in thought that I jump when I hear steps behind me.

"You can look now," he says.

The water is so murky, I could stand right in front of Kallias and not see anything under the water.

More's the pity.

He said he couldn't touch. He said nothing about looking. So why should he wish to avert his gaze? And why the hell did he force me to turn around?

Suddenly put out, I hurry to think of something to say before our outing turns awkward.

"Do the shadows make it easier to float?" I ask him.

"Yes, actually."

He's only up to his waist, giving me a nice view of his torso. There's not a mark on him. Not a scar or freckle in sight. How? How is he so perfect?

A silence builds, as we both think about the obvious. We're naked. In a lake. Doing nothing untoward.

How is this my life right now?

I need to say something else. But all of the topics racing through my mind are terribly inappropriate.

"Are you a virgin?" I ask.

Well done, Alessandra.

But he seems beyond amused by the question. "No. Are you?"

I should say yes. A lady's entire reputation hinges on that fact, as I well know. But the way he asks, in earnest, I can't help but wonder . . .

"Would it matter if I wasn't?" I dare to ask.

"Not at all," he says immediately.

My lips part. "But it's practically an unspoken law that ladies must be virgins on their wedding nights."

"It's no law of mine. In fact, I've made a point of doing my best to give ladies the same rights as men. It's what my mother would have wanted. And besides, how can men expect all the ladies to remain virgins while they don't? The numbers don't add up."

He's serious. All this time I worried about Myron ruining things, when I needn't have bothered at all.

First thing when we get back, I'm calling in his debts.

"No," I say at last. "I'm not a virgin." Then I hurry to add, "So you permit yourself to touch people after all, then?"

"I used to. Before I was king."

"And the ladies in question are not around to counteract your ability?"

"When I was younger," he explains, "I paid handsomely for the attentions of women. Courtesans, mostly, who I then gave small fortunes to so they could start their lives over in one of the other five kingdoms."

"That's . . . smart," I tell him.

He looks down at the water, watching droplets fall from his fingers. "I almost wish I hadn't. Then I would never know what I was missing."

Perhaps I should be sympathetic. Instead, I ask, "You've been celibate for an entire year?"

"Yes."

"And you plan to remain celibate?" There might be unnecessary pauses between each of the words, but I can't help it. "Surely it's not worth it?"

He shrugs. "I am the most powerful man in the world, and I will live forever. I imagine men would give up a lot more for immortality alone."

Hmm. What would I give up for such power?

I suppose it doesn't matter. All I have to do is invest my time. There's nothing I have to give up.

"Where did this shadow ability originate?" I ask.

"My family has been ruling since the dawn of time, or so I've been told. One of my ancestors—his name was Bachnamon—struggled to maintain his throne. Many attempts were made on his life. His own cousin tried to usurp him.

"He prayed to the gods for help first. The god of strength. The god of wisdom. The god of justice. He asked for the strength to maintain his power, to be strong enough to destroy his enemies. He wanted his line to remain in power forever. None answered.

"So he prayed to the devils next. The devil of suffering. The devil of vengeance. The devil of pain. The last one answered. Bachnamon was granted the power of the shadows. He was invulnerable to death and pain so long as he remained in his shadow form. But because the ability was gifted by a devil, it was not without its price. He was granted immortality, so long as he spent most of his days in shadow. But if he didn't, the ability would be passed on to his children."

I stand there, digesting that all for a moment while watching tendrils of shadow snake up his arms.

I look up to his eyes, only to find him watching a drop of water slide down my shoulder.

He coughs. "Now it's my turn for questions. Tell me of the men lucky enough to receive your favors. Was there more than one?" And then his voice changes. "Do you have a beau waiting for you now?"

The question seems to dawn on him with horror.

"I have no one right now. But as I said, I grew up receiving little attention from my family. So I sought it elsewhere."

"Oh, Alessandra. If only I'd known you sooner. I would never ignore you."

"Such a gallant king."

"How many men?" he wants to know.

Dozens.

Instead of answering, I shoot back, "How many women?"

Somehow, I think our answers might be similar.

"All right. Keep your answer, and I'll keep mine," he says.

"Fair enough. Now may I swim?"

"Certainly. But if I reach the other side of the lake before you do, you owe me an answer to any question I ask."

"Deal," I say at the same time I spring for the other side.

Damn him. He wins.

"I want to hear about the first boy," he says. "How did it start and end?"

The only thoughts of Hektor Galanis I have are when I reminisce upon his death. The beginning of our relationship is something I haven't thought on much.

"He was the fifth son of a baron," I start. And I realize that perhaps I shouldn't use the past tense when speaking about him. I'm practically admitting that I know he's dead, and an investigation is being conducted. I need to take better care with my words.

"My father had business with his father," I continue. "He came over to our estate with the rest of his brothers. The older ones all chased after Chrysantha the moment they arrived. But Hektor singled me out. And I was drawn to him because of that fact alone. I was fifteen.

"I didn't have any experience with men at the time. I'd hardly *seen* any, sequestered at home as I was. I devoured Hektor's compliments. I relished in his nearness. And the second time his father came to call, he led me to a quiet corner of the house and kissed me. The next time, he undressed me."

Kallias is perhaps the best listener I've ever encountered. He can be so still, his shadows stilling with him.

"It went on for two months. During that time, I thankfully had a maid who taught me how to prevent pregnancy. I learned the ways of the bedroom. Hektor was more than happy to instruct and pleasure me. Until he found someone new. Someone else fresh and inexperienced and willing to bed him. So then it ended." I pause, thinking I'm done here, but then I feel prompted to add, "And then I vowed I would never fall in love again. So every man after Hektor was used and discarded once I became bored with him."

I find a cold spot in the water, and I shift back over a few feet. I don't know if Kallias is disturbed by what I told him, or if he doesn't know how to respond, but I ask, "Have you ever been in love?"

"No," he says. "Not ever. What's it like?"

"Horrible."

The silence grows, but not in an unpleasant way. I feel closer to Kallias than I've ever been before. Exposed in a way that has nothing to do with my nakedness.

A spot of movement catches my attention.

"Who's that?" I ask, looking over Kallias's head. "Is that one of your guards?"

Kallias turns in place, looking back toward the shore and the hefty remains of our lunch still left there.

"No," he says. "Alessandra, stay where you are."

Kallias cleaves the water in wide strokes as he draws closer to shore, toward the figure hovering over our picnic, staring down at its contents. I think it's a man, but it's difficult to tell with the attire he wears. A cloak hides much of his figure. A hood conceals his face.

"Halt!" Kallias shouts, his torso coming out of the water while the rest of him remains submerged. "What do you think you're doing?"

The man turns, his hood falling away. Not that it reveals anything. A brown cloth covers his face from the nose up, only two slits allowing his eyes to see through.

"So much food for only two people," the man says, his voice unusually deep, as though he's trying to mask its true timbre. "Surely you've had your fill, and the poor grow hungrier by the minute. I will see that your leftovers are distributed to those who need it most."

It's him. The masked bandit who accosted the nobles.

The man in the brown mask gathers the blanket by the corners, sweeping all the food to the center. He places the entire bulge back into the discarded basket.

"That is the property of the king!" Kallias shouts back at him. "You will unhand it immediately."

"It's the king who demands too high of taxes so he can maintain troops in all the lands he's conquered. While you start new wars in harmless kingdoms, your own people suffer. It's time you took care of those who need your protection the most."

Without another word, the bandit leaps onto the back of a waiting horse and starts galloping for the nearest hill.

Kallias turns back to me. "Get dressed. Quickly." He races the rest of the way out of the water, yelling for his guards. I realize I'm staring once he reaches down to grab his pants, jumping into them seamlessly.

"Hurry!" he shouts to me again, then rushes back for the carriage.

Needing no further prompting, I swim for the shore, wringing out my hair, trying to shake the droplets of water from my skin. My clothes don't go on easily. Everything is tight, unwilling to slide over wet skin. After much struggling, I finally get myself covered up and race after Kallias.

CHAPTER

16

"How the hell did he get past you?" Kallias shouts at some ten men surrounding the carriage. Our driver has returned, carrying a bouquet of wildflowers he likely meant to take home to a sweetheart. But Kallias pays him no mind. "You are paid for one job. To protect your king. And you failed. How? What the devils were you all doing?"

Half of the men turn toward me.

"We were unprepared for the . . . um . . . distraction," one of the men says.

"Am I to understand you failed to protect me because you weren't paying the lady the respect she deserves?"

"You can hardly blame us, sire. She was *naked.*"

Kallias steps forward, draws his sword, and puts it through the one who spoke. The man looks down at the rapier stuck in his gut, eyes wide. He falls as Kallias draws his sword back out.

I'm reminded of Hektor and the last breaths he took. It's the only time I've ever seen death.

Until now.

The rest of the guards step back, likely worried that they'll be next.

"Anyone else wish to offer up excuses?" Kallias asks in a quiet voice. No one says a word.

"You." Kallias points to one of the guards. "Ride ahead and gather my council. We meet as soon as I return."

⋗—⊢⊰⟩⊷○⊷⟨⊱⊢—⊲

During the return carriage ride, Kallias has the back of his hand pressed to his lips as he thinks. He stares off into some corner. Not avoiding me, just lost in his own thoughts.

"Forgive me," he says, suddenly looking up. "You should not have seen that. I shouldn't have—in front of a lady—What must you think of me now?"

I've been perfectly calm the entire time. I didn't feel as though I were in danger when the bandit attacked. Not from the safety of the water. And I find Kallias's question perplexing.

"I believe you now," I say. "You do know how to use that sword."

His expression turns incredulous. "You're not frightened? Of me?"

"You defended my honor. Why should I fear you?"

"Because I killed a man in front of you."

I shrug. "You have to make tough decisions as king. You have to put down those who disobey you. Make an example of them. It's how you maintain order. You think I don't know that?"

"I still shouldn't have done it in front of you." He looks away.

"Kallias."

His gaze focuses on me once more.

"I do not fear the decisions you have to make as a king, and I would never think lesser of you for them. I'm surprised you killed only one of them, to be honest."

His voice lowers. "The rest will die as well, but I can't very well do it when I'm outnumbered and when we have to rely on them for protection on the road back."

The carriage draws to a halt in front of the palace, and Kallias jumps out. He's barefoot, clad only in pants as the rest of his clothing was left behind in our haste. Not that it's easy to tell. He has his shadows out in full force. Every inch of bare skin is haloed by smoky blackness.

I follow after him, and he says nothing as we tread up some stairs, down corridors, through doors. Ladies and servants startle at the sight of his bare chest and storming shadows as we pass them—until at last we find ourselves in a meeting room.

Five individuals are seated at a large table. Kallias takes the sixth seat. At the head. "Ikaros, fetch Lady Stathos a seat."

If the rest of the council thinks anything of my presence, they say nothing. Leandros's uncle grabs a chair from the outskirts of the room and places it at the corner of the table, next to the king.

"This masked bandit problem has gone on long enough," Kallias says once I'm seated. "How has our plan to catch him progressed?"

I hardly think Kallias is unnerved by the loss of some food. No, it is the fact that someone stole from the *king*, that this bandit would dare challenge his monarch. The problem has become personal, and Kallias must deal with it immediately.

"The coins are finished," Lady Terzi says.

"And I've allowed word to slip that they will be transported soon," Lady Mangas says.

Ikaros Vasco steeples his fingers over the table. "If the bandit has been spotted so close to the palace, then surely he intends to take the bait."

"Once he strikes and redistributes the gold, my troops will be ready to round up the peasants caught with them." This from Kaiser.

Ampelios shifts in his seat. "And then I'll be ready to question them. We'll get him, sire."

Kallias takes a few moments just to breathe, to think everything through. If any of the council members think anything of his partial nakedness or the dampness of our clothing, they wisely say nothing.

"Good," Kallias says. "I want daily reports on how this progresses. And, Kaiser? See that all the men who accompanied us on our outing are hanged."

>—•—○—•—<

THE SITTING ROOM IS abuzz with gossip the next day. I know immediately that it's about me, as everyone goes quiet as soon as I enter the room with my latest sewing project, the top to match my high-low skirt. (I've decided on something formfitting and low-cut down the front.) A few ladies hurriedly pick up their embroidery and try to look busy. Others stare, but my good friends have nothing but smiles for me.

"We saved you a seat!" Rhoda says, her fingers pointing to a cushioned chair across from her.

Light conversation starts up as I take the proffered spot.

"*Spill!*" Hestia says when my rump barely hits the cushion.

I look to Rhoda for help.

"You were swimming with the king!" Rhoda says, and the room goes quiet, holding their breath and waiting for me to divulge the whole story.

I say, "And we were *naked*."

Hestia's hands go to cover her mouth, while Rhoda grins with delight.

"He was a perfect gentleman," I assure the room, even though I'm directing my attention to my friends. "Didn't touch me. Didn't even look as I undressed."

A girl on the other side of the room coughs into her hand. "For your sake, I hope a proposal is underway. No other man will have you now. Whether you two were chaste or not. Naked is naked."

Another girl gasps at her remark, hardly daring she would be so bold with the king's beau.

"I had a nice talk with the king about virginity," I say, and I proceed to rehash the conversation. At the end, I say, "Considering at least half of you have already given yourselves to men, I should think you grateful that you no longer have to keep your exploits a closely guarded secret. I certainly won't bother to do so with mine."

In fact, this morning I called in my debt to Myron. He has a month to get the money to me before I hand the case over to the constabulary.

It's only a moment after I say the words that the whole room floods with new gossip. This time, of ladies sharing their secret exploits with others in the room or their wishes for such trysts. Satisfied with what I've started, I turn back to Rhoda and Hestia.

"And here I thought I was being bold coming out of mourning so soon," Rhoda says. "You're changing everything."

I shrug. "I merely think we should be afforded the same rights as the men. Even in the bedroom."

>─┼─◆─┼─O─┼─◆─┼─◁

WHEN BREAKFAST IS SERVED, I'm not yet dressed, still clad in a nightgown. This one is black and formfitting. Though the short sleeves cover my shoulders, the silky material opens on each side of my abdomen, from my lowest ribs to below my hips. I chose the design because men do so love to use my hips and waist as handholds when kissing me senseless.

I brush my hair out of my face before entering the sitting room to break my fast.

Kallias stands from the breakfast table as soon as I open the door, and his eyes immediately go to the openings in my nightgown, where he can see the smooth skin at my second-best curves.

"My maid didn't inform me you were joining me this morning," I say by way of explanation. "I'll go put on a robe."

"No," he objects.

I raise a brow.

"I mean, I'm the intruder. You may wear whatever you wish in your own rooms." He drags his eyes to my face. "Are you up for company this morning?"

"Certainly." I take the seat opposite him.

"Your nightwear is . . . different," he adds.

"It's breathable."

"Do you get overheated when you sleep?"

"Only when I'm not sleeping alone."

Kallias turns his head toward my door.

"There's no one else in there," I say. "I didn't mean I'd had company last night."

He returns his gaze to me. "You say that almost wistfully."

Well, now that we're being honest about our past exploits—"It's . . . been a long time."

"Longer than it's been for me?"

"Devils, no!"

He stares at me, and I find myself laughing at the conversation.

"Just how long has it been for you?" he wants to know.

Truth or lie?

"Just over a month."

He blinks. He tries to start a new sentence but stops himself three times, before, "Anyone I know?"

"He was a nobody. Someone to amuse myself with to pass the time, while I waited for Chrysantha to become engaged."

A silence spreads between us as we dance around such a dangerous topic.

Finally, he blurts, "A month? A *month* is long for you?"

"Not all of us have as much self-control as you do."

"I'm not so in control as you might think." He looks down at the shredded potatoes on the table. Our untouched breakfast.

"Oh? Are you dallying with some lady in secret?" The words come out friendly and aloof, but for some reason, I start to see red at the corners of my vision.

"That's not what I meant." Kallias puts a bite of food into his mouth and chews slowly, as though giving himself an excuse not to say more.

He's saved by a knock at the door. A maid goes to answer before returning with a letter for me.

"Put it on my desk. I'll attend to it later," I tell her.

"No," Kallias says hurriedly. "Please, don't let me keep you from your correspondence. It might be important."

He's stalling for more time. All right, I'll indulge him.

I take up the letter and read:

To Lady Alessandra Stathos,

I'm looking into the disappearance of my son Hektor, who has been absent since July 27, three years past. I have learned that you may have had some sort of relationship with my son, and it is my hope that you might have more information concerning his disappearance.

As a favor to me, will you please come to my estate so we can talk? I'd hate to bring this matter into the king's home.

Sincerely,
Faustus Galanis, Baron of Drivas

I don't miss the blatant threat. *Come to me or else I'll come to you.*

"Something wrong?" Kallias asks.

I look up and gather my thoughts quickly. "It's an invitation to the Baron of Drivas's estate." Not a lie.

"Oh. I know of the baron, but I can't say I've seen him more than a handful of times. But if you wish to go, I would be honored to accompany you."

My knuckles whiten on the letter. Kallias thinks I've been invited to a party or some event. Of course he does, and he's trying to show that he's all in now on our ruse.

"Actually, the baron makes me . . . uncomfortable."

At that word, I have Kallias's undivided attention.

"Has he done something untoward?"

"He's been talking with my father and my sister. Now he's all but threatened to come to the palace if I don't come to him. I think he's up to something."

I have done my best not ever to lie to Kallias. Lies are far too easy to get caught up in. Far too easy to discover. I let Kallias draw his own conclusions from my words.

"The baron has many sons, does he not?" Kallias asks.

"He does," I say with resignation.

"Perhaps I should have a talk with him about how you are unavailable."

"Oh, please don't make an issue of it," I say. "But if it's not too much to ask, should he attempt to come to the palace . . ."

"I won't let the guards admit him. Say nothing more."

I relax. As long as I'm in Kallias's confidence, I needn't worry about the baron. Hektor will not ruin this for me.

Kallias returns to his breakfast, while I think through a reply for the baron. I'll assure him that despite what he's heard, I barely knew his son, and I'm afraid I have no information to assist in his search. Then I will pass along my regrets.

Yes, that should take care of things for now. I certainly can't leave the palace to deal with this issue myself. Not when things are finally turning around for Kallias and me.

⊱—⊹⊱⊶⊙⊷⊰⊹—⊰

I SEE KALLIAS AGAIN at lunch.

Twice in one day.

"You will be happy to know that both of your plans are progressing splendidly," he says to me while a servant brings a fresh bowl of soup for the king. "The people of Pegai have cast their votes for representation on the council. The newly appointed voice of the people is being followed discreetly everywhere he goes. We will know all the ringleaders of the revolt soon enough. As for the bandit, he struck this morning and took the freshly stamped coins. We will begin searching nearby towns for the gold first thing tomorrow."

Kallias's leg bounces underneath the table. He's in a very fine mood.

A wave of pleasure washes over me at his words. "Excellent. I would be very interested to remain informed on both situations."

"Of course. I'm beginning to realize there is nothing I care to keep from you anymore."

An amiable silence sits between us as we enjoy the food. At one point, I find Kallias watching me out of the corner of my eye. When I turn my head, he only grins when caught staring.

"What are you looking at?"

"That should be obvious. Perhaps you'd like to ask me what I'm thinking instead?" His eyes are liquid fire, and I wonder just how dangerous it might be to ask that very question.

But I do anyway.

"I'm thinking," he answers, "that you are quite beautiful, and every man at this table wishes he were me right now."

My stomach starts to flutter. "You are king. Every man *does* wish he were you."

"No. Every man wishes he had you at his side."

"You said I wasn't beautiful enough to be tempting," I remind him.

He takes his napkin from his lap and brushes his fingers against it. "I lied. You're the most stunning thing to ever set foot in my palace."

Our eyes hold. I'm helpless but to maintain the connection sizzling between us.

And though I know he won't break the law—not yet—for me, knowing that I have some hold on him brings a slow smile to my lips.

He stares down at them, at the red stain that graces my skin.

"Why are you telling me this?" I ask finally. And then I realize, "You don't want me to spend any more time with Leandros."

He admits, "I want to keep you all to myself."

I shouldn't be surprised at all that a king would be selfish, demanding, even cruel at times. But he is other things as well. He is intelligent, handsome, and giving. And he is not entirely unchangeable. He is changing his ways already for me.

"I think, Your Majesty, that all this talk of past indulgences is getting to your head."

"Perhaps I am simply in a good mood. Everything is going quite splendidly."

And it is all due to me.

Really, everyone should be quite glad when I am the one ruling all the kingdoms.

When Kallias excuses himself sometime later, his back hasn't even disappeared around the exit of the great hall before Hestia and Rhoda take the empty seats near me.

"I heard the king dined in your rooms this morning," Hestia says with a waggle of her eyebrows.

"He did. But that was all. Breakfast."

"No new gossip for me, then?"

"I'm afraid not."

"Oh, very well. We shall have to turn to less exciting gossip to occupy our afternoon."

"How about we talk of all the dancing you did at last night's ball?" Rhoda asks. "With *Lord Paulos.*"

With everything else that's been going on, I neglected to ask my friends about the event I missed. It seems things went very well for Hestia.

"It was only a couple of dances," Hestia says. "It was nothing. Truly."

"If that's the case, then why is he watching you right now?"

"What?" Hestia swivels her head around in time to catch the man who must be Lord Paulos quickly look away.

He's a bit older than she is, with a little gray at his temples, but still quite handsome.

I grin.

"See?" Rhoda continues. "And I happened to overhear him tell his friends how you smelled like a berry patch in spring. Men don't say things like that unless they're smitten."

"They don't?" Hestia looks down at the wood grain of the table and grins shyly.

"And he obviously very much enjoyed the conversation you shared. What did you talk about?"

"Well, I started by discussing the latest fashions in the palace, but somehow the conversation morphed into talk of gaming."

"Gaming?" Rhoda repeats.

"My father loves to play cards, and he taught me. Lord Paulos and I were rehearsing some of our favorite moves seen played in the game of hach. We both are obsessed with the strategy of the game. I know it wasn't very ladylike of me to discuss such things, but it was so terribly fun."

Sometimes Hestia can be quite silly, but I know she is an only child, with an absent mother and a father who wasn't quite sure how to raise a daughter. She may be trying to imitate me in the extreme, but part of me wonders if she is so afraid of doing or saying the wrong thing that she thinks imitating others is the only way to be safe. Then it's not her who is the one being rejected.

"Hestia," I say. "Do you know how I was able to catch the king's attention?"

She shakes her head.

"By being myself. By discussing what I wished to discuss and behaving how I wished to behave and wearing what I wished to wear. It is not conforming to a standard that drew His Majesty's attention. If you wish to make a happy match, I think you should do the same. Don't be afraid of who you are. Say what you wish. Be who you wish. Don't try to be someone else. You don't want to catch a man who wants *me*. You want to catch a man who wants *you*."

Hestia blinks a few times before looking down at the clothes she's wearing, the ones that resemble my close-fitted dress from last week. She takes a full minute to think while staring at the smooth fabric about her waist. Suddenly, she rises, walks over to Lord Paulos, and takes the empty seat right next to him.

Rhoda takes up her empty seat, so we can converse more easily. "I've been trying to tell her the same thing for years. I think it just needed to come from the future queen."

"Do you expect we'll hear news of an engagement soon?"

"I expect we will."

We both lean back in our seats, letting our eyes trail down to Lord Paulos, who is now laughing at whatever Hestia has just said.

"What of you?" I ask. "Any progress on your search for passion?"

"Oh, I'm having a dreadful time of it."

"How can that be?"

Rhoda brushes a black curl over her shoulder. "I have come up with a ranking system for men who are in the running. But none of them are quite what I want."

"You must tell me of this system you've devised!" I say, thoroughly intrigued by the conversation.

"I have come up with three different categories by which to judge men. They are looks, manners, and personality. Each category is ranked from one to five, one being a low score, and five being a high score. Now take Lord Toles, for example. With his sculpted features and dark complexion, he is an easy five ranking in looks. He's fairly polite and thoughtful, resulting in a three in manners. But personality? Oh, he's as dry as a lake during a drought. Overall, he ranks only nine out of fifteen."

"How fascinating! What would your ideal future husband rank overall?"

"At least a thirteen, don't you think?"

I ponder it a moment. "Definitely. If we were only talking of bedding men, I would say you need to look only for fives in the good-looks category. If you were looking for a friend, all you would need is a five in the personality department. If you're hoping for an escort to an event, then you would need only a five in manners, perhaps looks as well if you're trying to leave a good impression. But for a love match? Definitely at least a thirteen."

Rhoda nods. "I thought Lord Cosse would be the one after the last party. Did you know he and I danced three times together? Not in a row, of course. But three in total! He's a four and a half in looks and a three and a half in personality. But manners? When I begged a break from the dancing because I was thirsty, he didn't bother to offer to grab something from the refreshment table. He only went in search of a different dance partner. Can you believe that?"

"An outrage," I say.

"My thoughts exactly. Lord Doukas has been after me for a while, but he's only a two in looks. If we're being kind," she adds in a whisper. "The man is a five in both manners and personality. So it's a real shame. I don't like to think of myself as being shallow, but surely I should find a man I think is attractive if I'm to pursue him?"

"I agree."

Rhoda sighs. "Sometimes, I don't think there are enough men at court. And I'm convinced the perfect man doesn't exist."

Without prompting, Kallias's visage rises to the front of my mind. The perfect symmetry of his face. The dark volume of his hair. His intelligent and bright green eyes. The view of his bare chest and bare . . . other things.

I think of our teasing and joking. Our discussions of bedding and reaching for the things we want. I think of the way he waited for me to arrive before starting on his dinner, how he waited up for me when I went out with Leandros.

Kallias has his flaws. Oh, so many flaws. I think of his temper. Of his selfishness to keep me to himself. Even though he doesn't want all of me.

Mouth dry, I say, "I don't think it's necessarily about finding the perfect man but finding the perfect man for you. One person may rank a man far differently than another, even if they are both using your ranking system. But . . ."

"What?" Rhoda asks.

"The king is a fifteen. Perhaps not for everyone. But he is a fifteen for me." And it's the starkest truth.

Rhoda quirks her mouth to the side. "I assure you, Alessandra. It is not just you. The king is most assuredly a fifteen. Perhaps I should have rephrased. No *attainable* man is a fifteen."

How very right she is.

But I'm far from giving up just yet.

CHAPTER

17

The next day is more bleak than the ones we've been having of late, with gray clouds blocking the entirety of the sky. The air is full of moisture and constantly threatening rain, though no drops have surfaced just yet.

Despite the weather, I'm in a fine mood after the most recent letter from my father.

Alessandra, what did you do? Lord Eliades just withdrew his marriage proposal. He said rumors were abounding about you and the king. What happened?

You know we were depending on this after your failure to secure marriage with the king. Now I will have to start from the beginning to find someone who will have you. Why must you be so trying?

I suppose word of my naked swimming adventure with the king got back to Orrin. I'm so delighted to be rid of him.

I wrap a thick shawl about my shoulders and head outdoors, thinking today to be the perfect opportunity to sneak away for some air. No one else is likely to be outside. Not in this weather.

I take a fresh sketchbook with me and go in search of the gardens Kallias mentioned his mother maintained while she was alive.

As I round the stables, an arm snakes through mine. I'd think it Hestia or Rhoda if I didn't feel the distinct muscles hidden beneath a copper-colored jacket.

"Alessandra," Leandros says, "I thought I saw you disappear outside. You aren't planning on abandoning us, are you?"

I adjust my grip on my shawl so that I might more easily hold on to the arm of the most narcissistic man in the palace.

"With naught but my sketchbook?" I ask.

"Fair point. What are we to be drawing today? It must have slipped your mind to ask me to model."

I let out an unladylike snort. "I don't draw people. I draw designs. For me to then sew."

"And we're out in this chill because . . ."

"Well, I'm here because I thought the gardens might be a lovely place to draw inspiration from. I can't fathom why you're here."

"I saw an opportunity to finally catch you alone. Any other time I try to approach you, Kallias shoots daggers at me with his shadowy glare."

"I hadn't noticed," I admit.

"That's because you're so taken with him. But he's not here now," he says in a naughty tone. "Tell me, when can I take you away from here again for another night of fun?"

A sad smile rises to my lips. I like Leandros. He's ridiculous at times, but fun and kind. Not to mention handsome. His manners run a bit short, but he has to be at least a thirteen by Rhoda's ranking.

But he can't make me a queen.

I'm about to open my lips, but Leandros turns and places a fingertip against them. "No, don't say whatever you're thinking. I can tell I won't like it. Take some time. Wait for Kallias to do something to upset you. Then come find me with your answer."

We come to a stop before an iron gate, through which I can see rows and rows of flowers. Leandros halts.

"I'll leave you to your sketching. But do come find me if you decide you're in need of a model. Nude or not." He gives me a wink before striding off.

Such a little devil, but I find a wide grin on my face as I let myself through the gate.

Brick-lined trails wend through patches of flowers. First, I pass by the roses. Each row varies by size and color. Some are all one shade, while others are tipped with pinks and yellows. They're cared for immaculately, with not a dying bloom among the plants.

Farther along, I see beds of other species. Chrysanthemums and daffodils and tulips, but I don't go exploring just yet. I stop before one of the rosebushes, the petals a sun-bright yellow. They flare to the most stunning red-orange at the tips, and I can't help but stare at the individual blossoms. How they remind me of the flickering colors of fire. One flower hasn't quite yet bloomed. With just a few orange tips peeling away, it looks like an ember slowly extinguishing. Growing smaller, rather than larger, as I know the blossom will do.

A dress takes shape before my eyes. A yellow gown with orange tips about the hem, individual petals pulling away from the skirts. Finding a nearby bench, I seat myself, flip open to an empty page, and move my pen rapidly against the parchment, letting the dress take shape.

"May I join you?" a deep voice asks.

His voice.

I look up, and I can hardly believe that Kallias has entered the garden. He looks so out of place with the black attire he's chosen for today, with the shadows surrounding his person. They don't seem to belong in a colorful garden.

Demodocus trots along beside him. But, as some idea gets in the beast's head, he takes off like a shot through the garden, jumping over a nearby hedge of flowers and giving out a loud *yip*.

Probably spotted a rabbit.

I turn back to his master.

May I join you? he'd asked. Such manners. Leandros assumed he would be welcome. And whether Kallias actually has any intention of leaving if I were to tell him so will remain unknown. I can't ever see myself turning him away.

Not just because I need to win his heart.

But because I like him, and I want him near me.

"Please do," I say, and turn my nose to the empty space beside me. He sits, keeping an appropriate two feet between us on the bench. "How did you know I was out here?" Or perhaps he didn't. Maybe he wanted to go for a turn about the gardens, seeking the outdoors and potential solitude as I was.

"I saw you out the window."

"And you followed? Were you not in a meeting?"

"I was."

I look up from my sketch, giving him an inquisitive look.

"I decided I'd rather be out here with you, and I cut it short."

Pleased, I return back to my sketch.

"Are you designing a new outfit?" he asks.

Again, I find myself pleased. Pleased that he would know exactly what I'm doing, because he knows what I like. "I feel at a disadvantage," I tell him. "You know my hobbies, but I have yet to learn yours."

Leandros mentioned fencing and riding when we went out together, but surely there is more.

Kallias cups his hands in front of him and leans his elbows on his knees. "I used to enjoy fencing above all else, but since I became king, I have been unable to have a partner who wasn't made of straw."

"Oh." I hadn't thought of that.

"I do like riding and spending time with Demodocus. I've always been fond of animals, but even more so of late."

As if hearing his name, Demodocus comes bounding back over, tongue lolling out the side of his mouth. He sits before me expectantly, waiting for a scratch behind the ears. I oblige him.

"What do you mean?" I ask.

"I can't touch another human, but my abilities aren't affected by animals. Demodocus is the only companion I can have. Some days, I even spoil him and let him in the bed."

I hadn't even considered that. That he would seek out contact in other ways.

With his turned-down head, a lock of hair sweeps over his brow. If he were any other man in the world, I would reach forward and smooth it back.

"I used to play the piano," he says more quietly. "Most everything I learned how to do, I learned from a tutor, but not the piano. My mother taught me herself. She loved music."

I swallow past a sudden lump in my throat. Is that sympathy? For him? Even softer than his utterance, I ask, "Would you play for me sometime?"

"Do you like music?"

"I think I would like your music."

He turns toward me, and just like on the first day we met, a jolt goes through me at the connection of our eyes meeting.

The breeze flutters now, sending that lock of hair brushing against his brow.

My fingers twitch, and I look down at my gloved hand.

Slowly, so very slowly, I raise it.

Moving as carefully as I would toward a startled horse or a frightened child, I let my hand drift toward Kallias, toward that lock of hair.

His gaze shifts to my glove, and I can't begin to guess the trail his thoughts take.

But I move at a pace that gives him what feels like all the time in the world to stop me.

Instead, his shadows disappear. He solidifies before me, so that when my finger touches his brow, it doesn't go through. It meets warm resistance and brushes that lock back.

Oh, but how I wish I could feel the exact texture of his hair.

When done, I let my hand fall back into my lap. But our eyes are still trapped upon each other.

Finally, Kallias looks down at my sketchbook. "What are you making? A day dress? Something with pants?" His voice is deeper than it was before, I note, and it almost rambles, as though he's making up the words just before he says them.

After a lengthy pause in which I'd forgotten that I'd held anything in my hands at all, I manage, "A ball gown, actually. I was inspired by your mother's roses." I look up at the blossoms in question.

"We must throw a ball, then, so you may show it off once it is finished."

"Could we? Oh, I've never organized a ball before."

"Would you like to?"

I nod.

"You name the date, and we will make it happen."

All of a sudden, I don't feel as though I need the shawl wrapped around my shoulders. I'm so very warm and light.

Once, there was another boy who made me feel this way. One who made me feel full and seen and loved.

Now the bugs of the earth have feasted on his flesh.

But I won't let Hektor ruin this moment I'm having with the king.

Something moves out of the corner of my vision. I turn, thinking perhaps it is only a flower stem swaying with the breeze.

But it is much bigger. Much sturdier. Much more alive.

"Kallias!"

I throw myself forward, but too late.

A shot sounds before I can move, filling the garden's quiet. Ruining its peace.

Striking the king.

Kallias falls backward, his back hitting a patch of grass first, before his legs follow, slipping over the sides of the bench.

I'm paralyzed to the spot, staring in horror at where Kallias lies, his vest a deeper black right in the middle of his gut, where the fabric has become damp with blood.

Demodocus leaps after the king. He whines lightly when Kallias doesn't move after he nudges him with his nose.

My hand shakes as I reach for Kallias, but what am I to do? I don't know anything of healing.

Help. I should go for help.

I stand abruptly, but then I notice a man running toward us. I don't process anything other than the fact that he's holding a semiautomatic handgun, which he returns to a holster on his side, and reaches for the rapier at his waist to replace it.

The assassin is coming to make sure his mark is dead.

I plant my feet before the bench and stare the assassin down. He comes to an abrupt halt before me and points his sword out in front of him.

"Out of the way, or I'll run you through."

All I can hear is my breathing in my ears. All I can feel is the rise and fall of my chest. But I don't move an inch to let the man by.

My single night of failed boxing comes to mind.

Unhelpful.

Words are my only ally in this situation.

"You hit him square in the chest," I say. "Now go before the guards come running to investigate the sound of the shot."

With his free hand, he shoves me away. I hit the ground hard, but I don't register the pain as I rise to a sitting position, reaching for my boot.

The rubies around the hilt of my dagger gleam as I bring the blade down in an arc, sinking it into the man's thigh.

He howls and backhands me with the hand not holding his rapier.

I go sprawling on the ground again, really hating the bricks that take the skin off my knees.

The assassin reaches down for my dagger. With a grunt, he pulls the blade from his skin and tosses it away.

His murderous eyes are turned to me now, but before he can take a step in my direction, we both snap our necks toward the dark shape rising from the other side of the bench.

Kallias is off the ground, standing firmly on two feet, swathed in shadows. He walks right through the bench, and as he does so something metal *plinks* onto the brick walkway below us.

The bullet.

Though his clothes still bear the stain of blood, he holds himself without a hunch or anything else to show signs of him being in pain. He takes one glance at me on the ground, at the red outline of a handprint on my cheek, before turning back to the assassin.

"You'll die for that," Kallias says, his voice a deep rumble.

"It's you who will die today," the man says, and he steps forward, thrusting the tip of his sword through Kallias.

The assassin nearly loses his footing when his sword doesn't meet the expected resistance, instead going clean through Kallias's shadow form.

"What the—?"

Kallias steps right through him, and a shiver goes through me, as I remember the smoky sensation of Kallias's shadow form all around me.

The assassin whirls, facing Kallias now that he's on the other side of him. He draws his gun once again, and this time deposits the entire round of bullets into Kallias's chest.

But of course, they go right through him.

He drops the gun as the king pulls his own sword from his side, the shadows disappearing from around the blade and hand that holds it.

And then they duel.

Indeed, Kallias hadn't lied when he said he knew how to use that blade. He sends out a series of quick thrusts that the assassin deflects just in time. He's slower with the injury I dealt him, but he just manages to evade each one.

After a time, I realize Kallias is toying with him. Though the two swords meet in the air with metallic clanks, every time the assassin attempts to make his own jabs toward the king, they go right through him.

Like he's dueling a ghost.

Unkillable. Untouchable.

Eventually, the assassin tires of the game. When the swords of the two men come together, he hurls his weight into the connection, sending Kallias stumbling backward.

Then the man takes off at a run, his steps hitching with the leg I stabbed. Kallias runs over to one of the flower beds, bends over the ground, and comes up with my dagger. He barely takes aim before the weapon goes twirling out of his hand.

It hits the assassin square in the back. He goes down.

Kallias whirls on me, bending at the knees on the bricks beside me. His shadows are gone.

"Are you hurt?" he asks.

"I'm fine."

But either he doesn't believe me, or he doesn't hear my answer at all, because his gloved hands sweep over me. First touching my cheeks and neck, then sliding down my sides, over my abdomen, down my legs. Checking for injuries.

But because I have none, my breathing hitches at the contact. And even though his hands are gloved, the heat of them reaches through my pant-clad legs.

By the time he finishes, he lets his gaze return to mine, and he freezes at what he sees there. His hands are wrapped around my ankles. They tighten their grip when his eyes latch on to mine, and a rush of heat steals up my spine.

His hands move to my knees, spreading them apart so he can settle there. We're close. So close. Too close. Closer than we've ever been before and—

"Sire?"

We startle apart at the same time, the two of us not having even heard the sound of the guards approaching. Kallias's shadows return in a flash, safely encasing his whole body.

Five men bearing the king's crest on their tunics stand before us, rapiers and pistols drawn.

Kallias stands and holds out a hand to me, the shadows about the offered limb disappearing as he hauls me to my feet. He releases me once I find my balance.

"There was an attacker. I felled him over there." Kallias points, and three of the men go in search of the body while the other two begin sweeping the area. "Take the assassin to the dungeons. If he doesn't die from his wounds before then, send for a healer to attend to him. And also send a healer to the queen's suite. Come, Alessandra."

Kallias and I walk side by side to the palace. Demodocus leaps over the bench to amble along beside us, the fur about his lips wet from lapping at the king's blood.

"Useless mutt," Kallias says, but he looks down at his dog fondly. "He's a lover, not a fighter. That's for sure."

Touching. So much touching. And heated gazes. And assassins with swords and a gun and—

"You were shot," I say, stopping in place. "How are you uninjured?" When Kallias stops beside me, I reach out a hand to hover over the bloodspot on his coat.

"If I have time to shift into shadow before an injury kills me, the shadows will heal it."

"I thought—" I can't even voice aloud what I thought. It's far too terrible.

"You placed yourself between the attacker and me."

I did? I hadn't been thinking. I'd just acted.

"Thank you," he says. "But do not ever put your life on the line for mine. I can heal. You cannot."

He resumes walking, and I stumble to follow him. I can't seem to focus a single thought in my mind. It just replays what happened over and over again.

"What did you notice about the attacker?" Kallias asks.

Notice? I try to bring his image to mind, thinking everything through.

"He was male." I silently curse myself. Obviously that hadn't been what Kallias meant. Why am I struggling to remember a person I just saw minutes ago? "He wore dark clothing."

"What kind of clothing?" Kallias prompts. I wonder for a moment why he bothers to ask me all of this when he saw the attacker for himself as well. But it feels important to answer, so I do.

"It was made of leather. The hems were lined in furs. It was . . . Pegain." An assassin from the kingdom Kallias most recently conquered. The weather is cooler there. That's why the women wear pants. The cold can't climb up their legs.

"Good," Kallias says, as though my answer pleases him. We enter the palace, and Kallias remains right at my side as we climb a set of stairs.

Something niggles at the back of my mind. Something wrong. Something off about the assassin.

"I spoke with him," I say.

"Yes, I heard."

"His accent wasn't Pegain. It was Naxosian."

"What does that tell you?" Kallias asks.

"The assassin is from here, but someone wanted to make it look as though the killer was a foreigner. He didn't shoot me. Only you. He was supposed to be seen before he got away."

"Very good," Kallias says.

"Why are you praising me like I'm some daft schoolgirl?"

"You're in shock, Alessandra. I'm trying to keep your mind busy."

I realize then that my hands are shaking. Kallias looks down at them as I do. He takes one of my hands within his own, not missing a step.

Kallias is like a specter as he moves through the palace, all flickering shadows floating from place to place. Though his feet still make the imitation of steps, I wonder if they need to. It looks as though his feet hardly touch the floor. The potted flowers sitting on tables in the corridors don't rustle as he walks by. The black carpet doesn't indent with his steps. The drapes around the windows don't whisper with movement as he brushes past them.

I follow beside him, fascinated by everything about him. From the way the muscles in his back flex as he walks, still visible through the shadows, to the way servants press themselves flush against the walls to let us pass. Everything about him exudes power.

We stride down a corridor leading . . . somewhere. I've never been in this part of the palace before.

Wait, what was it Kallias had ordered to the guard? Something about sending a healer to the queen's suite?

A couple floors up, Kallias stops in front of a door. A potted ivy plant rests upon each of two tables placed on either side of the doorway, the vines growing up the walls and connecting at the space above the doorway. It's easy to imagine a magical garden lying hidden on the other side.

Kallias, seeing me stare at the beautiful plants in wonder, says, "My mother loved plants. Roses were her favorite. I'm sure you've noticed them detailing all the woodwork throughout the palace. She'd grow them in her garden and paint them black."

"Black? Why?" I breathe.

"Because then they reminded her of my father. Of the shadows."

"Is this—?" I start, unable to finish.

Kallias walks through the solid door, leaving me alone in the dark corridor for a moment. Then I hear a latch clicking, and he opens the now unlocked door from the inside for me.

"These were my mother's rooms," he says. Though his hand must have become corporeal to open the door for me, it is already encased in shadow once more as I brush past him.

In the greeting chamber, a large table rests, fresh roses blooming in a vase. A grand piano sits against the far wall. And the wall behind me, next to the door I just stepped through? Stained glass covers every inch of it, little pieces of color forming together to make the picture of a flourishing forest. A deer drinks from a flowing lake. Butterflies hover below the leaves of a tree. And everywhere along the bottom, flowers bloom. The door was made to look like the trunk of a large tree, not detracting from the opulence in the least. Candles throughout the room cast the whole magnificence of the design aglow, the inner facets smoldering as though the flames live within the individual glass pieces.

"The whole palace has been fitted with electricity, but my mother preferred the way the candlelight made the glass shimmer. I still have servants light these. I think she would have liked that."

Kallias opens another door, which leads into the bedchamber. The bed sits high off the floor, so heaped with downy blankets and plump pillows, I wonder if I'd have to jump to reach into the expansiveness of it. Red bed hangings have been tied to each of the four posts around the bed, and I suspect they perfectly block out the light when let loose.

Red rugs cover the black carpet, making each step even softer. The wardrobe is massive, a design of rose thorns cut through the wooden sides. A vanity takes up nearly half the wall, an assortment of jewels and cosmetics heaped upon it.

Seeing where my eyes have landed, Kallias says, "They belonged to my mother. Use what you will. Anything else, you can have the servants remove."

"What?" My mind tries to wrap around everything. Assassin. Kallias's blood. The queen's rooms. "Why are we here?"

"These are your new rooms."

"What?" I ask again stupidly. "Why?"

"You saved my life by distracting the assassin and giving me time to heal. And I have never feared so much for your safety. You'll be sleeping right next to me now." And then he adds, as though it pains him to say it, "Unless you find that disagreeable?"

I'm speechless for a moment. "No," I say at last, my face softening. "No, I'll stay here. And I'd be honored to use your mother's things. Don't have them removed from the room."

Though his face doesn't change, I can tell he's pleased. Perhaps by the way the shadows about his face lighten.

"That door at the end of the room leads to the washroom. And this one"—he points to a door I hadn't noticed near the bed—"leads to my chambers."

My throat feels a little tight, and I can't quite think why. Because I'm so pleased? Humbled by this gesture? Perhaps even a little afraid by the intimacy of it?

Kallias rushes to say, "Also, keeping you in the queen's suite further helps our ruse. You can also barge in on me, if you like, as I have so rudely done to you several times." His eyes are still trained on the door leading to his own rooms.

"I don't know what to say," I say at last. The large windows set all the finery to near sparkling. The small potted trees in the corners of the room strain toward the light.

I feel like a woodland princess.

No, not a princess, I amend.

A queen.

I am in the queen's rooms.

"You could say whether or not you like it," Kallias offers. "If there's anything displeasing about the accommodations."

I smile, turning to him. "I don't find anything displeasing. This is beautiful. Thank you for sharing it with me."

"I'm glad," he says. Then he looks down to my hands.

I realize they're still shaking.

Kallias gently pushes on my shoulders to get me in a sitting position atop the bed. He grabs a blanket from an ottoman near the foot of the bed and wraps it around my shoulders.

"I'm fine," I insist.

"You will be, but it's fine if you're not."

"It's not the first time I've seen death, Kallias." I wish I could call back the words. I don't need him asking me questions about Hektor.

"Seeing me kill a guard is far different than watching me kill a man intent on killing us. Your life was in danger."

Oh, right.

"Why are *you* so collected?" I ask, glaring up at him. "You're the one who was shot, for gods' sake."

"Because I've known for a while that someone is trying to kill me. I've come to expect it."

Kallias doesn't leave me until a healer arrives. Some old woman who fusses over me, insisting she look at the red welt on my face. Unsurprisingly, she prescribes rest as a treatment.

"Do you have someone who could stay with you tonight?" the old crone asks.

"Why?"

"After such an encounter, some find it difficult to sleep. Another body in the room might help."

"I'm not a small child. I don't need someone to check my closets for monsters."

"Not monsters. Assassins. Men who would use you to get to the king," she remarks unhelpfully.

"Get out," I snap.

The healer gathers her things before quitting the room and leaving me in blessed quiet.

CHAPTER 18

I take supper in my new rooms. After the excitement of the day, I have no desire to be around lots of people. Kallias doesn't join me, and I assume it must be because he's looking into the man who managed to get into his mother's gardens undetected.

And likely killing the men who allowed it to happen.

When I am finished with my meal, a maid comes to help me undress.

"I brought your correspondences with me, my lady, in case you wish to respond to any tonight. I'll have the staff move the rest of your belongings up here first thing tomorrow."

She sets two neat piles of letters on the nightstand beside my bed. At the top, I note Orrin's love letter and cringe at it distastefully.

She lays one of my simpler nightgowns on the bed for me to change into, but I send her away, not needing her help anymore.

I ensure the door is securely locked behind her. I check the windows, making sure each one is latched. I look into every nook in the room large enough for an intruder to hide. I turn on every light in the entirety of my rooms before drawing myself a bath and washing away everything that happened today.

I dry myself methodically, pull on the simple white nightgown, blow out the candles and turn off the lights, and climb into the bed.

As soon as I do, my heart races. Every shadow in the room feels as though it's concealing an intruder. I try drawing the curtains about the bed, blocking out the rest of the room.

Somehow, that only makes it worse. Not being able to see what may or may not be out there.

After such an encounter, some find it difficult to sleep.

Damn the old crone!

Logically, I know there's nothing in the room. I know I'm alone. I know no one can get in without breaking down the door or shattering the glass of a window.

But I can't seem to get my body to relax enough for sleep.

Tonight, at least, I know I won't rest if I'm alone in the room.

I wonder if I could persuade Rhoda or Hestia to join me tonight, but that hardly seems fair to rouse them now. The hour is so very late. I couldn't possibly bother them.

A faint sound barely reaches me, and I startle at it, despite its gentility. It was only a soft yip. Demodocus and Kallias must have finally returned for the night. Nothing to be worried about.

I sit up in bed, pull the curtains away, and stare at the door adjoining our rooms. Before I can think twice about it, I'm up and running for that door like it's the key to my salvation.

I knock gently. Perhaps too timidly. Could Kallias have even heard it? Perhaps I don't *want* him to hear it. I'm being so ridiculous. Perhaps I should just attempt a few laps about the room to rid myself of the nervous energy and—

The door creaks open, suggesting it hasn't been opened in a very long time.

"Alessandra," Kallias says. As if it would be anyone else on the other side of the door, knocking for him.

His hair is mussed, as though he's been running his hands through it for hours. His shirt is untucked from his pants, all the buttons undone, exposing his smooth chest. I caught him in the middle of undressing. Though that didn't seem to matter to him if he still opened the door.

"I—I can't sleep," I say.

Before he can say or do anything, a furry body pushes its way past Kallias's legs and helps himself into my room. Demodocus sticks his nose along the wall, sniffing the new room's interior.

"Just a moment," Kallias says. He leaves the door open while he turns back into his room. Though the room is dark, I see the faint outline of a massive bed, big enough for five to fit comfortably, I should think. I wonder if it's the same bed his father used or if Kallias had it made specifically for himself. What is Kallias like when he sleeps? Is he still and quiet with nothing but the movement of his chest up and down to signal he's alive? Or does he toss and turn, let out little snores? Is he encased in shadow in his dreams or is he solid?

His form returns, blocking my view of the bed. He's clad in a long scarlet robe, his gloves returned to his hands. Perfectly covered from head to toe.

And not a shadow in sight, I notice with some relish.

I step aside, allowing him into the room. His eyes find Demodocus sticking his wet nostrils into the wardrobe to inspect the smells found there, the beast having risen on his back legs.

"Demodocus, down."

The dog listens and goes in search of other things to sniff.

"What troubles you?" Kallias asks.

I return to the bed, sitting on its edge, and he joins me.

"Nothing, but I can't seem to sleep."

"We had some excitement today, and the men who let the intruder in have been dealt with, but you're safe. I promise. There are men out in the corridor and men out in the courtyard, watching the windows.

Not that anything could reach us up here, but better more precautions than less."

I nod, already having known all of this.

"I'm next door, should you ever need anything. You're not helpless," Kallias says emphatically. "You stabbed the assailant with a dagger to the thigh, for gods' sake. You're very capable." He places a comforting hand on my thigh.

I turn to him. "Thank you. I know all of this, truly. I just can't seem to relax."

"Lie back," he instructs, and I do so, scooting over to the opposite side of the bed so there's room for him. He starts to recline, but his eyes catch on the bedside table to where my letters are piled up.

Kallias picks up one, and I'm about to thank him not to go snooping through my things, when I realize just what he's holding.

"*My dearest Alessandra,*" Kallias reads aloud. "*I hope you will forgive my boldness, but word has reached me that the king did not accompany you to your latest outing at the estate of the Christakoses.*"

I leap forward, trying to snatch the letter from his grip, but Kallias stands out of my reach, never ceasing in his reading. "*In fact, it's rumored you spent the evening with a childhood friend. This has dared me to hope that perhaps you've ended things with His Majesty. You, of course, know of my business travels. They've kept me from your side too long, but I think of you daily. I miss your conversation, your smile, the way you look away from me when you're overcome by my generosity.* Who the hell wrote this?" Kallias's eyes skip to the end to find the signature. Then he barks out a laugh. "Orrin wrote you a love letter!"

I stand, trying to rip the damned thing from his hands, but Kallias keeps jumping out of reach.

"*When I look at the night sky, I cease to see its beauty. All I can think of is you. Your sable hair and how I long to run my fingers through its lengths. Your lips, ripe as cherries—how I long to taste them. Your fingers are as dainty as butterfly wings, and your eyes have a shine to rival the light of stars."*

"Damn you, Kallias, give it here!" I throw myself at him, and this time, instead of dancing out of reach, he turns to shadow.

Along with the letter, which is now safely out of my reach for as long as Kallias likes.

"That is unfair," I say.

Kallias wipes a shadowed tear of mirth from his eyes. "How could you keep this treasure from me?" He reads, *"Your voice could command the world to stop spinning, the plants to stop growing, the wind to cease blowing, the bugs to stop chirping."* The king erupts into a fit of laughter.

"Chirping bugs. In his love letter to you!" Kallias clenches his stomach with both hands, and in doing so, he loses his grip on the letter. It solidifies instantly, and I snatch it up before it even hits the ground.

I tear the damn thing to shreds and let the pieces fall to the floor.

"Not all men have skill with a pen," I say through gritted teeth.

Kallias turns toward my stack of letters. "Tell me this isn't his first letter. Oh, please say there's more!"

"There isn't," I assure him.

"A pity. Oh, I haven't laughed that hard in—well, at least a year. Alessandra, are you blushing!"

"No. If my face is heated, it is from the fury I feel toward you."

"For making fun of Orrin?"

"For making fun of me. For thinking it humorous that anyone should want to write me a love letter."

Will he never see me as a romantic prospect?

Instantly, the joviality disappears from his face, replaced with utter seriousness. "Alessandra, I do not tease you. It is only Orrin's attempt at poetry that amuses me. You are worthy of all the poets' notice, but that"—he points to the shredded pieces on the ground—"is not worthy of you."

Somewhat appeased, I challenge, "And I suppose you could do better?"

"I most certainly could." He looks sadly upon the torn scraps at the floor. "Did you have to destroy it? I could have framed it and saved it for whenever I'm having a bad day."

"Shut your mouth." I return to the bed, staring up at the ceiling. I refuse to let a smile grace my face.

But Kallias's mirth is so very contagious. And I enjoy his smile more than I care to admit.

A large weight joins me on the bed, but since it's half on top of me, I know it isn't Kallias.

"Well, hello there," I say to Demodocus.

Kallias snaps his fingers and points to the foot of the bed. With a sad, downcast face, Demodocus rises and lies down by my feet instead.

Kallias claims the spot beside me. He interlaces his fingers over his chest, staring up at the canopy.

"I haven't done this in a while," Kallias says.

"Lie next to a woman?"

"Climb into my mother's bed."

There are several feet between us, but I manage to reach over and clasp a gloved hand in mine. He doesn't pull it away.

"You don't have to stay with me. I can—" I start.

"Hush. Go to sleep."

The interruption brings a smile to my lips. I try to do as he suggests. I really do, but it's been a while since I've had a man in my bed. Sleep is the last thing on my mind. Even if anything else is impossible.

And then I remember what happened in the garden. After the attack. Kallias had his hands on me. Checking for injuries, but then things changed. His touch changed. His eyes changed. His breathing changed.

I don't consider it an improvement. We almost died. Afterward, he was likely drunk on the energy from such an ordeal. And it made him . . . impassioned.

Just what would he have done if the guards hadn't come?

I ask, "Did the assassin survive?"

"No. Between your wound and mine, he didn't have a chance."

"Then you weren't able to learn anything from him?"

"Nothing, save what we already discussed about his clothing and accent. He didn't have anything in his pockets. No note from whoever hired him, nor any money. Whoever sent him was quite careful."

I give Kallias's hand a gentle squeeze. "Then what's to be done?"

His free hand rises to rest above his head on the pillow. "I thought I would have answers by now. Everyone has been questioned again and again regarding the night my parents died. There are too many people unaccounted for. Everyone was terrified when the break-in happened. No one can remember who was in the safe rooms with them, save the person on their immediate right and left. Half my nobles claim to be in places where no one else seems to have seen them.

"Ampelios has been looking into who might have poisoned my gloves two months ago. He's found nothing. And the terrible thing is, I don't know if that's true, or if he's in on it because he's one of my council members.

"Now we've had a new attack, which should present us with new leads. But the assassin is dead. His body has no secrets to reveal. And all his accent and clothing suggest is that someone within my court killed my parents and is now trying to kill me. Which I already knew."

I let my thumb stroke over his as he talks, hoping to silently comfort him.

"You know," Kallias says, his voice dropping a little, "I wouldn't blame you if you left."

"Left?"

"The palace. Being close to me puts you in danger, too. You don't have to stay. I would never force you to remain here."

I turn my neck, but he won't meet my eyes. "I'm not going anywhere. You're not facing this alone." Besides, when I'm queen, people will be trying to kill me anyway. Might as well get used to it now.

His breath leaves him, as though he'd been holding it while waiting to hear what I would say.

"We will figure this out together," I say.

Kallias nods, but I can tell it gives his troubled mind no relief.

><+>-+>--O--<+>-+-<

WHEN I WAKE, the heat of another body curls into me, suffusing me with warmth. At first, I think to drape an arm over the man, whoever he is, but then I register two things simultaneously.

First, I'm dressed.

Second, the body next to mine is unusually fuzzy.

Demodocus, it would seem, maneuvered his way back to the front of the bed whenever Kallias left. He probably went back to his own room as soon as I was out. He can't risk falling asleep in my bed. What if I were to roll over and touch him?

I scratch my bed companion behind the ears. "Good morning."

Demodocus tries to reach my face with his tongue, but I roll over and exit the bed.

"No slobbery kisses, thank you."

When my maid comes to help me in the morning, a manservant also arrives to let Demodocus outside. She brings with her a simple gown, but that is no matter. Today I will begin the preparations for the ball Kallias is allowing me to throw. I think I'll set the date for one month's time, which means I have much to get ready. Invitations to send out. A theme to select. Decorations. Food. Table arrangements.

But I know just the two ladies to enlist for help.

A knock sounds at my door as soon as I'm dressed and ready to leave to start the day.

"Lady Stathos," a man says from the other side as he bows.

"Lord Vasco." The head of Kallias's council.

"Please do call me Ikaros."

I don't return the gesture of goodwill.

"May I come in?" he asks, glancing behind me to the queen's greeting chamber.

Who does he think he is, inviting himself to my room? He most certainly may not come in. And how did he know I was staying here already? He must have a spy close to Kallias. Or me.

"I'm actually on my way out." I pick up my skirts to cross the threshold, then head down the corridor. A small army of servants passes us by, carrying my belongings into my new rooms. "And forgive me, but I haven't particularly enjoyed any of our past conversations. I have a hard time believing this one will be any better."

Ikaros follows me as I walk away.

"I'm so very glad you were there yesterday to assist the king," he says, ignoring everything I just said.

I nearly trip as I come to an abrupt stop in the middle of the corridor. "Assist? Do you mean save his life?"

He crosses his arms in front of himself as he pauses with me. "That's a bit of a stretch, don't you think, considering he wouldn't have been out there in the first place if you hadn't been?"

"Are you trying to suggest that I had something to do with the attempt on the king's life?"

He brushes invisible lint from off his robes. "Not at all. I hardly see what you would have to gain by killing the king. Your prosperous future comes from keeping him alive. Which begs the question: Why do you persist in spending time with my nephew when you are being courted by a king?"

I continue walking, not bothering to answer things that are none of his business.

"I know you spent an entire night with Leandros, doing gods know what. You dance with him at parties. You were seen with him outside shortly before the attack in the gardens."

"Are you having me followed?" I lift my skirts as we descend a set of stairs, refusing to look in his direction.

"There are eyes everywhere. Nothing you do goes unnoticed. And if you persist in acting like a strumpet—"

"Vasco," I say, rounding on him, showing the utmost disrespect by neglecting his title and refusing to use his first name once he's given me permission. "You should be very careful of what you say to me. Right now, the king trusts me more than he does you. And someday, I will be his queen. When he comes of age and has no need of you anymore, how hard do you think it will be for me to convince him to rid you from the palace?"

Before he can say anything, I continue, "I will spend time with whomever I like. Just because I'm courting the king, it doesn't mean I cannot have friends. Thankfully, your nephew is nothing like you. Do not follow me from here."

To my back, he says, "Do try to stay focused, Alessandra. The king needs an heir, and if you do not show the proper amount of interest, he may just look elsewhere."

"When I'm told not to do something, I only desire to do it more," I say before rounding the corner out of sight.

But something bothers me about the council's insistence on an heir from Kallias. Wouldn't they know exactly how his powers work? And if so, wouldn't they want him to avoid touching anyone?

Unless they are indeed the ones trying to have him killed.

I'm beginning to think Kallias's fears are perfectly warranted.

CHAPTER 19

I stand in the middle of the ballroom and turn in a slow circle. "We'll need potted flowers. I want the entire ballroom lined with them. They'll form pathways just like a flower garden."

Epaphras, Kallias's appointment keeper, is less than thrilled to be in my employ for the day. (Apparently I got on his bad side when I ignored him and barged into Kallias's meeting.) But Kallias insisted he could keep his meetings straight for one day so I could have the best of his schedulers taking notes for me. My ball is to have the utmost priority.

At first, I thought it strange he would insist when an attempt was just made on his life. But then I realize he doesn't want that attention on himself. He doesn't want his people to think he's in danger, that there's any threat at all to him. He wants things to appear normal.

"Why bother with pots?" Epaphras asks sarcastically. "Why don't we just dump dirt right onto the ballroom floor?"

"I think it's brilliant!" Hestia says. "*Jewels of the Queen's Garden* is a wonderful theme! The ballroom will look splendid once you're done with it."

"All the ladies can dress to look like different blossoms," Rhoda adds. "Oh, we better commission our seamstresses quickly before they're all booked!"

"You're at an advantage," I assure them, "since I have yet to send out invitations. Epaphras! I will need stationery and penmanship samples, of course. The invitations must go out by this weekend."

"Naturally," Epaphras bites out.

"Best inform Kallias I am in far greater need of your services than he is. I shall need you for at least the next week, I should think."

The scribe goes pale, and I share a secret smile with Rhoda.

"Galen," Rhoda says to the shadow behind her. "Do contact my seamstress and set up an appointment. Make sure she knows it's urgent."

"Of course, my lady."

Epaphras stomps off, muttering something about his skills being wasted, as he exits the ballroom.

As soon as he's gone, Hestia fairly leaps upon me. "At last we're alone! Now tell me quickly, *is it true*?"

"If I'm to answer, I need to first know the question, Hestia," I reply, though she no doubt wishes to discuss the attempt on the king's life.

"My lady's maid heard it from her sister, who works as a laundress, who heard it from a gardener, who heard it from—"

"Dearest," Rhoda interrupts, "I don't think we need to know the precise line the news traveled."

"Right." Hestia turns to me. "Are you staying in the queen's rooms?"

I blink. Oh. Then I offer her a sincere smile. "Yes."

Hestia groans with jealousy. "You are the most fortunate girl in all of the six kingdoms. What are they like?"

"Last night, I bathed in a tub large enough for three to fit comfortably. The walls are lined with oils and fragrances. I put fresh rose petals and lavender oils in the water. If I didn't fear drowning, I would have slept in it."

"You must make me a list. I need a copy of the labels from all the bottles."

"Perhaps I could just—"

"Every. Label," she says, cutting me off. "I simply must know what brands the queen used!"

"I thought we already discussed that you smell nice all on your own," Rhoda says. "That you don't need to copy everything that—"

"This has nothing to do with that! You're telling me you're not the least bit curious whether the queen bathed in lavender oil from Rondo's or Blasios's?"

Rhoda thinks a moment. "I'll grant you that."

"Ha!"

Our work done for the day, we see ourselves out of the ballroom. As soon as we hit the main receiving area, I spot a figure entering the palace.

Orrin.

He's finally back.

Our eyes meet, and a look resembling a wounded animal crosses his face before he turns away from me.

"He looks so heartbroken," Hestia leans over to say.

"It's not me he's heartbroken over. It's my sister. He's somehow so misguided as to think we're the same person."

"He does seem quite . . . daft at times," Rhoda intones. "However did that man inherit an earldom?"

"All of his father's intelligent offspring must not have made it to adulthood," I reply with distaste. "I'll meet up with you two later," I add, before steeling myself to talk with Orrin.

"Lord Eliades!" I call, striding up to him. I'm doing this for Rhouben. He held up his end of the bargain, and now it's time for me to do mine. "I wonder if we might talk in private? Perhaps in your rooms?"

"There's nothing more to say, Lady Stathos. You've made your feelings quite clear."

"But perhaps if I could just explain," I try.

"That won't be necessary," he says, and heads after his footman, who carries a trunk of his things up to his room.

Among all his things will be his seal. I need it if our act is to work. Orrin won't let me into his room directly, so I'll have to find another way.

>–⟨⟩–○–⟨⟩–⟨

I HAVE A NEW plan by the time Kallias joins me in the library for dinner, though I've no clue if it will work. Just to be safe, I retrieved the forged letter from Rhouben and had Petros fill in the date. With all the players finally in the palace, all we need is that seal.

"I'm told you and Lord Eliades had a bit of a disagreement in the greeting hall this afternoon."

As Kallias takes his seat, Demodocus lies on the floor next to me, placing his head atop my foot, like a pillow.

"Yes, well, he was somehow under the impression that he and I were courting. A notion I'm afraid my father encouraged. After our escapades at the lake, Orrin wanted to make it very clear that he no longer wishes anything to do with me."

"Does your father know of our ruse?"

"Of course not. He only wanted a backup plan should I not succeed in securing your hand. My father is quite set on achieving an enormous bride-price for me. His estate is . . . bankrupt."

Kallias blinks. "And so he thought to *sell* you to me?"

"Is that not how things are done?"

"Well, yes, but not in such crass terms. Hmm. Perhaps I should do something about that."

I know *I* will certainly do something about it once I'm queen.

A pause in the conversation allows us both to sample our supper.

"Tell me," Kallias says, "when it is safe for our charade to be done with, do you not wish to marry and have a family of your own?"

"Of course I do. Marriage at least. I'm not certain about children just yet." I want to slap myself as soon as the words are out of my mouth. How does he do that to me? Sometimes I'm convinced we're real friends, and I can be honest. But that is the true charade, isn't it? He is a mark, and I cannot make the mistake of becoming too comfortable with him.

If I want to marry the king, I most assuredly should have said I want children. That is the duty of a queen. To bear heirs. Never mind Kallias won't live long enough to produce any.

"I feel the same way," Kallias says, surprising me. "So why don't you have any interest in Orrin? I happen to know he's quite rich. The ladies at court seem to think him attractive."

"They obviously have never had a conversation with him."

Pleased with my answer, Kallias turns his attention back to his food. My foot has fallen asleep thanks to Demodocus's significant weight, and his breath warms my other foot.

"Why do you choose the library for us to dine in?" I ask. "Do you even like to read? I've never seen you with a book in hand."

"My father loved to read. He was an old man. He liked to acquire knowledge. This room not only reminds me of him, it sort of smells like him."

Though Kallias has always been quick to speak of his mother, this is the first that he's said anything personal of his father.

"I don't have time to read," Kallias says. "But even if I did, I wouldn't. It's not a hobby of mine. I'd much prefer to run with Demodocus or spend time with you."

"Was he the oldest man in history, your father?"

"No. I have a great-great-grandfather who lived to be seven hundred and fifty-eight."

"He lasted more than seven hundred years before taking a wife and having children?"

He nods.

"How long do you think you will last?" I ask.

"You doubt my resolve?" he asks, switching out courses.

"I'm trying to picture you at seven hundred years old and not having read a whole book. Will both your body *and* mind stay the same?" I hide my smile behind a drink of wine.

"Books are not the only way to learn. I will grow smarter and more powerful as my empire spreads. As I discover new strategies in leading my armies. As wise men and women council me."

"And you will grow lonelier. Don't you think you will forget how to be human if you push away all the mortals in your life?" I'm not even trying to convince him to court me at this point. I'm honestly curious.

"I haven't pushed you away."

"But someday I will die. I will age, and you won't, so long as you live your life in shadow."

Kallias jerks away from the food he'd been bringing to his lips, as though that thought had never occurred to him. Finally he says, "That is a very long time from now." But he won't meet my gaze.

No matter. That's enough friendly chatter for one night. Time to move on to putting my plan into action for helping Rhouben.

"Kallias, I heard a story about you stealing frogs from a lake to put into one of your tutor's beds."

He grins wickedly at the memory. "She was a terrible bore."

I size up Kallias.

"What?" he asks.

"I'm wondering. With your ability, is it only inanimate objects you can turn to shadow with a touch?"

Demodocus leaves me and goes to sit by his master, finally restoring blood flow to my foot.

"Why?" Kallias asks.

"I have to sneak into someone's rooms. For a friend. I wondered if you could let me in through the door. And I do mean, *through* it."

"You think I will just help you break into someone's rooms? Someone of my own court?"

"For me? Yes."

A light dances behind Kallias's eyes. "Whose rooms?"

"Orrin's."

"Do I even want to know what you're planning?"

"I think it would be far more fun if you watched things play out."

Kallias reaches down to pet the top of Demodocus's head.

"Don't pretend to be above such things with me," I add. "I know exactly how much you like slipping into courtiers' rooms. And with all the responsibilities you've been dealing with lately, you could really use a bit of sneaking."

His smile shows his teeth. "All right, but only because it's Orrin. And if you're caught, I will deny having any part of it. For appearance's sake."

"And will you berate me in public only to pardon me in private?"

"Something like that. Now let's be off while everyone is still at dinner downstairs."

Kallias helps me out of my chair and holds the door to the library open for us. I pause outside.

"What is it?" he asks.

"I don't actually know where Orrin's rooms are."

"I'd be concerned if you did. This way."

I follow him down the corridor. Up a flight of stairs. Down another hallway. He stops before a door that looks just like all the others.

"How do *you* know where his rooms are?" I ask.

"I know where everyone's rooms are. I like to know where all potential threats come from."

"But you keep the most dangerous persons closest to you?"

"Not at all." He flicks the tip of my nose with a leather-clad finger before grabbing my hand in his. Kallias glances down both ends of the hallway, ensuring we're alone.

Then I feel myself disappear.

I never noticed how heavy my limbs are until I suddenly can't feel their weight at all. Shadows trail along my skin, curling around my fingers, sliding over the fine hairs on my arms.

I clasp Kallias's hand more firmly, as I'm overcome with the sensation that I'll float away and disappear into the heavens if he doesn't keep me grounded.

"You get used to it," he says. "Now let's do this."

Kallias goes first, leaning his head forward to poke through the door. Confirming it's empty, he then tugs me with him.

The sensation of sliding through a solid wall is akin to slicing a knife through soft butter. Very little friction. And almost satisfying in a way.

Then we're through.

Orrin's room is quaint compared to my queenly quarters. The drapes and bedspread are a royal blue with silver embellishments on the hems. As I try to spot the personal touches, I realize there really aren't any. No pictures of family (as some people are possessed to have), no trinkets or baubles—there aren't even any books on the shelves.

Perhaps with how often he travels for business, he doesn't bother with such things.

But then I forget about my surroundings entirely, as I realize I'm still holding Kallias's hand.

"What would happen," I ask, "if we were to touch in this state?"

Kallias brings his free hand to his lips and tugs off his glove with his teeth. He brings his fingers to my cheek.

I register the contact, and I feel it distantly, but there's no heat. No sensation that comes from touching someone you find attractive.

It's rather awful, actually. Wanting that contact and not getting it. Even with a touch.

"I know," he says, reading the look on my face. "It's, well, a shadow of what real contact feels like." He bends over to retrieve the glove he dropped. "I'll wait outside and warn you if he comes. Just knock if you need anything."

And then he slides back out into the hallway with a wisp of shadow.

I feel my limbs return to normal, watch as the shadows fade away. That feels much better.

Orrin's desk faces the large window in the main room. His quarters consist of a bedroom and a washroom. No greeting room or study, as is in mine.

I open the first drawer and find everything I need in one neat place. The seal, wax, and the tools for lighting it.

I light the wick and set the wax above it, waiting for it to melt. Since I've never been very patient, I decide to poke through Orrin's things. The rest of the drawers on his desk are filled with writing implements and some unfinished letters.

Orrin has a few chests and a wardrobe. One of the chests is locked. The other holds extra linens. His wardrobe contains nothing but his bland clothing in beiges and whites and browns.

I eye the locked chest.

"Whatever could be inside you?" I whisper to myself. Nothing else in the room is locked. Not the drawers with his correspondences. Not even the drawer that holds a pouch of necos.

I test the weight of the locked chest. I can lift it clean off the ground. It's not heavy at all, save for the wood it's made out of. Nor is it terribly large. Just a bit wider than my own body.

I stand after setting the chest back on the floor and look about the room. If I were Orrin, where would I hide the key, assuming he doesn't have it on him?

I find myself back at the desk, examining the individual drawers a bit more closely.

And I note that one doesn't appear to be as deep as the others.

A false bottom.

With a bronze key nestled underneath.

Eliades, you simple fool.

I turn back toward the chest, let out a sigh of relief when the key fits perfectly within the lock, and lift up the lid.

There's clothing inside. Rather foul-smelling ones at that.

Why the devils would he want to lock this away?

First, I pull out a rumpled shirt in shades of brown. A smudge comes away on my own gloves after handling it, and I bemoan the loss of the garment.

Then I find a pair of unremarkable trousers. Beneath those are a pair of boots.

Orrin certainly isn't clever enough for misdirection, so what—

And that's when I see the final item in the bottom of the chest.

The incriminating one.

I hold up the fabric and let it dangle by the fingertips of my already-soiled glove.

A mask.

The mask.

Of the bandit. The very same one who robbed Kallias and me.

I let out a giggle. Oh, Orrin.

But of course it's Orrin. The pious do-gooder who wants to adopt orphans. Of course he would steal from his own class and help the poor.

The fool.

At first, I think to rush out and show Kallias, but then I realize he'll lock Orrin away. I can't let that happen just yet. He has a part to play to save Rhouben.

So I tuck the mask into a pocket of my dress, replace everything else within the chest and lock it, return the key, and finally seal the letter I brought with me before putting all the supplies back in their proper places.

Then I knock on the door. Kallias reaches a hand through, grabs me, and tugs me back onto the other side.

We begin walking.

"Did everything go according to plan?" he asks.

"Even better."

Kallias looks me over carefully as we round a corner. "I don't recall ever seeing you quite this elated. I'm feeling jealous knowing that Orrin is what caused it."

"Don't be," I say. "I just found incriminating evidence in Orrin's room."

Kallias narrows his eyes. "Did you put it there?"

I laugh. "No, actually. I came for an entirely different purpose and stumbled upon it."

"And do I get to know what it is?"

"Yes, but later. I need Orrin to do something for me first. Do you trust me?"

Kallias pauses and sizes me up, honestly considering the question. "I do," he says at last, as though the words surprise him. He rushes to add, "I'm bursting with curiosity, but I'll try to be patient."

"You are so very good at being patient." I mean the words jokingly, but somehow, I think a bitter note enters my voice.

CHAPTER
20

I t's time.

Rhouben has delivered the letter to Melita. His father, Lord Tho-ricus, is at court, though reluctantly. Orrin is back from his travels, which I now realize had nothing to do with business at all but were an excuse for his illegal activities as the bandit.

I still can hardly believe he has the capability and brain capacity for such deception.

But it is of no matter. Orrin will be exposed soon enough.

Rhouben arrives at my rooms at half past eight.

"She just excused herself from our outing in the gardens, saying she was fatigued and would turn in early tonight. She's taking the bait, Alessandra!" Rhouben's excitement brings a smile to my lips. "What do we do now?"

"I've bribed a servant to follow Orrin all day and send me regular letters with his whereabouts. What's next is for me to get him to Melita's rooms."

Rhouben's legs fidget under his well-tailored pants. "How are you going to do that? Everyone's heard of the way he dismissed you in the entrance hall."

I toss my hair over my shoulder. "By appealing to his better nature. Don't you worry about that. Do you remember your part?"

Rhouben wipes his brow with a handkerchief. "I tell my father Melita said she wasn't feeling well. I ask if he would like to accompany me to check on her in her rooms. I need to act as though I'm concerned for my bride-to-be." He grimaces as he says the words.

"You can do this," I tell him. "But remember, timing is everything. The good news is your father and Melita are staying on the same floor. Still, you must wait until you have Orrin and me in your sights."

Rhouben lets out a deep breath as he pockets his handkerchief. "All right. I'm ready."

Rhouben leaves me to retrieve his father, the Viscount of Thoricus, and I put on my best smile before seeking out Orrin, a small bouquet of flowers in my hands. The last letter I received said he was turning in to his rooms for the evening.

Good thing I now know right where they are.

He answers after two knocks. The earl is still dressed, and his face falls upon seeing me.

"Lady Stathos, I don't want to see you." He starts to close the door in my face.

"Lord Eliades, please wait a moment, won't you? I have something I need to say."

He stops with the door cracked open only wide enough for his face to be visible. I take a deep breath. If this doesn't work, I suppose I could always pull his bandit mask from my pocket and *make* him do what I need. But something tells me Orrin wouldn't make a great actor.

"I admire your good deeds greatly," I start, careful not to wince at the outright lie. "I've been thinking about my actions of late and how I hurt you. I wish to change. No one is a more devout follower of the gods, and I can think of no man more righteous than yourself. I hoped you might be willing to help me change my character." I try for a humble tone, but since I've no idea what that sounds like, I'm not so sure that I manage it.

I relax as Orrin smiles, though faintly. "This is most admirable of you, Alessandra. May I call you Alessandra?"

"Please do."

"The gods are always willing to forgive. It is mortals like myself who need more time to heed their example."

"It is I who am in need of an example," I hurry to say. "Yours, in fact. Listen, I've always been at odds with Lady Xenakis."

"Why? She's so delightful."

If one considers the sourness of a lemon delightful.

"I wish to do something nice for her," I continue, ignoring his question. "I've just learned that she's retired early and is ill. I thought I might take these to her." I lift up the flowers. "But I am not so sure I have the courage to go alone. Not after how terrible I've been to her in the past. Will you accompany me?"

"You make it so impossible to say no to you."

I beam. "Thank you!"

I put my arm in his before we take the stairs to the floor below.

"Tell me of your latest business trip," I say as we head down the corridor for Melita's rooms. Orrin doesn't even notice Rhouben standing outside his father's door as he tells me lies of selling crops and tending to his duties as landlord of various tenants. I nod politely and offer a few appropriate responses.

Rhouben immediately knocks on his father's door as we round the corner out of sight. I hear the faint taps echoing behind us.

When Melita's room is finally in sight, I pause with Orrin outside of it.

"Would you hold these for just a moment?"

Orrin takes the bouquet without question, ever the gentleman.

The corridor is far too quiet. Where is Rhouben? Perhaps his father is being difficult to coerce out of his room.

"Aren't you going to knock?" Orrin asks as we just stand there.

"In just a moment."

Awkward silence fills the space.

Orrin cocks his head. "What are we waiting for?"

Where the hell is Rhouben? We cannot go in without knowing he's right behind us.

"I just need a moment to gather my courage."

Orrin nods in understanding. "Doing the right thing is not always easy. And being the bigger person, the first to reach out with kindness, takes great strength of character. You needn't fear, though, Alessandra. Doing the right thing is never the wrong answer."

Orrin has an oddly twisted sense of right and wrong. He lies to me about his business trip. He steals from his peers. Are those not wrong?

And then I hear it. Soft footsteps on the carpet and the deep baritone of male voices.

Oh, thank the devils.

"Thank you," I say. "I needed to hear that. However, perhaps you wouldn't mind entering the room first? Maybe I could follow your lead in this instance?"

Sympathy alights in his eyes. "Of course." He turns and taps three times on the door.

"Come in!" calls Melita's bright voice from within.

Orrin lets himself into the room, and I continue walking down the corridor as the voices grow loud behind me.

"The poor dear!" Rhouben's father is saying. "Do you suppose we should have the cook send something up?"

"Best to check on her first," Rhouben says. "If it's a stomachache, we don't want to make things worse by sending up food."

"Quite right," the viscount responds.

I round the next corner as I hear the door to the room open.

"What the devils!" the viscount booms. "Melita! What—what are you doing?" There's a sound of shuffling feet.

"I—I don't know what's happening." That's Orrin.

"You were kissing my son's fiancée! That's what was happening."

A voice clears. "I'm sorry, Lord Thoricus," Melita says. "I didn't mean to disrespect you or your son."

"Oh, this is far past disrespectful. How dare you ruin yourself while engaged to my son! What would your father say? This is a horrid scandal, and we will have no part of it! I can't believe you would tell him you were ill so you could meet up with your lover!"

"I still don't know what's happening," Orrin says. "I came to support Lady Stathos. Lady Xenakis just threw herself at me!"

"Lady Stathos? Are you dallying with *two* promised women, then, Eliades? Shame on you," Thoricus says. "And you, Melita? I can't even imagine how disappointed your father will be. Come, Rhouben. Your engagement to Lady Xenakis is officially over."

And then the two men depart the way they came, Rhouben with far much more spring in his step, I imagine.

"Are those flowers for me?" Melita asks.

"Yes, but they're not from me," Orrin says. "They're from Alessandra. She should be right out in the hall. I—I have to go."

I still can't see anything from where I hide around the corner of the corridor, but the viscount must have left the door to Melita's rooms open, allowing me to hear the voices of the two still inside.

"No, we must talk," Melita says. "I never knew you cared for me so! Why didn't you tell me sooner? Was it seeing me with Rhouben? Did it make you so jealous? Oh, Orrin you are one of the most handsome men at court! Of course I would choose you over Rhouben. Rhouben doesn't care for me one whit."

"You are mistaken. I don't even know your given name."

"But of course you do! You wrote it in your letter."

"My letter?"

There's a sound like paper unfolding.

"It's remarkably close to my handwriting and that's my seal, but I'm afraid I didn't write this."

"But of course you did!" Melita's voice grows frantic.

"I'm so sorry for your distress, but here." I imagine him handing her the flowers. "I must go find Lady Stathos."

"Lady Stathos? Why would you bring her into this?"

I take off down the corridor, making myself scarce before Orrin has a chance to discover me.

⊱ ⊰

KALLIAS AND I HAD arranged for a late dinner that evening, due to a meeting he knew would run late.

When I join him in the library, I don't walk, I dance my way through the door, twirling my skirts after me.

"Whatever are you doing?" Kallias wants to know.

"I'm in an excellent mood tonight."

"I can see that."

I pause in my twirling to take note of Kallias and his big grin. "What?"

"I'm in an excellent mood, too. We learned many things during tonight's meeting. We've rounded up all the Pegain revolutionaries. They're to be put to death first thing tomorrow. And we've found several peasants carrying the bandit's stolen money. One of them is ready to talk! Though he doesn't know the bandit by his true name, he can identify him by sight. All we need to do is have him take a look at all the nobles."

I laugh a little before pulling the mask from my pocket. "We don't need to do that."

Kallias rises from his chair so fast it almost tips over. He startles Demodocus into taking a few steps to the side. The king strides over and takes the mask from my fingers.

"Where did you get this?"

"From Orrin's room."

"Eliades?" Kallias says with disbelief. "This is the incriminating evidence you found? How could you not tell me straightaway?"

"I made a promise to Rhouben. I told him I would get him out of his engagement with Melita, and I did. Now you are free to lock up Orrin."

Kallias is too pleased over the sight of the mask in his hands to give me any more grief over the timing. He fairly runs to the door and barks orders to throw Eliades into the dungeon until Kallias can come deal with him.

When he returns to the table, Kallias holds up a glass of wine. "I think a toast is in order."

I find my own glass and lift it.

"To you, Alessandra. May your wit never be used against me."

I laugh before tipping the contents of my glass into my mouth. "And to you, Your Majesty. To your fine leadership. This growing empire wouldn't be what it is without you."

His eyes are on mine as he tips back his glass a second time. And something about that gaze, the way it drinks me in—it curls my toes within my slippers.

But our celebrating is interrupted by a presence at the door.

"Come in," Kallias calls after a pause in which I think he seriously considered turning the intruder away.

A servant enters with a platter held atop the fingertips of his right hand. He lowers it before me.

"A letter for you, my lady."

I take the parchment and look to the handwriting spelling my name on the front. I do not recognize it.

"I have no guesses as to whom it's from. There's no seal," I tell Kallias as I read the note to myself.

"What is it?" Kallias asks when he sees the look on my face.

I know who is trying to kill the king. The assassin was a distraction. Something to occupy the king's mind before the real attempt on his life is made. I cannot divulge the individual's identity in a letter. They are much too powerful. If this note should be intercepted, I fear for my life. Suffice it to say, the king cannot trust his councilors.

I'm told you are one of the few whom the king trusts. That is enough for me to trust you as well. Meet me at the address listed below in two nights' time. I will find you then. Wear a flower in your hair, so I may know you.

May the gods bless the king.

"There's no signature," I say as I pass the note over to him.

He must read it three times over before focusing on me again. Then he stands abruptly, rushes to the doorway, and calls back for the servant who delivered the letter.

"Who gave this to you?" Kallias demands of him.

"A guard at the palace's entrance."

"Which guard?"

The servant coils inward. "Couldn't say, sire. They all wear hats. He didn't look up. Your Majesty, I don't think it would help. I doubt he was the one to initially deliver it. It could have gone through one of the groundsmen first and before that—"

"Enough," Kallias says. "I understand. Resume your duties." He shuts the door after him and turns to me. "What do you make of it?"

I take the note from him, looking over its contents again before answering. "Whoever wrote this letter knew I would show it to you."

"How can you tell?"

"They praise you far too much. You are not well liked among your people. If it were a member of your nobility, he would just come to you himself."

Kallias bristles at the words, but I continue. "He *or she* hopes to lure you out. Either because it's a trap to do you harm or because they wish to speak with you in person. Since they didn't outright ask for your presence, I'm inclined to believe the former."

"They left too much up to coincidence for it to be a trap," Kallias says.

"Or they did their job well enough to make you think so."

"Either way, I'm going."

"You can't go. Not if it's an attempt on your life."

"I'll go in disguise."

I eye the shadows swirling about his figure. "You cannot disguise those."

The shadows disappear in a heartbeat, and Kallias in all of his solid beauty stands before me. The difference really is astonishing.

"And now you're vulnerable to attack," I point out.

"Only if I'm recognized. I won't be by the time I'm done."

I shake my head. "Don't be stupid. If they see you with me—"

"You intend to join me?" he asks, cutting off the rest of my sentence. A boyish hope lingers around his eyes. I don't know if I can see it because they're so bright without the shadows, or if it's the first time he's shown me such an expression.

"Of course I'm going. I'm not letting you go alone to this—what is this address? Do you know it?"

The hope is instantly replaced with a mischievous raise of his brows. "I know it. I'm rather shocked you don't."

"What is it? A public place? A tavern of some sort?"

"Not exactly. It's a club. A private one. But I can get us in."

"If it's private, how are we to get in without our identities being discovered?"

"Leave that to me." He thinks a moment. "I wonder why our contact wishes to meet you there. It's a gentleman's club."

"So I will stand out in a sea of men?"

"Well, there are ladies there. They're just not the kind who wear very much clothing." He fades back into shadow, as though he's trying to hide his expression. "Will that be a problem?"

"Are you asking if I have a problem dressing like a harlot for a night?"

"I wouldn't have said it exactly that way, but yes."

An excuse to show off my best assets to Kallias?

"How exactly would you say it?"

"I would ask if you have any issue with letting men believe you to be a lady of the night."

I laugh lightly. "Will I be in disguise?"

"Of course. Just in case our contact does know what you look like and is only trying to mislead you."

"Mislead us."

Kallias brushes away the comment with a hand. "In two nights' time, we will be the ones doing the misleading."

CHAPTER

21

have a sense of déjà vu when Kallias shows up in my rooms holding
a dress. It was not long ago when Leandros was the one offering me
a dress to enjoy a night of fun with him.

Only tonight is far more likely to be a night of danger and deception.

I hold out the garment so I can get a proper look at it. "Do I want to
know where you got this?"

"It's clean, if that's what you're worried about. Freshly washed."

"There's more to it than I would have thought."

"I need your arms covered," he explains. Without his shadows, we
are at the highest risk of touching. Though I'm sure he will wear his
own gloves, there can't be any mistakes.

"It won't be a problem," I say. "With this low neckline, no one will
be looking at my arms."

"I'm counting on it."

Kallias waits outside for me while I lace up what little there is of
the bodice. I can't wear boots to hide my knife, so I find a way to tie the
sheath into one of my garters. Since I can't very well be seen leaving
my quarters like this, I don a scarlet cape over the top of everything.
With the way it clasps about my throat, the sides cover my cleavage and

shoulders. No one will think anything of the absence of petticoats. I'm known to wear all kinds of oddities.

When I find Kallias, he's holding a red rose, the thorns already having been plucked from the stem. I hold out my hand for it.

"It's not for you," he says.

"But I'm supposed to wear a flower to mark myself."

"And that would put you in danger. I'll give the flower to some girl at the club to draw our contact out. Then we'll question him properly once we have the upper hand. I have men already canvassing the area. Dressed as civilians. Some are already stationed at the club discreetly."

"And what if your own men are in on the attempts made against your life?"

"Then I suppose we'd best hope they can't see through our disguises." He pulls out a blond wig for me, curled ringlets bouncing every which way. Kallias helps me to secure the whole mess over the top of my head, tucking all the strands of my dark hair beneath it.

For himself, a light brown wig and a slight beard, which he attaches with some sort of adhesive.

"How do I look?" he asks.

Actually, he looks a lot like Leandros now. The hair color and beard length are the same, though I doubt he would appreciate such a comment.

"Less kingly," I offer.

"Good. Then let's be off."

⊱┈┈◈┈◯┈◈┈┈⊰

DAWSON'S IS LOCATED SMACK-DAB in the middle of the city. It's the largest building in the entire block, as well as the loudest.

"Damn," Kallias says from the horse next to me. "I just realized we can't go in together."

"Why not?"

ᑦᔕᐤ 222 ᐤᔕᑕ

"A man doesn't take his mistress to a place like this. He goes here for a break from his mistress."

"What about his wife?" I ask.

"He needs a mistress for a break from his wife."

"What about your parents?"

"That's a different case entirely. The men in my family don't give up their power for anything less than the most all-consuming love. Something that they're willing to give their lives for."

His words make my mouth go dry, and I can't quite meet his eyes.

"Then I suppose we'd better head in so we can better protect yours," I say. "What should I do?"

"I don't want to separate."

"You just said we have to. We'll draw too much attention if we enter together."

He thinks a moment, not bothering to climb down from his horse yet. "There should be other entrances in the back. We just need to get you in. Try to get to the gaming room. I will find you from there. But if anything happens, if any man tries to . . . grab you or do anything at all—you leave. You get out. And I will do this on my own. I should do it on my own anyway."

"Too late," I say. "Friends don't let friends go to gentleman's clubs alone when someone is trying to kill them."

He doesn't bother to laugh at the lame joke.

I slide down from my horse. Catching myself on my feet, I hand the reins to Kallias before he can utter another word of protest.

I feel my way around to the side of the building. Music and laughter spill out through an open window when I reach the back, the light helping me to find a door.

There's nothing left but to use my talents of manipulation to get myself where I need to be.

I pull the unlocked door open, my eyes blinking at the sudden onslaught of light. Taking a few hesitant steps into the room, I try to make sense of where I am. Tubs of water. Stacks of used mugs. A strong scent of stew.

Kitchens.

A young girl—perhaps ten or so—looks up from where she's scrubbing at pots in one of the tubs of hot water, her hands red and raw from the task.

"Oh," she says upon my sudden entrance. She flicks her head back in an attempt to get an errant strand of thick black hair out of her eyes. Her hair doesn't look as though it's ever been brushed in its life. A relief. She doesn't work here as a prostitute. She's merely a kitchen girl.

"Sorry," I say. "I think I came in the wrong way. I'm a new hire. Can you point me to the gaming room?"

"That door. Down the hallway. Up the stairs. Second door." Her hands never cease their scrubbing.

As I exit the room, another girl is entering, and we collide. The fall sends my cape sprawling open, and the older woman gets a good look at me. A good look at more of me than has ever been seen in public.

"Who are you?" The new voice is stern and exhausted. She's broader than I am, which I tell myself is why she was able keep her feet and I wasn't.

"New hire," I say as I catch my feet.

"I don't think so. I do the hiring for the working girls."

Damn. New tactic. "I need the money. Thought if I came ready to work, you might have need of me."

She steps up to me and unclasps my cloak. It falls to the ground in a tangled heap.

"You're wearing gloves? Honey, the men here aren't worried about getting dirty." She pinches my fingers as she slides each one off and pockets them. She examines me as she walks in a circle about me. "You know your way around a bedroom?"

"Yes, ma'am."

"You don't have much for a man to hold on to up top. Open your mouth."

A bit startled by the question, I do so. It is the only reason I'm able to let slide the insult to my décolletage.

"You've got nice teeth. That's a rarity around here. All right. You're in luck. I'm short a girl tonight. I can't give you regular work. But I'll give you a quarter necos if you finish out the week."

"A quarter necos!" I shout back without thinking, forgetting myself for a moment.

"Fine. A half. Just because of the teeth. But if I get one complaint about you, you're out."

I have to remind myself that I'm not posing as a noblewoman tonight. I'm a poor working girl.

"Done," I say.

"Take this. You'll save me a trip." She hands me a tray full of mugs spilling over with ale. Then Madam Dawson gives me the same instructions up to the gaming room. "Let the men have a good look at you. Most of them are regulars, so they already know where the rooms are. They can show you where to go to receive your services."

I take the proffered drinks and push at the swinging door with my hip, so very glad to be out of that room. I couldn't believe all the things Madam Dawson said in front of the little girl. Though if she works here, she's probably heard much worse.

Even without the directions, I'm sure I could have found the right room. Music from fiddles and other stringed instruments pours down the stairs, along with the tinkling of coins hitting tabletops. Cigar smoke clogs the air.

As soon as I walk in, I hold back the urge to cough.

How the hell am I supposed to find Kallias in this?

How did I let the *king* talk me into bringing him to a place like this?

Round tables are spread throughout the room. Girls dance atop a stage to the fiddle music. More girls wearing significantly less than I am walk around or sit perched on men's laps. I walk past a couple tucked into a corner, the man sucking on the neck of the prostitute.

After a minute more, he grabs her by the hand and hauls her past me. To wherever the rooms are.

Cards and dice seem to be the games of choice. I walk around the outskirts of the spacious room, trying to catch sight of Kallias. It takes me a moment to remember I'm not looking for a dark head of hair but a light one. A wig. And he won't have his shadows to aid me.

Devils, anything could happen to him in here.

At least all the firearms are checked at the doors. But it's hardly difficult to hide a knife under one's clothing. Even when wearing as little as I am.

A man suddenly runs up to me, and I panic before remembering I'm holding a tray of ale. He grabs a glass and peers at my exposed cleavage the entire time.

"Hm," he says, slapping my rump before turning back the way he came.

I freeze for a moment, battling with the noblewoman I am and the light-skirt I'm pretending to be tonight.

No one touches me without permission.

But being here. In this dress. That is permission. It's the job.

Oh, but my fingers itch for the ruby-handled knife strapped to my thigh. I could so easily drive it into his turned back.

"I don't recognize you," a voice thick with drink says, pulling me from my thoughts.

A man with a bloated belly from too many nights indulging in drink looks me up and down.

"I'm new," I manage to say, while finding my feet to resume my trek around the room's edges.

"And fast. Get back here."

A tug on my skirts nearly has me dropping the tray. Checking my irritation, I spin and hold out the tray. "Drink?"

"No. I need someone to keep me company at my table. I've made it a point to sample every lady Madam Dawson has under her employ."

"I'm only a fill-in," I say around the disgust crawling up my throat.

"Come here," he says more forcefully.

Oh gods.

"This one's already spoken for," a new voice says, and my shoulders sink with relief.

Kallias.

He has his eyes on the horrible man propositioning me.

"Shove off," the drunk man says. "I found her first."

In just a few steps, Kallias grabs the tray from my hands and thrusts it upon the other man. "You're welcome to fight me for her once you're sober, but I think you know better than to try now."

With one gloved hand clamped firmly along my bare arm, Kallias leads me to a table, weaving through men and girls as we go.

"Just give her back to me once you're done!" the other man shouts after us.

I gag.

"Easy now," Kallias says.

And before I can register anything else, Kallias is lowering himself into a chair, and I'm in his lap.

Just the knowledge of this has my neck heating.

"Never did see a blushing light-skirt," a man on the other side of the table says. "Must be new on the job. Good on you, Remes. Your turn, by the way."

One hand slides against my abdomen while the other picks up a hand of cards. I'm unfamiliar with the game, but Kallias must know it. He throws some necos onto the growing pile on the table and sets down a card before the man next to him takes a turn. There's five of them at the table. I don't recognize any of them. I suspect none are nobles currently living at the palace.

I feel warm breath against my ear as Kallias whispers, "Are you all right?"

I turn so I can look up at him, careful not to let my face get too close to his. "Yes."

He presses his lips to my ear, where my wig keeps his face from touching me skin to skin. To the men around the table, we must look like we're whispering flirtations.

I try to hide the shiver that goes down my spine from the contact, but I'm certain Kallias can feel it.

"What happened to your gloves?" he asks.

"The madam said they weren't appropriate for my line of work."

"We'll have to be careful."

"I'm always careful."

"Good. Now laugh like I just said something naughty."

His words catch me off guard, but I let my eyes drift down to half-hooded before giving him a short laugh filled with promise. I slap his shoulder playfully for good measure.

"Remes, your turn again."

Kallias takes less than five seconds to look at his cards and throw down a new one.

"It's like you're not even trying," the man across the table says, before throwing down his own card. The other three people groan as he sweeps the pile of money toward himself. "If it's the lady distracting you, then she has my deepest thanks."

"Just deal another hand," Kallias says. He lets the hand on my abdomen drift up to my side, before letting a gloved finger trail down my bare arm.

I wonder if the men across the table can see the goose bumps rising on my flesh as clearly as I can.

For gods' sake, it's only his glove. I shouldn't be turning into a liquid heap.

But, as if he's found a new game he likes far better, Kallias doesn't glance at his cards. His gaze holds mine as he lets his fingers trail up the side of my neck, across my collarbone, a little lower. Watching my face for any reaction at all. As if he's asking a question and waiting for my expression to tell him the answer.

And damn him, but my breathing hitches, the muscles in my legs tightening. His answering smile is that of a predator, masculine pride at its finest.

Oh, but two can play at that game.

I sit a little higher up on his lap, let one hand travel up his chest from lower abdomen to his shoulder, letting my fingers reach under his waistcoat, so there's less fabric between our skin.

A low sound comes out of Kallias's throat. He tries to hide it behind a cough.

"Just take her upstairs and get a room already," another man at the table says.

"No!" the first one shouts back. "She's our ticket to winning everything in his wallet."

Kallias reaches for the new hand of cards, but I beat him to it, grabbing the deck and holding them up where he can also see. I let my head rest back in the space between his neck and shoulder, my wig protecting us from any contact.

But with my free hand, I grip the side of his thigh and squeeze.

He pitches forward slightly, his chest barreling into my back. But then I realize it was no doing of mine.

"Sorry!" a girl with a fresh tray of ale says. She rights herself from behind Kallias, only having spilt a little bit of the dark liquid down the sides of the cups before moving on.

She's wearing my rose in her hair, I note. I wonder when Kallias gave it to her. And how he convinced her to wear it. Now that she's in the room with us, Kallias tries to be subtle as he follows her every movement. Waiting to see if our contact—whomever he or she might be—will approach her.

I turn toward Kallias again. "Did you touch me?" I whisper, worried that the klutz pushed us too close together.

For some reason, Kallias doesn't seem worried. He holds a gloved finger under the table. I watch as a swirl of shadow appears around it.

"No," he says.

The fear receding, I breathe onto his neck as I say, "Oh, good."

And, as if that breath of air were too much, he scoots me down his lap a bit toward his knees.

"Are you going to go or what?" the irritated man to our left asks.

"I think I'm done," Kallias says, his voice deeper than it was a moment ago. With one arm slung around my waist, he stands and leads me toward the edge of the room. He steps past a partitioned-off area, where cushioned seats line against the wall. He gently sets me down before sitting beside me, our legs just touching.

"I'd hoped to blend into the room, but it's too hard to watch our girl," he says. "We have a better vantage point here."

"Well, we can't just sit here. We stand out too much. You don't take a whore to the cushions just to talk to her."

He reaches down, grabs my legs, and throws them over his lap. One hand goes under my skirts to trace against my calves.

"More convincing?" he asks.

I swallow. "Yes."

And as I sit there with my legs in the lap of the king, one thing becomes abundantly clear.

I can't believe how much I want him to touch me. I want to rip off those cursed gloves and burn them in a fire, bury the ashes in a hole deeper than the one in which I dumped Hektor.

I want to know what his lips feel like. I want to know what kind of kisser he is. What kind of lover. A selfish, pampered royal? Or a man willing to give pleasure as well as receive it?

Kallias grabs my knees and scoots me closer, my skirts rising up to show off my stockings. He brings his face within inches of mine. "I want to know what you're thinking about right now."

"You couldn't handle it."

His fingers tighten subtly, and his face draws even closer. Were he any other man in the world, I would have closed that distance weeks ago. As the king, he has to be the one to decide to take this risk. It makes him so vulnerable.

My face retreats an inch, before I realize what I'm doing. I don't want him to be vulnerable. I—

"Careful," I manage.

Kallias lets out a breath of air as he leans himself back into the cushions, his hand under my skirts making more progress north.

What am I doing? Did I just retreat from him?

My mind is a tornado of thoughts, but I drop them all as we see a man approach our girl with the rose.

But it is a false alarm. He grabs a drink before moving on.

>-+-+>-+-O-+-+-+-<

TORTURE.

Being in these cushioned seats is absolute torture. Touching but not touching.

Kallias and I stay seated for about half an hour. Altering our positions. Trying to be convincing. But who in the world would take so long on the cushions with a whore without taking her upstairs?

I have my face turned into his neck, trying to look as though I'm nuzzling into him, playing with his ear.

My entire body is alive with heat. I don't know how much longer I can take it. The lavender-mint smell of him is everywhere. I can't believe I haven't grown used to it yet.

"Hey! You've had enough time to sample her. Either take my new girl upstairs or hand her over to someone else. I'm not running a charity here."

I crane my neck to find Madam Dawson with her hands on her hips.

"We were just on our way," Kallias says. He scoops me up and sets me on the floor as he stands.

"What now?" I ask as we make our way toward the exit.

"We—"

I lose my footing before I even realize what's happening. My body makes painful contact with the floor, Kallias landing on top of me. Our heads bang together in a painful clash.

There's murmuring in the gaming room. Guests lean out of their chairs to investigate. So many people are surrounding us, the space suddenly feeling crowded.

A dampness reaches me. Dropped food or drink or something soaking into my skirts. And then Kallias's weight leaves me. Several people are helping me up, brushing food off my skirts.

"Are you all right?" another of Dawson's girls asks.

"Yes," I say.

I look around, trying to figure out who barreled into us, but several of Dawson's girls have gone to the floor to clean up the mess, including the little one from the kitchen, who appears to have shown up to clear off empty dishes from tables.

What the devils?

Kallias practically pushes me toward the exit. We squeeze past more of Dawson's patrons before finally getting out into the empty hallway.

"Are you all right?" I ask, placing a hand over my throbbing hip.

But Kallias is staring down at his gloved hands.

"What is it?" I ask.

"I can't call on my shadows."

CHAPTER

22

Kallias has the two of us sprinting for the exit. He hits the main floor and flings open the doors to the outside. Then he barks orders at the stable boy to bring our horses.

"That stumble in there was no accident. They meant to knock me over. To overwhelm me. I didn't see who touched me. Too many tried to help me to my feet."

"I think the girl you gave your rose to might be involved. She ran into us once, do you remember? I think . . . someone was trying to force us to touch."

Kallias spreads the fingers of his right hand in front of him, and shadows swirl about his hand. "It wasn't you. I can still use them around you. We were lucky with that head bash, but—"

"Now you're a target. Whoever sent that assassin will try again. Now that they know you are corporeal in their presence."

The horses finally come around, and Kallias throws me onto mine before taking his own, not even bothering to tip the boy before we take off into the night.

When we're some distance from Dawson's, Kallias finally slows his horse's gallop, and I pull up alongside him.

"I was right," Kallias says at last. "It was no servant who killed my parents. Who wants me dead. Only a nobleman could have gained access to that club. I didn't see anyone I recognized from court. Did you?"

"No. They could have been in disguise, as we were."

Kallias pulls the wig and facial hair from his face before dropping them onto the stones at our horses' feet. "Not that they did us any good. Whoever our contact was, he spotted us anyway." He sighs. "I should have listened to you. We never should have gone. I'll be dead within the week."

"Oh, hush," I snap. "Perfectly normal and *mortal* kings live to ripe old ages. You're just used to protecting yourself. All you need is to take precautions. More guards stationed in the palace. And you hire for yourself a personal guard of only the best soldiers to follow you wherever you go."

"That didn't save my father."

"Your father didn't know to look for danger within his own court. You do. When we get back to the palace, you will make the proper arrangements. And don't let Kaiser select the men. If he's in on it, he will not pick the best candidates for your protection. You find the best men for the job yourself."

Kallias doesn't say anything in response.

"I don't want to hear any more talk of you *resigning* yourself to death. Yes, you're a target. That's part of being born a royal. But you're not stupid, and you're *not dying on me*. Do you understand?"

A grin has replaced his solemn expression. "If you command it."

"I do."

"Well, a lady must always get what she wants."

When we reach the palace, Kallias walks me to my room. He promises to make arrangements for his safety as soon as he leaves me.

"See that you do," I say. "I have no intention of losing my best friend."

Kallias opens his mouth. Shuts it again. Then, "You and I are playing a very dangerous game."

I pull off my wig, letting it dangle from my fingers as I shake out my real hair. "It was only a little bit of dress-up. And a small fall. Hardly dangerous," I assure him, offering a smile.

Kallias's eyes bore into me with all the force of a burning comet. "I wasn't speaking of that game." His eyes dart down to my lips briefly, before he turns on one heel and walks away.

⊱·–‹◊›··◯··‹◊›·–·⊰

WHEN MY EYES FLUTTER open the next morning, the most delicious feeling of happiness wafts over me. Confused, I search through my memory. Thinking perhaps I'd had a pleasant dream.

Kallias's face rises to the surface, and my whole body heats. Yes, I'd dreamed of him. We'd finally grown close physically. But as I try to remember the details—where exactly he touched me, where he kissed me, where his teeth had nipped at my skin—there is nothing. Only a haze. And frustration overcomes the feeling of happiness.

I throw my head back onto my pillow. What is happening to me?

I do not *like* the king. He is a means to an end. And while I will deeply enjoy consummating our marriage, there is nothing else Kallias is useful for.

I don't care if he makes me laugh. Or if at times he seems to know me better than I do myself. And who the devils cares if he's a perfect fifteen?

These thoughts won't do at all.

My maid draws me a bath, and she blessedly doesn't ask any questions as she washes the cigar smoke from my hair. Once I'm dressed and all done up, I've decided on the proper course of action for the day. I need to do something to remind myself of why I'm here.

The old crone who serves as the castle's royal healer will have a number of medicinal herbs within her storeroom, if I can find it. I will take the necessary ingredients with which to poison Kallias when it comes time.

⪼⊶⊙⊷⪻

SOMETIME LATER I'M ON my way back to my rooms, my pocket holding a vial of distilled minalen, a plant native to Pegai. Might as well keep with the ruse used by the other assassin.

My mind eases as I feel much more resolute in my task.

As I pass by a window, a blur catches my attention. Outside, Kallias walks with a small troop of men surrounding him. His shadows rise about him in full force. Even from here, when I can't see the details of his face, my heart skips a beat.

This man who gives me what I ask. Who makes time for me when he's so dreadfully busy ruling six kingdoms. Who takes me with him on dangerous missions because he trusts me. A man who challenges me in wits, in scheming. Who values my opinion and implements my ideas for catching bandits and traitors.

A man who sets my blood to racing without even touching me. Who can warm my heart with a look.

Suddenly, the treasonous vial within my pocket feels heavier than a bag of rocks. I hurry along to my room, casting it into the deepest recesses of my wardrobe.

I don't know what I'm doing anymore. But I do know one thing.

No one but *me* is allowed to decide when Kallias Maheras, king of six realms and counting, is going to die.

⪼⊶⊙⊷⪻

I DON'T SIT BY Kallias at lunch that day. Instead, I cram myself into the seat next to Rhoda before another lady can take it. The lady in question gives me an affronted look, but I ignore her. Just as I ignore the heat on the side of my face that is no doubt a result of the look Kallias must be giving me. He saw me stride with purpose into this seat. And he thankfully doesn't demand I join him at the front. Perhaps he can tell I need a little space.

Maybe that space will set everything to rights.

"You're not sitting with the king today?" Rhoda asks, eyeing the empty seat at Kallias's right.

"I want to sit with my friend. Is that a crime?"

Rhoda looks at me doubtfully. "Are you and Kallias fighting?"

"No." Before she can ask another question, I add, "I would rather not speak of it."

"Very well."

Rhoda's manservant, Galen, trots over to her and places her napkin in her lap. He proceeds to do the same for me before another servant gets the chance.

"Thank you, Galen," I say.

"Of course, my lady."

Then he returns to stand by the wall, but I let my gaze linger on Galen a moment longer.

He's staring at Rhoda. Not in the way an attentive servant would stare, waiting to be of some use. But in the way a man stares at a woman he wants.

I've noticed this before, and I still can't quite believe how blind to it Rhoda seems.

I tuck the thought away as I note the extra guards by every exit of the room. Good. Kallias still has his shadows cloaked about him, however, so whoever touched him at Dawson's isn't in the room with us now.

I turn my back, spot all five council members there. Kallias meets my gaze as I swivel back around.

Yes, not them, that looks says.

But it could have been that they ordered someone to touch him. A whore or other member of the nobility not stationed at court. Someone who would never be suspect, because they're not involved. Until now. Until someone in Kallias's court offered them something they couldn't resist. Something to risk treason. Or perhaps they don't even know. Kallias was in disguise. They could have been paid simply to run into him. To touch him. They'd think it an odd request. But given enough money, people won't ask questions.

"Where's Hestia?" I ask as food is placed before me.

"Don't you spot her?" Rhoda inclines her head farther down the table.

My eyes widen. I'd been looking for someone wearing purple, as that is what I'd worn yesterday. But Hestia is wearing a cream-colored gown that suits her skin tone nicely. She's seated next to Lord Paulos.

"That must be going well, then."

"I daresay it is. She looks happy. Now you both have your beaus, and I'll be alone at the table forevermore."

"Nonsense," I say as I bring a spoon of broth up to my lips. "You will find your love match, Rhoda. It's only a matter of time. What about Rhouben?"

"He was engaged to Melita not long ago."

"So? He's not anymore."

"Doesn't matter. I don't think he's right for me. Didn't you see the way he would nag at Melita? I don't put up with that sort of thing."

"But he wouldn't nag *you*," I protest. "He'll adore you!"

"No. I don't think we're suited for each other."

"What about Petros? It is well known he likes ladies as well as lords."

"Courtiers are too drawn to him. I'd get jealous."

"But he'd never betray your trust, physically or otherwise."

"I would still get jealous."

"Then what of Leandros?" I ask.

She quirks a brow. "Are you just going through the names of everyone you know at court? Besides, I thought you might have something with Leandros—something on the side for when the king upsets you."

As if he can sense we're talking about him, Leandros looks up from farther down the table. He sees me watching him and smiles warmly.

"I take that back," Rhoda says. "I don't want anyone who is already smitten with you."

I grin, realizing she's left me the perfect opening. "What you need is to start paying attention to someone who is already smitten with *you*."

Rhoda looks around the room meaningfully. "Who?"

"He's not sitting at the tables. He's against the wall."

Her eyes zero in on the man instantly. "You mean *Galen*?"

"He is in love with you, Rhoda. You spend most of your time with him; surely you've noticed?"

She purses her lips in thought, as though replaying in her mind every moment she's ever shared with him. "He's my servant. A *commoner*."

So very true, and if it were me, that would mean the man is far beneath my notice. But this is Rhoda, and she isn't like me at all.

"I've never taken you for the kind of woman who would care for class distinctions, especially when you've said yourself you don't need to marry for money or a title. Besides, your ranking system went for looks, manners, and personality. Title wasn't included. And Galen is a fifteen for you, Rhoda. By your own designs, you really should have snatched him up already."

"I . . ." Her voice drifts off as she stares at Galen against the wall in a new light, a carefully considering look upon her face.

"Just invite him to my ball. Get him something to wear. Tell him it's an honor for being so devoted to you all these years. You can have a night of no expectations, yet a moment to see him in a new light. You don't have to marry him to have some fun with him."

She looks unconvinced.

"If you don't invite him," I say. "I will."

She shoots me a glare before turning her focus to her food. But I can see I've planted a strong seed in her mind. She only needs time for it to grow.

I DON'T SAY ANOTHER word about Galen during our time in the sitting room that afternoon. Having already completed my last outfit, I work on my dress for my upcoming ball in silence. Hestia regales the whole room with how romantic and delightful her Lord Paulos is.

"We play quite a lot of cards," she says. "I love how he challenges me during our games. And do you know? He used to smoke a cigar during every game, but I finally admitted how much I detest the smell. He hasn't smoked anything since. He said"—she pauses to lower her voice dramatically—"that when he kisses me the first time, he doesn't want to taste like ash, now knowing how I loathe it. Can you think of anything more romantic?"

"How long do you think it will be before he kisses you?" Rhoda asks.

"I don't know! I can only guess he must intend to do it soon if he quit those awful things."

Afterward, I return my work in progress up to my rooms and try to decide what to do with myself until dinnertime. Perhaps I should see what Rhouben and Petros and Leandros are up to. It has been a while since I've spent time with them. I haven't even seen Rhouben since I got him out of his marriage with Melita.

I close the door to my rooms without properly looking down the hallway first. That must be why Leandros is so easily able to surprise me.

I place a hand over my heart. "Don't scare me like that."

"Sorry! I thought you saw me."

I wave away his apology as I deposit the key to my room into a pocket of my dress. "I was actually going in search of you and your friends. Thought I'd see what the lot of you were up to this afternoon. My schedule is quite free."

"I'm glad to hear it. I was hoping to speak with you." He points his face toward the ground, as though suddenly shy. It's a rather odd look for Leandros, who is usually so full of himself, I fear his large head might explode.

I duck down to find his eyes and bring his head back up. "Concerning?"

"Could we perhaps talk in your rooms?"

I don't know why, but I have the distinct feeling I should not invite him into my rooms. It's not that I fear being alone with him or fear him in any way, but I think this might be a better conversation to have out in the open.

"We're alone here," I say lamely. "Go on."

If he's put out by my indirect refusal, he doesn't show it. "I received your invitation to your ball. I'm quite eager to attend. I thought to ask what you're wearing, so we might match."

"We can't match," I say, allowing my voice to raise in volume playfully. "However would that look?"

"Like I'm besotted with you," he says, his voice a tad too serious for comfort.

"No, it would look as though I'm a woman whose attentions stray far too easily."

"It isn't straying, if you agreed to be mine."

"Leandros—"

"No, let me finish, Alessandra. I know I joke quite a bit, but let me assure you I'm very serious right now. I *am* besotted with you. And I don't want to be an afterthought. I don't want to be who you turn to when Kallias casts you aside.

"I want to be your first choice. And maybe I've never made it clear that I *am* a choice for you. I like you, and if you let me, I know I could love you. My title might not be as fancy as Kallias's, nor my pocketbook quite as deep, nor my estate quite so large.

"But my heart is bigger, Alessandra. And I would love you completely, wholly, as a woman ought to be loved. I won't hide behind shadows. I won't love you from afar. I won't only take parts of you. I want all of you. Mind, body, soul. I want to be with you. Always.

"I tend to hide myself behind humor, but not this time. Not with you. I am interested. You are the only woman at court who interests me, and I would make you mine if you also wanted me." He takes a breath. "I don't expect you to answer now. I've had weeks to think this all through. And you haven't had even a minute, but I do hope you will think on it."

His body turns as if to leave, but, realizing he's not quite done yet, he reaches for my fingers. He keeps his eyes on mine as he slides off my glove, slowly releasing each finger before tugging the whole thing off. The kiss he gives the back of my hand is not soft, not gentle. But purposeful, lingering, full of the passion he feels.

It's a reminder that he can touch me. He *will* touch me if I choose him, and Kallias won't.

I cannot lie, the contact is delicious, but that is all it is. Skin touching skin. My feelings for Leandros don't traverse so deep.

"You've always been a good friend to me," I say when at last he drops my hand. "I have treasured our time together. And I know that if I were to choose you, I would be . . ." Not quite happy. Content, perhaps. For a time. "It would be a smart match. I know you would be kind and fun always. And I'm more than tempted because of all the things you can offer me that he can't."

His face falls. "But."

Oh, but this hurts. What am I doing? It's not in me to be kind.

Especially not to men. But it's so unfair to him to treat him this way. To give him hope.

"But," I intone, "I've already promised myself in courtship to him. It's not fair to you to pretend that my intentions might be changed." There's no need to clarify who *him* is, and it seems wrong to say another man's name aloud when Leandros is professing his love.

"He will never love you," Leandros says. His tone isn't unkind, only explanatory. "He will never marry you or touch you or be with you in all the ways you deserve. What do you plan? To forever live a half-life with him?"

I am shocked by the sudden realization that I would rather have this life. This life of Kallias's trust and friendship, of helping him to rule a kingdom without having any real power, just a king's ear—I would rather have all of that than another fling with a man who will just give me jewels because he likes the things I do to him in bed.

Of course, it wouldn't be like that with Leandros. He would care for me more than that, but I can't do that to him. Not when he has always been so kind to me.

"It is my life to do with what I will," I say. "And I've told you my decision."

Leandros nods to himself. "Do you love him?"

Of course not, I think. I do not do such childish things as fall in love. Love made me into a murderess. It broke me for a time. I had to build myself back up.

But there is certainly *something* brewing between the king and me.

"I don't know," I whisper.

And either that is answer enough, or Leandros sees the truth of it on his own, because he bows low, gentlemanly.

"Excuse me," he says.

And he's gone.

I wrap my arms around myself, saddened by the exchange.

But as I turn back toward my room, thinking to lie down for a bit in misery, I see the barest wisp of a shadow disappearing through the wall housing Kallias's rooms. It's so slight, I think perhaps I might have imagined it.

But if not, I can't decide if it's a good or bad thing for Kallias to have heard all of that.

CHAPTER

23

I debate whether to show up for dinner in the library.

On the one hand, I haven't spoken with Kallias all day. There is much we should discuss, including his safety measures and what happened at the club.

But then I know he will ask me why I've opted to avoid him all day. And gods forbid he overheard my conversation with Leandros and brings it up.

In the end, I decide I want to see him, and that is enough to put up with all the rest.

I expect to find him at the table, already starting on his supper. Instead, he's seated at an armchair before the fire, stroking Demodocus on the top of the head with one hand and sipping wine from a cup held in the other.

Upon hearing my entrance, he says, "I can't decide if those who wish me dead are unable to get through my new guards stationed around the clock, or if they're simply biding their time, waiting for me to grow comfortable before striking."

"The former, I hope," I say, taking the other armchair pointed toward the low fire.

"It's not so bad being followed around everywhere I go. Honestly, it's preferable to the isolation I've resigned myself to."

I say nothing. I think perhaps he might need me to listen.

"In other news, I've sentenced Lord Eliades to life in prison. He's been stripped of all his lands and his title. He won't trouble us anymore. We've also located most of the gold coins he took and redistributed. All the peasants caught with them have also been imprisoned. They knew very well they were being given stolen goods."

"You don't seem terribly happy about all of this."

He stares at the flames and downs the rest of his cup. "The roundup did not go well. Several peasants died in the process. They resisted the guards. And many of the merchants did not want to give up the coin they'd already received in exchange for their goods."

I settle deeper into my chair. "And you blame me."

His hand stills from where it is reaching for a decanter beside him to refill his glass. "Why would I blame you?"

"Because it was my idea to catch the bandit in this manner."

"That's not at all what I'm trying to say. My guards did a poor job of handling the matter. It is they who are to blame, not the plan. Besides, I couldn't care less about a little public unrest."

"Then what is the problem?" I ask.

"The council wishes to do something about the stir we've caused. They're considering a royal parade through the streets of Naxos."

I blink. "You can't do that. That's the perfect opportunity for our contact to assassinate you."

He starts on another glass of wine. "I know, but I'm afraid the council has voted against me. I have no choice."

My skin glows with the reflection of the flames, and I feel my body grow hot all over. And not in a good way. "One of them is in on it! They have to be. Why else would they make you do this?"

"It would generate some goodwill. Remind the people that I'm not a monster putting all his focus on foreign kingdoms. It humanizes me, apparently. Makes them more likely to pay their taxes or some nonsense."

He finishes refilling his drink yet again. "Oh, and the Kingdom of Pegai is officially at peace once more."

I finally turn in his direction. "I'm having a hard time reading you. Are you upset? Worried? Pleased?" *Terrified?* I don't say aloud.

"I'm remarkably calm for someone who knows there will be another attempt on his life soon."

"An attempt, perhaps, but nothing more. Your would-be killer will not succeed. They will be caught."

He swallows the rest of his cup and finally sets the empty glass aside, letting his head fall back against the armchair as he does so. "Well, now that all the pleasant conversation is done with, shall we move on to whatever the reason is for you avoiding me all day?"

"That was the pleasant conversation?"

He stops petting Demodocus, and the dog slumps down to the floor, out as soon as his head falls atop his paws.

"What bothers you, Alessandra?"

"I don't think you've had enough to drink for us to have this conversation."

"Meaning?"

"I'd rather you not remember it."

A small smile grazes his lips. "I could drink some more if you'd like."

"No, you should be alert at all times. In case anything happens."

He shakes his head once. "Quit stalling. The fact is that . . . you were—um—not treated well last night." As if the words bother him, he reaches for his glass once more and refills it.

"I wasn't?" I ask.

"You were treated and touched like a whore, and it must have been disgraceful and humiliating. I don't blame you in the least for hating me for it."

"Oh." I try to mask my surprise at his words.

"You are a true friend, Alessandra. Someone I consider my equal in all things, save title. I did not treat you as such last night."

"Kallias, you let me help you last night. You treated me as you would a friend. Nothing less. Don't think any more on it."

He stands suddenly, and his legs are a bit wobbly, as he steadies himself against the nearby table. "Perhaps I drank more than I thought."

"Let me help you up to bed."

I take Kallias's arm, and though I've never done so where anyone can see before (save when we were in disguise), I keep a firm grip on him as we exit the library. I order the guards to escort us up to the king's rooms, but no one else dares to lay a hand on the king. I couldn't ask them for help if I wanted to. They wouldn't risk their lives. I'll leave Kallias to do the pardoning for our touching later.

Demodocus trails behind us, ever the faithful pup.

We pass by a series of windows in the hallway, and the sound of thunder and pelting rain reaches us. Quite a storm is gracing us this evening.

The guards leave us be at the end of the hallway, and Demodocus and I continue on. I try Kallias's door first, but since it's locked, and I'm not about to go through his pockets for a key that he likely doesn't have on him when he can walk right through walls, I let him into my room instead.

I think to help him into my own bed, but he says, "No, through there."

I try the door connecting our two rooms. It's unlocked.

"Why wouldn't you lock this?" I ask.

"Why would I when it's you on the other side?"

I help angle his fall onto the bed, then lift up both of his feet. I even take off his boots one at a time.

"Kallias, I'm not mad at you," I reassure him, continuing the conversation from before. "I don't care about yesterday. It was quite fun playacting, actually."

Demodocus hops onto the bed next to him, placing his head atop the king's stomach. Kallias lolls his neck over in my direction. "Even if you're not mad about that, you should be mad at me for other reasons."

"What reasons?"

His eyes close. "I saw you with Leandros. He offered you happiness, and you refused him. Because I'm forcing you to go through this ruse of courting me. I should release you from it."

I smile. "But you won't."

"I can't. I need you too much."

Perhaps it's just the drink, but I would very much like to think he didn't just mean as a ruse.

His eyes shoot back open then, and his arm swings about before it catches my gloved hand and brings it toward his mouth but stops before he makes contact. He looks down at my glove as though it offends him. Then he's sliding the garment off. I hold perfectly still.

"He kissed you. Here." A leather-clad finger trails along my skin.

"Yes, he did."

"I don't want him doing that. *I* want to do that."

He lowers his lips, but I jerk back my hand violently before he can make contact. "You're not allowed to do that until you're sober," I tell him.

"Nonsense. Give that back!"

I laugh at him. "Go to sleep, Your Majesty." I push against his shoulder, and he falls back onto his pillows, his eyes shutting once more. The fight has left him.

I step toward my room, taking one last look at my king. "I didn't tell Leandros no because of some deal I have with you. I told him no because it would take me away from you."

Satisfied that he's too fast asleep to remember any of it, I shut the door on him and make ready for bed.

KALLIAS LETS HIMSELF THROUGH the wall into my room the next morning for breakfast. "Well, that answers that question."

He has one hand pressed against his head, and he's still in his clothes from last night.

"What question?"

"I can still call my shadows around you."

"Was there any doubt you would be able to?" I ask, trying to ignore the way the thin material of his shirt outlines all the muscled parts of him.

"I don't remember much. You helped me to my room. I thought perhaps I might have thrown myself at you."

I hide my smile behind a teacup. "You did. I had to fend you off."

"Typical. I haven't been drunk since I was made king. Naturally I throw myself at the first female in sight."

"Naturally."

"Was it bad? What did I say?"

"You tried to kiss my ungloved hand. You're so polite, Kallias, even as a drunk." Then I laugh at him.

"My mother raised me to be proper," he says, unapologetic.

"She would be proud of you."

Kallias lets a sad smile grace his lips. Then he looks down at himself. "We should get dressed and join the other nobles for breakfast."

"Why? We never attend breakfast with the nobles."

"I have something to show you, and I'm too impatient to wait until the lunch hour. I had it commissioned some time ago, and I've just received word that it's done."

"And it's . . . in the great hall?" What did he do? Commission a tablecloth with our initials?

"Yes. No more questions. You'll understand. I'll be back in half an hour to collect you."

Then he disappears back through the wall.

"You clearly have no idea how long it takes a lady to get ready!" I shout after him.

⊱┄◈┄◯┄◈┄⊰

THE GUARDS FOLLOW US at a not-so-discreet distance, but I don't mind. Not when they are keeping Kallias safe.

He takes my arm this morning, not caring who looks on. Perhaps with a killer on the loose, it doesn't matter to him who sees us touching through our clothes.

Kallias somehow found the time to bathe *and* dress this morning. His hair looks slightly damp, but it still manages to maintain impressive volume. I wonder if he doesn't keep his hair out of his face because he knows just how delicious his facial features are. His nose is so straight and perfect, I want to run the tip of a finger down its slope before tracing his full lips.

Even his ears—decidedly unattractive body parts—manage to look pristine. And I can't help but imagine what sound he would make if I tugged down on his lobe with my teeth.

"You seem distracted this morning," Kallias says. "Did something happen I'm not aware of?"

"No." I turn my face away from him as I feel heat rush to my cheeks. Am I blushing? I haven't blushed at being caught staring at a man in—

"Here we are."

The doors to the great hall are open already, the sound of the nobles' chatter wafting out to us.

Kallias doesn't pause as we enter, though the nobles instantly quiet, perhaps at the way we're walking arm in arm, when no one else is permitted to touch the king without suffering death.

I scan the faces and the seating arrangements, trying to figure out what the surprise is. He didn't redo the walls or the rugs. The table appears the same, except—Is it my imagination or is it a bit bigger?

The king and I traipse past openmouthed nobles on our way to our usual seats, my mind whirring as I try to figure out what I've missed.

And that's when I see our seats.

I freeze in place, bringing Kallias to a jerking stop beside me.

The table *is* bigger. He commissioned a new one. And at the head of the table, where Kallias always sits, there are two chairs.

Two.

The table is twice as wide, allowing for us to sit side by side at the head of the massive oak piece.

This isn't just some polite gesture. This is a statement. One all of the nobility can see and understand.

But *I* don't understand.

"Why?" I ask.

Kallias looks around at the quieted nobles and coughs meaningfully. They instantly resume their morning chatter. So we can't be overheard.

"I told you, you're my equal. You've assisted me in more ways than one. You've been my constant companion these last couple of months, and I don't ever want you to leave, Alessandra. I want to show you how I respect and appreciate you."

"But this—in front of all the nobles. You might as well have proposed."

"Actually, I want to talk about that later."

My head snaps in his direction so fast my neck cracks.

"When we're alone," he clarifies. "Come." He gently tugs me toward our seats.

I somehow manage to make my feet move, despite the way my head is spinning. First elation, then disappointment, take turns occupying my thoughts.

He's going to propose.

But he said it so offhandedly. It was hardly romantic. I don't think he means romantically. He means for a practical alliance, surely.

But he's going to give me power. Share his power. Just like he's sharing the head of the table.

But I still won't be able to touch him. I won't have him.

Which is more important?

I know the answer to that. Obviously the power. But then—why do I feel so miserable inside?

"Your Majesty, the new table is simply divine!" a voice says from my immediate right.

I startle. When did Rhoda sit down? To her right is Hestia, who is also seated next to her Lord Paulos. The two chairs closest to Kallias are left empty, but my side is full. Kallias is practically in full shadow form to supplement the new table arrangements.

"I'm glad you approve," Kallias says.

"You seem surprised, Alessandra. Did you not know?" Rhoda asks.

"I didn't."

"It's a terribly romantic gesture," she says, only slightly lowering her voice.

Kallias heard her. "I'm glad *you* think so, Lady Nikolaides. Lady Stathos doesn't seem to know how to react just yet."

"I'm pleased, of course!" I hurry to say. "It was only unexpected."

"I make romantic gestures all the time," he says in mock defense, putting on a show for those seated closest to us.

"He has a point," Hestia says, pulling her attention away from Lord Paulos for a moment. "He showers you with gifts. We've all seen the gorgeous trinkets. This should be no different."

"It's a table," I say. "Not a necklace. Very different. And very unexpected."

Kallias brings a spoonful of porridge to his lips. "I have to continue to surprise you, else you'd find me boring and be done with me."

Rhoda laughs. "Not likely, Your Majesty." She looks up and down what she can see of his profile before giving me a meaningful glance. *Fifteen*, her eyes say. As if I could ever forget.

Kallias grins at her politely, and the meal resumes.

As my eyes trail down the table, I spot Rhouben and Petros laughing about something together. They look so carefree and happy, but I can't help but note that one noble is missing from the new table, as though its very existence has prevented him from joining us.

Poor Leandros.

⊱┈❈┈⊰

"DON'T YOU HAVE MEETINGS TODAY?" I ask once we finish breakfast and Kallias escorts me from the room.

"No. I've cleared my schedule. Your ball is coming up quickly. I thought I could help with the rest of the preparations. And as I mentioned, there's something we need to talk about."

I clear my throat. "Yes, I'm . . . curious to hear more about this topic we're going to discuss."

Well, that sounded overtly formal.

The man wants to propose for devils' sake, and I find myself wanting to run far away.

But this is what I wanted. It's the whole reason I came here.

So why am I dreading this conversation?

"Shall we go to the library?" he asks.

I don't say anything, but he leads me in that direction all the same, his guards following.

"It's a beautiful day," Kallias comments, as he glances out a window we pass by. "Storm passed quickly." Then he curses. "Why am I talking about the damned weather?"

Still I say nothing. The guards leave us to enter the library alone, and Kallias closes the door behind us.

"Do you want to sit?" he asks.

I shake my head.

"I'm sorry," he says. "I was stupid. I didn't mean to bring it up like that."

"Proposing, you mean?"

"Yes. I shouldn't have surprised you with the table, either. I should have talked with you before I had it made. I just thought you would like it."

I stare down at my boots. "But it's not just a table, is it, Kallias?"

"No. No, it's not."

It's silent for a moment, and I lift my gaze to study the spines of the books around the room. Anything to avoid looking at him and his perfect features. For this conversation, I don't think I can bear to look at him.

"We just do so well together," he says at last. "You have a mind for scheming better than any of my councilors. You've proven yourself time and again as an invaluable ally. Simply put, you're brilliant.

"I enjoy myself whenever I'm in your presence. Even if we're quarreling over something. I enjoy our trips away from the palace. Being in disguise, going on adventures—it's more fun than I've had in years. I've been so lonely lately, but ever since you've arrived, I've been . . . happy.

"But this isn't just about me. It's about you, too, and I've been trying to think of what this arrangement could offer you. We've already talked about the invitations to parties and balls. I promise to start attending with you. I want you to join me in all of my meetings—"

That has me looking away from the walls instantly.

Seeing that he has my full attention now, he continues, "I want you by my side, helping me make decisions for the kingdom. I want you to help me conquer the last three kingdoms in this vast world. I want you to be my equal, Alessandra. My queen. You would have power. A guard of your own. We would talk before making decisions. We would get the council off my back once and for all, and you would be free from your family. You'd of course have access to the treasury and the kingdom's funds. You wouldn't be without your own means."

Equal power. Rule the kingdom . . . *with* him?

That means—

I wouldn't have to kill him. He'll give me everything I want, and I won't have to get rid of him. My friend and companion.

But what about . . . more?

I swallow. "You want me to be your queen. But in name only. Is that right?"

Kallias loses his voice as he searches my face for something. "That's right. We would be married. So it would be official. But you'll keep your quarters, and I'll keep mine. No one would ever need know we don't consummate the marriage. Very few know the reason why I can't touch people. Most won't be able to tell whether we're intimate."

This is it. It's everything I've ever wanted. He's offering me the world.

He's just not offering me himself with it.

When did I start to want that?

A rough knock raps on the door.

"Go away!" Kallias says, never taking his eyes from me.

"Begging your pardon, Your Majesty"—I recognize Epaphras, the appointment keeper, as the owner of the voice on the other side of the door—"but you wished to be informed immediately if Baron Drivas came to the palace. He was quite forceful, and the guards had to restrain him. He's also accompanied by a constable."

My breath leaves me at the knowledge that Hektor's father is in the palace.

Kallias turns to me. "Why would the baron bring a constable into the matter of trying to get you to marry one of his sons? Did you sign some sort of contract with him?"

I swallow. "No, I didn't."

"This is ridiculous," he says to himself. "Epaphras, have the guards send them up. Let's deal with this immediately."

"Of course, sire."

I feel my stomach sink beneath the floorboards. "Must we?"

"You don't have to remain here. I can scare off the baron on my own, but this harassment of you is ridiculous. I should have dealt with it the moment you brought it to my attention."

"I'll stay," I say feebly, thinking of no way to delay this moment. Or to get out of it. I should have quickly said I'd marry Kallias, though I don't know that that would have offered me any more protection for what's about to happen.

The door opens minutes later. The guards surround two figures. One, I recognize as Faustus Galanis, Hektor's father. The woman with him must be the previously mentioned constable.

"Your Majesty," Faustus says. "At last! I've been attempting—"

"You will not speak until I allow it," Kallias says with all the authority of a king. "Who are you?" he asks, turning to the woman.

"Constable Damali Hallas, Your Majesty."

"And what is your purpose in being here?"

"Baron Drivas hired me to look into the disappearance of his youngest son, Hektor."

Kallias doesn't turn his head, but he glances to me briefly out of the corner of his eyes. "Disappearance?"

"So it was when we started the investigation, Your Majesty, but we now know the young nobleman was murdered."

CHAPTER

24

My stomach drops once more, but I allow nothing but surprise to flit across my face. "Hektor's *dead*?" I ask.

I note that Constable Hallas watches my face with a perceptive eye. Looking for any tells. She's a woman with hard features. A slightly too large nose, eyes too close together, a square chin. She has her ebony hair swept out of her face in a neat bun.

"For several years, I'm told," she says. "Some days ago, his body was discovered in the Undatia Forest. Apparently there have been a series of mudslides in the area. A couple of horsemen found and reported the body."

"Hold on a moment," Kallias says. "Who is this Hektor?" He directs the question to me, and I understand the true meaning: *Who is this man to you?*

"My first lover," I answer.

"And his murderer!" the baron flings at me.

"One more word out of you, Drivas," Kallias says, "and I will have you sent to the dungeons."

The guards surrounding him step inward, ready to pounce on the baron should the need arise.

"Your Majesty," the constable says, "with your permission, I have some questions for Lady Stathos."

Kallias turns to me. *Defers* to me.

How would it look if I sent them away without a word? No, I must appear innocent.

"I will answer her questions."

The constable steps forward. "Do you admit, then, to having a relationship with the deceased?"

"Yes, we were intimate, but not for years now. What happened to Hektor?"

"There was naught left of him but bones by this point."

A sob breaks out of the baron, but he doesn't say a word to accompany it.

"We identified him by the family crest he wore on his finger," the constable continues. "I had the remains examined yesterday. One of the ribs was nicked. Definitely points to a knife wound. I'm told you carry a knife on your person at all times."

I startle backward, as though affronted. "You're not seriously suggesting *I* killed him? And *who* told you I carry a knife?"

"Your sister." Hallas pulls a notebook from her pocket and glances through it. "A Chrysantha Stathos."

"Yes, I know my sister's name," I say bitterly. Chrysantha. The bane of my existence. Why won't she just die in a hole? "Many people carry knives. Why should that matter?"

"That alone doesn't, but the remains of a wooden chest were found with him. And one of the planks bore the initials *AS*. Those are your initials, are they not?" Hallas asks the question like she's done every single other one. Coolly, unemotionally, as though she really couldn't care about the answer. Even though she already knows the answers to all of them.

I dare a glance at Kallias. He's looking me over with the most peculiar expression. One I cannot place. As though he's seeing me anew.

He can't believe her!

I lose the strength in my legs and topple slightly. Kallias is there, though, holding me up.

"Surely plenty of people in the kingdom have the initials *AS*," Kallias offers.

"Perhaps," Hallas says. "But not all of them also had a relationship with the deceased. Who ended that relationship, Lady Stathos? It was Hektor, was it not? He broke your heart, and you retaliated by stabbing him, locking him in a chest, and then burying him in the forest."

Oh gods.

"You're speculating," I spit back. "There is no proof that Hektor ended the relationship or that I had any cause at all to harm him."

"Perhaps not yet, but I will find it. I've already spoken to the staff of your father's estate. I'm told you certainly would have had the ability and the means to get Hektor's body out of the estate unseen. You frequently snuck out at night unnoticed, only to return well past noon the following day. And I would like to request the king's permission to seize the knife on your person to compare it to the nick in the deceased's ribs."

I keep my gaze cool and collected as I turn toward Kallias, deferring to him this time.

Please read my calmness as innocence.

I haven't lost everything yet. Hektor will not come back to ruin me one last time. I am *this close* to becoming queen.

"Constable," Kallias says with a calmness that scares me, "you and the baron will excuse us. I appreciate you bringing this matter to my attention. As Lady Stathos is a member of my court, I will handle the investigation from here and get to the bottom of it."

The baron looks as though he has much more he wishes to say, but wanting to remain in good standing with the king, he allows the guards to escort him and the constable away.

Epaphras follows them out, closing the door behind himself. I manage to walk to the nearest armchair and fall into it. Waiting.

Waiting. Waiting.

Kallias is going to explode on me at any moment. He'll have me thrown into prison until he decides on the proper day and manner for killing me. He'll—

Kallias laughs so loudly and abruptly, I nearly topple out of the armchair. He has his hands on his knees while his whole body shakes from the force of the laughter. What the devils?

Did I break the king?

He manages to straighten after a moment and look over at me, but then his face contorts and he's back to uncontrollable laughter.

I feel my limbs grow tight, my face grow hot, anger pooling into every muscle.

"What the hell is wrong with you?" I snap, shouting over the top of his laughter. He wasn't even this bad when he read Orrin's love letter.

He says something I can't quite make out, then rubs tears from his eyes and tries again. "You killed him!" He throws his head back and laughs and laughs.

And somehow, I know that I'm not in trouble. How can I be if he's this jovial over the fact?

I could deny it. Plead on my behalf. But Kallias isn't stupid. Though the constable doesn't have enough evidence to convict me, Kallias knows the truth of it.

"I've an inclination to kill again," I say, glaring at him.

Kallias props himself up on the nearest wall of books, catching his breath. Once he's calm, he strides over to me and places his gloved hands on either side of my head.

"My little hellion. Quite the force to be reckoned with, aren't you? Oh, say you'll marry me, Alessandra!"

I swallow, thoroughly confused. "You're not going to hang me?"

"Hang you?" he repeats, letting his hands fall to his sides. "The man did you wrong, Alessandra. Honestly, you've saved me the trouble of tracking him down and killing him myself."

"But—"

"I pardon you," he says simply.

I blink. "Just like that?"

"Just like that. Anything for my friend."

I don't know that I've ever hated that word more than when it comes out of Kallias's mouth.

"Will you marry me?" he repeats, easily turning back to our previous conversation.

"What will happen if I say no?"

"You're still pardoned, if that's what you're worried about. I would never blackmail you into marriage! You'll be free to remain at the palace as long as you wish or to go." His face drops a little. "But I would be . . . most saddened if you left."

I think for a moment, but Kallias can't bear the silence.

"I need you, Alessandra. Say you'll be mine and I'll be yours."

He needs me. But he doesn't want me. He's giving me power. Everything I could ever want.

Why is this a hard decision?

Finally, I say, "I want a proper proposal. A public one." I cross my arms over my chest. "And no more laughing at me over Hektor Galanis. In fact, I never want to hear his name again."

Kallias grabs my gloved hand and kisses it. "Done. Now, let's discuss what you've done so far for the upcoming ball. Don't you think it will be the perfect opportunity for a proper and public proposal?"

>─┤─◆⟩─◯─⟨◆─┤─◁

I'M MARRYING THE KING.

The crimes of my past are forgiven.

I'll be free of my family once and for all. I can banish them from court forever!

But there is a killer out there. Someone who wants to take Kallias and this future from me.

I will not let that happen.

I realize that Kallias and I have perhaps been troubling over the wrong thing. The talk of a public parade through the streets had us worried, but I realize now that my ball is both sooner and just as public.

That will be when the killer strikes. I'm sure of it.

I share my concerns with Kallias while I sit in my rooms, working on my dress for the ball a couple of weeks later.

"I thought of that as well," he answers. "We'll double down on the guards. Check all the guests for weapons before they're admitted into the ballroom."

"Just what is the range on your abilities?" I ask him. "What is the farthest away the murderer need be to cancel your shadows?"

Kallias shrugs.

"You've never tested it?"

"Of course I have. I just don't want to worry you."

At my responding glare, he answers, "Fifty yards."

"That's all!" A talented marksman could manage that easily.

"I'll be safe, Alessandra. *We'll* be safe. It will be all right."

"I'd feel better if none of your council members were admitted."

"I would as well, but we can't very well uninvite them. Now stop fretting. Come show me what you're working on."

"No," I say. "I'd rather you see it on me when it's all done."

"That's quite a lot of fabric," he says sadly.

"Oh, hush."

CHAPTER

25

P otted roses line the entrances to the ballroom. They form a mazelike path to the refreshment table, before opening up in the center of the room to allow plenty of space for the dancing. Every member of the orchestra wears a black rose—the men in their breast pockets, the ladies in their hair—in honor of the late queen.

I had the ballroom painted, so it looks like ivy climbs up the columns. Green rugs line the floors, perfectly imitating grass. Rose petals have been sprinkled over the ground, giving off a soft fragrance.

It took several manservants and long ladders, but we also managed to dangle bouquets of roses from the ceiling. An occasional petal will fall, raining the floor with even more. I ordered tapestries to go along the walls, making them appear as though the edges of a garden rest all around us.

The electric chandeliers shine brightly. I wanted everything well lit. Not only to give the illusion of noonday in the garden, but so that any treachery or deceit would be impossible to hide behind shadows.

No one is killing my king tonight.

Guests have already started to pour in, though the ball doesn't officially start for another ten minutes. I can see everything from above, where I wait on the staircase, overlooking my arrangements. As it is my ball, I get to make a grand entrance, so I bide my time waiting until the right moment.

Really, I'm just waiting for Kallias to show up. I wouldn't want him to miss seeing me in my new dress.

I've outdone myself.

Overall, the dress is a light yellow. Every few inches, the fabric folds over itself as it moves upward, to give the shape of a rose's overlapping petals. I've stained the tip of each fold a bright red orange to match the fine roses found in the queen's garden. Normally I'm not overly fond of the color orange, but the queen's roses (and my dress by design) are simply divine. I wear a hoopskirt beneath the layers of silk, but the bodice is fitted, the top sleeveless, and my matching yellow gloves are dotted orange at my fingertips.

I've pinned my hair to one side, so it falls down my left shoulder, leaving my neck bare on the right side. I've curled the strands so they fall in perfect ringlets, a black wonder over the light fabric.

When Kallias does finally arrive, he doesn't have himself announced. Rather, he tries to enter quietly, going right for the throne on the dais. Having seen the fabric I was using to make my dress, he wears a matching yellow waistcoat—so light it could be mistaken for white. It looks remarkable against his bronze skin.

As soon as he is seated, I give the herald orders to announce me.

"Our hostess, Lady Alessandra Stathos, second daughter to the Earl of Masis."

I hold up my dress in both hands and let a light smile grace my features as I descend the stairs.

All heads turn in my direction.

And I know it's not just my stunning gown that causes their chattering. I'm the girl who caught the eye of the king. The girl who has the council following her strategies. The girl who saved the king from an assassination attack.

I've worked up quite a reputation indeed.

And tonight, Kallias will propose and shock everyone.

He watches me now, as I take each careful step. The dress is wide enough to allow my legs plenty of movement, but the floor-length hem and heeled boots make tripping an easy feat.

Yet I keep my eyes on him.

With that heated gaze on me, I can see just how much Kallias wants me. It is no longer a question of attraction between us. It is a matter of keeping himself safe from attack. We have a good arrangement. We'll both have what we want after tonight. He'll have a queen to help him manage and balance the council. He'll have someone on his side whom he trusts. The only person he trusts.

And in return I get power. The power to rule a kingdom at Kallias's side once he turns twenty-one. It'll only be another seventeen months.

When I reach the bottom of the steps, Kallias doesn't approach me. In fact, he turns away, engaging one of his nearby council members in conversation.

Disappointment and irritation mingle within me, but I keep my face in a pleasant smile.

I think to start welcoming my guests, but as I take a few steps in one direction, the partygoers . . . scatter.

What the devils?

Perhaps I've only imagined it? I head for the refreshment table, thinking to check on the food arrangements. Skirts sway from my path, and a group of gentlemen cut off their conversation midsentence to turn away from me and find somewhere else to stand.

What is the matter with everyone?

When I'm steps away from the table, I relax as someone approaches me. Until I realize it's my father.

"I don't recall sending you an invitation," I say, distracting myself with a glass of champagne from the table.

"Must have slipped your mind," Father says. But once he gets close enough not to be overheard, he adds, "I'm here to rescue you, Alessandra."

I take a sip from my glass as though I don't hear him. Father is hoping to get a reaction from me. It won't happen.

"Did you hear me, Alessandra? I'm going to save you and your reputation."

Again, I say nothing.

"What with the rumors of your crime spreading like wildfire, we must keep you safe by wedding you off right away to a powerful man."

My eyes flit to Father's face. "Rumors of my crime?"

"Yes, the murder of Hektor Galanis. Everyone is talking of it."

That's why everyone is suddenly giving me a wide berth. They think me a murderess.

Damn Faustus. He must know the king cleared me of all charges, but that didn't stop him from running his tongue.

"Don't worry, darling," Father says. "A hasty marriage will offer you some protection. I've been talking with the Viscount of Thoricus—"

"Rhouben's father?"

"You're familiar with his son, then? Wonderful. He recently ended his engagement with a baron's daughter. The two of you will make a smart match."

I nearly spit out the champagne in my mouth. "So now I'm to marry someone beneath my station?"

"He has money, Alessandra. And with my dear friend Eliades behind bars, we can't very well rely on him anymore."

I set my empty champagne glass down on a tray as a servant walks by. Then I face my father fully. "So nothing less than a duke will do for Chrysantha, but I'm to wed a future viscount. Is that it?"

"You can hardly afford to be picky with the way people are talking about you."

I startle my father when I start laughing. "You never listen to me. You never have, but let me be clear. I don't need you to save me. I don't need a hasty marriage. I have the king, and he has pardoned me of all charges. You would know this if you ever bothered to ask me about the situation instead of coming to your own conclusions and solutions.

"He's proposing to me tonight," I finish.

"He hasn't asked my permission—"

"He doesn't need to. He's the king, and as I said, you're not getting a cent out of the treasury for me."

He tries to get in another sentence, but I don't let him.

"No. This is my party. My night. You do not get to ruin it." I eye a couple of guards against the walls. When I catch their attention, I beckon them to me with a hand.

I half expect them not to listen. But they do. Two young men come striding forward, rifles slung over their shoulders.

"Yes, my lady?" one of them asks.

"Have the earl escorted from the ball. He's not welcome. If he does not leave willingly, you have my permission to use force."

Father lets out one laugh. "Who do you think you are? The queen?"

But the two guards step between me and my father. "This way, my lord."

Father looks upon me with bewilderment. And then, for the briefest of moments, I feel that he finally sees me. My ambition. My cunning. My achievements. The guards heeding my commands are proof enough of what I've been trying to explain to my father for weeks.

I have achieved exactly what I set out to do.

And then Father seems to realize that if that's true, then what I said about not receiving a bride-price for me must be true as well. His face turns to one of panic as the guards grip his arms firmly and escort him away.

Everyone in the ballroom has paused to watch the spectacle, though neither the music nor the chatter has ceased.

And now, not a soul seems to have a problem approaching me. Not when I can have them thrown from the party. Not when the king's guards obey my commands. In fact, I'm greeted by no fewer than ten nobles as they grab drinks and sample hors d'oeuvres.

"An astonishing party. Are those chocolates shaped like rosebuds?" Rhouben plucks a candy from the table and tosses it into his mouth. After swallowing, he adds, "I could kiss you right now."

"Best not to do it in public," I say.

"Seriously, Alessandra. Thank you. I know I've already said it, but I'll say it again. You freed me from Melita. She's left the palace, she was so distraught over the breakup, Eliades's rejection, and then Eliades's imprisonment. I'm a free man again."

And he doesn't even know I just saved him from marriage to me, as well.

"How are you enjoying your bachelorhood?" I ask.

"I'm going to celebrate by dancing with every single gorgeous woman in attendance tonight. That includes you. Save me a dance?"

"Of course."

He kisses my hand, and I watch him take off to a corner where Petros and Leandros laugh together.

It's nice to see Leandros. I worried he wouldn't come.

As if sensing my gaze, he looks over. Upon seeing me watching, he offers a small smile. I offer him a grand one in return.

Leandros is clad in all black, just as Kallias was the first time I laid eyes on him. Only Leandros wears a painted black rose near his lapels. I almost miss the plant, since it blends in so well with his waistcoat. The sight of the flower endears Leandros to me even more. Kallias hasn't spoken to him in a year, and yet, he shows up at a party in honor of the king's mother and wears her favorite blossom. The rest of his dark attire makes Leandros's golden skin look lighter, and it really brings out the darker undertones in his pale brown hair.

It doesn't matter what he wears—he's so handsome and thoughtful. He really will make some girl very happy.

I force my gaze away and survey more of the room. I'm pleased to find that most everyone is showing up in the proper attire. I see a group of ladies dressed as tulips, their necklines rising in the back to a standing collar, curving around their heads and to the sides of their faces, shaping like a tulip's petals. Bands around their heads have the protruding stamen.

One lady is ambitious enough to attempt what I think is supposed to be a daffodil. With a gold hat shaped like the flower's horn, she looks rather . . . different.

The men are predictably boring, with nothing more than flowers in their breast pockets to match the ladies.

I spot Hestia and Rhoda and rush over to them. Rhoda is dressed like her namesake. The hem at the base of her dress is gathered into clusters that look like purple-pink rhododendrons. Simple, yet quite elegant.

Hestia is a marvel in dusty pink. She, too, went for roses, but instead of shaping the entire dress like one, she simply had her seamstress sew exquisite beading over the entire skirt, shaping trails of thorny vines and blossoming flowers.

"You both look exquisite," I say.

"Thank you," Hestia says. "Did you notice my shawl?"

I take the time to examine the pink silk about her shoulders. "Oh, you sewed it yourself, didn't you?"

It's a simple task, sewing down the ends to give the accessory a smooth edge all around, but I know how terrible Hestia was when she started learning to sew, unable to keep her stitches straight. And while the shawl isn't perfect, as I can see a loose thread hanging off one end, most of the stitches look fantastic.

"It looks amazing," I tell her.

"I had a good teacher," she says in return.

"The decor turned out even better than you described," Rhoda offers. "And you put everyone to shame with your dress. How do you manage to look like a flower without looking ridiculous?"

"I spent a lot of time on it," I admit. When I wasn't with Kallias, I was sewing.

"Something is missing," I note as I survey Rhoda. "Ah, I told you to bring Galen! Where is he?"

Rhoda flicks a black lock over her shoulder, discreetly pointing her head toward a spot against the wall.

It takes me three tries before I spot him. I was looking for a servant, dressed in simple cotton and drab colors. I wasn't prepared for a dashing man in purple-pink brocade. He even fixed his hair, somehow getting the ends to smooth back out of his face. Despite the improved attire, the man looks terribly uncomfortable with the way his hands twitch at his sides and the way he eyes the guards nearby as though expecting to be thrown out.

"Whatever is he doing over there?" I ask.

Rhoda sighs. "He's waiting to, well, wait on me."

"But didn't you tell him he was to be your escort?"

"I did, but I think he misunderstood me. He only accepted the clothing I had made for him because he knew he couldn't *serve* me tonight if he wasn't dressed for the occasion."

"Oh, Rhoda, you must set things straight for him."

"That's what I told her," Hestia says.

"I tried," Rhoda says. "I told him to walk with me and be at my side, but he insisted he could see if I needed anything from the corners of the room."

I shake my head. "Stop being so timid with him. Sometimes men need a little help. Do something that he can't mistake as being a servant's task."

"Like what?"

"Invite him to dance with you."

Her eyes turn down, and she fiddles with her own fingers.

"What's the matter?" Hestia asks.

"What if he tells me no?" Rhoda says. "What if he's trying to tell me he's not interested by purposely misunderstanding my intentions? What if I'm harassing him? Or worse, what if he feels *obligated* to abide my wishes when I do make myself clear because I am his employer?"

"Oh, Rhoda," Hestia says. "All that uncertainty and fear? It comes with being in love. But once you're past it, everything is wonderful! Of course Galen cares for you. He's been at your side for *years*. No servant is obligated to become your friend and confidant, yet Galen has always been both for you. He loves you. It's obvious to everyone. Now, go and get your man."

Rhoda steels herself before marching in Galen's direction.

I turn to Hestia. "Very sage advice."

"I only learned it myself a short time ago."

I pause a moment. "How—how do you get past that fear? How is it worth what might come later? The heartbreak?"

She considers my questions before answering, "I think that when you care enough for someone, you reach a point where it's far more painful not to have him at all than to have him and risk losing him. You realize the risk is worth it. Because happiness, however short-lived, is always worth it."

We both watch as Rhoda reaches Galen. She says something to him, and he nods. She says something more, and he looks at her, his head quirking in curiosity. Then she throws her head back, grabs his arm, and drags him to the dance floor.

It's awkward to watch at first. Rhoda leads, because Galen has not been taught the dances. Not as a commoner. But after a moment, his arms hold her more firmly, his feet find the steps, and he has eyes for nothing but the dazzling woman in front of him. He has the look of a man who has just been handed the world.

"Now, isn't that worth it?" Hestia says.

"Where is your Lord Paulos this evening?" I ask, changing the subject.

"Oh, he said he'd be a little late. Some business he had to attend to."

"Men are always attending to business."

"But the king isn't. Is he not just sitting on the dais? Why haven't you gone to him?"

"He hasn't come to me."

"He knows you're in charge of this party. Perhaps he fears getting in the way."

"The party is already all planned out. I am simply enjoying it now. He should be enjoying it with me. But he won't even look at me now."

Hestia purses her lips. "Sometimes I wish we could know exactly what ridiculous thoughts were going through their heads."

"Indeed."

CHAPTER 26

Hestia leaves my side once Lord Paulos arrives a short time later. She offers to stay with me and chat, but I shoo her away.

Just because my man is ignoring me, it doesn't me she should ignore hers.

"You look lovely tonight, Lady Stathos," comes a voice at my back.

Lady Zervas hasn't bothered to match my theme. I suppose it would be stranger if she did. I doubt there's anyone in the world who bears more ill will toward the late queen than the other woman who competed for the king's heart. The woman who lost.

"You're not in costume," I respond, taking in her simple emerald-colored gown that doesn't bear any added ornamentation.

"I wore green, didn't I? What says 'garden' more than that?"

I have nothing to say in response.

"I was surprised to receive your invitation," she says. "I didn't think you particularly liked our last conversation."

"I didn't, but who could use a ball more than cranky old spinsters?"

She laughs at the jibe—a response I hadn't expected. "I like you," she says. "I think you will make a fine queen. I only thought to tell you how to protect yourself when last we spoke."

"It's too late for that," I say, more to myself than to her.

She nods, as though understanding what I mean completely, before walking on.

⤞⊶⊶○⊷⊷⤜

THE BALL IS IN full swing, and my friends couldn't be happier. Hestia and Lord Paulos share a dance. Rhoda and Galen are in a corner, talking and giving each other light touches. A few judgmental stares are eyeing them, but Rhoda is blind to them. I'll have a thing or two to say if anyone tries to interrupt my friend's happiness.

Petros has a new lord in his arms, and the two are the most elegant dancers in the room, I'm convinced. Meanwhile, Rhouben is eyeing a lady over the rim of his wineglass. Even Leandros has found a dance partner, a pretty girl in lavender.

The guards are quiet sentinels at the edges of the room. All weapons have been checked at the entrances.

And Kallias—

Kallias is still on his throne, watching me. Not participating, but present. As he always must live his life.

I sigh and turn away. I suppose this is about to become my life full-time. Might as well get used to it. But that doesn't mean I can't enjoy my own ball. Rhouben still hasn't worked up the nerve to ask the lady to dance, so at the next lull in between songs, I start to stride over to him.

A gentle hand comes down on my shoulder, and I turn.

"Dance with me."

Kallias pulls me into his arms before I can answer, holding me right there for the whole world to see. The song strikes up, and he moves us in time to the gentle thrumming of the violins. He lets his shadows swirl about his face, to let any onlookers know he is still in full control of his powers. But his arms are tangible for our dance, so he can spin me, lift me, clutch me against him. His gloved hands move over my back and arms as he leads me through the steps.

I'm unprepared for the sudden sensation of being on fire. Everywhere his gloves touch burns. I can barely feel my feet—I even trip once—I'm so aware of where his body touches mine.

Damn him.

"What are you doing?" I finally manage to get out. "You don't get to ignore me all evening only to dance with me now!"

He leans forward. "You're so beautiful it hurts."

"What kind of answer is that?"

"I kept my distance to keep myself from doing something stupid. Something like this." He pulls me so close it's indecent as we go through the next steps.

I can't even hear the music anymore. All I hear is Kallias's frantic heartbeats, his warm breath against my hair.

When I dare to look up into his eyes, I realize it's the wrong thing to do.

I'm burning. My core goes up in flames. His gaze looks hungry, heated, *desirous*. The look of a man who hasn't had human contact in a year.

Kallias said it himself. No man would give up the power of the shadows except for the deepest and most all-consuming of loves.

Not that I *want* him to love me.

He met me two months ago.

And I used to want to kill him.

But now everything is different, and I want so much more. At the same time, I'm terrified of having more and so glad he cannot touch me, that he will never hurt me because we will never be allowed to get that close.

The music comes to an end, but Kallias keeps one of my hands in his. "Come with me," he says.

He leads us up to the dais where the throne is.

No.

Now there are two thrones. When was the second brought in?

Oh gods. It's happening now.

At some signal from Kallias, the beginnings of another song cut off. My guests go silent, and all eyes are on the king.

He seats me into the second throne, before dropping to his knees before me and brandishing a ring between two fingers.

It glistens in the light. I don't take in any details, because my gaze is locked on Kallias's. Little gasps and exclamations sound throughout the ballroom.

"Alessandra," the king says in a voice only I can hear. "You've made me happy again. You've given me hope and become an invaluable confidante and the greatest of friends. A—a woman I could love."

Love.

Could love. If he let himself. Which he won't.

Then he raises his voice for the whole room to hear. "Lady Alessandra Stathos, will you be my queen? My equal in all things? A protector and ruler of Naxos and the conquered realms? Will you marry me?"

"Yes."

An ear-wrenching cheer goes up from the crowd, and I bask in it. In the attention. In the offer of marriage from the most powerful man in the world. In achieving my greatest goal.

He's mine.

But then a stroke of fear rides in, as I remember someone wants to kill my king. And should we catch *this* assassin, Kallias will still be a target his entire life. He could be taken from me at any moment.

Kallias is ignorant to my thoughts as he slides the ring onto my finger, a silver band bearing a black diamond cut into the shape of a rose.

"A toast!" Lord Vasco says from somewhere nearby. I hate that he has to be a part of this moment.

Glasses of wine are passed around to all the revelers in just a few short minutes. But those minutes seem to take forever, and dread sinks low in my chest. There are so many people in the room. An assassin could easily sneak in.

He's safe, I remind myself. We banned weapons from entering the room. All the guests were thoroughly searched, much to their own irritation. No one can get past the guards surrounding the dais.

The council members stand below us. Serving maids spread throughout the room to fill glasses to the brim. Kallias thanks the woman who pours deep red liquid into his cup.

"To the king and future queen!" Lord Ikaros Vasco says, and the crowd repeats the words heartily.

That's when I see her. Hidden through the crowd, carrying a load of dirty dishes from the refreshment table.

It's the little girl from the gentleman's club.

From the place where Kallias was touched. And now, I note with horror, the shadows that had been about his head are completely gone.

He either hasn't noticed or isn't using them.

"Kallias, don't!" I shriek. I bat the cup that's raised to his lips away.

But it's too late. He already drank.

He immediately falls to the ground and starts convulsing. Liquid foams at his mouth, and he closes his eyes.

Screams go up, and the council tries to rush onto the stage.

"No!" I yell. "Everyone stay back."

The guards close ranks, barring anyone from joining the king and me on the dais. I try to think. I need to keep people from touching him. We don't know who the murderer is yet and—

Except we do.

It was Vasco who proposed the toast and had everyone's cups filled. We knew one of Kallias's council members had to be in on it.

I'm torn. I have to get the little girl out of here, but I don't want to leave the king's side.

And then Leandros, Petros, and Rhouben are trying to get past the guards.

"Let them through," I order.

The guards part just enough to let the three men by.

"What do we do?" Leandros asks. "He needs a physician."

"Don't let anyone touch him!" I shout. "No one. Stay here with him!"

I leap from the stage and kick off my heeled boots before running for that little girl. When I'm upon her, I lift her into my arms and sprint for the exit.

She drops her dirty dishes and grips me for dear life, fearing I will drop her. She makes little protestations, but I ignore her.

Run, run, run.

How far is far enough? What did Kallias say? Fifty yards?

We duck through the kitchens, swerve around overworked kitchen staff, and bound through the back doors. My feet step over rough pebbles and other refuse on the streets, cutting into my skin, but I don't let that stop me.

I have to get her away from Kallias. I'm not counting my steps. I'm too frantic. I have no clue where I'm going, but I don't stop until I'm exhausted, which admittedly, isn't that far away.

It's not often that I have to exert myself.

We collapse on the ground, and only then do I register that the girl is sobbing, her little hands grasping my neck.

"I didn't want to be there," she's saying. "They told me to. I didn't know why, but I knew something was wrong. First they had me touch him and then—and then—"

She bursts into more tears, her wracking heaves making it impossible to hear anything else she says.

I don't want to listen to her crying. I want to go see if Kallias is all right. But I can't let her get away. She must know or be able to point out who is behind everything.

"Who are *they*?" I ask. "Who told you to be here tonight? Who made you touch him?"

She can't get any words out. She's still so shaken from the way I dragged her away from the party and from the sight of the dying man she must now know is partly her fault.

I want to shake her, to get her to listen. But I know that won't help. And I know it's not really her fault. She's been used by people older and far more powerful than she. I just want her to say Vasco is behind it and have the whole thing done with.

"Alessandra?" It's Leandros.

"Over here." I bother to actually look around to where "here" is. We're in some sort of gap between the stables and a small runoff from the mountain.

When Leandros comes into view, I ask, "How is he?"

"He's all right, but he's asking for you."

I look down at the girl. "I can't leave her."

"I'll stay with her. She'll be here when you get back."

I hand her over, and the little girl allows herself to be held by a new stranger, though somewhat reluctantly. "It's all right," I tell her. "He's a good man."

At those words, she lets her face fall into his chest and resumes her sobbing.

And then I take off again. This time, I actually feel the pinpricks of pain that go through my feet with every step. The scenery is a blur around me as I hurry back in through the kitchens and into the ballroom, a nice streak of brown coating the bottom of my once-yellow dress.

Kallias is standing, his back to a wall, no shadows in sight, but I hope that is a good thing, not a bad one. His council is trying to order about the guards, escorting party guests away.

"Are you all right?" I ask.

Seeing me, Kallias grabs me and pulls me to him. "I'm fine. Look at you! Are you hurt? Where did you go?"

In as few words as possible, I explain about the little girl and how I rushed her from the room. I tell him Leandros is with her now.

"Thank goodness for Leandros and this lot." He points to Petros and Rhouben, who stand on either side of him. "My councilors kept trying to approach me. Vasco has already been carried off to rot in the cells until I'm ready to talk to him. My father's best friend . . ."

I'd forgotten what this means for him. It's not only about catching the person who is trying to kill him. It's about obtaining justice for his dead parents.

"There was more than one," I say. "I couldn't get much out of the serving girl, but she clearly said there was more than one person involved in this plot. I'll go back and question her as soon as we're done here."

"Someone else can do it," Kallias says as his arms tighten around me.

"It can't be you. You must stay away from her. We need to figure out what to do with her. But later. For now, we need to know what she knows, and there are too few people to trust. Where are your shadows?" I tack on at the end.

"Once I healed from the poison, I wanted to hit things. Vasco's face, in particular."

I resist an eye roll. "You should go upstairs. Rest from this ordeal. I'll join you as soon as I have more information."

Kallias sighs. Then he looks over at the men flanking him. "Go with her. Help her with anything she needs."

Somehow, my chest warms at the absence of him telling them to protect me. He knows I can protect myself. He doesn't even need to mention it.

I sit upon the dais and hastily brush off my feet before shrugging on my boots once again. Now that haste isn't required, I can afford to wear them. Then the three of us return to where I left Leandros and the girl, who appears to have finally calmed down.

I kneel down to her height. "What's your name?"

"Drea," she says after a sniffle. "Please, I didn't know he was the king until today. I never saw him before."

"It's okay, Drea," Leandros says, stroking a hand through her hair, "tell them what you just told me."

"There were two of them," she says. "That man, the one who announced the toast to the king and queen. And the lady."

"What lady?" I ask. *There's a woman involved?*

"The one who's always wearing black. But tonight she's in green."

CHAPTER 27

feel my brows shoot up to my hairline. "Lady Zervas."

Of course. Poison is a woman's weapon. She hated Kallias's father for not choosing her. Of course she would have him and his wife murdered. And Kallias. She tried to warn me to stay away from him because he wouldn't be long for this world. Her hatred must run so deep that she would want to kill the offspring of the romantic union that should have been hers.

Leandros hangs his head. "My uncle. I'm so sorry, Alessandra. I had no idea."

"I know," I say. "It's all right. We've already apprehended him, but I need to alert the guards to Lady Zervas's treachery as well."

"No need. I'll do it. You—Will you just take care of him and tell him I'm sorry?"

I place a hand on his shoulder. "You have nothing to be sorry for."

"I should have noticed something, surely. I could have—"

"Stop it. There's nothing to do but let it go. You helped Kallias today. And you two as well," I add, turning around to where Petros and Rhouben are keeping a lookout. "I'll make sure the king remembers it. It's time he stopped pushing his friends away. Especially with his parents' murderers finally caught."

>─◄►─O─◄►─┤◄

I PLACE THE GIRL in a room on the opposite side of the castle from Kallias and me, giving her over to one of the kitchen staff for safekeeping. I'll of course have to make more permanent arrangements later, but for now, I'm utterly spent.

Lady Zervas and Lord Vasco are in separate cells of the dungeon. I finally managed to shoo away the nobles and their questions and congratulations.

Who was behind it?

Was my drink poisoned as well? I think I better see a physician.

Let's see the ring, Lady Stathos!

You two are a smart match. Of course, my Clarissa would have also been a good choice for the king.

I shut the door to my rooms and lean against it for a moment, rubbing at my temples.

Managing people can be tiresome, but there's still nothing more satisfying than watching people do exactly what I say.

"You look how I feel," Kallias says from my bedroom. He sits on my bed, one foot crossed over the other.

"I had to assuage the worries of the nobles."

"You're already a fine queen."

I kick off my boots, wincing as my torn feet hit the floor. Walking on my heels, I make it over to a cushioned chair and collapse.

"You're hurt."

"Nothing that a long soak in hot water won't fix."

"I'll draw you a bath." Kallias moves methodically to my washroom. I hear him fiddling with the faucets and soaps before the sound of heated water filling a basin can be heard.

He pads over to me on bare feet, scooping me up in his arms and carrying me over to the tub.

"It was Zervas," I tell him when he doesn't ask. "She was working with Vasco. The girl from the club confirmed his treachery and named her as well. We've got them both in the dungeons."

When Kallias moves us to the washroom, he's careful to position me so my rump can sit on the edge of the tub, my back leaning against him, and my feet dangling in the water. I wince once the cuts on my feet make contact. The hem of my now-dirty gown soaks up the water, but I don't care. It's already ruined.

It feels so nice to wiggle my toes in the warm water, and Kallias's hands start kneading at the knots in my shoulders.

I'm a little worried by his silence at my revelation, but I give him the time he needs to process everything. I don't say anything. Just let him focus on me if that's what he needs right now.

"I'm relieved that it's over," he says at last. "I really am. But I'm also done with this."

I swallow, and I'm certain Kallias must feel the sudden tension in me. "Done with what?"

I don't know what I'll do if he says me.

His hands are in my hair now, letting the strands sift through his fingers. "The whole night, I watched you from afar, save at the end, when I couldn't stand it any longer. And just now? I stayed hidden from a little girl for fear that someone would be able to touch me." He gives one shake of his head. "It doesn't matter what precautions I take. I could lock myself up in a concrete box so nothing could ever hurt me, but that's no way to live.

"Being king comes with risks. I'm willing to take those. In the end it's worth it." He looks at me now. "You are worth it, Alessandra. I'm done living separately from everyone else. My parents' murderers will finally be brought to justice. But even if they weren't, I would still make this choice."

"What choice?"

His hand comes down to the side of my face, and he turns me, tilting my mouth upward.

I draw in a startled breath, and Kallias uses that parting to place his lips around my lower lip. He licks lightly at my skin as he gently pulls upward.

Forgetting my injured feet, I stand and shove him so hard, I nearly fall over in the almost-full tub.

I take the time to shut off the water before stepping out on the other side, keeping the basin between us.

But it's already too late.

"What did you do?" I yell.

"I kissed you," he answers simply.

"You *touched* me."

He stands straight, unafraid of this fight, it would seem. "Weren't you listening to me? I'm done with it all! I'm not my father. I'm not going to spend my life alone so I can reach a hundred. Three hundred. A millennium. I don't care about a long life anymore. I can't stand being alone for one second longer. I can't stand being apart from you for one second longer." His face falls as something occurs to him. "But if you don't feel the same way, I'm sorry I accosted you."

Water pools around me on the floor from my dress, but I ignore it. "The same way," I repeat. "How? How do you feel?"

Kallias reaches into a pocket of his dress pants and pulls out a folded parchment. "I wrote it on paper." He opens it, looks at the words, and shakes his head. "I can't read it aloud. It's for you to read. Later. Really, I just wanted to prove I could write a better one than Eliades. But I'll leave it here and go."

He turns around and places the letter on a nightstand before heading toward his room.

"Kallias Maheras, don't you dare leave me right now."

He pauses and manages to find my eyes.

"Tell me," I say. "You don't need to read a letter. Just tell me."

He closes his hands into fists at his sides. "I want you."

I wait for him to say more. When he doesn't, I say, "Surely you can do better than that."

He narrows his eyes at the challenge. "I'm done watching you flirt with other men. I'm sick of it. I don't want you kissing or touching anyone but me."

I keep a straight face as I rub one hand up my other arm. "That's awfully selfish of you."

"You be quiet now. I'm not done talking. You wanted me to say it. So I'll say it all. Selfish or not.

"When I first saw you, it infuriated me that you never looked at me. Not once during that inane ball. It wasn't until I approached you that you deigned to meet my eyes. And then you insulted me. You mocked me every chance you got. You didn't bow and roll over like every other human alive. You challenged me.

"That's when I first knew I was doomed." He takes a step forward. "And then we spent all those meals together, separated by a damned table. And you told me about your dreams. About your fears. And I wanted nothing more than to grant your dreams and remove your fears."

He takes another step. "You asked to spend more time with me. It was the one thing I thought I could not give. Because if I spent more time with you, I would fall for you even harder. This girl who didn't care that I was a king. But then you spent that evening with Leandros, and I realized the one thing worse than not having you was not having you and watching you be with someone else. So I tortured myself by spending more time with you.

"And you let me talk about my mother. You helped me challenge the council. You put a stop to nearly every problem in my kingdom. You were not only perfect for me, you were perfect for Naxos. So then I knew that marrying you was what I had to do. For the good of the kingdom. Even if it meant I would be miserable every day having you near and not *having you*.

"But the most exquisite torture of all was the night at the gentleman's club, when I could feel your reactions to me touching you. I didn't know if it was because it was *me* touching you or if it was just because you hadn't been touched in a while, as you'd mentioned before.

"I want a life with you, Alessandra, one without the shadows between us. And I don't care about being vulnerable. That's what my guards are for. I'll get a poison taster. I will live as other kings do. I don't need this centuries' old gift that is really just a curse.

"And even if you don't want me in return, I am still going to remove the law about people touching me. I don't want this anymore. I'm tired of living a shadowed life."

By now, Kallias's knees dig into the other side of the tub, he's so close. I can't move. I'm both terrified and desperate to believe him. To let him be what he wants to be. To marry him for real.

Because there was Hektor.

But—

Kallias knows I killed Hektor. He knows all my secrets, and he doesn't care. He wants me in spite of them. Because of them, even.

"Please say something," he says.

"You made this decision before the attack tonight?"

He nods.

"You've wanted me . . . from the beginning?"

Another nod.

And I realize that if I tell him no, I'll be just as he was. Alone because

I'm terrified to be vulnerable. But I can get past that, as he is now, and I can have it all.

The power.

The kingdom.

The man.

"Come here," I say, because my feet still ache slightly, and I also don't know if I can move with the way he's looking at me.

Kallias keeps his eyes on mine as he removes his gloves and lets them fall to the floor.

I swallow.

Between one blink and the next he's before me. He raises one hand, cups my cheek. I lean into that touch. The one I've been craving for so long.

Then Kallias lifts me, holds me with one arm at my back and the other beneath my knees. My arms go to his neck, and I draw his face toward mine.

"I wanted to do this the very first time I saw you," I say before our lips touch.

And then I'm aflame.

There is no softness or patience to this kiss. For Kallias, it is one he has waited a whole year for. And for me, I feel as though I've waited my whole life.

He stumbles slightly as he tries to veer around the tub without breaking the kiss, and I laugh against his lips before he silences me with his mouth.

I don't know how he manages not to drop me. But he makes it all the way to my bed. All while giving the utmost attention to my lips.

I'm flat on my back while he holds himself above me, his mouth moving to investigate the slope of my neck.

"Promise me—" I start, and then I lose my train of thought as he finds a spot at the base of my throat and runs his teeth across it.

I put my hands on his shoulders, pushing him away for a moment, just so I can collect my thoughts. "Promise me you won't send me away because I'm the one making you mortal. Promise me you won't change your mind later and decide I'm not enough for the price of mortality."

His breathing is ragged, but he manages to focus. "I swear it, Alessandra. You're not going anywhere. You're mine."

He sits back on his knees and starts unbuttoning his shirt.

I follow his fingers with my eyes, watching as each inch of his beautiful skin is revealed.

I don't like being on uneven footing, so I sit up, too. He draws his shirt away from his chest and tosses it to the ground, and I understand.

I place the palm of my hand flat against his chest, and he closes his eyes. He hasn't been touched in so long. And what he wants right now—what he needs—is to be touched.

My hands do a thorough search of his chest, and then I replace them with my lips, feeling every muscle, every slope, every smooth and coarse surface.

I lay him back, climb atop him, let him feel the weight of my body. My hair slides against his cheeks as I kiss the stubble at his chin, and then I move to his neck, up to his ear, grab the lobe between my teeth and tongue.

And then, as though he can't stand it anymore, he rolls us, effectively sliding me underneath him. My dress hitches up, and one of his thighs goes between mine, nudging upward—

And then I'm gasping, but he covers the sound with his mouth.

I can't think. I can't breathe. I can't—

Kallias slows the kiss. Draws each connection of our lips out almost lazily, as if he has all the time in the world.

My senses return, and I just enjoy the feel of him, the heat of him, the way his clever lips move across mine.

The Shadow King is the most patient man in the world. He kisses me for hours. He plays with me, speeding the kisses up for a time and then slowing them down, as if to see how close he can bring himself to the brink of control before calming back down.

He never takes off his pants. He never takes off my dress. He doesn't even let his hands stray to fun places.

And I'm so terrified that he'll change his mind. That he'll send me away. That he'll decide he doesn't want me anymore—as Hektor did—that I don't try to push anything. As badly as I want him, I let him control the pace and speed at which we go.

Just for tonight. When things are new and terrifying.

Perhaps that is what he needs. To ease himself back into remembering what it is like to *feel*.

>—⊹—◦—⊹—<

WHEN I WAKE, I try to cling to the remnants of a delicious dream. There was me and Kallias and—

But when my eyes open, I find him in bed next to me, one gloveless, shirtless arm slung over my middle.

Not a dream.

A beautiful reality.

My Shadow King.

His eyes crack open, and he just stares at me, as though startled. But then he collects himself. "That'll take some getting used to."

"Waking up to another face?"

"Waking up to a face that isn't Demodocus's. As much as I love him, I much prefer yours." His hand snakes forward to cup my face, and he draws me in for a sweet kiss.

An hour or so later, he leaves me to dress in his own room, but he doesn't bother to shut the door that usually separates us, so that we might talk.

"I'm having your things moved in here," he says.

"Moved where? Into your room?"

"Into our room. We'll knock down this wall. Make it one great room. I don't care. But you're sleeping with me. There will be no your-bed-and-my-bed nonsense." His next words are muffled, as though he says them while pulling a shirt over his head. "Unless you really want your own bedroom . . ." It sounds as though the words cost him greatly.

I smile, not answering right away because it'll drive him mad. Finally, I say, "I don't need my own room."

"Good. I'll order the staff to move your things over immediately. We'll get some builders up here to take out the wall while we're away on our honeymoon."

"We're going away for our honeymoon?"

He appears in the doorway, not having bothered to ask if I'm dressed. "A *very* long one."

While I managed to get my dress over my head, I can't do the laces in the back. "Will you help me, or should I ring for a maid?"

He doesn't say anything, and in the next instant I feel his fingers sweeping my hair over my shoulder. He works at the strings on my back, pausing every other one to add a kiss to the back of my neck. When he's done, I reach for my gloves, but Kallias plucks them out of my fingers and tosses them away.

"No gloves." And he grabs my fingers with his, lacing them together.

"You've suddenly become so much more demanding."

"And I think you love it," he says, pulling me close, running his nose along my neck.

Oh, but I do.

>—⟩—○—⟨—⟨

A WHOLE SLEW OF guards accompanies us down to the dungeons.

It will take some time, I think, to adjust to how many are appropriate throughout the castle, now that Kallias will be vulnerable to attack constantly, just like any normal man.

When we're let through a thick door with a barred opening at the top, I'm glad I didn't wear one of my own designs down here. The ground is positively filthy. I suspect it's never been cleaned.

Every step echoes loudly, and lit torches shine from their sconces. Electric wires must never have been installed down here. Why would they need to be? Criminals don't need the light.

"Ikaros first," Kallias says, and a burly man with a ring of keys leads us through a maze of cells before stopping before an occupied one.

Lord Vasco—just Vasco now that I suppose he'll be stripped of his title—stands with his back toward the bars, facing an abandoned corner. The other corner holds naught but a bucket, and I don't want to think about what it's used for.

No plumbing down in the dungeons, either, it would seem.

"I just want to know one question," Kallias says. "Why?"

Vasco doesn't turn, doesn't make any movements to indicate he heard our approach at all. He keeps his head firmly toward the corner as though it's the most interesting thing in the world.

"My father and mother—" Kallias swallows. "They loved you. You had their respect. Why would you do that to them?"

Again, no response.

"You wanted the power, is that it? Without the Maheras line, you thought you would rule instead? Well, you wouldn't have. I have third cousins. They would take the throne before you ever would. So why?"

When Vasco doesn't move, Kallias screams. "WHY?" The sound bounces off the walls, and I resist the urge to cover my ears with my hands. I only stand by Kallias's side, holding his hand for support. This issue is personal to him. I will respect him by letting him deal with it in any way he sees fit.

When the echoes die completely, Kallias tries again. "Did you think I would be easy to control? Is that it? You thought I would be your puppet king? And when I wasn't, you thought to get rid of me as well?"

Still, no movement.

Kallias turns, taking me with him back down the hallway, but he says over his shoulder, "You have three days to think it over. After that, we resort to less pleasant means of getting information out of you." To the guard, "Take us to Zervas now."

"Your parents weren't who you thought they were," a cold voice says from behind us. Kallias halts but doesn't turn.

"You were never supposed to be king," Vasco continues. "Your father deserved what happened."

Kallias's grip tightens on my fingers, and I wrap my free hand around his upper arm.

"To Lady Zervas's cell," I tell the guard. And we put Vasco behind us.

We're led down another corridor, and where Vasco's cell was initially as silent as a tomb, Zervas's rings with music.

She's singing.

I can't make out the words with the horrid way the cells echo, but it's probably some little tune sung to her as a child.

I suppose one has to pass the time somehow.

Once she hears our footsteps, she silences, watching us as we come into view.

She sighs dramatically. "Are you here to let me out?"

"No," Kallias says.

"Well, then, let me know when you are here to let me out." And she resumes her singing.

What the devils?

"You're locked up for *murder*," I tell her. "You should take this more seriously."

Her voice cuts off again. "I'm not the one responsible for the late king's and queen's deaths. I've never raised a hand to Kallias. When the real murderer strikes again, I will be released."

"You matched a description perfectly."

"A description given by whom?" she asks.

Neither Kallias nor I dare to say, "A little girl."

"Either it was from a highly unreliable source, or it was from someone who was in on it. Someone who wants you to think it's me so you will let down your guard. Honestly, the person behind the attack has my utmost respect. I'm a perfect scapegoat. I have the means and the motive. But while I did want your dear father to suffer as he did, I'm not the one who killed him. And there's no reason why I should want to kill *you*.

"If I were you, I'd be very careful. And honestly, perhaps you should take a closer look at *her*." It takes me a moment to realize she's speaking about me. "After all, love is an excellent motivator to kill."

And then she resumes singing.

CHAPTER 26

Kallias and I join the rest of the nobles for lunch in the great hall. We need to be a strong and united front for all the courtiers to see. Kallias is undaunted by the attack on his life. He is as strong as ever. And everyone is here to witness it.

Save Vasco, Zervas, and Orrin, of course.

I lean forward in my seat. "Rhoda, where is Galen? Why isn't he joining us?"

Rhoda turns her head to stare at the man leaning against the wall with the other servants. She pivots back around, a forlorn look on her face. "He wouldn't come. Said it would put too much pressure and attention on me. Can you believe it? He's worried about me!"

Kallias looks up from his meal. "You're pursuing your manservant? Romantically?"

Rhoda meets Kallias's gaze without shame. "I am." She raises a bite of food to her mouth.

Kallias nods. "Would it help if I made him a lord? Gave him some land and a title?"

Rhoda chokes.

"I think it would," I say.

Rhoda takes a deep drink from her cup. "Your Majesty, I could never ask such a thing!"

"If it would make Alessandra happy, then it's already done." Kallias switches his fork to his left hand. His right goes under the table.

To my leg.

I try to keep my face neutral at the sudden weight.

"Oh, sire, thank you! But I have plenty of land for the two of us. He doesn't need it. But a title! We would be honored to accept that."

"Then I will make it all official and have my man draw up all the particulars. We'll gift it to him in public to help do away with the suspicion about you two."

Rhoda leaves the table abruptly and runs over to Galen. She takes him by the hand before leading him from the room.

Meanwhile, Kallias's hand slides to the inside of my thigh. I don't know how he manages it while also bringing food to his lips. I nearly drop my spoon when his thumb rubs over an especially sensitive spot. I'm so glad I opted for a dress with thin skirts today.

Even though it makes it impossible to focus on a single word Hestia is saying.

Something about inviting me to visit with her at Lord Paulos's estate. Or maybe—

Kallias's hand slides higher.

Oh, that wicked man.

"Forgive me," I say, standing from the table, "but I'm not feeling so well. I think I'll retire to my rooms."

I practically run from the table, hoping to hide the heat in my cheeks and my quickened breath. I don't spare Kallias a glance.

⋆·❈·❖·❈·⋆

WHEN I REACH MY ROOM, I dismiss all the servants who had begun moving my things over to Kallias's rooms. They appear to have made it through my vanity and washroom but stopped just shy of the wardrobe.

Perhaps I should consider a cool bath.

There's a knock, followed by the door opening. Kallias, of course.

"You're unwell? Why didn't you say—"

I throw myself at him, layering hot, openmouthed kisses on him. Though startled at first, he soon returns them in kind. Lavender-mint fills my senses, and his mouth has the light taste of wine.

I lean him against the nearest wall, fusing our bodies together, let my hands slide the jacket off his shoulders.

"I'm just fine," I say as I pull back slightly to deal with a button that's impeding my progress. "You, however, are in trouble."

"For what?" he asks innocently.

"Distracting me to the point of not being able to eat my meal."

He spins us around, spins *me* around, so my front is pressed against the wall, my head turned to the side to look at him.

"That doesn't seem right," he says. "All I did was . . ."

And then he's bending down, pulling up my skirts so he can trace the same path he did under the table, only this time on my bare skin. Meanwhile, his lips are exploring the back of my neck, and I'm trapped, helpless to do anything but feel him as his fingers explore higher and higher.

When I can't take it any longer, I push off from the wall, spin to face him. His lips find mine, and his fingers are in my hair, pulling out the pins I used to hold it up this morning.

I place my hands at my back, trying to reach the laces holding my dress together. I need it off. Now. There is too much between his body and mine.

Once he realizes what I'm doing, he says, "No." He steps backward. "No," he repeats.

And I think I might scream if he tries to stop this, if he—

"Let me," he adds.

In mere seconds my dress is gone, and I'm before him in my chemise.

He looks me over slowly, at the skin he can view beneath the practically see-through material.

"If I were a better man, I would send you away," he says. "My life is dangerous. There's always someone trying to kill me. Even if this threat has been dealt with, there will be others. You could get hurt by being close to me."

"Good thing you're not a better man." I take off his cravat, start on the buttons of his shirt. "Why?" I ask. "Why didn't you take me last night?"

"I wasn't sure if you wanted to. Or if you wanted to wait until after the wedding. You didn't—"

"I want to." I rip off the last button after it slips through my fingers for the second time.

And then he carries me to the bed.

The Shadow King, it turns out, was well worth the wait.

>—⟡—○—⟡—⟨

THE FORMER QUEEN'S SITTING room is now *my* sitting room. I still have a mind to redecorate it, but for now it's the perfect place for Rhoda, Hestia, and I to spend some time alone.

Especially when I have so much to tell them.

"What was it like?" Hestia wants to know. "Being with a king?"

"It was . . . better than anything I could have imagined," I say. "But I don't think it had anything to do with the fact that Kallias is a king."

It is his patience, his ability to hold himself back until the right moment that makes him such a good lover.

"What of you and Lord Paulos?" I ask. "Have you two . . . ?"

"No," she says simply. "I asked him if we could wait until after the wedding."

"Has he pressured you?" I ask, suddenly growing protective of my friend.

"Oh, no. He's been wonderful about it. You might think I'm silly, but I just want to wait until I'm his wife."

I take her hand in mine. "There is nothing silly about waiting until you want to. Don't let anyone ever tell you otherwise. It is your body to do with as you will."

She smiles at me then, and I worry that I might be the first person to tell her that.

Waiting. Not waiting. One lover. A hundred lovers. There should be no judgment either way. A woman is not defined by what she does or doesn't do in the bedroom.

"What of you, Rhoda?" Hestia asks. "What's the latest with you and Galen?"

"If it were up to me, I would have bedded him after the ball," Rhoda says. "Galen wants to wait. He muttered some nonsense about preserving my virtue. But if you ask me? He wants to wait until we're married so I can't change my mind. As if he has anything to worry about!"

"Perhaps you need to be a bit more persuasive," I suggest.

"I'm open to ideas."

"Have you tried waiting for him in his bed at night?"

"Yes!"

"Already naked?"

She opens her mouth. Pauses. "No."

"He won't resist that." In a more practical voice, I add, "You'd think he'd be a little more grateful after being made a lord. He should be worshipping you."

"So true," Rhoda says. She sighs.

And I look at my two friends. My first real friends. I thought women were always my competitors, people to be jealous of. How wrong I was.

We're all just so happy. I hope it lasts forever.

The door to the sitting room bursts open, nearly flying off its hinges.

"Lady Stathos, you're ordered to appear before the king immediately." Some nondescript guard issues the command. He's flanked by two other men wearing the crest of the king.

"Is Kallias all right?" I ask as I stand abruptly.

"Take her," the first guard says, and the other two flank me, each grabbing one of my arms, and start physically pulling me toward the doorway.

"What do you think you're doing?" Rhoda yells from behind me. "That's the future queen. Unhand her at once."

But she's ignored, and my arms are bruised as I'm dragged up the stairs, toward the library that Kallias and I use for our private meals.

After a while, I stop struggling and just bear the humiliation. I will deal with these three men once I'm with Kallias. Oh, how they'll pay then.

This is some sort of mistake. They must have misunderstood the king's orders. I can't imagine what he said to give them the impression I should be treated as a prisoner.

But when they finally release me, I find Kallias alone in the library, his back to the door.

"Wait outside," he says to the guards. They do, shoving me unceremoniously toward the king.

"Kallias, what is this? Gods, I have bruises from the guards!"

He turns, his eyes going to my arms to assess the damage. Then, as if remembering himself, he looks away, hardening his features.

"Why did you come to court?" he asks in a low tone.

"Because you asked me to!" I'm fuming now.

"No. What was your real purpose? Why were you at the ball, the one specifically set up by my advisers because they wanted me to select someone to court? Why did you ignore me, practically force me to come to you?"

Dread sinks low in my chest, but how—how could he know?

"Where are these questions coming from? Have I done something wrong? Kallias, it's *me*."

Did Zervas spout more drivel about me being involved in his attacks?

"The servants finished moving your things over to my room. This was found in your wardrobe."

He holds up the vial of minalen—the one I stole from the healer and then shoved into the back of my wardrobe ages ago.

And promptly forgot about.

"Kallias—"

"You are suspected of treason," he bites out. "And you will address me as *Your Majesty* for these proceedings."

Something in my heart twists, breaks, dissolves away. Leaving a gaping wound in its place. I need a lie. A convincing one. Fast. Now.

But I, conniving, scheming Alessandra Stathos cannot think of a single thing to say when he looks at me with such loathing.

"Why was this in your wardrobe?" he demands. "I've already had it examined by one of my healers. It's the same kind of poison that was found in my cup after your ball."

Oh, a horrid coincidence.

I open my mouth.

"I don't think you've ever lied to me, Alessandra."

I haven't. Not really.

"You've misled me, of course, when it came to Hektor and the baron. But I don't think you've ever spoken an outright lie to me. Do you think I'd be able to tell if you were? Let's find out. Now tell me what you used this for."

I look down at my fingers to find them shaking.

"Look at me!" he says.

I do. Any hesitation on my part would only seem as though I'm trying to come up with a lie. So the truth starts to spill out of me.

"I—" I cough and force my face to remain calm. "I went to that ball with the intention of catching your eye," I start.

"I don't need the whole story. What I need is for you to tell me who the poison was for and why." He considers the vial. "It's unopened, and it does you little good to kill me before we are wed. Were you working with Vasco? Did he put his plan into action too soon without you? Or were you working for him? Distracting me so that I would touch you and make myself vulnerable to him?"

"No! I was not working for or with Vasco in any manner. I had nothing to do with what happened at the ball."

"Then what did you intend it for, Alessandra!"

A single tear slides down my cheek. "You. I intended it for you."

The cruel man before me disappears for the briefest of moments. Kallias's face falls, hurt softening his features. Then the villain is back.

"Why?"

"I had a plan. There were three simple steps. I was going to woo you. I was going to marry you. And then—"

"And then *what*?"

"And then I was going to kill you and take your kingdom for myself."

A bitter smile stretches across his lips. "That does sound like you."

"But, Kallias, I threw out that plan weeks ago. I no longer had any desire to kill you because I—"

"What? You *what*, Alessandra?"

Now the tears are coming quickly. I can't look at him as I say it. I don't *want* to say it, but my life is on the line. "I fell in love with you."

He laughs. The sound is not kind, and the empty space where my heart once was burns with pain. "All this time, I worried about old threats, when I should have also been looking for new ones. I suppose a king is never permitted friends or lovers. Not when every person in the world wants something from me."

"It wasn't like that. Not anymore. I swear it. I never lied to you. I never pretended anything with you. I didn't *have* to. Don't you see?"

"I don't want to hear any more."

"Kallias, please."

His neck snaps in my direction. "I told you. You are no longer allowed to address me in that way, Lady Stathos."

The hurt is so deep, but so is the anger.

And that night with Hektor flashes into my mind.

My knife is in my boot, of course. I could draw it much faster than Kallias could his rapier. Especially when he's mostly turned away from me.

And though my anger is rich and raw, I have no desire to reach down for my knife.

I could never, *never* wish Kallias any harm.

"You will leave," he says. "I don't care where you go, so long as I never have to see you again. If you come back here—if I ever have to look upon your face again, I'll kill you myself."

I rub at the tears as they fall. Try to gather my thoughts, but the ache in my chest is all consuming.

"Leave, dammit! Before I change my mind!" He stomps toward me, and I think he might physically remove me from the room if I don't find my feet.

So I flee.

"Be out of the castle by nightfall!" he says to my retreating back. "I don't care if you have to leave your things behind."

That's the last thing I hear. Out in the hallway, I see Hestia and Rhoda, waiting. They've brought my other friends, Leandros, Rhouben, and Petros. What do they mean to do? Plead on my behalf? They don't know what I've done. Will Kallias tell them?

"Alessandra—" Rhoda begins, but I ignore her. I rush past them all, streak up the stairs, ignoring the looks the servants give me as they see my red face and tearstained cheeks.

"I'll go after her," I think I hear someone say distantly. "You speak with the king." But I barely make sense of anything. Everything is a blur through the moisture at my eyes. I fumble for the key to my room three times before I get the door open. The space is completely empty.

Right. I've been moved into his room.

The tears start afresh as I stride over to the adjoining door. And I look into the room that's been made to fit both his things and mine. Our wardrobes are side by side. Extra pillows have been added to the bed. My vanity has been placed on a free wall, near the washroom that smells like the soaps he used this morning.

Looking at it all, at the evidence of the life I could have had, with *him*, I fall to the floor in a heap of skirts, my head dropping into my hands.

How long until nightfall? I don't know. I don't care. Not when everything is ruined.

I don't know how long I sit there before the softest tapping reaches me.

"Alessandra? May I come in?"

I don't answer. I try to rub my tears off on my sleeves.

He comes in anyway.

Leandros. He looks as though he has recently bathed, his hair still damp. The smell of roses wafts over me. He must have had petals in the water.

"Oh dear," he says when he sees me. Then he falls to the floor and gathers me to him, letting my head rest against his chest. One of his hands strokes my hair while his voice lets out soothing sounds.

I've already cried myself dry, though. My tears cease.

"Do you want to talk about it?" he asks.

"There isn't anything to say. He's sent me away. I have until nightfall to collect my things." My voice sounds hoarse.

Leandros tightens his grip. "How could he send you away? What did you do?"

"Nothing," I say. And it's true. I'd been caught with the vial of poison, but I didn't use it. I hadn't actually done anything. I wasn't going to do anything. Why did I ever steal it in the first place?

"Then he's a fool." Leandros pulls back just enough to look at me, to wipe the last undried tear from my chin. "I know you're hurting, but you will get past this. All will be well."

And as I sit there, staring at Leandros, I'm overcome with a sudden urge.

The urge to hurt Kallias.

He made me feel for him and then sent me away. Tossed me aside as has happened to me once before.

How dare he?

So I lean forward and kiss Leandros. He doesn't return it. He's rigid as a board before me, so I use my hands to scoot closer, before letting them drift around his neck. I catch his lower lip with my teeth, and that results in the most delicious noise from his throat.

Then he returns everything in kind.

He is an exceptional kisser, but he is not Kallias.

I don't care.

My hands drift to his hair, still slightly damp. There's a hint of some other scent about him, but I can't quite place it. It mixes nicely with the rose.

I wish Kallias would walk in. I wish he would think to check my progress. Wish he would change his mind and ask me to stay. Beg me for forgiveness. Get on his knees and—

"Are you all right?" Leandros asks, pulling away. "You seem distracted."

All the years of practice with my previous lovers makes it easy to pretend. "You make it hard for me to think."

He grins.

"You are too good for me," I say. "How can you be so kind when I rejected you? Leandros, I'm so sorry. I never should have said no."

He leans forward and kisses the tip of my nose. "Think nothing of it. I knew you would see my merits eventually."

I smile as my eyes catch sight of the window. The sun is beginning to set. "I have to go. He ordered me away before sunset."

"Don't worry. You won't be gone long."

I reach for what I can find. A small purse of money. My favorite jacket to protect me from the cold. "You saw how angry he was."

"Give me some time to talk with him. You'll be back at court, this time on my arm, in no time."

I feel sick. No, just miserable. Kallias would never permit me back at court, and even if he did, I couldn't bear it to be here and not with him. I kissed Leandros, and for what? It didn't make me feel better. It didn't enrage Kallias. All it did was give Leandros false hope.

Perhaps not entirely false. I can't go back to my father. He'll probably throw me out just like I did to him at my ball. My best chance is to marry quickly. Perhaps I can persuade Leandros to make an offer for me and then keep me in his country estate.

"I will write to you," I say.

"I will collect you," he answers. "When it's time."

So optimistic. How does he manage it all the time? Surely it must be exhausting.

CHAPTER

29

The carriage clops along the street, wending down the slope of the mountain, carrying me to an inn located at the base.

In all my misery, I failed to realize one thing.

I'm lucky to be alive. Kallias had every right and authority to order my immediate death. He could have me hanged along with Vasco and Zervas.

But he told me to go.

Why?

Why would he do that?

Not a single reason comes to mind.

The passing scenery makes me sick. It reminds me of when Kallias and I rode up the mountain together. When I fell into him. When he trusted me with his secrets. When he remained a gentleman while we went swimming.

He was anything but a gentleman last night.

My heart seems to break all over again when I remember our time together. When I think of his touches and kisses. When I think of the things he whispered into my hair.

Oh, but I did love him.

But he was cruel in forcing the confession from me. And when I told him how I loved him, he laughed in my face.

That person is not the Kallias I know.

I have at least three more hours in the carriage to go, so I try to get comfortable, letting my legs rest against the opposite seat.

He can't do this to me. To us.

We were perfect together. We were made for each other. As rulers. As lovers. There is no reason why we shouldn't be together.

My hands close into fists. I have to make him see it. I have to convince him. But is it worth the risk of my own life? He swore he'd kill me himself if I returned.

How could I convince him I meant him no harm? How can I convince him I want the life he carved for us?

My shoulders loosen and my hands fall open. A new wave of pain hits me as I see Kallias's ring on my finger, but then my eyes catch on something below it.

"Ugh." A spot of dirt smudges the lower part of my hand. I attempt to rub it on the seat of the carriage. Kallias's carriage.

It doesn't come off.

I take a knuckle to it, and when that also doesn't work, I wet a finger with my tongue and rub at it.

But it won't come off.

Hesitantly, I lower my nose and sniff.

That aroma from before, the one mixed with Leandros's roses, wafts gently toward me.

I know this smell. How do I know this smell?

My hands. They were in Leandros's hair while I kissed him.

Yes, hair! There is a product used in the dying of ladies' hair. It smells just like this.

But why would Leandros dye his hair?

As I sit there, I remember Lady Zervas's insistence that she is innocent, that she'll be freed when the real killer shows themselves.

Vasco is guilty. Of that I'm certain, but could he have roped his nephew into helping him?

No, Leandros would never. Why would he? He was Kallias's friend. He came to court after the death of Kallias's brother. Why should Leandros have any motive to harm the king?

But then I remember how he insisted I would be back in the palace soon and by his side. Still, why should he want to harm Kallias?

I stare down at the spot on my hand.

He came to court after the death of Kallias's brother.

When Kallias and I went to the gentleman's club in disguise, I'd noticed how Kallias looked so much like Leandros with the lighter hair.

What would Leandros have to gain from harming Kallias, unless . . .

Devils!

"Turn the carriage around!" I scream the words, and the carriage comes to a severe halt. I'm almost thrown onto the opposite seat.

"My lady?" the coachman asks.

"The king's life is in peril. We must turn around at once."

"I'm—I'm to take you away. King's orders."

I toss my head out the window, so I can glare up at the simple man. "And what do you think will happen when the king dies, and I tell the council you could have prevented it?"

He still looks unsure.

"I have fifty necos in my purse," I say.

At that, he turns the horses around, and we veer back up the mountain, this time at breakneck speed.

>─┼─◆≻─◯─≺◆─┼─<

I DON'T KNOW WHAT I'm doing.

Kallias is going to kill me. The moment he sees me, I'm dead. Not long ago, I wouldn't have hesitated to save myself, even if it meant someone else's death. I still would—if it were anyone except for Kallias.

I hate him.

But I love him more.

He needs to know the truth. Even if he kills me for it. He needs to know who murdered his parents. It wasn't Zervas, and it wasn't Leandros. It wasn't even Vasco, but he must be involved somehow. I don't quite have the whole of it figured out.

But I know enough.

I leap from the carriage once we reach the palace again. I curse the skirts that impede my speed. If I had just worn pants today—but I hadn't thought I'd be running anywhere. I just remember what Kallias did the last time I wore skirts . . .

The sun has long since set; the palace is as quiet as a tomb. Guards stand watch at every opening into the palace, but I suspect they haven't been told of my treachery yet. None prevent me from entering, and fortunately I don't spot the three who delivered me to the library to await the king's judgment.

I'm panting by the time I reach the corridor—our corridor.

"Is the king in his rooms?" I ask the guards on watch.

"No, Lady Stathos. He hasn't turned in for bed yet."

My voice turns into a growl. "Where is he?"

"We're not assigned to his personal guard. I couldn't tell you."

"The king's life is in danger. I need to know where he is now!" But yelling doesn't help. It doesn't suddenly give them the answers I want.

I turn, flying back down the stairs. When I hear the guards follow, I shout back, "No, stay put in case he does turn in. Do not leave your posts."

Where would he be this late at night? If he doesn't have any meetings, where would he go?

He was in the library the last time I saw him, so I make my way there instead. But on a hunch, I change course halfway there, making for the queen's sitting room instead.

His mother's day use room.

I curse myself for my foolishness when I don't spot any guards outside the doors. But then, what if Kallias ditched his guards?

I plunge into the room at full speed, the door slamming into the wall behind it. A pair of arms catches me before I go sprawling on the ground.

"Alessandra?"

I push myself out of Kallias's arms, still fearful of the way he treated me when last we saw each other. "You're alive!"

He gives me a look like I've gone mad. "Yes."

"Where is your guard?" I get the words out around heaving breaths.

"I gave them the night off. With all the threats against me dealt with—including *you*, I might add—I thought I'd have some time without them. Never mind that, what are you doing back here? I—"

"You're alone?" I say over the top of him.

"No, I'm here, too."

Leandros steps out of the alcove he'd been standing in. "We were catching up. What are you doing here?"

I spin to Kallias. "You need to run. Now. Go to your guards. Wherever the nearest ones are."

"Why? Are you going to try to kill me again?" he asks with bitter sarcasm.

"I've never tried to kill you, and I'm not the one who poses a threat to your life. He is!" I point to Leandros, whose eyes widen at the accusation.

"What?" Kallias asks. "Leandros didn't help his uncle. He protected me from him when Ikaros tried to approach me after I'd swallowed the poison."

"He didn't protect you," I say as realization dawns on me. "He used the opportunity to touch you. Have you been able to use your shadows since entering this room?"

"I haven't tried, and they're not about to work with you here. Now get out!" Kallias grabs my arm, trying to drag me away.

"He isn't who he says he is. Lord Vasco has no nephew!"

Kallias's grip loosens at the words, and I tug my arm free. "What are you talking about?" he asks.

"I have the same question," Leandros says, and his voice is much closer now.

Without thinking, I shove myself between the two men, using my body as a shield for Kallias. Even as I spot the sword hanging from Leandros's hips, I don't lose my footing.

"Look at him, Kallias. Look at him closely. You know him."

"Yes," his voice comes from behind me. "He's my best friend. Or was, until I—"

"No, you know him from before that. He looked a little different then, with hair as black as yours, a nose that wasn't broken. The mind sees what it wants to see when it can't make sense of anything else. Your brother died, so how could he return disguised as someone else?"

And then Leandros—*Xanthos*—narrows his eyes at me.

"What happened to you?" I ask. "You were beaten; that much is obvious. But why fake your death? Why come back and kill your parents and try to kill your brother? It doesn't make sense."

Xanthos looks over my head to Kallias. "I think she's feeling guilty. She kissed me this evening, you know. After you sent her away."

"Stop it!" I shout, feeling shame and anger all at once. But I don't dare look at Kallias. I can't take my eyes from Xanthos, from the threat. "I was hurt," I say by way of explanation. "That doesn't excuse it, but it did reveal to me your treachery."

I hold my hand above my head, so the stain is pointed toward Kallias. "Hair dye. It came off on my hands. He caught up to me right after using it. I suspected he wanted to see me off. Make sure he could really get you alone for once, without anyone witnessing him murdering you."

The room goes silent.

"No," Kallias says at last. "No, he can't be Xanthos. I loved my brother, but he was taunting. Cruel. Leandros has been nothing but—"

"An actor," I finish. "An assassin in disguise."

Again, silence. It stretches for so long, I think I might turn around just from the pain of not being able to read Kallias's face.

And then the heat at my back retreats as Kallias steps backward. "It *is* you."

Xanthos looks heavenward. "Great, Alessandra. Well done." He draws his sword. "I've been working on this for four long years, and then you have to go and ruin it."

"You're the one who ruined it," I point out, showing him the brown mark.

"I thought to take one last thing from my brother. He had everything that should have been mine. The kingdom. The empire. The shadows. The only thing that was truly his was you, and I wanted to take that, too."

I step back when I feel Kallias's hand come down on my shoulder, tugging me toward him.

"The assassin in the gardens," I say. "He was there on your orders." I'd seen Leandros right before Kallias showed up. I can't believe I didn't make the connection sooner.

"He'd been serving as a manservant for a week," Xanthos says. "We were just waiting for the right moment. When there weren't guards around. When Kallias would let his shadows down."

"And the letter?" I ask. "The gentleman's club?"

Xanthos shakes his head. "No, that was Vasco's doing. I would never agree to such a stupid and convoluted plan. He's lucky he saw through Kallias's disguise. Lucky he wasn't seen at the club."

A lead weight sinks low in my chest. "I left you on the dais with him at the ball. I told you to look over him!"

"And he would have died if Petros hadn't seen me touch him. He thought it was an accident, but he ordered me away so Kallias could heal."

"Xanthos," Kallias says finally, as though he still can't quite believe it, as though he didn't hear any of the conversation we just had. "What happened to you? Why didn't you tell me it was you? I would have—"

"You would have *what*?" Xanthos snaps. "Stepped down from being king? Given the title over willingly and happily? You and I both know you wouldn't have. Not after you'd had a taste of the power. Besides, I couldn't reveal myself until Mother and Father were dead. Until you were dead, so no one could stand with you to contest my claim to the throne."

"Oh," I say, as realization dawns. "You didn't have the ability. The shadows. Your father didn't want you to become king. You embarrassed him, didn't you?"

Xanthos raises his sword so the point presses against my throat. "I would stay silent if I were you."

"Leave her out of this," Kallias says, tugging me out of reach of the sword. He places his body between me and his older brother. "I don't understand. Father ordered you beaten?"

Xanthos's nostrils flare as his face hardens. "He beat me himself. To death, almost. That was surely his intention. He left me by the side of the road, near a carriage he had his men tip over, to make it look like an accident. And then he left, not a shred of guilt to be found."

"That's when Vasco found you," I say.

"When he found out what my father did, he pledged his loyalty to me. The true king. He took care of me. Helped me disguise myself, vowed to help me take back my throne. We hired those men to enter the palace, put the whole place on lockdown. I killed Father before he even knew what was happening. It was much too quick. He should have been beaten first, as I was. But I knew I didn't have much time."

Kallias's breathing has hastened. "And Mother?" he asks, his voice breaking at the end.

"I couldn't be sure she wasn't in on it. It was harder to kill her, but I knew I had to. She was already beginning to suspect who I was."

But that was too much. Kallias launches himself at Xanthos, dodging the sword and tackling him to the ground. The sword goes flying off to the side, and I run to retrieve it. Then I stand back, watching the two men.

Kallias has the fight in hand.

He's landed atop Xanthos. Straddling him, he unleashes his fists on the fallen man. "She. Was. My. Mother." He punctuates each word with a slam of his knuckles.

Xanthos surges upward, slamming his forehead into Kallias's nose. He shoves him to the side, freeing himself from his younger brother's clutches.

And then he kicks him. Kallias goes down.

"Don't think you were the only one who loved her," Xanthos says. He pulls at his cuff links almost without noticing, and I remember that he liked to wear ones shaped like roses. Their mother's favorite flower. "It nearly killed me to end her, too. But you? You I will enjoy killing."

Kallias rolls away and manages to find his feet, but a steady drip of blood comes from his nose.

They tangle together again. Dodging and throwing fists. I can't do anything but watch. What if I slash the wrong man with the sword? Should I run for the guards?

Not if I want to risk Xanthos winning the fight.

"How have you enjoyed my birthright, Kallias? Did you like ruling behind the council? Did you enjoy the king's suite? Sitting at the head of the dinner table?"

"I did," Kallias says. "I never would have given it up. Not for a powerless, pathetic, matricidal whelp like you."

Xanthos screams as he flings himself at Kallias. They roll over each other on the floor, until Xanthos comes up on top this time.

Kallias takes a fist to his lips, to his left eye, to his throat.

Xanthos will kill him, I'm sure of it.

I step forward with the sword, place it under his throat. "Off. Now."

He ignores me, tries to slap the sword away with his fingers, so I let the edge dig into his skin, drawing a line of blood.

That gets his attention. He rises at my next insistence and backs away, retreating until his back hits a wall.

"Let me go, Alessandra!" he shrieks.

"No."

"He sent you away! He said he'd *kill* you if you returned." Had he been listening in on our last conversation? "Why would you defend him?"

I shrug. "Just feel like it, really." I'm hardly about to profess my love yet again where Kallias can hear it.

"He doesn't want you. Saving him won't change that. Move away. Now."

"I won't."

"If you want to stop me, you'll have to kill me. I think we both know you don't have it in you."

When he tries to move, I let the tip of the sword break his skin, sliding in until it hits the wall.

Xanthos's eyes widen in surprise, as a choking noise comes out of his throat. Where blood oozes from his airway.

"You didn't really know me," I say. "If you had, you'd know I've already killed for love once before."

And then he slumps forward, tacked to the wall like some macabre tapestry. Dead.

I turn to Kallias, find him watching me from the floor, his eyes going in and out of focus.

Then I run for the guards.

CHAPTER 30

As soon as I knew Kallias was safe, that a healer was tending to him and a whole platoon of guards were watching over him, I left. I knew he would only send me away again once he had the strength to do so. Unless of course he decided to kill me.

I saved him, but somehow, I'm as miserable as ever.

Perhaps Zervas was right. It is far better to know he was mine before death than to know he will go on to be with someone else.

I plump my pillow before adjusting it below my chest, wrapping my arms around it, and letting my chin sink onto the edge of the downy softness.

Rhoda is letting me stay at her estate for as long as I wish. She's away with Galen, staying at some country inn, far, far away from gossip and anyone who knows them.

I try not to be bitter about the romantic getaway they're having. How can I be so jealous when I have a glorious duchess's estate to stay in?

Alone.

Cast aside.

Threatened with death by the man I love.

Loved.

I cannot still care for him after what he's done. It's been a week since he threw me out of the palace. Since the duel in the sitting room. A week of sleeping in dreadfully late each morning, or afternoon, really. A week of selling off the trinkets Kallias gave me to pad my purse. A week of walking down the vast halls of this estate, touring the grounds (yet avoiding the gardens). I go for a horse ride each afternoon. Enjoy delicious dishes prepared by Rhoda's exquisite cook. And try to decide what the next step is for me.

I don't need to marry anymore. I have all the money I could need and a free place to stay indefinitely.

I have nothing to scheme for. And I find I don't have a taste for men at the moment.

Hestia has written to me, asking me if she might visit. She also sent a wedding invitation.

I don't know if I can stand the sight of my friends and their happiness right now.

What I need is to feel in control. Perhaps I'll purchase my own estate. Order my own servants about. That should make me happy.

I ring for a maid to help me dress and fix my hair. Then I let myself into Rhoda's study, where I sit before a desk. I'll inquire after any land for sale. Or perhaps I'll see if Vasco's estate is up for grabs. He lost it along with his title when he was sentenced.

After some time, a letter arrives from my sister. She pleads Father's case, telling me how desperately he wishes me to come home. She apologizes for being away from me so long.

If only I'd been with you to set an example.
Perhaps you might not be alone and without any
prospects. Would you like to come stay with me and the

*duke for a time? Of course, you can't carry on as you
have while you're here.*

*You were so young when Mother died, and as your
older sister I should have taken better care of you.
Father and I certainly don't blame you for turning into
a trollop. How else were you to entertain yourself while
I was at parties and balls?*

"I'm not a trollop," I announce to the empty room. "I'm a sexually empowered woman, and there is nothing wrong with that."

How dare she try to argue morality with me. Through a *letter*. And how could Father go to her to convince me to come home? He only wants a bride-price for me. Without me, he's left figuring out how to save his estate alone.

Good, I think. It's his problem to deal with. Not mine. He never should have tried to use me. I'm worth so much more than that. I wish he would have treated me so.

I turn back to the letter I'm composing, when the handle at the door catches.

"I'd prefer not to be disturbed with any more correspondences," I say without looking up to the servant. For good measure, I tear my sister's note to pieces before tossing the paper to the floor for someone else to clean up.

"Will you permit a visitor, then?"

I stand abruptly, turning at the sound of the voice that has come to be sweeter to me than music.

"I'm afraid I bullied the servants into letting me enter without being announced," Kallias says. "I worried you'd order them to send me away before I had a chance to see you."

He has a few yellow bruises on his face that are still fading. Though his eye and lip are no longer swollen, a few lines of scabs cover his cheeks and brow. But he's alive and well.

"You didn't heal yourself. With your shadows. I'll leave. Then you can—"

"I wish to heal from these the long way. I've earned the pain that comes with them."

Silence fills Rhoda's study. When I can't take it anymore, I ask him, "Did you change your mind?"

He looks somewhat puzzled by the question. "Yes, of course."

I nod and let my eyes trail along the floor. "How is it to happen, then?"

He's silent for a moment. "I thought we'd take the carriage."

"And then?"

The quiet stretches out so long that I look up. "Well?" I snap. "How am I to die? Am I to be hanged? Drawn and quartered? Are you going to push me off a cliff? Strangle me with your bare hands? What's it to be, Kallias?" And then, remembering what he said before, I amend, "I mean, what's it to be, *Your Majesty*?" Perhaps if I'm civil now it will be a quick death.

A look of horror crosses his features before he removes the space between us. He falls to his knees before me, taking my hands in his bare ones. His thumb brushes over the ring on my finger. His ring. Which I hadn't brought myself to remove yet. He stares at it for a moment before saying, "You've misunderstood. When I said I changed my mind, I meant about sending you away. About destroying our life together."

I go so still; I think my heart might stop beating.

"You could have let me die," he says. "You could have let Leandros—I mean, Xanthos—kill me and then ruled as queen with him. But you didn't. You killed him. You killed for me.

"But I knew before then. I was hurt, yes, but I was going to come back for you right before Xanthos approached me. I was in my mother's sitting room, because I tried to imagine a future where that room wouldn't be yours, and I couldn't."

He rises then, keeping my hands clasped in his. "I was scared. I was so scared to trust anyone, and I hurt you as a result. I said things I shouldn't have. And I'm so unbelievably sorry, Alessandra."

Before I can get in a word, he's jerking his hands away and struggling to reach for something in the pocket of his jacket.

In an unusual bit of clumsiness, he drops a letter onto the floor and scoops down to retrieve it. "You never read this. I started it right after the night I read Orrin's letter to you. I realized that words can be so hard to find when spoken aloud in the moment. But writing? It gives me the time to articulate just what I feel. I was too much of a coward to read it to you before. But I'm going to now.

"My Alessandra,

"All the poets in all the world could write odes to your beauty. You are lovely, stunningly beautiful. Even a fool could see it.

"But that is not what drew me to you. It was your eyes. It was the way you didn't look at me that made me realize you are special. You didn't look at me like I was a king, someone to be respected and worshipped. You looked on me as a man. A man who says foolish things and makes terrible decisions. You made me remember what it is to be human.

"I'd forgotten. Having spent a full year with no one to touch, no one to talk to—it was you who reminded me what it is to live.

"Your eyes spoke of a mind that loves to tease and loves to win. But they also showed me your heart, one that could be so reserved but ready to love if I could only earn it.

"I haven't earned it. I will never earn it. I could spend a million years trying to worship you, and I still wouldn't be worthy of you.

"But I'm desperate for you all the same. And though I will not have millennia to live, I want to give however many years I have left to you. Because I love you. I love the woman who saved me. And though she doesn't need me, I want her. Fiercely.

"All the time in the world is worth nothing if I don't get to spend it with you.

"Forever yours, Kallias."

When done reading, Kallias folds the letter back up methodically, taking his time, scared to look up, I think.

"Why did it take you so long to come see me?" I ask, keeping the emotion from my voice.

He shrugs and laughs uncomfortably. "I was a mess. I thought I might have a better chance of you taking me back if my face weren't all beat up."

I let a hand slide against one cheek, resting my palm there. "I couldn't care less how your face looks."

I feel the pull of muscle as his lips twitch. "No?"

"I do like it when it's healthy and beautiful, but it is not why I love you."

His breath hitches as he says, "The money and power help, too."

"It is what originally caught my interest, but I lose interest in everything sooner or later. Everything save you. Because in you, I found my match. In you, I found my equal."

Kallias, my Shadow King, grabs me, pulls me into his arms. "I love you, Alessandra. What can I say to make you forgive me and take me back?"

"Words only mean so much. Actions speak far louder, don't you think?"

"I do."

He lowers his head, brushes my lips with his.

And we start our new life together. Never to be alone again.

Acknowledgments

Let's try for short and sweet this time around! I have so many people to thank for their help with this one!

Rachel Brooks: Thank you for being you! You're so on top of everything all the time. I couldn't have asked for a better agent. I'm so glad you have my back for every step of the process!

Holly West: Thank you for getting as excited about this project as I was when I first pitched it! You really helped me shape it into what it is now. I couldn't have done it without your enthusiasm.

Jean Feiwel: We've never met or spoken, but thank you for allowing Holly to keep buying my books! (And special thanks for approving this idea!)

Nekro: Thank you for another stunning cover! I'm still drooling over your work!

Liz Dresner: Thanks for all the design magic you work on my books!

Erica Ferguson and Starr Baer: Thanks for all the copyedits!

Charlie N. Holmberg: Thank you for being my critique partner! I'm so glad to have you. I rest easier knowing you read my work before I send it anywhere else.

Cale Dietrich: You are the best! Thank you for reading this one early and providing helpful feedback!

Caitlyn Hair and Mikki Helmer: Thank you for the lunches and brainstorming sessions! I'm so grateful for your friendship!

Bridget Howard: You're a great cheerleader and friend and photo-taking badass!

Taralyn Johnson: Sorry you had to skip over the sexy parts, but thank you for reading this anyway!

My family: Mom, Dad, Becki, Johnny, and Alisa, thanks for continuing to support me and show up to my book events. It's always nice to know you're out there rooting for me.

My fans: Thanks for sticking with me for another book! Or if you're picking up my work for the first time, thanks for joining us! It's you who make it possible for me to keep writing. A million thank-yous! I'll see if I can work in extra kissing scenes in my next book just for you.

THANK YOU FOR READING THIS FEIWEL AND FRIENDS BOOK.

THE FRIENDS WHO MADE

POSSIBLE ARE:

JEAN FEIWEL, Publisher

LIZ SZABLA, Associate Publisher

RICH DEAS, Senior Creative Director

HOLLY WEST, Senior Editor

ANNA ROBERTO, Senior Editor

KAT BRZOZOWSKI, Senior Editor

ALEXEI ESIKOFF, Senior Managing Editor

RAYMOND ERNESTO COLÓN, Senior Production Manager

ERIN SIU, Assistant Editor

EMILY SETTLE, Associate Editor

FOYINSI ADEGBONMIRE, Editorial Assistant

LIZ DRESNER, Associate Art Director

STARR BAER, Associate Copy Chief

FOLLOW US ON FACEBOOK OR VISIT US ONLINE AT MACKIDS.COM

OUR BOOKS ARE FRIENDS FOR LIFE.